Purview of Flashbulbs

An Alexis Parker novel

G.K. Parks

Copyright © 2019 G.K. Parks

A Modus Operandi imprint

All rights reserved.

ISBN: 1942710135
ISBN-13: 978-1-942710-13-4

For my mom

ONE

"Miss Parker, the car is out front."

I pressed the speaker button on my desk phone. "Thanks, I'm on my way."

Taking a final sip of coffee, I checked my reflection in the mirror and smoothed my skirt in place. I hated interviews. I moved briskly down the corridor and smiled at the assistant who was standing beside the waiting elevator. The office building wasn't exactly bustling at six a.m.

"Good luck," she called as the doors shut.

When I exited the building, I saw the stretch limousine idling directly in front of me. The hazards were blinking, but that was the only sign of life. I took a step forward, and the driver opened his door. His attire was beyond anything a federal agent could afford. Private security really did have its perks.

"Alexis Parker?" he asked, even as he moved down the length of the vehicle to the rear door. "We've been waiting."

Refraining from stating that it was six o'clock in the morning and I was only awakened and told to get to the office an hour earlier, I muttered an apology and climbed into the back seat. While my eyes adjusted to the dark interior, I couldn't help but think that every time I got into a car with strangers, things never went well.

A woman sat on the bench seat. A silk scarf covered her hair and was tied in a decorative knot at the side of her neck. She wore large Jackie O sunglasses and looked like one of the Old Hollywood film stars of the 1950s. Her lips were painted a glossy red, and she stared straight at me. Although, I wasn't certain she could see through the dark lenses in the dimly lit interior.

"Would you care for something to drink?" Her voice sounded husky, but I didn't recognize it or her.

"One of us just woke up," I retorted.

Her laugh came out as a soft lilt. "Coffee then?" She pushed a button, and the built-in cabinet beside her opened to reveal several mugs and a single-cup brewer.

"No. What is this about?" I asked.

"Lucien didn't tell you?"

"He doesn't tell me much. He just told me to get to the office because a client was waiting."

She selected a delicate white cup and placed it beneath the brewer before pushing a button. It hissed, and steam rose, filling the air with the scent of an exotic dark roast. She carefully removed her beverage, closed the cabinet, and pushed a button for the intercom. "Dennis, let's circle for a bit. The park might be nice." She waited for the slight lurch of the limousine going into motion before she settled back against the seat and took a sip. "Miss Parker, I was told until recently you were an FBI field agent."

"Technically, I was part of the OIO, an elite branch of the FBI."

"Even better." She held the cup securely on her lap, and my eyes were drawn to the dark red half-moon smudge. "Have you ever fired your weapon?"

"Yes."

"Not in training, my dear. Out there." She gestured with her free hand at the tinted windows.

"Yes."

"What else have you done?"

"Whatever I had to."

She put the cup into a round depression at the top of the

cabinet and reached for a notepad and pen. "That's clever." She scribbled something down. "Do you have experience dealing with drug dealers, terrorists, or serial killers?"

I studied her, unsure what type of job she needed fulfilled. "Yes," I said uncertainly.

She looked up from her notepad. "To which?"

"All of them."

"That is excellent." She leaned forward. "Tell me, have you killed anyone?"

"Look, I'm not entirely sure what my boss promised you, but this would go a little easier if you told me why you contacted Cross Security. I'm a private investigator. He has others at the firm who deal with security issues. Perhaps it'd be best if you spoke to one of them."

She bit her lip. "No, it wouldn't." She found my answer irksome and cocked her head from side to side. "Have you ever provided private protection?"

"Not for Cross Security."

A knowing look played across her face. She was intelligent. She could read between the lines. "I take it you have killed someone. Was that while you were at the FBI or working in the private sector?"

Whatever this was, I wanted it to be over. I wanted out of the car. My gaze darted to the door and out the window. Maybe when we stopped for a light, I'd make a break for it.

She watched me with utter fascination, like I was some kind of specimen. "You don't want to talk about it."

"I want to know what this is about."

"I understand that, but I need you to answer my questions. If you won't, I'm sure Lucien has a file he could provide."

My boss put me in the back of this car, which meant this was a client he wanted. The limousine and driver meant whoever this woman was, she had money. Lots of it. Even if I wouldn't play ball, I knew he would. I looked at the privacy window separating the rear of the limo from the driver. "Yes."

"While on the job or off?"

"Both."

"I'm sorry. I imagine that must have been difficult." She

wrote something else on her sheet of paper. "Have you ever been wounded? Is that the proper term?"

"It is. Do you want to see the scars?" I asked flippantly.

She sat up straighter. Her entire appearance seemingly lighting up. "Actually, that might be incredibly useful. Are they bullet wounds?"

"I was being sarcastic."

She slumped against the seat and reached for her coffee. "Oh." She thought for a moment, trying to understand something. "So was that a yes to being shot?"

I rolled my eyes. "You know, I actually would prefer if you hash the rest of this out with Mr. Cross. I don't think I'll be of any use to you, ma'am. But I'm sure he'll find someone who is."

"Why did you leave the FBI?"

"An assignment went south. Things happened."

"Now was that the first time or second time you left?"

Her latest question cut through the bullshit. She knew a lot more than she should, and I wasn't sure if that was Cross's doing. "Who are you? Why are you asking these questions?"

"I mean you no harm, Miss Parker. These are just background questions. We did our research, and we asked Lucien for his help and input. You seem to be the perfect candidate."

"Candidate for what? I already have a job."

"I know. This won't take long. A couple of weeks. Cross Security is already under contract with the production company. We're in need of a technical consultant, but I was hoping for a ride-along. Someone I can mimic and learn from. You'll do nicely."

My brows scrunched. "A ride-along?"

She pushed the intercom button. "Take us back, Dennis." She finished her cup of coffee. "Our legal team will meet with you this afternoon. Once the NDA is signed, you'll be given additional details. I find this cloak and dagger routine rather entertaining, but I can comprehend why you would find it unnerving and potentially dangerous." Her eyes narrowed on my purse. "Are you carrying a weapon?"

"Always."

She made a note of that also. "That might cause an issue. We'll let our bosses figure that out." She looked contrite. "I hope you weren't offended by my questions or this meeting. That was not my intention. I hope we can be friends. There's a lot I can learn from you." She opened the cabinet again and placed her cup inside. "Are you sure I can't get you a cup of coffee? It really is the least I can do after dragging you out at this horrible hour."

"Not unless it's going to provide some kind of insight into what you hoped to accomplish with this meeting."

"You'll see soon enough."

The limo stopped in the exact place it had been when I entered, and Dennis opened my door. I stepped out, casting a final wary look at the unidentified woman before going back inside the office building. Lucien had a lot of explaining to do.

By the time I made it upstairs, he had already started the morning meeting. For some reason, he decided to call everyone else in a few hours early too. He probably figured there would be safety in numbers and didn't want to deal with one of my outbursts. No matter how hard he tried, I refused to grasp the boss-employee dynamic. And he despised my insistence on autonomy.

Barging into the room, I took my usual spot at the conference table. A few of my colleagues stifled their snickers. Lucien Cross slid a blue folder in front of me while he continued speaking about our newest clients. Lancaster asked a few questions about the specific case he had been assigned, and while the men were talking, I looked to see what the boss had in store for me. Answers to what just happened would be great.

"Really?" I looked around the conference table, suspecting this was some sort of trick. "This is a joke, right?" At least that would explain the snickers.

"Of course not," Cross replied.

Bennett Renner, one of my colleagues, diverted his eyes and coughed in an attempt to hide his laughter. Darwin, Lancaster, and Simms were distracted by the assignments they had just been handed and didn't seem to care one way or the other about what I had been tasked to do. Kellan Dey, on the other hand, gazed at me with pity in his eyes. At least someone seemed to understand.

"Is there a problem, Miss Parker?" Lucien asked. His tone became prickly, and I knew he expected me to answer in the negative.

"Several. Let's start with why me," I said, disappointing him as usual.

He cast looks around the table. "Does anyone else have any questions or concerns?"

"No, sir," several of the others responded.

"Then get to work." Cross leaned back in his chair and waited for his team of investigators to file out.

Renner clapped me on the back on his way to the door. "This could be your big break, Alex. Maybe they'll ask you to do a bit part, and you'll be discovered. I'll be able to say I knew you when."

"That's enough, Bennett," Cross hissed.

The former police detective smiled. "Whatever you say, boss." He was the last to leave the room.

"So this is a bullshit assignment?" I asked once we were alone. "Is this some hazing ritual? Is this even real?" I gestured at the contract. Aside from the name of the production company and a generic list of required duties, no other details were provided. I scanned the page again, wondering if Cross had one of the techs upstairs draft it just to see how I'd react. Hell, he probably hired the woman and limo driver just to make me think this was real. The one thing I'd learned about my boss in the six weeks since I'd started working for him, he liked to test people.

"I assure you it's quite real." He let out a lengthy exhale. "Cross Security has been providing protection and consultants to Broadway Films for the last seven years. Whenever they film locally, my firm handles their security. *We* handle their security. Depending on their requirements, I have also provided the film company with technical advisors." He glanced down at the contract on the table. "You'll be given additional details when you meet with their legal team." He looked at his watch. "I suggest you lose the attitude. And try not to act starstruck. We're professionals. This firm has a reputation to uphold."

"Then why is Renner acting like this is some big joke?"

"It is not, and you have more important things to do than waste time trying to figure him out." Cross stood, but I remained seated. "Is there something else you wanted to say?"

"What was the deal with the woman in the car? Who is she?"

"She wanted to make sure you were just as promising in person as you are on paper." Subconsciously, he looked at his phone, and I knew she sent him a message as soon as I got out of the car. A brief smile danced across his lips. "Alexis, you are the only person with the unique set of attributes for which they are looking. They wanted a female federal agent with field experience, preferably former FBI."

"And I can check all those boxes."

"Precisely." He went to the door. "They'll send a car to pick you up this afternoon. Someone from reception will let you know when it arrives. Until then, make sure you have the rest of your case work in order. Once you start with Broadway Films, you won't have much time to check in at the office. If you have anything ongoing that is time-sensitive, pass it off to Mr. Dey."

"Do I have a choice?"

He studied me for a moment. "This is a great opportunity, Alex. It isn't dangerous, and honestly, after your audition with my firm, I feel I owe you something easy and safe. Just meet with their legal team, and if you decide you still want to pass, I'll find someone else to do it."

"Thank you."

He gave me a final look. "Just give it a chance." That wasn't a suggestion.

I collected my belongings and went to my office. Kellan was across the hall, and as soon as I settled in behind my desk, he knocked on my open door. I looked up, jerking my chin at the client chair in front of me while I flipped through the papers to make sure everything had been completed.

"Spill," I said as soon as he sat down. "What do you

know about Broadway Films?"

"Plenty."

"Like?"

Kellan sighed. "What Cross didn't tell you is this is the worst assignment you can get. We've all served our time on set. The good news is no one will shoot you, unless it's with a prop gun. The bad news is you will be bored out of your mind, and the hours are absolute shit."

"That doesn't sound so bad. It's like any other day stuck in the office."

"Not in the least. The first day will be lovely. They'll try to woo you. Make you feel like a real asset. Someone they value and cherish. That will stop just as soon as your input contradicts their cinematic vision. Also, working on set will completely decimate whatever glamourous view you have of Hollywood and the movie business. And don't even get me started on the mind fuck the questions can be."

"I'm a big girl. I can survive a look behind the curtain." I just wasn't sure if I could deal with that woman or her prying questions. "What exactly do they want to know?"

"The basics — how to hold a gun, if shouting *freeze* is realistic, the proper way of breaching a house." He shrugged. "Things like that. Y'know, the muscle memory stuff that we don't even think about."

That didn't sound so bad, just tedious and boring. "Great," I said nonplussed. "I was afraid it was more cerebral than that."

"It can be. It just depends on the writers and actors and how badly they want to incorporate real life," he put air quotes around the words, "into their film."

"That's what I was afraid of."

"You like movies, don't you?"

"Who doesn't?"

"That might change after this." He stood and tapped the edge of my desk. "I'll see you in a few weeks, and you can bitch all about it. In the meantime, I offer you a few parting words of advice. Actors are assholes. Drugs will be on the set; it's just a matter of looking. And don't hesitate to ask craft services to make you something special. If you eat what they leave out for the crew, you'll gain twenty pounds and feel like you've been stuck on the world's most boring stakeout for the entire duration."

"Is that all the advice you have?"

"Pretty much. It's not difficult, just draining."

"I'll keep that in mind." I held a manila envelope in his direction. "Cross said to pass off any open cases to you. Have fun."

He glanced down at the paperwork. "Searching for hidden assets?"

"Yep."

"Fabulous."

TWO

I reread the NDA again. The two attorneys seated across the table were getting fidgety. I picked up a pen, practically hearing their collective intake of breath. They wanted me to sign on the dotted line. Instead, I tapped the pen against the edge of the paper and read through a few of the clauses again.

"Let me get this straight." I leaned back. "You want me to agree to these terms when I don't even know what this is?"

One of the lawyers practically growled. "This is a boilerplate nondisclosure, Miss Parker. I'm sure you've encountered these before. If you desire someone to review it or explain the features to you, I'll be more than happy to invite a member of Cross Security's legal team to join us. But this is the same agreement we've used in all of our previous dealings with your firm. Until now, there has never been a problem."

"Yeah, well, I went to law school. They told us we need to read contracts before signing them."

His eyes practically rolled back in his head, and he got up from the table and turned to look out the window behind him. The mere sight of me was making him ill, and

I couldn't help but take a perverse joy in his misery. If the production company decided I was too much trouble, they would request another consultant, and I would be off the hook.

"Miss Parker," the more patient attorney said, reaching across the table and taking the contract from me, "let's make this easier on all of us. The conditions are simple. You will be given access to the set and production personnel. That includes writers, actors, producers, and directors. You're going to see and hear things that are not yet available for public consumption. The movie we are making is going to be a blockbuster. We've been in talks about turning this into another hit franchise, and we need to do all we can to avoid leaks on set. We have no intention of confiscating your phone or searching you before, during, or after you leave, but should you share, remove, or otherwise spread any information, whether it's for profit or not, Broadway Films needs to have legal recourse available."

"The woman I spoke to this morning asked a lot of personal questions. I don't have an issue with maintaining your production secrets, but I'm not signing anything until I know what you want from me."

The attorney at the window turned around. "Agreeing to the NDA does not automatically bring you under contract with Broadway Films. That arrangement has already been signed by Cross Security. Your firm is under contract."

I gave him a *no shit* look and said, "With the stipulation that your technical consultant agrees to the terms of the nondisclosure, so once I sign this, I become your technical consultant. Do you see my problem?"

He rubbed both hands down his face. "We're at an impasse."

"Or you can choose to trust me with some of these top-secret details. Honestly, my government security clearance is still valid. Doesn't that indicate I'm trustworthy?"

"Andrew, why don't you see what Dinah wants to do?" the seated man suggested.

"Fine." He stepped into the hallway, and I let out a breath.

I offered the remaining attorney a small smile. "I'd like to state, for the record, that I'm not always this difficult. Normally, I'm the one asking clients questions, not the other way around, and I didn't quite care for the third degree."

He scratched his eyebrow. "I get it. I wouldn't want to end up going for a ride in the back of a limo. It's a little too *sleep with the fishes* if you ask me."

I grinned. "Have you always been an entertainment lawyer?"

"It shows, doesn't it? If you stick around long enough, you'll undoubtedly witness my Christopher Walken impression and hear several lines from *Jerry Maguire.*"

"Please don't," a woman said, and I turned to see a statuesque brunette with expertly executed highlights entering the room. The only similarity between her and the woman in the car was the glossy red lipstick. She smiled warmly and took a seat beside me. "I'm Dinah Allen."

The introduction was pointless. She was featured on the covers of half the entertainment and fashion magazines on the shelf this month. She was a few years older than me, having started her career as a fashion model after being discovered working behind the scenes for one of the big labels in Paris. After a decade of modeling, her agent had gotten her cast in some independent film that swept through Cannes like wildfire. Now she was a rising film star.

"Nice to meet you," I said. I'd seen clips of the indie film on several late night programs, but the film itself wasn't my cup of tea. Honestly, I might have just been too self-absorbed to care about the newest Hollywood darling or the trendiest flavor of the week. "Were you rehearsing for an Audrey Hepburn biopic this morning?"

"I was hoping for more of a Lauren Bacall vibe." She grinned wickedly. "Tell me I didn't miss my mark?"

"I guess I can see the Bacall thing," I admitted.

"Great." She gestured at the contract. "Andrew says we have a problem, and seeing as how I'm the one who caused it, I should be the one to fix it." Her French manicured fingers swept her hair behind her ear. "Miss Parker, what

G.K. Parks

I'm about to tell you cannot leave this room. I've been cast to play an FBI agent, and I want to get it right. This isn't just some shoot 'em up, sexy, action flick. We aren't doing popcorn films. My character has depth and a troubled past. I need insight on how to approach the role from someone who lived this and, based on your reaction, is probably still living with this. I don't want to do a disservice to the women who fulfill these roles in real life. I need your help. I want to talk to you and learn from you."

Kellan hit the nail on the head. "Wow, that sounds like one very boring movie."

She laughed. "It won't be. There are chase sequences and shootouts. The studio needs a technical consultant for those matters, and I figured two birds, one stone. I'm not exactly a veteran of this industry, and they are only offering me some slight indulgences. They couldn't get the actual FBI to agree to let me shadow them. They said it was for insurance, but I imagine the federal government has better things to do than babysit some newbie actor."

"But I don't."

"That's not what I meant."

"Regardless, I suppose it's true." I sighed. "Don't come at me with a million loaded questions and drop a bomb in my lap. It won't get you very far, and contract or not, I will walk away."

"Okay."

"How did you know those things about me?"

"Lucien mentioned your revolving door career."

"I'll be having a chat with him." I reached across the table for the contract. "I'll sign this on one condition, and it is non-negotiable."

"You can't reveal the nature of the film, plot points, lines of script, scenes, or anything related to the actors' professional or private antics to the press, paparazzi, or the media in general, especially social media," Andrew warned.

I glared at him before turning my attention back to Dinah. "If I tell you something is out of bounds, we aren't discussing it further. I'll provide as much help as I can for your preparation of the role, but some things aren't about the job, they're about me. And they're private."

"I can appreciate that."

I picked up the pen and signed my name. If I hated being here, Lucien would pull me and assign another investigator. That was our agreement, and since he'd blatantly violated my trust by sharing details of my life with the client, he owed me. "Now what happens?"

"I'll see you tomorrow morning, Miss Parker," Dinah said.

"It's Alex." I'd been nothing but hostile, and since she was the client, or at least one of them, it was time to mend fences.

"Dinah." She held out her hand, and we shook. "Andrew will have someone take you on a tour of the set, get you a pass, and a copy of the call sheet. Be prepared to hit the ground running." She went to the door. "Gentlemen."

"Miss Allen," they both replied in a dreamy tone. And Cross was afraid I would be starstruck. Ha. "We'll take you by security and go from there. I hope those are comfortable walking shoes." He glanced down at my heels. "This is a small lot by most studio standards, but it is nearly two acres and spans multiple buildings. You won't need to familiarize yourself with everything, but we'll show you around anyway." He went to the door, waiting impatiently for me to join him. "Come along. I don't have all day."

And Kellan said they were going to be nice to me at the beginning. Surely, it wouldn't all be downhill from here.

*   *   *

It was a little after seven p.m. when I made it back to the office. Most of my colleagues had called it a night, so I went up another two levels to Lucien's office. Normally, his assistant was stationed in the outer office, but he wasn't there. However, my boss's open door clued me in that the big man was still hard at work. I knocked against the doorframe, waiting for him to look up before I stepped inside.

"How was the rest of your day?" he asked. "I had a feeling you'd be stopping by tonight."

Licking my lips, I struggled to figure out what to say.

"You gave them access to my résumé?"

"Just the bullet points. Broadway Films wanted to be certain we could tick off their requirements." He gestured to the seat in front of his desk, and I dropped into it. My feet hurt from too much walking.

"All of your investigators are qualified. I'm not the only woman who works here, and I'm not the only one who served her time with the FBI. Tell me why you chose me."

"You fit the profile," he stated coolly.

"Bullshit. The first case I worked was messy, and ever since, you've given me these easy tasks to complete."

"Maybe I thought you were working on something on the side." He glowered. "Correct me if I'm wrong, but you forced me to strike the noncompete from your contract before you agreed to sign with my firm."

"And I appreciate that." I blinked, recalling the vast amount of resources I'd used and overseas phone calls I'd made since I began working here. It was no secret Cross monitored office communications. "Am I to assume these assignments are some sort of punishment?"

"Was the OIO that punitive?"

"No." Something about his question and the look in his eyes gave him away. "This is about the missing persons case I worked, isn't it? You don't trust me to be out in the field."

He shrugged.

An irritated laugh escaped my throat. "I didn't take you for a sexist."

"I'm not." He stood, circling his desk before pacing back and forth, a sure sign of stress. He found this conversation vexing.

"Afraid I can't handle myself?" Granted, he and Detective Nick O'Connell had come to my rescue, but the situation had been beyond my control.

"Even though I haven't seen you use the company gym, I have no doubts that it would be difficult to best you in a fight."

"Do you really think you'd win?"

He considered the question carefully. "Honestly, I don't know, and I'd rather not find out." A compliment, I should have been overjoyed. Instead, I feared the follow-up. "Like you said, the first case you worked was messy. Shit happened. Since then, you've come to work exhausted, jumpy, and in constant need of visits to the coffeemaker."

"I'm not a morning person, and as you know, I was assisting on a case in England. The time difference sucks." He didn't speak, and I knew what he was thinking. "I'm not traumatized," I insisted.

"Then you're the only person on this entire planet that could go through something like that and not be." He returned to his desk chair. "Along with medics on staff, there is a counselor equipped to deal with the fallout from these unpleasant experiences should you wish to speak to someone."

I chuckled. "Really, Cross, I'm okay." I eyed him. "Is that why you've been giving me these ridiculous cases? You want me to see the shrink?"

"The federal government mandates psychological evaluations."

"I hated those."

"I imagine more so than most. You're a woman operating in a traditionally male-dominated field. You had to be stronger, faster, better, and more capable than your male counterparts. Anything that indicated weakness made your life exponentially harder. You should know it isn't like that here. You earned your position on the merits. You made it through the audition phase. You have nothing to prove."

"Who said I have anything to prove?"

A smirk played across his lips. "Regardless, I'm not in the business of endangering the lives of my people. Our security teams deal with the more dangerous situations, bodyguarding and such, but there is a reason every one of my investigators carries a piece. Typically, our case load doesn't get messy, but..."

"I bring out the messy." Leaning my head back, I rolled my neck from side to side. "Kellan said everyone on staff has served as a technical consultant for Broadway Films at one point or another. It's only fair I serve my time as well." I gave him a stern look. "You say I have nothing to prove, so stop lobbing softballs. I can handle whatever you throw at me."

"Then you shouldn't have any problems handling the creative minds at Broadway Films or dealing with Dinah Allen."

THREE

Pressing my palms into my eyes, I wondered if I fell asleep in this position if anyone at the table would notice. The studio hadn't exactly started production yet, or maybe they had. I wasn't exactly aware of what was happening outside this tiny room. It was cramped, smelled like feet and pepperoni pizza, and three of the four walls were painted cinderblock. Kellan was right; I no longer believed in any of the glitz and glamour broadcast during award shows or red carpet appearances. This wasn't even as ritzy as a TSA interrogation room in some third-rate airport.

"Moving on to the next scene," Travis Kreecher said, and every person, excluding myself, turned the page on the script. The group assembled at the table was the writing staff. Travis was in charge. I was given strict instructions to interrupt if the jargon used was incorrect or if the dialogue was off the mark. He tapped his highlighter against my elbow. "Did you find a mistake?"

I pulled my hands away from my eyes and looked down at the 150 page script. "No, we're all good."

"Keep up then. We're on a tight schedule. They want to start shooting tonight."

I want to start shooting right now, I thought. Fortunately, my nine millimeter was locked in my glove box. The studio didn't want to risk having an actual weapon on set with so many fake guns around. Granted, the fakes had a bright orange strip on them, but one could never be too careful.

The hours dragged on. At some point, someone from craft services came in with a box of sandwiches and salads and put them in the center of the table. I watched the feeding frenzy begin. Lions in the wild weren't as voracious. Taking a moment, I went in search of coffee.

When I returned, Travis was anxiously pacing the hallway. "Where have you been? We're on a deadline. You should have been here days ago. I don't understand why Neil waited until the last minute before hiring a consultant. We could have already gone over this with someone in L.A."

"How dare he," I deadpanned.

"Damn straight," Travis replied, leading me back into the room. "We have four hours to get through the rest of the script, and we still have," he flipped to the end, "forty-three more pages to go."

"You're assuming we aren't going to be doing last minute rewrites," Artie, another of the writers, said. "Lance always has his own ideas and ad-libs. You know we'll be tweaking it until production closes."

"And have to clean it up further in post," Dallas added glumly. He shot a smile in my direction. "You aren't the problem, Alex. It's the director and the talent. They seem to forget without us they wouldn't have anything. But we're just little worker bees. What do we know?"

"I can relate," I said.

Having convinced them I was onboard and wouldn't cause any more delays with my annoying desire to stretch my legs, use the bathroom, or drink coffee to stay awake, I followed along as Travis pointed out the relevant parts of dialogue and asked a few questions. We spent the next four hours going through the last of the script, but at least that was finally over.

As soon as we finished, Travis printed a new copy from the master file and brought it to the director. A production assistant came into the room as the writers cleared out. She picked up the sticky note that was on top of the pages. Once the director approved the changes, she would be responsible for making sure everyone had new copies, and since secrecy was tantamount on this production, she'd have to collect each of the old scripts and replace them with the new ones. That wasn't my problem, but now that we were done, I wasn't entirely sure what I was supposed to do.

"You're Alex, right?" she asked as I lingered just outside the room, wondering if I could leave for the day.

"Guilty."

She yanked the radio free from her waistband. "Tell Dinah she's finished." She waited for a quick reply. "Just wait over there." She pointed to the end of the hallway which led to the wide open expanse of the soundstage. I looked to see where she was pointing, and by the time I turned around, she was gone.

"Okay."

I went to the spot she indicated. One of the indoor sets was being constructed, and I watched as they moved the backdrop around, checking the tape markings on the floors for proper placement. Someone else said something, and a cable lowered to the floor. Before I could see what it was going to be used for, another PA appeared at my side.

"Miss Allen is waiting." She didn't even give me a chance to respond before turning and heading for the large exit at the far end of the building. At least today I wore my running shoes.

When we stepped outside, I was surprised to find the sun had set. It was dark, or it would have been if floodlights weren't lighting up the sky. Dinah was seated in a chair with her name stamped on the back in bright white lettering. She wore a long coat which seemed way too warm for this time of year and was typing something on her phone. She held up a single digit when I approached, not even bothering to look up until she was finished. Then she put the device in her coat pocket and smiled.

"Finished dealing with the writers?" she asked, even though she already knew the answer.

"I think so."

"They'll probably check-in from time to time with modifications, but the hard part should be over." She brushed an invisible strand of hair out of her eyes, blinking rapidly and getting frustrated. "Stupid fake lashes." She brushed again before forcing her hand into her lap. "You would think after years of modeling I would be used to them." Her phone buzzed, and a smile tugged at her lips. "I'm sorry, Alex. I'm out of my element. I've never been on a set like this either, and I'm entirely overwhelmed. I only did that one film, and it was nothing like this. We didn't even have sets. Everything was shot on location. The prep was nothing. This," she watched as a stuntman hooked to wires ran through an elaborate routine while another checked the light levels and someone with a boom mic tested out sound, "is unbelievable." She grabbed the arm of the closest chair and dragged it next to her. "Do you want to sit down?"

I sat in the offered chair, practically jumping out of my skin when the mic let out a shrill whine. I laughed at myself and tried to keep one eye on the action and the other on her. "Now that I'm done with the writers, what's next?"

"The stunt coordinator will want your input on a few of the action sequences, and I'm sure the director will want a word at some point. Tomorrow morning, you're going to instruct the actors on the proper way of holding and firing a handgun." She reached for a schedule no one bothered to share with me. "And in the afternoon, fight training."

"No one told me any of this."

She looked a little guilty and handed me the paper. "Sorry, I said I'd give that to you, but time got away. I spent my day in the wardrobe trailer, getting fitted, and in the makeup trailer while they worked on perfecting the various color palettes."

"So I'm supposed to teach you how to fight and shoot in a matter of hours?"

"We already went through a six week boot camp back in Los Angeles. This is a refresher. And it's not just for me. Lance, Gemma, and Clay will be there too. The stuntmen have previous training and their own coordinator. You actually don't have to teach us anything, except how to make it look like we know what we're doing."

"Sure." Maybe it wasn't too late to get Cross to send a replacement.

As if reading my mind, she settled back in her seat and assessed me, subtly shifting until she was in the exact same position I was in. "Unlike today, most of your time from here on out will be spent in my company. I'll be shadowing you while you follow me around." She laughed "I know it's rather counterintuitive, but we're under time constraints. Elodie will get you copies of my call sheet, so you'll know when you have to be here and where to be."

"Okay." My head throbbed. The only place I wanted to be was home.

Her assistant, probably the previously mentioned Elodie, appeared with a salad of some sort and a bottle of water. She handed the items to Dinah as inconspicuously as possible. Dinah looked down and thanked her, stabbing a piece of fish with her fork. "Have you eaten yet?"

"No, but I'm okay."

Dinah looked at me through her lashes. "Elodie, see if crafty can toss together another one of these. Do you have any food sensitivities, Alex?"

"No." I jerked my chin at the bowl. "What is that?"

"I call it a California poke salad." She shrugged. "Wow, I just heard myself. That sounded pretentious. It's lettuce with cucumber and carrot ribbons, poached tuna, avocado, and a honey lime dressing." She smirked. "Sounds good, doesn't it?" She looked back at Elodie and winked. The assistant disappeared, and Dinah took another bite. "Did you ever think you'd be on a movie set telling writers how to make the lines better?"

"Not quite, but life tends to throw me curveballs."

"I bet." She took another bite, balancing the bowl on her lap while she reached for her water. "If someone asked you ten years ago where you'd be right now, what would you have said?"

A pang of sadness came over me. "I would have said that I hoped to be working at an FBI field office."

"You miss it?"

"Not really."

She raised an eyebrow, her dinner completely forgotten. "Do you miss the life you thought you were going to have?"

"I actually ended up with something much better than I ever imagined." The look on her face told me she didn't believe it. "I am grateful to be alive and where I am."

"Then what's the problem?" she asked.

"It came at a price."

She quirked an eyebrow and reached into her pocket for a notepad. "Professional or personal?"

"Damn, you're inquisitive." I shook it off. This was why I was here. "Both. Professionally, I wanted out of the OIO. I needed to break free. When I went back, it was a mistake. Leaving this time closed the door for good."

She wasn't following along, probably because I was being rather cryptic. "Were those issues gender-related? Women in a lot of industries face glass ceilings."

"That wasn't my problem. Sometimes, things just go wrong, and when they do, people die. I didn't want to be there anymore, so I left. And my boss spent a very long time convincing me to go back. I did some consulting work which bridged the gap, and then some factors beyond my control came into play. I went back because, at the time, it seemed like the right thing. It wasn't." I bit my lip and looked away.

"People die," she mumbled, latching on to the one thing I shouldn't have said. "You lost someone to the job."

"My first partner. We went through Quantico together." I glanced at her. "That's all you get. I'm not talking about this."

She held up her palms and tucked the notepad back into her pocket. She had just picked up her bowl and resumed eating when Elodie returned with a carbon copy. She handed it to me, asked if Dinah needed anything else, and went to check on something in the trailer.

"This is really good," I said, hoping to change the subject.

She swallowed and dabbed carefully at her glossed lips. Before she could respond, her phone buzzed again. She looked down at the device, a flirtatious grin skirting across her face.

"Is that someone special?" I asked.

My comment caught her off guard, and she looked rather alarmed. "How did you do that?"

"I am a trained investigator. And I'm here all week," I teased. She continued to stare at me. "The look on your face. I've seen it a million times. It looks like someone has a crush."

"Had," she corrected. "We haven't seen each other in nearly fifteen years. He was my first love. It turns out he still lives in the city. He recently contacted me in regards to a business proposal, and we've been texting a lot ever since. He's going to stop by the set later. My people tell me he's single and still gorgeous. I guess we'll see."

"Actor?" I asked.

"No, I've made my fair share of mistakes with those." Her eyes darted in the direction of her costar, Lance Smoke, and I wondered exactly what the story was. "I knew him from my fashion days."

"Model? Photographer?"

"He should have been a model." Her eyes closed, and for a moment, she looked absolutely content. "I guess you'd say he was a designer. We worked closely on several lines. But I ended up taking a job in Paris, and he stayed behind." She typed out a quick response and tucked the phone away. "Actually, I was quite surprised to hear he was looking for some of the original sketches and an unfinished line we had worked on. Sure, fashion is circular and trends basically repeat with a few alterations, but I never expected him to reach out, especially now. It's kind of crazy."

"Do you think it's because you're a big star? You're on the front of every magazine this month."

"That could be." Her expression soured. "And the tabloids too."

"Goes with the territory, right?"

She rolled her eyes. "Unless you help me, I'm going to be a laughingstock in Hollywood." She lowered her voice. "Do you think I have any idea what I'm doing?"

"Join the club."

The look she gave me said *yeah, right.* Before such thoughts could be verbalized, Elodie returned, carrying an ugly arrangement of flowers. Most of them looked black, but it might be on account of the dark.

"I just found another one. What do you want me to do?"

Dinah frowned, her gaze on the bouquet. "Is there a card?"

Elodie held it out, and Dinah tentatively reached for it. After reading it, she crushed it in her hand and tossed it to the ground. "Get rid of it, and notify security. I don't want anyone going inside my trailer without my permission."

I finished eating as I watched the situation play out. "What's that about?" I asked.

"Just a fan." Someone called to Dinah from across the lot, and she took off her coat. Underneath, she was in costume, ready to film some sort of nighttime outdoor scene. From what she was wearing, I could only imagine it was romantic in nature. "You should call it a night. We have a long day tomorrow and more long days ahead after that." She offered a smile that was far from genuine. It was obvious she was worried. "Good night, Alex."

"Night." I watched her cross the lot, and then I reached down and picked up the crumpled note.

Flowers for my flower. You're mine, Dinah. You don't need anyone else, and I'm going to make certain the world knows it.

FOUR

"We found three sets of prints. The only match we've made so far is to you," Amir said. He worked on the thirty-first floor in Cross's lab. "I'll expand the database search and see if we get a hit."

"Don't bother. Whoever left the note didn't leave a print."

"Are you certain?"

Actually, I wasn't, but that didn't matter. I needed to speak to the security team Cross assigned to Broadway Films. They would have access to surveillance footage. If someone entered Dinah Allen's trailer, they would know about it. "You wouldn't happen to have a spare portable modem, would you?"

The question amused him. "For your laptop?"

"Yes."

"Give me a sec." He crossed the lab and opened a cabinet. Inside were plenty of high-tech toys. This was one of my first visits upstairs, and frankly, I was impressed. I'd only glimpsed some of Cross's gear during my first assignment at his firm, but this was definitely top of the line. It put the OIO and PD to shame, perhaps even the DEA, and out of the three agencies, the DEA seemed to have confiscated more than their fair share of shiny gadgets. He handed me a clipboard. "Sign there." He pointed to the bottom line.

That was easy. Maybe too easy. My eyes went back to the crumpled note. "What about DNA?"

"That's a lot more complicated than fingerprints. I can get started tonight."

"I don't know. I'm not sure any of this is important."

Amir picked up the card and held it up to the light. "It's doubtful there's anything on it, but I'll check. If there is DNA, it could be a few weeks. I'll leave you a message in the morning and let you know either way."

"Thanks."

Just as I reached for the elevator button, the doors opened. Lucien Cross stood on the other side. His hands shoved in his pockets. The lines of his suit remained pristine. To this day, I had no idea how he accomplished such a feat. He stepped to the side and gazed at me expectantly.

"Were you coming to see me?" He sounded smug, as if he already knew the answer, which he did.

"Don't you have anything better to do than watch the security feed?" I stepped into the elevator, and he pushed the button for the lobby.

"Why did you request fingerprint analysis?" His reflection in the mirrored doors glared at me. "Have you already moved on to another case? It would have been courteous to at least notify me before reneging on Cross Security's contract with Broadway Films."

"I'm not reneging." I stepped in front of him so he couldn't continue to stare at himself in the doors. "Something weird happened, and I thought I'd check it out. Speaking of, I need to get into contact with our security team."

"This is about the breach in Miss Allen's trailer." Lucien nodded to himself. "Did she ask you to look into it? Does she have any suspicions as to who left the flowers?"

"No." I licked my lips. As usual, he knew more than he should. "Tell me what's going on."

"Nothing. It's my understanding the delivery was a

miscommunication. The studio delivered the gift. Whoever entered her trailer belonged there. They probably didn't realize fan mail and gifts were being rerouted. Protocols concerning Miss Allen aren't set in stone yet. This is their first experience working with her, and it's not like her manager or agent care about anything other than publicity."

It sounded like excuses. "So your team isn't responsible? They didn't screw up?"

"Absolutely not." He looked stern. "Should Miss Allen require additional information concerning the identity of the sender or the delivery person, feel free to direct her concerns to the security team."

"You don't want me to investigate."

He smirked. "There's nothing to investigate." My gut said otherwise, and Lucien knew it. "Use your best judgment. Just remember what your actual duties are."

"I will."

"And Alex, don't forget the terms of the NDA." The doors opened in the lobby, and Lucien waited for me to step out first. "If any other issues arise, please let me know. I will expand the security team if you believe there is an unaddressed threat, but you might want to do some research into Dinah Allen before you jump to conclusions. Any one of her people could have delivered those flowers."

"I thought it was a closed set."

He resembled a Cheshire cat. "There are always exceptions." He moved through the lobby like he owned the whole damn building and not just the three floors where his offices were located. "Would you care for a ride home?"

"My car is in the garage."

He nodded and climbed into the back of his town car. Maybe one of these days I would actually figure him out, or he could just make my life simpler by laying his cards on the table and sharing his intel. Pondering the unlikelihood of that, I worked myself into a tizzy while I drove to the apartment I shared.

Even though I was tired from the long day, my muscles craved movement, but my treadmill was across town at my place. There was a twenty-four hour gym within walking distance, but I didn't have a membership. So I had to improvise. I changed into workout clothes, road the elevator down to the lobby, opened the door to the stairwell, and ran up twenty-one flights.

By the time I made it back to the apartment, I was covered in sweat. My legs were dead, and my glutes were cramped. My heart beat so hard in my chest I wondered if that workout would be my last. I showered in record time, just so I could sit down, and changed into pajama shorts and a t-shirt. It was only after I settled onto the couch with my computer to research Dinah Allen that I realized just how exhausted I was.

According to the schedule on the call sheet, I would have to get up by 4:30 in order to get to the studio on time. Didn't actors need their beauty sleep? It was nearly eleven. I scanned through the top stories concerning Dinah Allen. Hollywood's newest It girl was rumored to be in a torrid affair with Lance Smoke. The rumor mill continued to churn around their on again, off again romance. From the photos, it appeared Lance wasn't ready to be tied down to just one woman.

Several articles concerned the casting of the new movie. No wonder the studio was determined to keep a lid on things. The paparazzi loved on set romances, and the model turned actress who hooked up with one of the most sought after actors on the planet was definitely at the top of their list. Cross Security would need to remain on their toes, but at least I understood why Lucien was certain there hadn't been a breach. It would have been all over the internet by now. Maybe Lance had one of the assistants deliver the flowers. The more I thought about it, the more sense it made.

After packing my laptop and the modem to take with me, I filled my gym bag for tomorrow and made sure I had everything ready to go. I planned to stumble out of bed, grab my things, and drive to work. I'd be lucky if I was awake enough to remember to get dressed. Craft services better have coffee waiting.

I crawled under the covers, but something nagged at the

corners of my mind. I twisted and turned, checking the clock every few minutes. Finally, I managed to fall into a light sleep.

The sound of the front door opening jolted me upright. My hand sought out my nine millimeter in the dark, but I retracted it when a familiar voice called out. A moment later, James Martin stepped into the bedroom. His tie hung in a loose knot, but aside from that, he appeared to be the powerful CEO he was.

"Sweetheart, I'm home," he cooed, leaning down and kissing me. "I'm sorry I'm so late. I sent you a text, but you didn't respond."

"What time is it?" I mumbled.

"Late." He continued to kiss me. "I haven't been able to get you off my mind all day. It made for some rather interesting meetings." He laughed softly, his breath against my ear. "The only thing I wanted to do was come home. My last meeting ran late." He nuzzled against my neck, running one hand through my hair while the other worked on removing his tie.

I inhaled. "Why do you smell like perfume?"

He stepped back, standing up straight. "Samantha was sitting next to me. I guess I got too close. I'll just jump in the shower and wash off." He grinned roguishly. "I'll be right out."

Before I could say a word, he disappeared into the bathroom, and I relaxed. He was home. That knowledge put my overactive imagination at ease, and I turned onto my side. Now maybe I could get some sleep.

A few minutes later, he climbed into bed. He wrapped his arms around me and nibbled on my earlobe. I sighed, and his mouth moved downward. It wasn't fair he knew every single thing that drove me wild, and tonight, he seemed determined to arouse me to wakefulness.

"Martin," I rolled onto my back and looked at him, "not tonight, handsome."

"In that case, it's a good thing it's morning," he teased, stealing another kiss.

If he kept this up, I would give in, and he knew it. Normally, he wasn't this persistent. "Is everything okay?" I asked.

"I just missed you. You're the most important person in my life, and instead of spending time with you, I was stuck in pointless meetings for half the night." He kissed me again. "With the way you've run out of here the last two mornings, I've barely seen you, let alone kiss you." He hovered closer. "I've really missed you."

"I can tell. What time is it?"

"Almost three."

"I have to get up in less than two hours. I hate to say it, but I need sleep."

"Fine, but you owe me," he said playfully before checking to make sure the alarm was set. He curled around me, burying his nose in my hair. "I love you, Alexis. You're my whole world."

I barely closed my eyes when the alarm sounded. For a moment, I gave careful consideration to smashing it into the wall. Instead, I hit the snooze button and thought about calling in sick. Martin stirred beside me.

"Not yet," he murmured, his words barely coherent. He tucked me against his body, his chest pressing against my back. I could feel his measured breaths and the tension leave his arms. The bastard fell asleep, and I wanted nothing more than to join him. We remained in that embrace until the alarm sounded the second time. "I'll make you breakfast," he mumbled.

"Don't. I'll grab something at work. Go back to sleep."

Carefully, I disentangled myself from him. He was unconscious before I even climbed out of bed, and I envied him. The point of this apartment was so we'd have a weekend getaway where we could escape from work and the outside world. Unfortunately, that idea went out the window after our first weekend inside the apartment. Now we were cohabitating on an almost regular basis, except, as he pointed out only a couple hours ago, that didn't mean we had actually spent any time together. Now with the long hours at the studio, I wasn't sure how long we'd continue to be ships passing in the night.

Grabbing my clothes, I went into the bathroom to change and face another day. The glare of the lights was harsh on my eyes, and I looked out the window at the pitch black night. I was used to working late, but being up so early that I would have considered it late was a new experience. And one I despised. I went to check my reflection in the mirror, but it was still covered in a layer of condensation from Martin's shower.

I wiped it off and looked around the bathroom. Normally, Martin was rather neat and orderly, but he had been in such a rush last night to jump into bed he hadn't bothered to tidy up. After seeing the slight disarray, I couldn't help but think the entire thing was a bit odd. He had quite the sexual appetite, but waking me up at three a.m. wasn't one of his go-to moves.

One of his shirt sleeves escaped the hamper and dangled freely. A stain on his cuff caught my eye. I opened the cover and picked up his shirt. It smelled of floral perfume. A second stain was on the side of his collar, and I couldn't help but think it looked like makeup transfer. I also knew it wasn't from me. I showered before bed, not that I even wore enough makeup to leave a smudge like that.

My insides went cold. I wasn't thinking clearly. Surely, there was a reasonable explanation for everything. Shaking it off, I dropped the shirt into the hamper and finished getting ready. Then I grabbed my bags, tossed a final look in the direction of our bedroom, and left the apartment. This was the last thing I needed right now.

FIVE

"Can you show me that again?" Clay Chaffey asked. He was in his mid-twenties, fresh-faced, and excited to play with toy guns. Unlike Gemma and Lance who seemed rather indifferent to the firearm instruction, Clay was obsessed. "How come every time you spin to disarm it looks so cool, and when I do it," he spun, grabbing the barrel of the gun from the stuntman and attempting to take control, only to drop the weapon to the ground, "that happens?"

"You don't have the magic touch," Kurt Wen, the stunt coordinator, insisted. He was in charge of this training session; I was simply consulting. "Alex, if you'd be so kind." He held the barrel of one of the prop guns, and I took it from him. "Pay attention, Mr. Chaffey."

I aimed the prop gun at Wen, and he put his hands up. He crossed his right over the top while maneuvering his left into position. He did this exaggeratingly slow so Clay could see how it was done. Then he popped the weapon free from my grip, spinning it, and aiming it perfectly at me.

"Okay, I see." Clay scooped up the weapon and handed it back to the stuntman. He tried again, and it clattered to the ground. "Dammit."

Wen chuckled, ducking his head down. When he looked up, his eyes met mine. "Any other suggestions? You're the expert."

"Don't let the kid anywhere near a real gun," I whispered.

Chaffey glanced in my direction. "What?" From the look on his face, I knew he didn't hear what I said.

"You'll get it. You just need practice." I took a step back, catching a glimpse of Dinah working on the proper hold and grip. "Straighten out your arm." I knew what scene she had in mind, thanks to the readthrough yesterday. "Shift your weight to the balls of your feet. You're moving. You want to keep it fluid."

Dinah looked at me. "Holding the gun one-handed is what you'd do? Two feels better. More natural, like the way Kurt showed us and the trainers taught us back in L.A. Those six weeks of weapons and fight training were for a reason, right? We shouldn't be switching everything up now."

"You aren't. We're adding to the skills you've already learned. The difference here is you're moving down a hallway. You're alone. You can't see the enemy, but they might be able to see you. So you want to make yourself the smallest target possible. Your back will be against the wall, and you're sliding forward. Two hands mean you have to be squared to the front. One means you can stay sideways. However, when you come to a doorway or the end of the hall, you can place both hands on the grip, pull your elbows in, take a breath, and pivot into the unfamiliar area. If a hostile were present, you'd be in position to fire in the preferred two-handed style."

"Show her what you mean," Kurt said, having caught the tail-end of the conversation.

I executed the maneuver in the makeshift hallway. Dinah watched, and as soon as we broke up the session so the actors and stuntmen could perform a few more practices before going on with their day, she scribbled the notes I'd given her in her pad. At least she wanted to do a good job, unlike Lance who was sprawled out in his chair, one leg thrown over the arm while the other dangled in front of him. He was on his phone with his agent while his assistant ran to fetch him some water and a clean shirt.

"All right," Kurt declared, "let's break for lunch. Afterward, we'll run through a few of the fight sequences so our consultant can make any necessary changes to the routines before we break it down for you."

Clay continued to work on his disarming technique. Lance barked at his assistant who apparently returned with the wrong shirt. The PA turned and disappeared in the direction he just came. Dinah headed in my direction, but Gemma intercepted. Something happened in the wardrobe trailer concerning yesterday's fittings, so they had to get refitted for a few costumes.

Just because everyone else was too busy for lunch, that didn't mean I was. There was also a good chance most of the talent just didn't eat. I stood next to the table craft services had set up at the side of the soundstage and waited for an espresso. So far, everything Kellan told me was true. Actors were assholes, or at least Lance was. And craft services didn't seem to have an issue fulfilling my requests. The only thing I hadn't witnessed yet was drug use, but since Kellan said it was here, it probably was.

"Hey," Kurt came up beside me, "FBI, right?"

"Yeah."

"I did not expect you." He narrowed his eyes. "Current or retired?"

"Shit. I know I look terrible today, but retired, really?"

He smiled. "I'm sorry. For the record, I don't believe you're old enough to be retired. You don't even look old enough to buy liquor. But most active agents have better things to do than spend days on set."

"Do you have a lot of experience with consultants?"

"What's a lot?" He reached for a bottle of soda from the cooler and twisted off the cap. "I just think it's weird we managed to get an FBI consultant this late in the game. The script's been done for weeks, minus the constant tweaking, and for the last two months, I've been in charge of working out the action sequences. The actors have been in boot camp training for the last month and a half. It's just weird."

"Tell me about it. I got the call two mornings ago to meet with a client. The next thing I know, I'm on set."

"So you are active?"

"Nope."

"Retired?"

I gestured at my face. "Do you think the makeup artists can do something to fix whatever has you convinced I'm at least twenty years older than I am?"

"There's nothing to fix." He grabbed a scone off the table and took a bite. "You're not active or retired, but you are FBI."

"Was." I glanced at the table, but the thought of eating made me ill. "I just started in the private sector a couple of months ago."

"How do you like it so far?"

"It's a job."

He snickered. "You are not what I was expecting. I've been doing this for twenty-five years, and I've worked with a lot of consultants. The last movie I worked on had three former special forces guys advising us on boot camp, weapons training, and what deployment is actually like. Let's just say I never would have known they had been special forces. They looked like a bunch of beach bums who spent their days drinking, and every time they opened their mouths, they regaled us with stories from their glory days that were even less believable than a lot of scripts I've read."

"Are you asking why I don't have a beer belly?" I rather enjoyed being a ballbuster.

"This is coming out wrong. When I was told an FBI agent would be consulting on the film, I expected someone older who likes to blow smoke, not someone who could kick my ass seven ways from Sunday." He pointed a finger in my face. "You look more like the idealized version than the real thing. Are you sure you're not an actor?"

"Positive."

"Yeah, so anyway, about the fight training. They should have most of the moves down, but as you saw with the weapons training, it doesn't always stick."

"What are you going to do about Clay's lack of

coordination?"

"Probably CGI in his face on someone else's body or the director will cut around it."

For the next thirty minutes, Kurt rambled on about grappling techniques, throwing punches, and what looks best on film compared to what might be most effective in real life. He was a talker, but more than that, he wanted to convince me he knew what he was doing for fear that I might ruin the choreography he'd already spent weeks perfecting. The most I could do was promise that wasn't my intention.

Filled with enough espresso to keep a herd of elephants awake for several days, I took a seat next to Kurt and watched the stuntmen demonstrate a few scenes. Obviously, the actors would replace them at some point, but this was to give me an idea of what it should look like. And it looked good. Since part of the film revolved around training at Quantico, I shared my personal experiences, but Kurt had done his research. The good thing about being a consultant was I didn't have to teach or train, just offer insight. Although, that wasn't exactly how weapons training had gone.

My phone buzzed, and I took a step away from the group. It was Amir. "What's up?" I asked.

"I couldn't pull any DNA off the card. Have you spoken to the security detail yet?"

"No. Why?"

He smacked his lips, the sound reverberating through the earpiece. "No reason."

"Amir," I hissed, but he hung up. I cursed, wondering what that was about.

Dinah avidly watched me instead of her instructor. Her brows scrunched, and she nearly took a blow to the face. I rubbed my eyes and went back to my chair, trying not to be a distraction. After an hour of watching what was starting to look more like a dance routine rather than a fight sequence, Kurt called it quits. Gemma and Clay were scheduled to shoot a few scenes in three hours and needed to get to hair and makeup before changing into their costumes.

Kurt returned to my side, talking a mile a minute. I smiled and nodded, but Dinah had made it obvious she wanted my attention earlier. While she waited for Kurt to leave, she bent over to pick up her water bottle. Lance came up beside her. His hand traced the curve of her spine, stopping at the waistband of her yoga pants. He was careful not to be inappropriate but only by a small margin. He was smiling with one of those patented sexy grins that begged forgiveness even though it oozed nothing but trouble. I'd seen that look plenty of times, and a pit settled in my stomach.

I came out of my chair, pretending to stretch but trying to get a bit closer to hear what the bastard was saying and to block out Kurt's incessant yammering. I could barely make out the words. However, I could read body language.

Dinah stood up straight, holding her water bottle in both hands directly in front of her. Lance, on the other hand, kept his posture loose and arrogant. He had something to say and nothing to fear.

"C'mon, Lance," she said, "we've talked about this. I don't think it's a good idea."

"Why not?" As if those dimples could get him anything he wanted. "My agent thinks it's a good idea. Even the studio is on board. What's the problem?"

"The problem is you."

His smile dropped. "What's that supposed to mean?"

"When you're stumbling out of some club at four a.m. and the flashbulbs are going off all over the place, who's going to be hanging off your arm?"

He stared at her as if the question didn't compute.

"That's what I thought," she snapped. "Do whatever you want, but I'm not agreeing to it. And my team won't either." She turned on her heel, and he grabbed her arm. Spinning, she batted his hand away. The sound of her smack drew the attention of several of the nearby crew who all quickly diverted their eyes.

"Don't play like that," Lance said, his voice full of swagger in his attempt to save face. "You know you can't say no to this. What about Maui? Did you already forget how great that was?"

She put her bottle down on the chair. "We are not talking about this now." She looked around, her eyes catching mine for the briefest moment. "Not here."

"Then when?"

"Later."

"Promise?" he asked, and she nodded. "Good." He gave her a quick peck on the cheek and called to his assistant who was hovering a few feet away.

As soon as he was gone, Dinah deflated slightly. She glanced around, but Elodie wasn't nearby. "Alex, are you busy?"

I glanced at Kurt, who was still droning on about the differences between Brazilian jujitsu and Japanese jujitsu or koryu. "Maybe you should focus more on incorporating Krav Maga," I said, causing the light bulb to flick on over his head. While his wheels started spinning in another direction, I excused myself and followed Dinah out of the building. "Is everything okay?" I asked.

"Yeah. Nothing I can't handle."

"Okay."

SIX

"Kurt brought up an interesting point," I said as we walked back to her trailer. "You and the rest of the actors have been training for six weeks in preparation for this movie. Why didn't you go on your so-called ride-along then?"

She snorted. "I'm the new kid on the block. I'm also one of the oldest actors on the set. Gemma and Clay are barely old enough to vote, and Lance is Hollywood's heartthrob. My manager didn't have the pull to ask the studio for all the things I wanted. And they aren't exactly thrilled to be investing in me at this point, not when I only have one indie feature under my belt. After we flew here to film, I asked the director. Neil pulled some strings and negotiated you into the current contract we had with Cross Security."

"And to justify it, I've had to act like a technical consultant to the writing staff and stunt coordinator."

She glanced at me from the corner of her eye. "Pretty much. Are you mad?"

"No. Tired, yes."

"The worst should be over now. Aside from weighing in on a few scenes Neil has already cherry-picked, your work here is done. I just need to get to know you. See how you function and think. Watch how you carry yourself and handle yourself in real situations." We reached her trailer, and she carefully opened the door. After a wary look inside, she climbed up the steps. "This would probably be easier if I could have gone with you while you conducted an investigation, but since you're not an agent and the insurance wouldn't give me clearance for a stunt like that anyway, I guess I'll just have to settle for hearing your stories and taking a few unauthorized field trips." She gestured at the white couch against one wall. "Make yourself comfortable."

I took a seat, resisting the urge to flop onto my back and close my eyes. Instead, I watched her pull two bottles of water from the fridge. She put one on the table next to me and took a seat.

"I don't enjoy being the center of attention. I like to blend into the background," I said.

She laughed. "We must be polar opposites."

A thought crossed my mind, and I wondered how impolite it would be to ask. But given the questions she'd been asking me, it seemed fair. "Did you become an actress because you aged out of the modeling biz?"

"In case you haven't noticed, I've practically aged out of the film industry too. This script was one of the only exceptions I've seen to the norm." I raised an eyebrow, silently asking what that was. "You know, playing the mom." She exaggerated the word. "We live in one incredibly sexist society." Her eyes narrowed. "Isn't law enforcement a boys' club?"

"It can be. Things are changing, but change can be slow. It's funny. Mr. Cross actually suggested the reason I work as hard as I do and strive to be the best I can is because I have the need to prove myself due to my gender. To be perfectly honest, I never really thought about it. I don't think that's been a factor, at least not a conscious one. The insane drive to find answers is just me, probably a side effect from the way I was raised."

"Are your parents proud?"

I scoffed at the notion. "Next question."

"Dammit, you really won't give me anything to work with. Why did you even join the FBI?"

"When everything goes to hell, someone needs to do something to fix it."

Her eyes narrowed, and she pulled the damn notepad out of her pocket again. "Something happened to you, didn't it?"

"No."

She raised an eyebrow. "I don't believe you."

She wanted some dramatic answer to incorporate into her character's backstory, so I decided I could perform a little acting of my own and came up with a reasonable lie. "If you must know, when I was a freshman in college, my dormmate and several of her friends were killed while on spring break. I could have been with them, but I had a paper due the next week. After that happened, several police officers and federal agents questioned me and a number of other people on campus. That's when I knew what I wanted to do with my life."

"You must have been close."

I let out a slight chuckle. "Strangely enough, no. She liked to party, and I was determined to keep my head above water. She only asked me to go with them out of pity." At least my characterization was the truth.

"But you felt guilty afterward?"

"Are you my shrink?" I gave her a look.

She tilted her head to the side. "In case you're wondering, I'm very curious as to a person's motivation for choosing your former profession. The incident with your roommate makes sense. Is it like that for everyone?"

"It depends on the person. A lot of field agents come from military or law enforcement backgrounds, so the jump to the FBI makes sense. Some are recruited because they excel in a specific field. Others just want job security and good benefits. Honestly, it's like any other job. Why does anyone work anywhere? Some have a passion for it. Others just like to be able to put food on the table."

"My professions have been a bit different."

"That's because you're an artist."

She smiled at the compliment and glanced down at her notepad. "So that was it? You finished your education, applied, and was accepted?" I nodded. "Then what happened? What was training like?"

"Honestly, I loved it. After spending three years with asshole law professors and the Socratic method, I was overjoyed to be handed information. There were a lot of seminars, weapons training, self-defense tactics, investigative procedures, but it only really just brushed the surface. After Quantico, I was placed with another agent and spent two years learning from him." My mind went to Mark Jablonsky, and I smiled. I owed him a phone call and a dinner. "My mentor was great. Is great. But he's one stubborn pain in the ass. He hates that I went private sector."

"Why did you quit?"

"Nope. You've asked that before. Do I need to remind you of the terms of this arrangement?"

She looked mortified. "Sorry."

"So that's me in a nutshell," I volunteered, getting us back on track. "Like I said, choosing me as your model for a film is a bad idea. I'm boring as hell."

"What about actual investigations? Tell me about a case. Something exciting. The morning I interviewed you, you mentioned you went up against terrorists and serial killers. Tell me about one of them. Isn't it scary?"

"Yep."

She rolled her eyes and let out an unhappy harrumph. "Alex, come on. I need something I can work with."

"Look, when the danger is real, it is scary, but you learn not to think about it. You've been trained. Your body functions on autopilot. Someone shoots at you, you shoot back. You radio for back-up. You give chase. You do whatever you have to. In those moments, there's nothing but the immediate consequences. Maybe you have to save a life or save your own. So you do. Or you at least try. Everything happens in the blink of an eye, but it seems much slower. Decisions have to be made, and you do it in a split second."

"What happens after?"

"You fill out paperwork."

"No. Not procedure. Not protocol. What happens when you go home at night?"

"Some people drink. A few probably use recreationally, which is a very bad idea in general but it's even worse if you're in law enforcement. Personally, I run or hit the heavy bag. Maybe both."

"And you don't think about it again?"

I wondered if she could possibly be that naïve or stupid. "When something happens in your life, do you just put it behind you and never think about it again?"

"No, I think about it a lot," she admitted.

"Yeah, so do I."

"How do you cope with killing someone?"

My eye twitched. "You just eventually move on."

"That's not an answer."

I climbed off the couch, feeling antsy and trapped. "It's the only one I have."

"What about the people you lost? You said–"

"I know what I said," I snapped. I waited a beat, my heart racing, probably from the espresso. "You spend every waking moment wishing it had been you instead."

She fell silent and tucked her pen inside her notepad. I opened the bottle and took a sip. Then I excused myself, went into her bathroom, and threw up. Too much coffee on an empty stomach is never a good idea.

When I came out, she was flipping through a memoir written by a retired FBI agent. Since she had the book, I didn't see what she needed me for, but before I could voice my opinion, someone knocked on the door. She put her book down and went to answer it.

"Di," Lance's voice boomed in the enclosed space, "you left your water bottle on set." He handed it to her. "You're always forgetting things."

"You didn't have to return it. Elodie would have picked it up."

"Well, I wanted to make sure you didn't forget we were going to talk. Can we do that now? You've got me in this weird headspace, and I have to get over to makeup soon so I can start shooting the prison scene. I need to be in character and not thinking about us."

"Then stop thinking about us. There is no us."

"Don't say that." He pushed into the trailer, taken aback

when he found out they weren't alone. "We need some privacy," he said to me.

A million thoughts entered my mind, but I held my tongue. Instead, my gaze shifted to Dinah who looked desperate to keep me there. "We're waiting for a few more members of the security team to meet with us. That really is time-sensitive, but I guess we can reschedule. What do you want me to tell them, Dinah?" I asked.

"I'm sorry, Lance," she said.

"Di," he purred, switching from being controlling to pleading, "it won't take long. I just need you to get on board with this. We can be Hollywood's new power couple. A reporter is going to be on set to conduct interviews in two days. I want to go public. Our vacation photos are all over the internet. If we deny it, it'll just make the paparazzi even crazier."

"I'll discuss it with my publicist, but I'm not agreeing to anything."

"Fine." He moved closer, his voice dropping to a level I could barely hear. "You know I'm crazy about you."

"Yeah," she said, but her tone didn't fit her answer.

"Are you crazy about me?"

She sighed.

"Say it, Di," he insisted.

"Lance," she pushed gently against his chest, "we'll talk about this later."

He kissed her and threw another look in my direction. It was one of smug satisfaction, as if he won. That was the moment I decided I didn't like Lance Smoke. My opinion on Dinah was still up in the air. But I didn't like the way he treated her, and something told me it spelled trouble.

She closed the trailer door and flipped the lock. "I'm sorry about that. Thanks for the excuse."

"Do you want to tell me what's going on?"

"It's nothing, just some personal stuff that got mixed up with our business stuff."

"You wanted to know what me conducting an investigation looks like, so let me give you some perspective. Clues are key to any investigation. Yesterday, you were distraught someone entered your trailer without permission. You weren't happy about the flowers and even less enthused about the attached card. You said it was from a fan. Today, Lance seems pretty smitten. Dangerously so. Is there any chance the two could be connected?"

"You think he left the flowers?"

"I don't know." Something told me not to mention I read the card and ran it for prints, so I kept that information to myself. "It just seems like a strange coincidence."

Something flashed across her face. "He probably saw Elodie bring them to set last night. He must think I've moved on, so he wants to make sure it doesn't hurt the buzz around the film or whatever potential buzz his publicist is hoping to create about us."

I narrowed my eyes. She believed it. It sounded plausible, but it was also possible Lance left the flowers as a warning and didn't want anyone to trace them back to him. He probably had his assistant deliver them. Or one of Dinah's fans really did convince a PA to leave them in her trailer. Didn't Elodie mention that wasn't the first time someone left flowers?

Dinah snapped her fingers in front of my face. "Alex, you still with me? You zoned out."

"Just thinking." I bit my lip and looked at her. "What about your designer friend? Do you think he could have sent them?"

She laughed. "Secrecy isn't his style. If he sent flowers, it'd be a beautiful, elegant bouquet, and he would sign the card." She gave me a funny look. "Why the interest? Is your own love life on the fritz? Because you are more than welcome to my drama."

"I'm not a fan of drama."

Her cell phone buzzed, and she reached for it. After a few quick uh-huhs, she hung up. "Elodie says they need me in makeup. Another screw-up. I swear someone cursed this production. It's been one thing after another since we arrived." She looked at me. "Maybe we can talk some more when I get back, but in the meantime, make yourself comfortable. If someone needs you, I'll send Elodie to get you."

"I thought you didn't want anyone inside your trailer."

"You don't count."

"Gee, thanks." I looked at her for a moment. "You're hoping if someone stops by, I'll be here to catch him."

A friendly smile dotted her face. "Maybe."

"Fine, but as of this moment, you should consider me another part of the security team and not your personal information center."

"But you're under contract."

"Don't remind me."

SEVEN

Alone with my thoughts, I needed to find something to focus on before my mind could go to dark places. The first thing I did was snoop through Dinah's trailer. I didn't find any recording devices, so whoever left the flowers hadn't bugged the place. That was a good sign. After that, I opened my messenger bag, which I'd been lugging around, and took out my laptop and connected it to the portable modem. Since I had some time to kill, I wanted to discover what the story was between Dinah and Lance.

The internet was a cornucopia of information. The first few pages were speculation about the new film, the characters the actors would be portraying, and whether this would turn into a franchise. It had been loosely based on a collection of short thrillers. The more official news sources spoke at length about contract agreements, studio budget, projected release dates, and theoretical earning potential. This film could be a gold mine or a mega flop. It was too soon to say, but respected critics and entertainment gurus came down on both sides of the fence, which blew my mind since they only started shooting yesterday.

After that, I moved on to the celebrity gossip sites. *Are they together? Did they split? Was he unfaithful? Were they even in a relationship? He wants a family, but she said no.* And the list went on from there. I didn't care what the talking heads had to say on the subject. But pictures do speak a thousand words, and even though I knew things could be taken out of context, there were plenty of photos from their Maui vacation three months ago to prove Dinah and Lance had a relationship, even if it had been nothing more than a fling.

One hyperlink boasted about a sex tape, so I clicked. Thankfully, it had been shot using a long lens from somewhere down the beach. The Hollywood heartthrob at least had the decency to keep them mostly covered inside their canopy on what I could only assume was a private beach. The video didn't show much, but it was obvious what was going on beneath the beach towels.

I scanned the comments. The perverts complained about the quality of the footage and the distance. The shippers hoped this was a good sign and wanted to know when the news would officially break on the couple's relationship. The rest were either jealous fans or haters. Most women and a few men were extremely catty, calling Dinah all kinds of nasty names and complaining she wasn't pretty, young, or good enough for Lance. On the other side, Dinah's fans, most of whom seemed to have followed her from her modeling days, thought he was just a player and she deserved better. Frankly, I wondered why total strangers thought they should have a say in the matter, but everyone wants to feel important, I suppose.

After another thirty minutes of scouring the internet for details about Lance and Dinah, I found more photographs of the couple. They went to clubs, five-star restaurants, premieres, and parties. The coverage spanned the last six months. Prior to that, the two were never seen together. According to the reports, they met at Cannes when her indie film debuted. That would explain the six month timeline.

Mixed into the photos of the two together were several images of Lance with random women. A few were recognizable actresses, models, and singers, but some looked like ladies he met at clubs and parties. At least I understood Dinah's comment a little better. Maybe she was a woman scorned, but I didn't get the impression she cared deeply enough about Lance to be scorned.

For the briefest moment, I wondered if I was also a woman scorned. My mind went to Martin. In all the time I had known him, he never acted the way he did last night, not even when we were fighting or broken up. His behavior wasn't bad, just peculiar. The issue wasn't actually with him; it was the evidence of something sordid coupled with his desperation. The smell of a woman's perfume on his body, her makeup on his collar and sleeve, his late night shower, and his desire to show his affection all added up to trouble. Or maybe he was feeling randy and the rest happened to be coincidental, even if I'd been programmed to believe coincidences didn't happen.

Regardless, I did my best to shake it off. He wouldn't jeopardize us, not now. We'd been through so much. If he wanted to walk away, he would. Still, the tiny voice of doubt in the back of my head reminded me he was human, and humans make mistakes. I'd be a fool to turn a blind eye to the possibility. I hated that voice and decided to silence it by starting a new search centered solely on Dinah.

"Jesus." Dinah Allen had quite the following. A decade spent as one of the most sought after fashion models would do that to a person. It probably didn't hurt that she had dated a number of Hollywood A-listers and several names off the Top 40 Billboard charts. Now with her indie film debut and being cast in what everyone hoped would be next summer's biggest blockbuster, her stardom exploded.

Honestly, it was amazing she seemed as grounded as she did. Nothing about her career was simple. But if the last two days had taught me anything, her profession probably wasn't as glamourous as it appeared. Several entertainment sites had articles, and I scanned the comments. Quite a few seemed like fanatics, completely obsessed with the model turned actress.

It would take a deep dive to determine if any of these

fans had the potential to turn into stalkers, and that wasn't exactly in my job description. What did Dinah Allen's personal security detail look like? Did she have adequate protection? "Dammit, Alex, you're losing it," I said to the empty trailer. There was no threat or danger. The damage was a bouquet of flowers with a creepy note. Hell, they could have come from the director, Lance, the fashion designer she was texting, or just some overzealous fan who wouldn't hurt a fly. Maybe I needed sleep.

I looked around the trailer again. This was worse than any stakeout I'd ever been on. At least stakeouts had goals. What was mine? To stay awake? On the plus side, at least there was indoor plumbing.

I closed my computer and tucked it away. Then I checked my phone for what felt like the millionth time and made myself comfortable on the couch. A nap might help clear away the mental turmoil. Her inquisition into my job and the reasons I became an FBI agent didn't help matters, so maybe I just needed to start the day over again.

Closing my eyes, I wondered what Cross would think of his newest investigator sleeping on the job. He wouldn't like it, but he didn't exactly want me poking around into Miss Allen's private business either. If given the choice, he'd prefer me unconscious instead of causing trouble.

The first interruption was my phone buzzing. I fished it out of my bag. "I had a feeling you might call," I said.

"Am I that predictable?" Martin asked.

"You weren't last night."

He didn't offer an explanation. "What time do you think you'll get home? You are coming back to our place, right? You didn't say anything before you left, but I just assumed."

"You assumed correctly, unless you're not going to be there."

"Why wouldn't I?" He sounded confused. "All in means all in, Alex. I'll make dinner."

I glanced down at the call sheet. "I'm hoping to get back around seven, but it isn't set in stone. Considering this isn't even really a job, the hours shouldn't be shit, but they are."

"It's okay. I'll be here whenever you get home." Before I

could ask any questions about why he was so late coming home last night, someone called to him in the background. "Sorry, the meeting is about to start. I'll see you later." He disconnected, and I put the phone away.

I closed my eyes again, feeling slightly better about things. There was a rational explanation for everything. The flowers. Martin. Cross's insistence to assign me the worst cases ever. It could all be explained, but right now, I didn't want to think about any of it. However, my mind kept returning to Dinah.

From the photos I had seen from her early days as a model, she had spent a lot of time dating Christian Nykle. He might be the designer she was texting last night. After making a mental note to check into him just for my own peace of mind, since I had decided sometime between last night and just now that my mission was to determine who sent the flowers to her trailer, I attempted again to doze on the couch.

An hour passed, and I accomplished nothing more than counting the ceiling tiles. A noise outside caught my attention, and I cautiously went to the door. Throwing it open, I didn't see anyone outside, so I went down the steps, glancing around. "Hello?" I asked, but no one answered. Not that I expected someone who might have been attempting to break into Dinah's trailer to answer, but it was worth a try.

I circled the trailer, spotting Jett Trevino, Lance's assistant, letting himself into Lance's trailer. Nothing appeared to be disturbed, so I went back inside. I moved to the rear of the trailer and looked out the window. Something on the ground caught my eye, and I went back outside to find a couple of purplish black flower petals crushed into the pavement. They were wilted and crunchy on the ends. They might have fallen from the bouquet last night.

Picking them up, I gave the area a more thorough sweep, but I didn't spot any more flower petals or anyone suspicious. In fact, no one was around. I went back inside. Maybe I was losing it or desperate for something to do. Eventually, I called Cross.

"Anything to report?" I asked after his assistant put me through to his line.

"Shouldn't I be the one asking that question, Parker?"

"According to the lab, only three sets of prints were on the card that was delivered with the flowers, and I can name three people who touched it."

"I'm aware." As usual, Cross was acting dodgy. "Did you do as I suggested and check into Miss Allen?"

"Just a preliminary internet search." I glanced at the door, afraid she might reappear at any moment. "She and her costar have a recent history. From the conversations I've heard today, I'd say he wants her back."

"Do you believe he sent the flowers?"

"No."

Cross waited a beat before adding, "Neither do I. According to Miss Allen's security team, this isn't the first time she's received an anonymous gift. They have no idea who is responsible, but since the gifts have not been threatening in nature, they are chalking it up to a fan. At the present, they do not believe Miss Allen is in danger."

"What do our people think?"

Cross's voice contained a smile. *"Our people* are providing security on set. We are to safeguard the production and the property. Our role begins and ends at the gate. That being said, our security team does not believe the lot was breached. The flowers must have come in through official channels or were delivered by someone on set." He cleared his throat, as he often did. "Why do you care about the flower delivery? Has Miss Allen expressed a concern?" Those were the same questions he asked last night.

"She acted pretty damn concerned, but no, she hasn't said anything to me about it. I tried to ask her, but we were interrupted."

"What are you doing, Alex? Shouldn't you be providing insight into the mind of an FBI agent instead of chasing down some florist?" He waited a moment, but when I failed to respond, he pushed on. "Is this task too difficult for you?"

"No, sir," I growled. Truthfully, it was difficult, even if I wasn't entirely sure why. "But something is wrong with this situation. She was genuinely freaked out about the flowers. Are we sure there isn't more to the story?"

"She is an actress. How can you be positive any of her reactions are genuine? You probably haven't dealt with many thespians in the past, but I have. They are no different than con artists. Keep that in mind."

"What if you're wrong?"

"Her safety is an issue for her security team when she is off set, and I can assure you that when she's on the lot, she's perfectly safe. I only hire the best."

"Obviously," I teased, but Cross didn't get the joke.

He lowered his voice. "You should be aware Dinah Allen was recently involved in a scandal. She has a habit of crying wolf, or, at the very least, the people who work for her like to cry wolf. Her manager made several allegations in Los Angeles that Dinah was being stalked. The police investigated, but they found no truth to these claims. In fact, the surveillance footage from the Allen estate wholly disproved her manager's statements. Eventually, one of the members of her public relations team came forward quietly and admitted to faking the story in the hopes of gaining additional publicity. They wanted to make sure Dinah stayed in the public eye. Her manager denied knowing anything about this ploy and found someone to clean up the mess and bury the story once the truth came out."

"Then how did you hear about it?"

"My people are better."

"I'll keep that in mind."

"Focus on your assignment. It'll make life easier on all of us." Without so much as a goodbye, Lucien hung up.

That changed things. Even if Dinah wasn't responsible, someone who worked for her might be pulling the strings. And then I realized something. Dinah was merely a vehicle for someone else to profit. Sure, she made six and seven figures easily enough, but plenty of people were making a percentage off of that. The producers stood to make billions off a successful film. There was plenty of incentive to keep the paparazzi and press focused on Dinah. No wonder Lance wanted their relationship to go public, fake or not. I closed my eyes, trying to remember the production pages I glimpsed. I was almost positive Lance was listed as one of the producers.

I considered checking into Dinah's team but decided, in this instance, that it might actually be better to follow Cross's orders. If Dinah wanted my help or if the security team determined there was a legitimate threat, that would change things, but for now, I was just a walking, talking encyclopedia on what it was like to be a woman in the FBI. Maybe I should call my friend Kate at the OIO and have her handle this.

Snorting at the notion, I picked up the memoir. It wouldn't hurt if I found out what this *New York Times* bestseller had to say on the matter. Obviously, she was more of an expert than I was. Her career lasted longer, and she wrote a book about it. If nothing else, I might be able to copy some of her answers for the more difficult questions.

I was three chapters in, reading the details of her first investigation, when voices outside caught my attention. Climbing to my knees, I peered out the window. Clay and a few other people went into one of the neighboring trailers. Several PAs were running errands in the vicinity. A bike went by with one of the dozens of other cast members. Shooting must have concluded for the day. And now, this part of the lot looked like an RV park, but at least the actors and staff had places to rest and relax when they weren't needed. Truthfully, I was thankful to have a place to hide. Maybe tomorrow I'd bring a book of my own to read or ask Kellan if I could help look for those hidden assets since I had so much free time.

EIGHT

The drive home from the studio took longer than expected on account of rush hour traffic which gave me plenty of time to think, except the last thing I wanted to think about was Dinah Allen and the film. When she returned to the trailer, she grilled me on a million different things. She wanted to know everything about the day-to-day. That wasn't so bad, but her final question threw me for a loop. *Would you do it over again?*

I had no idea, and being stuck in traffic for twenty minutes was really screwing with my head. Instead of thinking about her question, my mind went to the only other topic of any concern — Martin.

Simply put, I loved him. I just wondered if anything could change that. I saved his life. He saved mine. Things had always been complicated between us, but fidelity was never a concern. Getting blown to smithereens or shot in the back of the head was. He even went so far as to convince the police department to let him train with one of their elite tactical units just to prove to me he could handle himself in dangerous situations. Someone who put in that much effort wouldn't risk throwing everything away for a casual fling.

But what if he did? That was the question that gnawed

at me. By the time I made it to our apartment, I had played out dozens of potential scenarios. None of them good. I ran through every approach, but FBI interrogation techniques would be the equivalent of throwing a live grenade into an already tense situation. Neither of us would walk away in one piece. Questioning him about last night wouldn't end well. It would mean I didn't trust him, and trust had been one of our problems. More in terms of him learning to trust me again, but still, if I doubted him, he would start doubting my conviction to us. And that would be it. After all, I was the liar who notoriously ran from our problems by calling it quits.

When I unlocked our door and saw him standing in front of the stove, I decided whatever happened last night didn't matter. I just needed to get my brain to fall in line with my heart. Too bad I suspected the former controlled my mouth rather than the latter.

I dropped my bags on the floor and locked the door. He turned at the sound and smiled. "Rough day?"

"Strangely enough, yes." I moved to the counter and watched as he turned the dial on the oven. "You're home early." *Easy, Alex*, the voice in my head whispered.

"Perks of being in charge." He tossed me a playful grin. "The entire Board was pretty much dead on its feet after last night." He ran a hand through his dark brown hair. "I owe you an apology."

My stomach roiled. "Why?" I forced my voice to stay light and my tone to convey obliviousness.

He grinned. "You don't remember the desperate, horny man that woke you up in the middle of the night?"

"Oh, him?" I shrugged. "I'm used to him, except he normally keeps better hours."

"Well, he was an ass." Martin stirred something on the stove. Then he turned around and put his hands on the edge of the counter and stared at me. "I know you've been having enough trouble sleeping lately, and with this new assignment, I should have made sure I was thinking with the right head." He watched me carefully. "What are you working on? You haven't said."

"I can't tell you much. I had to sign an NDA."

He laughed. "That's how it's going to be?"

"That's how it is." I thought about taking a seat but was afraid if I did, I'd never get up. "Cross loaned me out to a production company. They needed a consultant for their movie."

His eyes narrowed. "Shouldn't this be your dream job?" He suddenly grew serious. "Any attractive actors on set?"

"They're all attractive."

"No wonder you hate this assignment." He smirked. "It sounds torturous."

"It actually is," I said sincerely. "I don't like probing questions."

"I believe that's why we didn't do so well with couples counseling."

I gave him a look. "You didn't like the questions either." I thought for a moment. "Do you think we should go back?"

"To therapy?" He ran a hand through his hair, a gesture I recognized as a nervous tic. "Wow, you must have had one shitty day." His expression grew sincere. "Don't let some actor get you all twisted around. It's not worth it. What did he want to know?"

"She," I corrected, "wanted to know why I joined the OIO, why I left, if I killed anyone." I rolled my eyes. "The list goes on from there."

"Shit." He reached across the island counter and took my hand. "I'm sorry you had to deal with that."

"At one point, I just started fudging the details because it was easier than giving truthful answers."

"Yeah, I get that."

I didn't like his response, and I swallowed. Jerking my chin at the oven, I asked, "What's for dinner?"

He turned around, supplying an answer while checking to see if the oven was preheated, but my mind wasn't on his words. It was on last night. I moved around the counter and reached around him, turning the dials to off. He turned toward me, and I stood on my tiptoes so I could bury my face in the crook of his neck. It didn't matter, I reminded myself. It just didn't.

He grabbed my hips and hoisted me onto the island so we were closer in height and kissed me. "Don't you want to eat first?"

"No." I needed to put these stupid thoughts out of my head. I looked him in the eye, even as my fingers went to work on the buttons of his shirt. "Tell me you love me."

He cupped my face in his hands. "I do." He kissed me again, pulling slowly away and seeing something disconcerting in my eyes. "Is everything okay?"

I nodded, unsure what would come out of my mouth if I spoke. "Show me," I managed, and he lifted me off the counter and carried me into the bedroom.

*　　*　　*

I forced one eye open and then the other. Where was I? The only thing I could see was a solid, dark wall. Something was buzzing. Martin removed his arm from where it had been securely wrapped around my middle and blindly reached over his head. The angle didn't make sense, and I rolled onto my back.

From this position, our bedroom looked a lot different. Where the hell were the pillows? Martin's other arm was under my head, and we were lying sideways at the top of the mattress. Fortunately, we had a king-sized bed, so my feet didn't dangle over the edge. He couldn't say the same. The buzzing stopped, and I rolled over to face him. We didn't need pillows or bedding; the duvet he tossed on top of us was perfectly sufficient. Frankly, I just wanted to go back to sleep. I didn't even have the strength to keep my eyes open.

"Alex, it's your phone," he said.

"It stopped," I mumbled. And for the first time in as long as I could remember, the buzzing wasn't followed by the annoying beep of a waiting voicemail message. "Wrong number."

He pressed his lips to my forehead and wrapped his arm around me again, tracing patterns on my back. "Wrong numbers don't call at two a.m."

"Uh-huh." I fell back into the oblivion, the exhaustion winning out over rational thinking.

Twenty minutes later, the buzzing returned. I didn't

hear it. What woke me the second time was Martin gently nudging me with his shoulder. "It's Lucien."

I fought to keep my eyes open, but I was losing the battle. "Put it on speaker, and don't say anything," I slurred.

Martin pressed the button and put the device down on his chest next to my head. I closed my eyes and waited. Maybe this was a bad dream.

"Alex, where are you?" Cross's clipped tone sounded tinny from this angle.

"What do you want?" My voice was thick with sleep, and my eyes remained closed.

"There's been an incident."

My sleep-addled brain couldn't even begin to process what that meant. "What kind of incident?"

He cleared his throat, the sound causing my eyes to flutter open. Whatever happened was serious. "The security team just phoned. I'm on my way to the lot. Get there as soon as you can."

"What happened?" I asked again.

"We'll be waiting for you." He hung up.

When I failed to immediately jump into action, Martin took my phone and placed it back on the nightstand behind his head. "I have to get up," I mumbled. Even the urgency in my boss's voice wasn't enough to jumpstart my adrenaline. "I need coffee."

"You need sleep," Martin said. "You're exhausted. You passed out hours ago and haven't moved since."

Even now, I was still struggling to stay awake. "Just give me ten minutes. Then wake me up." The buzzing sounded again, and I opened my eyes. It had been more than ten minutes. It was closer to twenty. Lucien had sent a text asking for an ETA. "You were supposed to wake me," I growled.

"I'm sorry. I must have dozed off," Martin replied, but I knew it was a lie. He put my needs above my boss's. Too bad he didn't think about that before waking me up to take the call. I sent a quick reply and searched for something to slip into before getting out of bed. When I couldn't find anything, I wrapped the entire duvet around my body, leaving Martin fully exposed. My gaze swept briefly over him. "I bet those actors wish they had my washboard abs and other assets." He smiled. "Are you positive I can't convince you to come back to bed?"

"There's been an incident," I repeated, growing frustrated as I struggled to figure out what to wear. Finally, I went with jeans and a t-shirt. It was the middle of the night. I wasn't in any mood to dress for the office.

"That could mean craft services ran out of kombucha."

"It could mean something much worse." My thoughts went back to the flowers and Lance's behavior. An icy chill ran down my spine. "I have to shower. Please, make me some coffee and put it in a to-go cup."

He pulled on his boxer briefs and climbed out of bed. "I'll call you a car. You can't drive like this."

"I'm okay."

"Sweetheart, you can barely keep your eyes open. It's not worth risking your life or someone else's because Lucien expects you to come running when he calls."

"I'm fine," I repeated more forcefully.

I pushed past him and went into the bathroom. Taking a cold shower was guaranteed to keep me from wasting time and jolt me awake. It was also an absolutely terrible idea and put me in an even fouler mood. When I came out of the bathroom, he had my coffee waiting. We never ate dinner last night since I fell asleep and didn't wake up until Lucien interrupted my dreamless slumber. Bastard.

"The doorman has a cab waiting in case you changed your mind," Martin said. He assessed my appearance and decided that I looked awake and alert. He had an assortment of fruit and protein bars on the counter. "Maybe you should take something with you."

"I'm good." Picking up my nine millimeter, I made sure the safety was on, and shrugged into my shoulder holster. "You should get some sleep. I'll see you tomorrow. Later. Something." I picked up the coffee, taking a sip as I reached for my keys.

I was halfway out the door when Martin stopped me. He kissed me gently. "Be safe."

"Always."

He stood in the doorway until the elevator arrived and the doors started to close. Then he waved goodbye and shut the door. By the time I reached the lobby, half of the coffee was gone and my brain was in overdrive over what might have happened at the studio.

The doorman dismissed the cab, and I jogged across the street to the neighboring garage and went to Martin's reserved space which I had been borrowing. Once I was on my way, I called Lucien to update him on my imminent arrival. Traffic was light at three a.m., and I made it in less than fifteen minutes.

Security was waiting at the gate. Two men remained on watch while the third pointed me to Cross's parked Porsche. I pulled to a stop beside his car, surprised when the same member of the security team opened my car door.

"We need to get you up to speed. Mr. Cross wants to have a handle on this and a game plan before they start filming in the morning. Your input is vital." He walked at a brisk pace, and I jogged to keep up. Thankfully, I finished my coffee on the ride to work or else it would be splashing everywhere. "What do you know so far?"

"Nothing," I said. "I was just told to get here ASAP."

We entered one of the soundstages. A man was standing beside the director's chair in a leather jacket, dark jeans, and a black t-shirt. His hair was messy and spiked. It took a full thirty seconds before I realized it was my boss.

"We've been waiting," Cross said. His gaze went to the security guard. "There's been a breach. The studio executives have been notified. They believe it's nothing more than a harmless prank. I imagine you'll disagree."

He stepped to the side, his focus shifting to the set where a life-sized dummy dressed in one of Dinah Allen's costumes and wearing her makeup was posed in a provocative position. The prop knife through its heart didn't exactly scream out harmless prank.

"That's no prank."

"I concur." Cross's tone went hard as nails. "Tell her the rest of the story, Mr. Perry," he commanded. His angry look hardened on the security guard, and the man swallowed.

"There's more?" I asked.

"Oh, yes," Cross muttered, "considerably more, to which I was also unaware."

NINE

I stared at Cross, one thought obvious on my face; *I told you so*. Although, it would have been too juvenile to say it. He met my eyes, anger flashing across his features. This wasn't good, particularly for Cross Security.

"Why wasn't I aware?" Cross asked, glaring at Dwight Perry. "Broadway Films expected us to deal with any issues." He gestured at the dummy six feet away. "This is a big fucking issue. You should have called immediately."

Perry uttered an excuse that fell on deaf ears. "I'm sorry, Mr. Cross."

Cross wrung his hands together, circling our surroundings. "As soon as your replacement arrives, get back to the office. You will wait for me there."

"Yes, sir." Perry lingered, unsure if he was supposed to leave us alone or stay to answer questions.

"When did you realize someone broke into the costume and makeup trailers?" I asked.

Perry was a large man, but the look Cross shot him made him cower. "We realized something was off this morning, but it wasn't until they shut down production for the night that we learned of the break-in. No one on set notified us."

"That isn't their job. It's yours. You are supposed to detect and prevent breaches." Cross rubbed his eyes. "Collect the footage. I want copies of everything brought to the lab. We have to figure out who is responsible." Perry faltered, and Cross hissed, "Now, Mr. Perry."

The man disappeared, and I rubbed a hand over my mouth. "Dinah Allen and Gemma Kramer had to go through a second round of fittings today and another session in the makeup chair. From what I was told, they thought the costumes and makeup palettes were misplaced. I didn't realize it was more than that."

"Why would you?" He spun on his heel. "You told me something was brewing concerning Dinah Allen. Do you still believe that?"

"Yes."

"Things disappear from sets all the time. Actors walk off with costumes or props. PAs decide they want something to brag to their friends about or sell on the internet, and the other behind the scenes guys may decide to keep a memento or two. However, that happens after production wraps, not before it starts." He knelt next to the dummy. "What do you see?"

"A threat. Sexual undertones, possibly misguided romantic feelings." My gaze swept the rest of the large, cavernous room, but nothing else looked disturbed or out of place. "It's posed on the main soundstage. That isn't an accident. It's meant to attract attention." The one thing missing was a note.

"The weapon of choice is a knife." Cross leaned closer. No one had touched it yet. We were waiting. He wanted everything moved to the office, but that would only occur once he spoke to the powers that be. A police investigation might be more appropriate, but something told me our client would want things handled in-house if possible. "You know what they say about stabbings."

"You think whoever did this has a problem getting it up?"

Cross shrugged. "It depends. The knife might have been the easiest way of making a statement. This is a studio. Theatrics are a given."

My gaze fell to one of the million different wires and cords that cluttered the floor. "It would have been just as easy to leave the body hanging. It would also be far more obvious and shocking."

"I'll take that under advisement." Something buzzed, and he removed the phone from his pocket. "The studio has reached a decision." He typed out a quick reply before dialing a number and speaking into his phone. "We need to figure out if the property was penetrated. Call in every one of our techs. No one is going home until we determine what happened. Do I make myself clear?" He blew out a breath. "Set up a meeting with Miss Allen's personal security team. I need to speak to them as soon as possible." He listened to the response. "That should be all for now."

"I take it the police won't be getting involved," I said after he hung up.

"No. We will handle this. I need you on point. Until we know more, we should focus on the obvious. Someone broke into Dinah's trailer. The following day costumes and makeup were stolen. And now this." He crossed the room and went down the narrow hallway where the writers' room was. I waited, unsure if I should follow, but Lucien returned a moment later with some rubber gloves and a box of trash bags. "Help me."

While I put on a pair of gloves, he opened the box of bags and took one out. We already photographed the entire area and the dummy, so he didn't hesitate to pick it up and wrestle it into the bag. I helped get the body inside and tied off the top. We carried it back to his car and slid it into the passenger's seat.

"Guess this means you can use the carpool lane." For some reason, he didn't find my comment amusing.

"Meet me back at the office." Without another word, he climbed into his car and revved the engine.

He was already through the gate by the time I got into my car. The second security team arrived, and I stopped to speak to them. They looked pretty rough around the edges, but they were professionals.

"Listen, this is a big lot. I know we have dozens of security cameras, but someone needs to check the cameras to make sure they are working. If you notice a blind spot, put up some sticky cams until something more permanent can be done to fix it, and we need a physical check of the fence and the perimeter," I said, even though this was above and beyond my position at the firm.

One of the guys nodded. "It's being handled."

"It sounds like you have your bases covered. Can you let me know what you find?" I scribbled my number on the back of a business card.

The man turned it over and read my name. "That is standard, Miss Parker. Mr. Cross said you were going to be taking charge."

"Did he?" I resisted the urge to roll my eyes, offered a nod of encouragement, and drove away.

My thoughts went to what the scene at the soundstage could mean. Every part of me said this was a direct threat against Dinah. Surely, Cross assumed the same thing since he requested a meeting with her security detail. I didn't know the specifics concerning Dinah's alleged stalker back in Los Angeles, but when I spoke to Cross on the phone yesterday afternoon, he had been convinced it was a publicity stunt. I wondered if he still thought that.

If the dummy was meant to represent Dinah, whoever left it wanted her dead. Or they wanted her off the movie, or they wanted her to pay. A knife through the heart could only be interpreted as betrayal or heartbreak. Lance. He was my prime suspect, and he and his assistant had access to the costumes and makeup trailer.

By the time I parked my car and took the elevator to my office, I was working on a list of potential suspects. From the limited details I currently possessed, Lance remained number one, but Dinah did have a potential suitor who she had been texting and a possible stalker from L.A. That didn't take into account the possibility this could all be another elaborate attempt to garner free publicity for the movie. If what Cross said was true and someone faked the stalker story, this could be a second attempt.

"Dammit," I muttered. I was spinning. My office was empty. No one had left any intel or notes. Reception was empty, and almost all of the offices were dark. Obviously,

Cross hadn't bothered to call in the other investigators, just the techs. I stepped back into the elevator.

When I got out on his floor, his assistant was on the phone in the outer office, but he waved me back. I stepped through Lucien's door, knocking gently on the jamb. At first glance, the room was empty. Then I noticed Cross standing in front of the closet. He had exchanged his jeans for dress pants and shed his shirt. His entire back was covered in an extremely elaborate tattoo. It was a winged creature, maybe a dragon, but before I could get a better look, he slipped his dress shirt on and turned around. Unintentionally, I gave him the quick once-over.

"See anything you like?" he asked.

"Nice ink," I replied, catching sight of another tattoo across the left side of his ribcage. This entire evening was one surprise after another. From the outside, I never would have expected Cross to be anything other than an overcontrolling suit. Obviously, he had a wild streak.

"Angel of death," he replied, matter-of-factly.

"Cheery."

He tucked his shirt into his pants and fastened his belt. Then he removed a comb from his pocket and turned to the mirror hanging from the inside of the door. He smoothed his hair down as best he could and reached for his tie. "Dinah's people will be here in four hours. She isn't due on set until this afternoon. I'd like you to be here."

"Okay."

He turned his collar down and tilted his head from side to side. Annoyed by the imperfections in his appearance, he turned away from the mirror and shut the closet door. "The lab is already analyzing the evidence. We should know something shortly." He took a seat behind his desk and searched through his drawers. "What do we know so far?"

"I already told you everything. My money's on Lance."

Cross jotted a note. "Based on the call sheet, he was one of the last actors on set tonight." He grabbed a clipboard and held it out. "That's the time log. Run through it and see if anyone sticks out. The later someone left the lot, the greater the chances he could be involved or witnessed something peculiar."

"I do know how this works."

"Then stop wasting time and get to it. I want a plausible list of suspects in two hours."

"Are we even considering the possibility the threat came from an outsider?"

"Don't worry about that yet. We'll get to that after the security team completes its analysis and after I have a chance to discuss these matters with Dinah's personal detail."

"Roger." I took the clipboard and headed for the door, but I stopped, suddenly confused. "When I arrived, you said the set was breached. Now you're telling me it's an internal problem. Which is it?"

"Mr. Perry believes a breach must have occurred since everyone at the studio had a reason to be there, but at this time, we have no proof either way."

"Sounds like he was jumping to conclusions."

Cross let out an annoyed sound. "One more thing, Alex. Keep a lid on this. I don't want you mentioning anything to anyone at the studio. If someone approaches you, direct them to me."

"Yes, sir."

I took the stairs down to my office, needing to do something besides wait in the deserted hallway for the elevator. On the bright side, I had already gotten a preliminary glimpse into Dinah Allen and Lance Smoke. That would save time now.

Booting up my computer, I started with the basics. Criminal records were something Hollywood actors collected like trading cards. Lance had several DUIs and a few citations for reckless driving but nothing else. That didn't mean he was clean. That just meant he hired the right people to bury things. Dinah didn't have a record. I wasn't sure what I thought about that, but I wasn't getting paid to speculate. Cross wanted cold, hard facts.

Checking the clipboard, I noted a few interesting points. Dinah was one of the first actresses to leave the set. Perhaps the reason whoever posed the dummy used her costume was simply because she wasn't around. Could it be a prank? Some actors were notorious for pranks, but the macabre depiction looked real. Cross and I both agreed on that, but now that I was back in the office, I felt we shouldn't discount the possibility so quickly.

The production assistants were among the last to leave. They were responsible for making certain everyone had updated call sheets, the proper sides, and knew what the final shooting schedule would be in the morning. Things constantly changed on set. I'd already seen dialogue changes and scene adjustments, and we were only two days in. We would need to question them. One of them might have seen something.

With the exception of Lance and Clay, the rest of the talent left after the last scene shot. That was around one o'clock. Cross called me for the first time at two, so it wasn't a huge window of opportunity. Picking up the phone, I notified the tech department of the timeframe, which could be narrowed even further depending on what time security realized there was a problem.

The last people off the lot were Neil Larson, the director, Kurt Wen, Travis Kreecher, and Lance Smoke. Most of the PAs and Clay Chaffey left thirty minutes before the bigwigs. The rest of the cast was gone as soon as shooting stopped. It all happened in such a short span of time, I wasn't positive any of them would have had time to get everything together, sneak onto the main soundstage, and leave the prop dummy without being seen.

The dummy must have been ready to go, I concluded. It could have been outfitted hours before, possibly after the break-ins at the wardrobe and makeup trailers. I closed my eyes and thought about the section of lot with nothing but trailer after trailer. It would be simple enough to slip inside without being detected or being given a second glance.

Hours after the thefts, Dinah had taken me back to her trailer. Before that, I was sequestered to one of the smaller buildings where we had conducted the weapons and fight training. Anything could have been going on outside, and I wouldn't have known about it. Security was busy at the front gate and monitoring the perimeter, so they would have been just as oblivious. But the one problem with my theory was Lance had been with us the entire time, as were Clay, Gemma, and Dinah. Still, I didn't think that ruled any of them out. The A-listers each had assistants who could have done the deed for them.

Lifting the receiver, I dialed the security team at the lot. "I need to know when wardrobe first noticed a problem. Do we have cameras covering the trailers? I need to know who came and went and when. I want everything from the first night of shooting until the following afternoon. Send a list of names as soon as you have it." I hung up, belatedly wondering if Cross's attitude had already rubbed off on me.

I was on to something. I knew it. I just couldn't figure out what it was. I picked up the schedule Dinah handed me our first night on set. The reason I recognized the costume on the dummy was because it had been the slinky nightie she wore to shoot her first scene. Only someone watching her film would know to take that costume, but more than one had been taken since Dinah and Gemma had to get refitted. Something didn't make sense.

Actually, none of it made sense.

TEN

"Well?" Cross asked expectantly, his focus never leaving his desk.

"I don't know."

"I'm not paying you not to know." His eyes flicked to mine, misplaced anger burning in them. "Do you know anything?"

"The director, head writer, stunt coordinator, and actor with top billing all left moments before security discovered the posed dummy. And at least two dozen PAs were on set around the same time, including Jett Trevino and Elodie Smith, Lance and Dinah's PAs. We should talk to them. They might know something. Honestly, I'm surprised everyone cleared out so quickly after shooting concluded."

"We can't question them directly. The studio wants this kept quiet." Cross shook his head. "They left after wrapping in order to go back to their hotels and sleep before starting back at seven." He folded his hands and leaned back in his chair. "Tell me something I don't know."

I blew out a breath. "Dinah's afraid this movie will prove she isn't much of an actress. She doesn't want to get pigeonholed into playing the mom. She and Lance had some kind of steamy affair a few months back."

"I saw the sex tape."

"Of course, you did."

He raised an eyebrow. "Go on."

"He wants her back. I don't know if that's about ego or publicity. His people and the studio are backing the idea of taking their relationship public, but as far as I can tell, it's over. He's a dog, and she's moved on."

He clicked something on his computer. "She hasn't been sighted with anyone since. Do you have a name for her new suitor?"

"She was vague. All I know is it's someone from her modeling days. She suggested it was a designer, and from my research, it might be Christian Nykle. But that's purely speculation on my part."

"Like the metal?" Cross asked.

"No." I spelled the name for him, my mind already circling back to the flowers that had been left in her trailer. "Honestly, I don't know why we're doing this." I dropped into the chair, and he stopped writing. "More than likely, whoever sent the flowers to her trailer is the same person responsible for tonight's threat. We need to identify the sender."

Cross slid several pages to my side of the desk. "That is an inventory of the gifts fans have sent to the studio for Dinah since they announced she was cast in the film. I'm already having a list of the senders compiled. More than likely, one of them also sent the flowers to her trailer, if," he paused for effect, "it wasn't someone on set."

"I thought the production was supposed to be top-secret."

Cross rolled his eyes, an irritated growl escaping his pursed lips. "Nothing is secret. It's why you're under contract not to divulge anything about the actors, script, or filming to anyone. They are doing what they can to keep most of it from leaking ahead of time. That being said, this is a film. The point is to create a buzz. They want the fans salivating at the notion. They want to tease. Keeping things secret is the best way to raise speculation and work them into a frenzy." He looked through my notes. "We need to be certain this isn't an internal problem before we expand our investigation."

I checked the time, wondering when the security team would phone. "Did any unauthorized personnel breach the lot?"

"Security found some damage to the fence in the rear right quadrant." He picked up his phone from the edge of his desk and flipped through the images before holding it out to me. A few of the links near the bottom had been cut, but the gap was not large enough for a human to enter or exit. It was just big enough to bend the very bottom of the fence inward to retrieve an item. "It's insubstantial."

"So no one breached the set?"

"We can't be certain, but it's unlikely. If someone did, we haven't figured out how."

When he looked up, I knew we had the same thought. The only people who could shed light on this matter were Dinah Allen's security team. If she was dealing with an ongoing threat, they needed to know about tonight.

His eyes raked over my body. "Miss Allen's team will be here in an hour and a half."

"I know."

He let out a scoff. "You cannot meet with them dressed like that. Get changed. Just make sure you're back in time. Do not be tardy."

I stood, confused by his priorities. "Lucien," I began, "you can't be serious."

He leaned toward me. "Aren't I? This is on me. My firm has a reputation, and tonight, someone proved we can't live up to expectations. The least we can do right now is dress the part. We don't need our incompetence to show in our choice of attire or my choice of investigators."

I glared at him. "I told you there was a problem."

He rubbed his temples. "You did. I failed to listen, choosing instead to listen to the shit for brains security team. That is one mistake I will not make again. Now go." His jaw clenched, and I took a step back. Now wasn't the time to argue.

"Right away, boss."

Driving back to the apartment I shared with Martin rather than my place would save roughly thirty minutes. If I was late to the meeting, Cross would have my head on a platter. Curiously, I wondered what would become of the security guard. I'd never seen my boss this far out of his depth. Granted, I'd only been working for him for less than two months, so I didn't know what Lucien in crisis mode looked like, but if today was any indication, it wasn't a good thing. I couldn't risk having that fury turned on me.

"Miss Parker," the doorman eyed me curiously, "is everything okay?"

"I just need a quick wardrobe change." I winked at him. "Can you make sure my car doesn't get towed? I'll only be a few minutes." I left it on the street near a hydrant. More than likely, it'd get ticketed before it would get towed, but it just depended on how seriously the city wanted to take fire safety.

"I'll do my best."

"Thanks."

When I entered our apartment, I didn't notice anything amiss, but I wasn't exactly paying attention. I'd like to believe if a thief and assassin were lurking in the shadows I would have noticed, but since they weren't, there really was no way to tell. I quietly entered the bedroom, hoping not to disturb Martin. It was a little after 5:30. He would be getting up in a few minutes anyway, or so I thought.

I just opened the closet halfway when I realized the glaringly obvious discrepancy in our bedroom. He was gone. The bed was made. Our missing pillows were back in place.

"What the hell?" I reached over and flipped on the overhead light as if that would make him materialize, but it didn't. Abandoning my mission, I went into the bathroom. Also empty. "Martin?" I called. He didn't respond. I even checked the balcony, but he wasn't there.

I was halfway through dialing his number when I found the note stuck on the fridge. *Went home. Needed notes on a presentation. I have a long few days ahead. I'll stay at my place tonight so I don't disturb you. Hope your crisis at work is handled. If you need anything, call.*

My mouth felt cottony, and I tried to swallow the lump in my throat. Cursing, I stomped back into the bedroom. I changed into a Cross approved outfit, found a duffel, and threw the rest of my belongings into the bag. Was I irrational? Probably. Was I pissed? Definitely. Did I have time to deal with this? Absolutely not.

Tossing my copy of the apartment key on the counter, I gave the place one last look. "I knew this was a bad idea." I slammed the door and waited for the elevator. When it opened in the lobby, I approached the doorman. "Did you notice what time Mr. Martin left?"

He bit his lip. "It was a few minutes after you did."

"I bet it was," I snarled. He stepped back, and I tried to force my face into a less hostile expression. "Keep up the good work." It was the best I could muster as I went out the door and back to my car. By the time I got into the car, I had already dialed Martin's number.

He answered on the second ring, not a hint of sleep in his voice. "Sweetheart?"

I shoved the key in the ignition. "You seriously left our apartment in the middle of the night?"

"You left first."

"Are we in kindergarten? I didn't want to leave. I had to go to work. I wasn't literally lying in wait for you to disappear so I could sneak off."

"Is that what you think I did? Alex, what is going on?" Martin asked, his voice had a slight edge. "You've been acting off ever since you came home last night. Talk to me. Did I do something?"

I cut into traffic, hearing an angry horn blare. Like any good driver who made a mistake, I flipped the annoyed motorist the bird. "I don't know. Did you?"

Martin was getting agitated. "Stop playing games. Why are you mad at me?"

Reining in my thoughts before they could spill out of my mouth, I exhaled. "I'm not mad. I'm just tired. I don't know what's going on with you."

"Did you get my note?"

"Yes."

"Well, that should have cleared it up."

Maybe he'd been at a strip club the other night. A lap dance or two would have explained the perfume, makeup, and his friskiness. "You're keeping something from me."

"Alex," from his tone I knew it was true, "you're being paranoid. Is this because you aren't ready for us to move in together again? I said we were taking it slow, and then I sprung the all in thing on you and turned our weekend place into an everyday place. I'm sorry."

"Why do you keep apologizing?"

He sniffed, slightly indignant. "Fine. I'll stop."

"I thought we weren't keeping things from each other anymore. You said we needed to rebuild trust."

"Don't you trust me?"

"Why did you leave in the middle of the night?"

"I needed notes for a meeting. If you come over right now, I can prove it to you. I'm home. You can ping my phone. No one's here. Do you want to look through my security footage to verify it? I don't care. I'll get copies of my office footage for you too. Whatever it takes to put your mind at ease."

It scared me that he thought he needed an alibi. Innocent people didn't worry about such things. "That won't be necessary."

"What do you want me to say?" Apparently, he didn't realize I just conceded, so he still felt the need to defend himself. "What I'm working on doesn't concern you. It has nothing to do with us. It's something for me. It's something that I *need* to do. You of all people should understand that." How was I supposed to know if he thought an orgy was something he thought he *needed* to do? "Alexis, please, let this go. When it's over, I'll tell you everything, but I'm in the process of procuring some sensitive items. Business deals and all. I can't discuss it. Not even with you."

"Can't or won't?"

"Sweetheart," he begged, and my heart broke.

"It's fine. We're fine. I'm sorry I called and bothered you." I pulled into the garage and parked in my assigned spot.

"Don't be upset."

"I'm fine," I growled. "I have to go."

"Wait."

"Martin, I can't do this now. I'm already back at the office. I only went home to change. Cross is on the warpath. The studio might have been compromised." I clenched my jaw. "My focus needs to be on this, and yours has to be on your top-secret project. It's okay. We're okay. This is what we do, right?"

"Fuck it. I'll come home early tonight, and we'll talk about it."

"Don't bother."

"Alex," he warned.

"No," I said, forcing my voice to be calm, "you're right. I have things that I have to handle, and you have things you have to handle. I understand what it's like to have a personal mission. You are under no obligation to discuss it with me. And we both know I prefer not sharing things with you, so we're even.

"Great," he huffed.

"I have to go."

"I can't hang up this phone until I'm sure we're okay." He didn't sound desperate or hurt. He sounded annoyed.

"I love you." The words leaked out from somewhere deep inside. I wasn't sure why. I didn't think he deserved to hear them, but a part of me was terrified. Under no uncertain terms was I supposed to confront him on this. I had decided that less than twelve hours ago, and then I lost my ability to act reasonably. "Whatever you're doing, just be careful."

"I will." He exhaled. "The same goes for you."

ELEVEN

"We believe there is a credible threat," Mario Scaratilli, Dinah Allen's chief of security, declared. He held up a hard copy of one of the photographs Cross had taken. "That's definitely part of her wardrobe. She verified it as soon as you texted the image." He put the photo down on the table. "Have you determined how the breach occurred?"

Cross swallowed. "We aren't positive there was a breach."

"Interesting." Scaratilli's gaze swept over the folders on the table. "I see you've built a profile for Miss Allen."

"Several. It is not yet clear if she is the target."

"Isn't that a bit of an overstep?"

Muffled static came from the speakerphone in the center of the table before one of the studio heads spoke. We were teleconferencing with the studio while Dinah's team was present in the hopes of getting to the bottom of this as quickly as possible. "Broadway Films requested Cross Security handle this incident. In order to properly do that, we've given Mr. Cross clearance to quietly check into the talent and crew. Mr. Cross has promised to execute the utmost discretion in these matters. Haven't you, Lucien?"

"Absolutely. Nothing I discover will be disclosed to

anyone with the possible exception of the affected parties, unless such a time occurs in which law enforcement is required." Lucien had the legalese down to a science.

"Have you informed the other actors of the danger?" Scaratilli asked. He crossed his arms over his chest and leaned back in the chair.

"No," I said, drawing his attention away from my boss.

"Why not?"

"We wouldn't want to cause a panic." My eyebrow twitched slightly upward. "Have you addressed the previous threat Miss Allen received?"

His stony face slowly broke into a slight grin. "You're the FBI agent she's been raving about."

"FBI?" the studio head squawked.

"Alexis Parker, the technical consultant," Cross responded. His gaze came to rest on me, his eyes fixed in a warning; *do not screw this up.*

"That would be me," I replied.

Scaratilli nodded. "You're talking about the flowers. We have yet to track the sender. In Miss Allen's haste, she discarded the only piece of evidence we might have used. Since then, we've had to make several inquiries to local florists, but so far, we haven't determined where the bouquet originated, much less who sent it."

"It seems like you could use our help," Cross said, "and we certainly could use yours."

"Lucien," the studio head interrupted, hoping no one forgot about him since he wasn't present in the conference room, "I don't want a large-scale investigation being conducted while we're trying to make a movie. I need to know the lot is safe, the talent and crew are safe, and that nothing like this is going to happen again."

"We've upped security. The man who had been in charge of the detail no longer works here," Cross said, and my eyes went wide. He fired someone over what might have been an oversight or a stupid mistake. Shit. Cross took his reputation very seriously. "We've increased patrols, added additional surveillance equipment to monitor the perimeter, and have enacted more thorough checks for visitors. Like I told you earlier, our best chance of determining the seriousness of this," he paused, frowning at being forced to use the word, "potential prank is to question the people on set, but since you are opposed to that request, we will find another way."

"Thanks, Lucien. Let me know what you discover." The sound of the dial tone replaced the staticky voice, and Cross hit the disconnect button.

"What do you want from us?" Scaratilli asked, his eyes never wavering from mine.

Cross cleared his throat. "We were hoping to share intel. Parker retrieved the note attached to the flowers. We've analyzed it for prints, but the ones recovered were inconsequential. You can have it back to continue your investigation if you provide us with the list."

The list? I wasn't sure what Cross was talking about, but Scaratilli did. The security chief glowered. "Are you trying to show us up?"

"Not in the least," Lucien said.

Scaratilli rubbed a hand over his jaw. "Fine, but we'll need everything you've compiled." He gestured at the stack of profiles on the table. "Some stupid love note won't hack it."

Cross nodded. "I'll have digital copies forwarded."

Scaratilli's eyes narrowed ever so slightly. "If this is anything but what it appears to be, we will take legal measures."

"I would expect nothing less." Cross stood.

The security chief gave me another glance. "Miss Allen is waiting at reception. She would like to speak to you."

I stood and followed the human refrigerator out of the conference room and to the front desk. He didn't speak on the way, and I had no desire to make small talk.

"Alex," she greeted, standing and moving toward me.

"Miss Allen." I glanced at Scaratilli who was standing a polite two steps away doing his best impersonation of a coat rack, even though he would have been better suited to imitate a redwood.

She shot me an annoyed look. "Dinah," she insisted. "I thought after yesterday we were warming up to one another."

"Of course, ma'am."

She saw the slightest twinkle in my eyes. "Scar, wait downstairs." Before he could protest, she turned to face him. "I'm in a building full of private investigators and security personnel. Nothing will happen to me. I don't see any paparazzi hiding in the wings. Do you?"

"No, ma'am." He pressed a button on the radio clipped to his ear and spoke to the driver, ensuring photographers weren't lurking outside. "I will be waiting in the lobby." He pushed the button, and we stood in complete silence until he stepped into the already crowded elevator. I was surprised he fit and wondered what the maximum weight capacity was.

"Cross Security is only three floors," I said after he was gone.

She smiled. "In that case, you better show me around."

"Sure." I glanced at the receptionist, wondering what Lucien would think of it, but she just shrugged. We passed the conference rooms, a few of my colleagues' offices, and the breakroom before we made it to my office. I opened the door and waited for her to enter. "This is where the magic happens."

She surveyed the inside from the doorway. "This isn't what I pictured."

"Me neither. Make yourself at home." I moved to my desk, making certain nothing incriminating or sensitive was out in the open. Thankfully, I was never one to clutter my workspace with personal effects, so there wasn't much she could dig up by snooping. "Can I get you some coffee, tea, water," I noticed her attention was on the bar cart in the corner, "a shot of whiskey?"

"You're a whiskey girl?"

"No."

Her face scrunched in disbelief. "Really?"

"That was actually meant as a welcome to the company."

"Coffee would be nice."

Leaving her alone in my office, I went to the breakroom and filled two mugs. From the morning in the limo, I knew she took her coffee black, so I didn't bother with creamer or sugar. When I turned around, I almost bumped into

Cross who had snuck up behind me. He took a step back, warily eyeing the hot liquid which splashed out of one of the mugs and onto the floor inches from his foot.

"Do be careful. This is the only spare suit I have in the office." His voice sounded serious, but I saw a slight playfulness in his eyes. Or I was tired enough to hallucinate it. "Miss Allen is waiting in your office."

"I know." I held up the two mugs.

"Right. The receptionist informed me she would like a tour of our offices. Take her upstairs to the lab. Show her our equipment, explain the basics of what we do, and the situations we can handle. Do your best to impress her."

"What if she wants to know about last night and what we're doing about it?"

"Tell her it's under investigation and put her mind at ease. Alexis, you've already been welcomed into her inner circle and have unfettered access to the cast and crew. You're the only one who can investigate without arousing suspicion or drawing undue attention to the matter. I'll keep on top of the security teams and see what they discover. The techs will gather and analyze as much intel as possible, but you're on point. Play this as you see fit. I want to know how we screwed up in order to make sure it doesn't happen again."

Now you give me autonomy, I thought but chose not to voice it. Instead, I blew out a breath and went back to my office. As I expected, Dinah had used my absence as an opportunity to snoop.

"Find anything interesting?" I put the coffee on the table in front of the couch.

She ran a hand through her hair and laughed. "Do you have cameras in here?"

"No."

She picked up the cup and took a sip. "But you've figured me out, and it's only been three days." She swallowed and put the mug down. "And you know how I take my coffee and which blend I prefer. If you decide this private investigator thing isn't working out, I could really use another assistant. Elodie can barely juggle everything I throw her way."

"I'm not particularly subservient."

She chuckled. "I picked up on that somewhere between the limo ride and my trailer yesterday." She sobered slightly and bit her bottom lip. "Do you think someone wants to hurt me?"

"I don't know. It's possible you aren't the target. It could be the production, or it could be a prank. Do you know if that's common behavior for any of the actors or crew?"

"I don't. Lance might know."

"What's the deal with you two?"

She picked up her cup and stared into it. "We had a spark for about five seconds. He probably thought it wouldn't hurt to tie his name to a rising star."

"And you thought it might help your chances of getting a role in this film."

She glared daggers at me. "It wasn't like that."

"He's an executive producer. He's also your costar. And he wants to maintain some semblance of a romantic relationship, at least in the magazines and tabloids. Does he want your relationship to continue beyond the purview of flashbulbs?"

She rolled her shoulders back and sighed. "I have no idea. I've never known what he's thinking. That's the allure. He's unpredictable. Adventurous. A little crazy."

"Dangerous?"

"All bad boys are." She considered my questions. "You can't honestly believe he's responsible. Wouldn't this stunt jeopardize the film?"

"You'd know the answer to that better than I would." I gulped down some coffee, burning my throat in the process. "I need to know everything, particularly who you are currently seeing or recently broke up with."

"Besides Lance?"

"Yes." I picked up a pen. "You mentioned a designer."

"I don't want to do this." Abruptly, she stood. "You can't expect me to believe this is the entirety of Cross Security. Show me what's upstairs. Scar said you had fancy labs and top of the line technology. I want to see something cool." A thought came to mind that painted a smile on her face. "I want to watch you work an investigation. I want you to take

- 84 -

me step by step through the entire process from beginning to end."

"I'm not an FBI agent anymore. I don't have access."

"Fuck the FBI. You're a private investigator. That must require similar qualifications and tactics. This will be my ride-along. And it's my case, so what could be better? You were far from forthcoming while sitting in my trailer being bored out of your mind. This is more interactive. It's fun and exciting." Her eyes held a challenge. "And since Cross Security wasn't to blame for the breach and is supposed to be one of the best security firms in the country, I'd like to see what one of their investigations entails."

"You said the studio wouldn't insure you for this," I protested.

"We won't tell them." She looked at me. "Plus, according to Mr. Cross, I should be perfectly safe. He has things under control. Or is that a steaming pile of bullshit?"

I didn't like the turn our conversation had taken. Lucien would want me to affirm our firm was completely capable of offering protection and solving problems, but Dinah was asking for trouble. And somehow, I ended up in the middle of it.

"What do you say, Alex? It's either this or I recommend the studio finds new security to safeguard the production."

"You realize that's blackmail."

"Maybe, but it is incredibly effective." She clasped her hands together. "It'll be fun. I won't get in the way, I promise. And you'll get what you want too."

"What's that?"

"Since we'll be focused on a current real-life problem, I won't have to focus so much on your past, and you'll get to ask me whatever you want in the scope of the investigation. It'll be great."

Great is not how I would describe it, but I didn't think I had a choice. I took another swig of coffee, wishing I'd gone for the whiskey instead. "Let me show you the lab. That's where the real magic happens."

TWELVE

Dinah wasn't impressed. Dozens of computers, monitors, and lab equipment, no matter how shiny, just wasn't impressive unless you understood how valuable they were to an investigation. I tried to explain it. I even roped Amir into giving her an in-depth analysis on how he obtained, scanned, and searched the databases for the fingerprints and why hers and Elodie's were not in the system. Then he went into minute detail about epithelial cells, saliva, and hair follicles in regards to obtaining viable DNA samples, but her eyes glazed over.

When he was finished, she spotted the prop dummy on one of the exam tables. She stepped toward it, and I followed behind. Several techs, whose names I didn't know, were running various tests in the hopes of finding some kind of trace evidence that might point to the culprit.

"Anything?" I asked, and one of them looked at me before glancing at Dinah. "You can speak in front of her. Cross gave the okay."

The tech just stood there, practically stuttering. It took a moment before I realized the poor bastard was starstruck. Dinah caught on immediately, flashing him what I had dubbed her starlet smile. It was far from sincere, but it was the same smile used in every single one of her photoshoots.

It was a million watts of friendliness with just a hint of sex appeal. It was a nice trick, and one that she could turn on and off with the flip of a switch. While he fanboyed out, I scanned the preliminary reports.

"They're still working on it," I said, "but it doesn't look promising."

"Now what do we do?" She moved away from the tech who finally stopped ogling her as if she were a glowing, golden unicorn.

I looked at my watch. "Don't you need to return to set?"

"My scenes aren't shooting until three. Elodie already texted scanned PDFs of today's sides. There weren't any changes. I have my lines memorized, so I have a few hours."

"Sides?" I asked, hoping to distract her.

"Pieces of the script specific to the scenes I'm shooting."

"Fascinating," I deadpanned.

"No, it isn't." She jerked her chin up as we went to the stairwell since she decided she didn't want to risk a non-Cross Security employee spotting her. It could lead to a tweet or post, and the place would be swarming with fans. "Is sarcasm a requirement for your line of work?"

"I think so. You basically have three options. Sarcastic, bitchy, or both. Personally, I try to walk the line between sarcastic and bitchy. It keeps people on their toes."

She snickered, despite herself. "You're a laugh a minute," she shot back with an equal amount of sarcasm.

"I keep myself pretty entertained, which is all that really matters. Although, you're a professional, so my standards and yours don't exactly compare."

She stopped outside my office door and crossed her arms over her chest. "When the geeks upstairs can't provide a solution, how do you solve the case?" Obviously, my wit wasn't enough to keep her distracted.

"You pray luck is on your side."

"You can't be serious."

I stepped around her and into my office. She followed, and I closed the door. "Actually, the secret to doing this job and working for the FBI is simple; it's better to be lucky than good."

As predicted, she reached for her notebook and scribbled it down. She nibbled on the end of her pen and read the words. "Isn't that true for absolutely everything?"

"Yes."

"So you're really not that good at your job?"

"No matter how good I may be, other factors are always in play. The only way we ever solve anything is by getting lucky." She giggled at my word choice. At least she found something amusing. Hell, Martin would have her rolling in the floor with his double entendres and innuendo. "I'm serious." Opening the nearest filing cabinet, I pulled out a few empty folders. "From here, our next step is to build profiles. Do you want to help?"

The question actually thrilled her, and she took a seat on the lengthy side of the l-shaped sofa and leaned forward. "Yes."

"Great." I pushed a legal pad and pen in her direction. "Let's start with the people in your life. Write down everyone you dated in the last two years. That will give us a good starting point."

"You can't be serious." It was the question she had avoided earlier, and now after our little tour, we were back to where we left off. "What does that have to do with this?"

"Think like an investigator," I urged. "We can only work with the facts we possess. Fact number one, someone broke into your trailer and left flowers and a card. Fact number two, someone broke into the wardrobe trailer and stole the sexy little number you wore the other night. Fact number three, someone took your makeup. Fact number four, the missing costume and makeup were both used to paint up a prop dummy, who was wearing a wig eerily similar in color and length to your hair, and stabbed it through the heart. What do those facts say to you?"

"It wasn't just my costume and makeup. They took Gemma's too."

"I know, and when a dummy appears on set dressed like Gemma, we'll have a conversation with her about who she's been dating," another thought crossed my mind, "unless the two of you have someone in common." It was a theory I hadn't considered until now and blamed it on lack of sleep.

She looked at me. "Neil. Maybe Lance."

"Neil Larson, the director?"

She set her jaw. "Do I need to remind you that you signed an NDA, and Lucien did as well?"

"There is one other thing you should know about me," I said. "Unlike the gossipy twits that rule your world, I don't give a shit who you bang. That isn't my business. What is my business is determining who might want to hurt you, so I'll ask again. Neil Larson?"

"Yes."

"Recently?"

She did her best to look indignant. "Do I need to draft a timeline?"

"Yes. Y'see, men tend to have problems sharing. Women too, but men mostly. They like to keep their playthings to themselves."

She actually laughed. "That's so simple. Trust me, Alex, it's different in my industry. We jump in and out of beds faster than most people change clothes. We live on a constant high of praise and success. We drink too much. Smoke too much. Screw too much. We work hard. The shifts are long and the conditions oftentimes unpleasant. So we play harder." She stared at me. "I won't apologize for any of it."

"I don't want an apology. I just want some names and dates."

"Fine."

By the time she was finished, I couldn't tell if she was the most enlightened woman I'd ever met or the most deluded. There was a reason for the recent shift concerning sexual harassment in the workplace, especially in the entertainment industry. Historically, women were objectified, hired or fired based on how far they were willing to go for a role and that didn't just mean shaving their heads or gaining fifty pounds. Several were forced to prostitute themselves to become stars. It was a tradeoff to reach their dreams, but sex should never be the price, even when sex and sex appeal is what sold tickets, filled seats, and took Dinah Allen from behind-the-scenes fashion lackey to runway model and movie star. No wonder I couldn't figure out her motivation. It was tangled up in one giant knot that society shat out.

"Do you know if Gemma has received any threats or mysterious gifts?" I asked, and Dinah shook her head, "Okay." I glanced down at the names on the list. Considering her insistence that celebrities changed partners the way normal people changed clothes, her list wasn't that extensive. "Last two years?"

"Yeah. Lance was," she sighed, "is the only relationship out of the bunch. The rest were weekend trips or one night stands. Nothing really lasted until Lance." I read through the twenty names and approximate dates. "No one since?"

She laughed. "No, Alex, I haven't been seeing anyone, just the occasional text message."

"And Neil?"

"After I was cast, he invited me out to dinner. We celebrated. Then we celebrated a bit more. That was it."

We needed access to her phone records, but I wasn't sure if I wanted to ask. It had been hard enough to get her cooperation on the names. Truthfully, we probably could have surmised as much by reading the entertainment gossip sites. I took the list and moved to the computer. She followed and watched as I typed. The first thing I did was determine where these people were at the present. Since every name on the list was in the entertainment industry, it wasn't hard to figure out their current locations. We lived in an age in which social media was king.

Neil Larson and Lance Smoke were the only two people close enough to pull it off. And while I was aware money and affluence could lend itself to a quick flyover, I knew if any one of the names on the list had been on set, someone would have taken note, even if it was just some starstruck member of the crew.

I needed to speak to Gemma Kramer, preferably in private, or Cross needed to contact her people. If Gemma was also targeted, as Dinah had attempted to insist earlier, that would change things. The prankster's motive would be stopping production or causing the two main female leads to abandon the production. Whereas, if Dinah was the only target, that spelled out jilted lover or possible stalker.

Rubbing my eyes, I wasn't sure what to do since Dinah was overseeing every move I made.

"Has Mr. Scaratilli mentioned any possible threats?" I asked.

"Scar?" She thought for a moment. "Nothing out of the ordinary. At Cannes, he insisted on additional guards. Then in Maui, after some paparazzi filmed Lance and me on the beach, he insisted on securing the hotel and grounds, but things have been back to normal since we returned home. The incident at my estate was a misunderstanding." The words came out without any type of conviction behind them. "Honestly, he's probably been even laxer since we came here to shoot."

"Was he in the limo with us?"

"No, he followed behind in a separate car. Ty Johnson was riding shotgun in the event we encountered any issues."

"Okay." It didn't seem important, especially since Cross was getting these details from Dinah's security team. He could assess any weaknesses, and we would go from there. "Who's in charge of your fan mail? Whoever reached out with the flowers probably attempted to communicate before."

"That's what Scar thinks too. He had Cherise send everything over." Dinah saw the question in my eyes. "Cherise is my agent. She's in charge of correspondence. She and her team reply to messages, physical and virtual." Dinah returned to the couch and took a seat, looking down at some empty folders and legal pads. "This is how it's done? You ask questions and form a list of suspects?"

"They are persons of interest. It's possible someone you know might have noticed something that will lead to someone else, but we don't know until we figure out who is in a position to know something."

"It sounds like guesswork."

"That's where the luck part comes in. It is guesswork, but you develop a feel for it. Pretend our roles were reversed, where would you go from here?"

She thought for a moment. "Back to set. I'd want to talk to Gemma. Then I'd probably want to talk to the prop guy to see if anyone borrowed one of the dummies."

I pointed at her. "I have a feeling you might just pull off a convincing FBI agent."

She gave me a genuine smile. "Not if I don't get back to film my scenes on time." She reached for her phone. "You are coming to set with me, aren't you? Despite all of this," she waved her hand around my office, "you're still a technical consultant and my personal insight into what it's like to be a female FBI agent. I need you."

"I'll be there. I just need to check in with Cross first." I gave her an encouraging look. "Should I meet you at your trailer?"

"No. Meet me on the soundstage. This is one of the more complicated scenes. We have five cameras. Setup will take time and probably quite a few takes. It'd be best to have you there in case I need feedback or input, and Neil might have questions. You haven't met him yet, have you?"

"No, but it's about time we get to know one another."

For a moment, her expression was entirely unreadable, as if she couldn't show any emotion when she didn't know what emotion she was supposed to convey. "You aren't going to ask about us, are you?"

"I am aware of what is considered polite conversation. Decorum is my middle name."

"Good." She stopped for a moment. "What is your actual middle name?"

"How is that relevant?"

"It's not, but you know more about my sexual history than my therapist. It just seems fair that I know something about you. Do you want to make a list of your conquests for the past two years? I bet that would be enlightening. Aren't law enforcement officials notorious for one night stands? It has something to do with the near-death, might not live to see tomorrow mentality."

"I'm not that exciting."

"What about your fellow agents?"

I thought of Kate, one of the forensic accountants at the OIO. "It depends on the person. There no broad generalization. My last partner is married with a young child. My mentor was divorced three times and at the point of swearing off all sexual encounters. And my Quantico roommate will take home any guy with a nice smile and biceps the size of my thigh."

"That doesn't tell me anything."

"It depends on the person," I repeated, "but to answer your question, danger heightens everything. It skews perception, which is why we are warned not to make any life-altering decisions after a dangerous encounter."

She scribbled something down in her notepad and called Scar to tell him she was coming down and to have the car waiting. Then she went down the hall, slipping on the Jackie O's and burying her hair beneath a scarf she pulled from her purse. And people thought I could be dramatic.

THIRTEEN

The day was long. Extremely long. It began around three a.m., and it hadn't stopped yet. In between Dinah asking a million questions, I'd spoken to several people on set, including a few of the PAs, but none of them were helpful. No one saw anything, and if they did, they weren't telling me. In fact, it seemed no one actually knew anything about the Dinah dummy, which I found hard to believe.

Gemma Kramer was unaware of any security issues. She hadn't received any hate mail or odd gifts. No ugly floral bouquets to speak of. She'd been in the industry since her teenage years, and her team knew how to handle such matters. Her security had never been an issue. Unfortunately, I didn't exactly get to grill her on her relationship with the director. From what I gathered, she and Lance had never been an item. If they'd been together, that information never leaked to any of the tabloids.

The prop master didn't recall anyone using any of the dummies. No one borrowed any or checked them out. In fact, he didn't even realize one was missing until I inquired about it. It was no wonder things disappeared from sets all the time.

Someone from the costume department found Gemma's

missing clothes in a heap on the floor. It appeared they'd been knocked off the hangers and buried under shoes, handbags, belts, and other accessories. I hoped to take them back to Cross Security to be checked for clues, but the costumer adamantly opposed that idea. She even threatened to call security on me. Someone ought to clue her in that I was security or at least security adjacent. But she didn't care, and the studio didn't want us getting in the way. They didn't even want me asking questions, which is why I'd been doing my best to be discreet.

After a brief introduction, I sat down with Neil Larson, the director, for a whopping three minutes. He didn't pay any attention to the things I asked. His focus was entirely on the scene and the input I could provide. He wondered how many units would respond to a threat, what the response time would be, and if it would seem contrived if they arrived at the same time. This seemed more like a logical reasoning or math problem, but maybe he'd never been able to figure out the age-old question of what time train A and train B would meet. As soon as he had his answer, he barked commands to the DP and disappeared into his makeshift command center.

Returning to my seat, I leaned back in the metal folding chair which wasn't cushioned or particularly fabulous. Kellan was right; it only took three days for me to hate movies. Unfortunately, it was too late to be reassigned. My window slammed shut the moment security found the dummy.

Lance eyed me while he waited to shoot his scene, and I wondered what he wanted. I hadn't spoken to him yet. He was always busy. Always doing something important or sneaking off to his trailer. At one point, he had his assistant run interference just to keep me away, but now it looked like he had something to say. Maybe it was a confession.

While he was shooting, I cornered Jett Trevino, his assistant, to ask if he'd seen anything odd the previous night, but that didn't go so well. As soon as Neil called cut, Lance stormed toward us, dismissing Jett with a flourish of his hand.

"You're a distraction," Lance said. "If this happens

again, I'll have you removed."

"Dinah wants me here," I replied, my eyes narrowing.

"She doesn't have top billing or producer credits. It's my money. My show." He leaned in closer. "I'm not stupid. Yesterday, you kept her from speaking to me. You need to back off. This doesn't concern you."

I held my ground, wondering how anyone could think he was one of the sexiest men alive. "Did you notice anyone lurking around set last night? You were one of the last people to leave."

He stared down his perfectly straight nose at me. "Why?"

I shrugged, wondering if he knew what happened. From my conversations with Gemma and Neil, no one was aware of the threat or potential breach. The studio execs were keeping that information secret, and Cross was an expert at containment. Perhaps finding the one person who knew what happened would be enough to pinpoint the culprit.

"Wardrobe reported some missing costumes. Cross Security wanted to make sure there wasn't more to it."

"You should run along and check." He shooed me away with a flick of his wrist.

Taking a step back, I sighed and walked away. Dinah was having her makeup touched up, so I left the soundstage and went outside. An elaborate outdoor scene had been built on the backlot. The walls had been painted, and several large platforms of varying heights were erected. The platforms ran almost the entire length of the lot. Two stuntmen were on wires, and Kurt was watching from the side. I took a moment to watch one man chase the other, jumping and rolling from platform to platform. Some metal rails separated the platforms, and the chase continued from the lowest roof to the highest with lots of jumps, flips, and other impressive acrobatics. When they were finished, Kurt cupped his hands over his mouth and shouted to them that was enough for today. He turned and saw me watching.

"It's a closed set," he said, grinning.

"I'm aware."

The radio in his hand chirped, and he pressed the

button and gave a quick reply before closing the distance between us. "What do you think? It's for the rooftop chase scene. We just wanted to run through it tonight to see if it would fly." He looked proud.

"Is the bad guy an acrobat?" I asked, and he scowled.

"Come on, Alex. We need something flashy and cool. It's based on military obstacle courses."

"Parkour?"

"You're familiar with the practice?"

"Envious of people who can move like that, but it seems rather unbelievable, especially with the wires."

He took a step back and cocked his head to the side. "The wires are safety precautions. They aren't assisting in the jumps or flips. Those moves are one hundred percent my guys. You look like you're in good shape. You could probably run through the course without a problem. Do you want to try?"

I held up my palms. "No, but I will admit I am intrigued. How does one go about preparing for something like that?" Polite conversation might give me the chance to ask about last night.

"Honestly, it's a lot of lower body strength, stability, and agility. It might sound weird, but the skills required in yoga are incredibly valuable in parkour in addition to jumping and vaulting."

"Were you setting this up last night?"

"Yeah, we had the platforms placed late last night. Construction went to work on the railings, and set design came in this morning to give it that real world feel."

"I don't remember seeing it when I left yesterday. It's crazy how fast it got put up."

"It was literally the last thing we did before leaving. When the cameras stopped rolling, Neil and Lance came to check it out. They moved the schedule around so Lance would have more time to practice. He wants to do his own stunts, but we'll see how that goes."

"What did you guys do afterward? Just stand out here and watch it get built?"

"Pretty much, and then we called it a night."

I bit my lip, thinking. Something crossed his mind, and

he shouted to the stuntmen to try something else. Since I no longer had his attention, I continued on my path to the front gate. It had been nearly a day since the dummy was found; I hoped security knew something by now.

Unfortunately, surveillance cameras faced out, not in. Aside from the few obvious blind spots, which had been remedied, no unauthorized personnel had been caught entering the lot. Cross had people looking into yesterday's visitors, and even though the lot was considered closed, thirty-four people had dropped by, everyone from lawyers, agents, assistants, and managers to random friends and family members.

I watched the footage of people leaving for the night, but that didn't help. "What about the trailers? Do we have cameras set up over there?"

"No, ma'am. The actors won't allow it. They say it violates their privacy, and the studio agrees. It's why we have no idea who entered Dinah's trailer and left the flowers."

"Fine." My eyes met the guard's. "And it's Alex."

"Noted."

Trudging back to the soundstage, I waited outside for Dinah. Her security team wasn't on the lot, and I realized I hadn't seen any of the actors' security details. Obviously, they believed the site was secure, which indicated they weren't worried about a threat. Dinah should have been. She knew better. Scaratilli didn't seem like the type of man to leave anything to chance. It didn't add up.

Laughter sounded behind me, and I turned to see Clay, Dinah, and the DP leaving the building. She met my eyes, excused herself, and bounded over with way too much energy. "What are you doing out here?" she asked.

"Working."

She giggled like this was the funniest thing she ever heard. I caught a whiff of smoke and realized her eyes were glazed over. Kellan was right again. "You can call it a night," she said, dismissing me as if I were Elodie.

"Yeah, okay." Asking what she was on wouldn't be productive. "Just be careful."

She made a face. "You sound like Scar."

"Where is he?"

She looked around. "Not here."

"No shit."

She scowled. "He'll be here when I'm ready to leave. That's how this works." Clearly annoyed, she turned and jogged to catch up to Clay who was on his way to his trailer.

So much for wanting to figure out who left the flowers. Apparently, it was easier to get high and let someone else worry about the potential threat. Maybe I picked the wrong profession.

* * *

"What do we know?" Lucien asked the moment I set foot in his office. He was sprawled out on the sofa, his head propped against the arm with the file opened in front of him. He looked tired. Hell, with his shirt wrinkled and his jacket and tie off, he looked like a cop.

"Clay Chaffey has some primo weed, and that's about it. Cameras don't cover the trailers, and no one was caught on tape planting the dummy. We're back where we started."

"Shit." He closed the folder but made no attempt to sit up. "Is this our fault?"

"I don't know. No one's aware of what happened."

"That's strange. By most standards, that's a small lot. Broadway Films is the only company currently using it. Everyone there is part of the same film. Someone should have seen something."

"It was cleared out. Only your security team was present when the dummy was found."

He reached for a pen and scribbled a note. "Maybe I should have them investigated."

"Lucien, you can't be serious."

After pulling himself up, he put the folder on the table. "Need I remind you that I am in charge. I'll do whatever it takes to safeguard that set. You said no one else was there. I'm just following your leads. If you have something that contradicts that theory, by all means, I'd love to hear it."

"No, sir," I managed through gritted teeth, even though what I really wanted to say was don't be a prick.

With a satisfied smirk, he climbed off the couch and went to his desk. "Broadway Films is unaware of any threats to their company, the production, or the cast and crew. I've spoken at length with the personal reps of the big names, but no one's been experiencing any issues out of the norm. I've double-checked with the LAPD and several of the private security firms on the West Coast. While it's possible another nutjob has come out of the woodwork, it's probably best to assume this situation is related to Dinah."

"I agree, so did her security chief."

"Still, it bothers me."

"What does?" At this point, I wouldn't put it past him to say the pinstripes on his shirt were a problem.

"Not knowing if the lot was breached." He dropped into his chair, sifting through several aerial photos and diagrams of the property. "We can't address the problem unless we know the source. If this is internal, everything," he gestured at the stack of papers on the coffee table, "I've done today is a waste of time, but if it's external, then everything you did today was a waste of time. Fuck."

"We have no way of knowing."

A fire blazed behind his eyes. "We need to find out." Abruptly, he stood and went to the closet for his jacket. He put his tie back on and adjusted it. Then he went to his phone and pressed the intercom button. "Justin, tell my driver to have the car waiting, and get the head of our legal department on the phone and transfer the call to my cell." He pressed his lips together and waited for the affirmative. "Thanks." He pressed the intercom button again and wrote down a number. He held it out, and I took it. "That's the phone number for Mario Scaratilli. Try to charm some answers out of him."

"Me?"

He continued moving around his office. "Yes, you. Or is that beyond your capabilities?"

"Didn't you mention at one point that I lacked finesse?"

"Yes, but Mr. Scaratilli views me as a threat. He doesn't regard you in the same light."

"How can you tell?"

Lucien plucked another folder off the table on his way to

the door and held it out to me. "That's his profile. I had our techs run it before our meeting this morning. He's the typical protective, alpha male. To put it simply, he's afraid I plan to show him up and force him out. In essence, he believes Cross Security wants to take over Dinah Allen's personal security."

"Why?"

"Protective. Alpha. Male." Lucien led me to the elevator. "Since it's not your company and you lack a penis, he should be more forthcoming with you."

"But I work for you."

Lucien grinned. "Tell him if you don't come up with valuable intel, I'll fire you. After what I said about the head of security, he'll believe it."

I gave Cross a look. "Did you fire Dwight Perry?"

His lips curled in amusement, and he barked out a laugh. "You don't know me at all."

"No, sir, I don't." But I knew his response wasn't exactly an answer either.

FOURTEEN

We stood outside the club. A light rain was falling, and the wind had picked up. The temperature had dropped considerably since the sun went down, and I turned the collar of my jacket up in the hopes of keeping the rain out. Mario Scaratilli remained entirely unaffected by the drizzle. He stood with his hands folded in front of him at the side door to what was supposed to be the newest and trendiest club. The radio was clipped to his ear, and the street light glinted off the thin silver microphone.

"Shouldn't you be inside?" I finally asked.

His eyes never stopped scanning the area. "Additional members of my team are inside, but the club is safe."

I smiled, doing my best to fit the part I was told to play. "You sound confident." Maybe I should swoon. "You're obviously capable. I don't imagine Miss Allen has ever faced a threat you couldn't handle."

"No," for the briefest moment his eyes found mine, "she hasn't."

"Is it hard? She's a famous model. There must be thousands of obsessed fans. Stalkers. Psychos. Thieves. Maybe a few gypsies and tramps too. This morning you were convinced the threat was legit, but I haven't noticed any extra measures being taken by your team."

"You wouldn't." He didn't move or react. To any onlooker, it wouldn't even appear as if we were having a conversation. "Security is tight. We're careful. Her information isn't readily available. Anything untoward gets filtered through one of her representatives."

"Untoward," I repeated, "how poetic."

He glanced at me. "What the hell do you want?"

"I didn't see you on set. For someone who said Miss Allen might be in danger, it's weird you're not maintaining eyes on her. Shouldn't you be a bit more concerned? Or is this just a paycheck?"

His face remained impassive, but the undercurrent changed. "My people are looking after her." He jerked his chin ever so slightly to the left, and I looked past him to the growing mob of paparazzi and fans. "The paps pose the most risk. That crowd is a threat to her reputation and her safety. It's hard to determine with their gear if any are armed. Any one of them could be dangerous. So I stay out here and keep a handle on things. Inside is a private party. Security cameras are off. It's just her and her costars blowing off steam."

I looked at him again. "How exactly?"

He didn't respond.

"Maybe a bump of blow?"

"What Miss Allen does is irrelevant. It just needs to stay off the internet."

"You fucked up in Maui." He clasped his hands a little tighter but otherwise didn't react to my words. "That sex tape ended up on the internet." I jerked my head at the club. "Unless you know for certain that Lance or one of Dinah's other costars doesn't have an axe to grind, you can't be sure that leaving her unattended with them is a wise decision. If the lot wasn't breached last night, whoever dressed up the dummy and stabbed it through the heart is someone she works with. Records indicate two of the last people to leave set last night were Lance Smoke and Neil Larson. She's had relations with both of them, and they're inside with the security cameras turned off."

"As I said before, other members of my team are inside."

He was growing agitated.

"What about when she's working?"

He looked away. "When you called, you said you had additional information. Was that a lie?"

"Yes. Cross is going to fire me if I don't figure this out. I have no idea how someone keeps getting on the lot and targeting Dinah. Since you're in charge of protecting her, I thought you might be able to shed some light on the matter."

"I've evaluated Cross's methods of safeguarding the studio. His plan is adequate."

"That's high praise coming from a man with your reputation."

If Scar wasn't the consummate professional, he would have smiled. "The flowers are more troubling than the dummy. That's the second time she's received Bacarra roses. The sender must be the same, except the second delivery was left in her trailer, and no one saw who did it. That means whoever left them knew precisely which trailer to target. The lack of fingerprints on the card leads me to believe the person who wrote the note also left the flowers. A florist or PA wouldn't have been so careful."

"Maybe the delivery person just didn't touch the card, or he might have been wearing gloves."

"You may be right, but I had the vase checked. It only contained two sets of prints. Miss Allen's and her assistant's."

I thought back to that first night. "Elodie said someone left flowers again. When was the first batch delivered? What did that note say?"

"Something similar." He swallowed. "The first delivery was waiting at the front desk of the hotel when we arrived."

"Anything else odd happen since your arrival?"

"Only what's been going on at the studio." His accusation was unmistakable. He blamed Cross.

"I'd like access to the first card."

Scar looked down at me. "Ask your boss. I gave it to him, along with the list."

"What exactly is the list?"

Scar focused on our surroundings again and not me.

"Names of the crazies. People who have sent death threats and hate mail and the names of those who are a bit too obsessed. Fame has a price, Miss Parker. I do what I can to make sure there is a wall of privacy and protection between my client and the people who want to hurt her. In order to do that, I have to know who to keep out."

"You don't think someone at Broadway Films is responsible? Without any clear indication of a breach, it's possible one of her castmates or someone on the crew could be to blame."

"Like you said, the flowers could have been delivered by a third party, and I'm not convinced the stabbed dummy is an immediate concern. To be clear, pranks are commonplace. Actors and the crew get bored. Sometimes, it is meant as a bonding experience. Had Cross's men not found the posed dummy, it would have been addressed by the director the next morning, probably resulting in a sensitivity lecture. Quite frankly, your people don't know enough about what's going on to make a judgment call either way. While I appreciate the help you are attempting to offer, you and your boss need to keep something in mind. You are assisting my team in safeguarding Miss Allen. It is not the other way around. And I am already looking into the matter."

"Do you think this could be the same person who was stalking Dinah in Los Angeles?"

"No."

"Why not?"

His head jerked, as if he were fighting with himself over the answer. "This conversation falls under the purview of the NDA you signed."

"Sure."

He looked at me from the corner of his eye before returning his attention to the crowd near the front of the club. "According to the police, Miss Allen wasn't stalked." He pressed a hand to his ear and spoke into the radio. "I'll tell the driver to meet us at the side. Let me know when you're taking her out." He turned back to me. "I have a job to do. You're a distraction. Leave."

"Thanks for your time, Scar," I said with fake sweetness

before walking in the direction of the paparazzi. When I emerged from the alleyway, the crowd turned to face me. A collective, disappointed sigh was released when they realized I wasn't anybody special, and they went back to hovering near the door. Truthfully, it was nice to be a nobody.

When I made it back to my apartment, I caught a glimpse of my reflection in the mirror. I looked like a drowned rat. Even though it had been a light rain, the constant drizzle eventually soaked through my hair and pants. My shoes even made a squishing sound when I walked. Stripping out of everything, I took a hot shower and climbed into bed. Before going to sleep, I phoned Lucien and left a message. Someone needed to tell my boss Scaratilli was under the impression we were working for him.

I was too tired to think about the two flower deliveries or even how someone snuck onto set. Instead, I closed my eyes and didn't open them again until the alarm went off at 4:30 that morning. I was dressed and on my way to the lot when Cross called back.

"Lance Smoke complained to the studio. You're an unwanted interruption."

"What does that mean?" I asked, wondering if this meant I could go back home and sleep until the sun rose.

"You're allowed on set, but you're barred from areas where they are filming. Dinah wants you to remain as her advisor, so I'm sending another member of our team to act as technical consultant. It will allow more of our people to investigate," Cross said.

"I'm glad you approve," I replied, deciding it didn't hurt to take credit.

He probably realized it had been a coincidence and not a carefully laid plan. "You need to get close to Dinah and her team. We need to find out how many threats there have been. Once we establish a pattern, it should make it easier to determine who is behind the threat and whether he works for the studio or found a way to breach the lot."

"Lucien," I said, tired enough to be even ballsier than usual, "why do you care? Your job is lot security. My job is technical consultant. We have nothing to do with protecting Dinah."

"We do when these incidents happen in a place where my team is providing protection. If the only weaknesses to her safety occur when she's at work, that is my responsibility. And yours. Don't forget that." He disconnected before I could say anything else. So much for turning this into someone else's problem.

When I arrived at the front gate, the security guard smiled at me. I recognized him from the office and held out the extra cup of coffee. "Thought you could use a pick-me-up."

"Thanks." He took the cup and performed a quick inspection of my car, another newly implemented tactic Cross insisted on. "Someone left a note. You're to meet Miss Allen at her trailer and remain there."

"I heard."

He chuckled. "Who did you piss off?"

"Everyone."

He looked inside my car. "Too bad you didn't bring enough coffee to win them over."

"Unfortunately, no matter what I bring them, it won't compare to what craft services can whip up."

He pressed a switch, and the gate lifted. I said good-bye and drove to the parking lot near the trailers.

The floodlights illuminated the dark lot, and I could already see crew working on one of the outdoor sets. Getting out of my car, I decided to take the long way around and walked the perimeter. The fence surrounding the lot was at least twelve feet high. It wouldn't have been easy to climb over, and it was impossible to go under. If there was a breach, someone must have come in through the main gate. The guard station was manned twenty-four hours, but distractions happened. It was also possible someone could have created a fake pass. I looked down at the lanyard around my neck. It wouldn't be difficult to create a facsimile.

Cross had gone over the list of visitors or was in the process of doing so. Think, Parker, was it someone on the outside or someone on the inside? My gut didn't have an answer, and my brain refused to function properly due to the limited amounts of sleep it had been getting.

It took a good thirty minutes to circle the entire lot. When I made it back to what looked like an RV park with the dozens of trailers crammed together, I spotted Scar waiting outside Dinah's trailer. His arms were folded over his chest, and he looked agitated. To be fair, he looked exactly as he did when I saw him a few hours ago, but since he was waiting for me, I knew he was agitated.

"Miss Allen is waiting inside." He looked as if he wanted to say something else but refrained.

I knocked on the door. A moment later, she opened it. Her eyes were red and puffy, and her face was splotchy. She didn't speak, only stepped away from the door and dropped onto one of the two sofas that lined the walls of the main room of the trailer. I glanced back at Scar, but he remained a statue, his gaze focused in front of him.

"What's wrong?" I asked.

Elodie handed her a tissue. The assistant looked tired and nearly as frazzled as Dinah.

"Thank you," Dinah sniffled and dabbed at her eyes. "You always take such good care of me."

"Of course. That's why I'm here. Is there anything else I can do?" Elodie asked.

"No. I just need to speak to Alex." Elodie moved the tissue box closer to Dinah, offered a tight smile, and went out the door. After it was closed, Dinah spoke. "Something happened last night."

I took a seat across from her. We sat in silence for several long minutes. She didn't feel the need to say anything, and I wasn't sure I wanted to know. The silence was usually too much for most people, but she didn't seem to be aware of it. Maybe she wasn't aware I was still in the room.

"It's not my business, unless you want to tell me," I finally said.

She blinked. "The morning I interviewed you I got the distinct impression you worked private security."

"Once."

"You don't do it anymore?"

"Cross has teams better equipped to handle personal security. I've used them myself. They are good at what they do."

Her brow scrunched for a moment. "Why did you need personal security?"

"I have a habit of pissing people off. In my line of work, those people occasionally decide to shoot at me."

She studied me. "That doesn't bother you?"

"Oh, no. It bothers me, but there isn't much I can do about it."

"You could go into a different line of work."

For a moment, I didn't think this conversation was actually about me. "I tried, but it didn't take. Good or bad, this is what I'm meant to do. This is what makes me happy and miserable. It's necessary."

"I can see that." We sat in the silence again. Finally, she spoke, "Scar is a good man. He takes care of me. He always has. He's been with me since my early days modeling."

I waited for her to go on.

"Asking for outside help seems like a betrayal, but you took the initiative without even asking. You want to know what happened, and I get the distinct impression you would focus less on keeping the paps off the set and more on making sure I'm okay."

"Priorities. What can I say?"

Her lips curled into a smile, but it didn't make it to her eyes. She ducked her head down and thought for a moment. "Lance doesn't want you involved in the production. Broadway Films has already spoken to Mr. Cross about finding a replacement who isn't as disruptive." Disruptive, maybe I would add that to my business card. When she brought her head up, there was newfound determination. "I want to hire you to identify my stalker."

That's why she felt she was betraying Scar. Before I could say as much, she read my mind. "Scar protects me, and while there could be some potential overlap, I want you to figure out who is doing this. My lawyer has already drawn up a new NDA." She pointed to an official looking document on the coffee table. "You can handle the investigation, and I can watch you do it. I will want daily progress reports and updates, and I might follow you to your office or the lab and watch your process. It isn't the FBI, but I've watched you long enough to know that you're doing the same job even without the badge. The way I see it, it's two birds with one stone."

"The difference is following the letter of the law," I supplied. "Nowadays, it's more the spirit of the law that is being followed."

"Good." She jerked her chin at the nondisclosure. "Let's get the formalities out of the way first, and then I'll tell you what happened two hours ago."

FIFTEEN

I made no move for the contract. "I'm not signing it. If you want me to investigate, I will. Cross Security is already investigating the dummy left on the lot. We can broaden the scope of that investigation to encompass identifying your stalker, but I need to be able to discuss these matters with my colleagues. I can't have my hands tied." I gave her a look. "You can choose to believe I won't unnecessarily divulge your private life, or you can find someone else."

She picked up the contract and tore it in half. "I had a feeling you would say that, but Cherise insisted. Everyone is so afraid a secret will leak and ruin my career. I'm so tired of it. Honestly, Alex, I'm tired of this." She gestured around the trailer. "Don't get me wrong. I want to do this movie and more in the future, but I'm tired of hiding in these trailers and having a bodyguard with me at all times. The last time I felt normal was when I was twenty-one years old. It's been a decade and a half of this shit, and instead of getting better, it's getting worse."

"What happened?"

"After we left the club, a group of us went back to Clay's suite. We're staying in the same hotel, so it shouldn't have been an issue. He's two floors below me. We were already buzzed, and we got blitzed."

At this point, I interrupted. "On?"

"Oh god," her eyes fluttered, "booze and pot. I haven't touched the harder stuff in months."

"Who was there?"

She blinked a few times. "Clay, Gemma, Neil, a bunch of people. I don't know."

"It's okay. Go on."

"Anyway, things had died down. Most people had left, and I was on my way out. I didn't bother to call Scar for an escort upstairs. It was only two floors, and it was the middle of the night. Nothing should have happened." She glanced out the window. "The elevator was taking too long, so I took the stairs." She swallowed. "He was waiting in the stairwell. He came up behind me. I screamed. God, I think I woke the entire building. Scar burst through the door on the floor above and scared him away."

"Did you get a good look at him?" I asked.

"Honestly, I didn't see anyone. I just heard him thundering up the steps behind me."

"Did he say anything to you? Did he touch you?"

"No." She sniffed and rubbed her eye. "I've never been so scared in my entire life. The way those footsteps sounded, I was sure he was going to kill me. Probably stab me just like the prop dummy."

I inched to the edge of the seat. "What did the police say?"

"I didn't call them?"

"Why didn't the hotel?" I asked. Her eyes went to the door. "Scar's handling it?" I was already on my feet and halfway to the door when she spoke again.

"Alex, I don't want people to know about this. It'll encourage this type of behavior."

"I'm just going to ask your security chief what he knows. That's it. In the meantime, I need you to try to remember everyone who went back to Clay's suite and note who stayed after you left. I also need an approximation of your timeline from last night. What time you went to the club, left the club, left Clay's, et cetera." Without waiting for an inevitable protest or more questions, I opened the door on the trailer and pulled it closed behind me.

"She told you what happened," he said.

"Yeah." I copied his pose and stood on the other side of the stairs. "Where the hell were you when this was happening?"

"I was upstairs. Clay Chaffey has ample security. My team and his team coordinated. They were providing protection for him and his guests. My people were making sure Dinah's floor was secure."

"Did you get a look at the guy?"

He sucked something free from between his teeth. His eyes remained facing forward. "When I opened the stairwell door, Miss Allen was the only person there."

"He heard you coming and escaped?"

"Possibly." He put his hands on his hips and exhaled. "The hotel has cameras covering the hallways on every floor. No one came out of the stairwell except Miss Allen and me."

"Not on any level?" I asked. He shook his head. "What do you think that means?"

"I don't know."

"You think she's crying wolf again?"

He looked at me. "She didn't cry wolf the last time. One of her handlers did. Dinah simply went along with the story. Honestly, they fill her head with enough lies and half-truths she might even believe it." He was protective. For a moment, I wondered if he cared a little too much for his client.

"But you're clear-headed. You should know what's really going on. Was someone waiting for her last night?"

Scaratilli wasn't comfortable with the question. "I personally checked for threats. The rest of the team was stationed in the adjacent suite to Miss Allen's room. We were given access to the hotel's security feed due to the special circumstances, and none of my men spotted anything amiss. We might not have been in physical proximity to Dinah, but we were monitoring the area. I would never let her out of my sight."

"Maybe the drinking and drugs made her paranoid. Perhaps someone laced her marijuana with hallucinogens.

Does that seem possible?" I didn't believe it, but I wanted to give him a noble way of saying Dinah was full of shit. It was also possible she'd been dropping acid or doing something else and failed to disclose.

"She's never acted irrationally before."

"It could be the stress of a big budget movie and knowing someone is out there," I suggested.

"That's unlikely." He turned and looked at the door to the trailer. "I've upped Dinah's security to ensure someone is accompanying her at all times. I was wondering if Cross could send a team to look for clues. Investigations are the cornerstone of his business."

Dinah again. Once could be a slip, but twice might be love. "You should call and ask."

He glowered. "I'm asking you. Aren't you a Cross Security investigator? Or does the master keep you on a tight leash?"

"What do you think?"

"You're a strong woman who does what she wants." His eyes held a challenge. "Will you have your people look for clues?"

"That is why Dinah hired me." I turned and opened the door to the trailer. "Make sure your team knows we're on the same side of this."

Dinah was busy writing out her list. As she thought, she chewed on the end of the pen. I lingered near the tiny kitchenette which wasn't more than a hot plate, microwave, and mini-fridge. Everything about this job was off. It had been from the beginning. Scar said there was no one else on the stairs. Fingerprint analysis indicated no one else touched the flowers except Dinah and her assistant. I'd been told the stalker in Los Angeles had been bogus. I watched as she continued to write, wondering if she wasn't using Cross Security to make her claims sound legitimate. Could this be a publicity stunt? Was she faking it? She was an actress or a con artist as Cross insisted.

"Here." She held out the notepad.

I tore off the two sheets of paper she had written on and read through the names. "Lance wasn't there?"

"No. Clay asked him to come back to party, but he

declined." Anger flashed across her face. "He was probably having a threesome. A few of the extras were all over him yesterday. He actually brought them to the club. Can you believe that?"

"I thought the two of you were over. No hard feelings."

"Yeah, well, I wouldn't care, except he keeps insisting we are meant to be. It's what the studio wants and what he wants."

"Is it what you want?"

She brushed her hands on her pants and got off the couch. "I don't know. We had fun, but if we aren't working together on a movie, I'm sure he'll be having fun with someone else. He has plenty of options."

"So do you."

Her eyes darted to the side, and a sly smile spread across her lips. "Touché." At least she didn't look as upset as she had when I first entered her trailer, and I couldn't help but wonder if the puffy eyes were part of the act.

Since I was banned from set and didn't want to spend any more time with Dinah Allen who was proving more and more difficult to read, I begged off, insisting I needed to get a jump on the investigation while it was still fresh. She bought my excuse easily, saying she had a long day of filming and would likely have questions tomorrow. When I left her trailer, Scar remained stationed outside.

"Airport rules," I said to him. "See something, say something."

If he wasn't doing his best to look like a tough guy, he would have smiled.

I checked the time. Perfect. On my way to the office, I considered everything I'd been told and the few things I knew to be true. Most of it came from Dinah Allen and her team, but they couldn't be trusted. It was all about spin, but I knew Dinah couldn't have planted the dummy. The flowers, yes. The invisible man in the stairwell, another yes. But the dummy, which was obviously a threat, happened after she left for the day.

When I arrived, I went straight to my office. Keying in my user name and password, I searched for additional information concerning the incident inside the hotel.

Nothing was mentioned on any of the official news channels, so I checked social media. Dinah claimed she screamed so loud she must have woken the entire building. Perhaps someone mentioned something about it on their feed or left an angry review on the hotel's website. Nothing. No sightings of Dinah Allen, Clay Chaffey, or any of the other celebs.

"What are you doing here?" Cross asked. He looked less exhausted than the last time I saw him. His suit was sleek and wrinkle free. My boss was back to his impeccable self. "Shouldn't you be at the lot?"

"Did Dinah Allen's people call you?" I asked. It was a little after six, early for Cross to be here.

"No."

Shaking my head, I let out an annoyed grunt. "They should have. There was an alleged incident at her hotel last night."

"Alleged?" Cross found that one word more intriguing than the possible incident. He shut my door and took a seat in one of the two client chairs. I told him what Dinah and Scar had said. "I'll have a contract couriered over for her to sign. We should keep this official." He seemed pleased to be able to add another A-list celebrity to his client list. "Good job."

"Who's covering for me at the studio?" I asked.

"Lancaster. He came from Chicago's FBI field office. He's been a consultant before. It'll be fine. He'll do what is expected and see what he can find out while he's there."

"Great." I didn't know Lancaster had been FBI, but then again, I only knew most of my coworkers by name alone. "What about the list?"

"So far, nothing concrete. A few names have criminal records, arson, sexual assaults, aggravated battery. You get the point."

"Lots of possibilities."

"I have people narrowing it down based on last known locations. Scaratilli did a decent job. He knows what he's doing which is why none of this makes much sense."

"There is another possibility." I wondered if I needed to voice it. Cross knew his shit, and he probably knew what I was thinking. "Dinah could be faking it."

"I considered it and have yet to rule it out. You've spent the most time with her. What do you think?"

"I don't know yet. After the morning briefing, I'll drop by the hotel and see what they can do for me. Then I might check with a few friends in case they've seen or heard anything troubling."

"Remember, there's a nondisclosure in place."

"I refused to sign. My investigation into Dinah's stalker isn't covered by that."

"It might not be, but anything that happened on set most definitely is." He reached across my desk and picked up the phone. He dialed an extension and waited. "This is Cross. Review the terms of our NDA with Broadway Films and let me know what Miss Parker is permitted to discuss with outsiders. I'll need your answer in an hour." He put the phone down. "You need to be careful. I have no desire to be in litigation for the next two years."

"Yes, sir."

He gave me a look, as if trying to determine if my remark was sarcastic. "If you need assistance, let me know. I'm handling this personally per the terms of our agreement with Broadway Films."

"What did you discover last night?" I asked, remembering the phone calls he placed before leaving the office.

"Dinah Allen's phone records."

"I'm intrigued."

"As am I." He tapped on the table. "Staff meeting in twenty minutes. Don't be late."

"No, sir." And that time, he heard the sarcasm.

SIXTEEN

Nothing. The hotel cameras showed nothing. The stairwell didn't have cameras, but the doorway to the stairwell was in clear view of a security camera. With a bit of cajoling and several phone calls, the hotel let me watch the footage. I checked the feeds from every level in the building from the time Dinah left the club until she left Clay's room. Hardly anyone took the stairs, and the few who did either exited in the lobby or exited on another floor and presumably went to their rooms.

"I don't suppose it's possible to question those guests," I wheedled, hoping hotel security might throw me a bone. They did not. However, I paid attention and had a handful of room numbers memorized. I didn't exactly need their blessing.

After thanking them for their time, I took the elevator to Dinah's floor and stepped out. Scar's team was comprised of eight men. Four on, four off. I stood outside the security suite and knocked. A man who looked like a college linebacker opened the door in a pair of sweats and a t-shirt.

"Alex Parker." I held out my hand. "Mr. Scaratilli said you'd be expecting me."

"Yeah, nice to meet you." He shook my hand and

stepped away from the door. "This is our command center. Miss Allen's room is across the hallway. Someone keeps watch outside whenever she's there. One of us should have been outside Mr. Chaffey's room last night, but he has his own security team who assured us they had it covered."

"But they didn't."

"Nope."

"Did you check the stairwell after the incident?"

"Scar did. He didn't find anything. I went through the hotel's security feed, but it didn't catch anything. I don't know what to tell you."

"Do you have a key to Miss Allen's suite?"

"Yes."

"Can I look around?"

"Afraid not. Miss Allen would have to give you permission, and she hasn't said anything to us."

"No one's been in her room?"

"I didn't say that."

"You're not making my job any easier, mister." I waited for him to offer a name.

"Johnson, but you can call me Ty." He offered a conciliatory smile. Unlike his boss, he was actually capable of showing emotion. "We sent the requested materials over to Cross Security. Did you not receive them?"

"No, we did. I'm just following up with the hotel, and since I was here, I thought I'd stop by and say hi."

"Hi." He grinned again, dazzling me with his pearly whites. A yawn escaped, and I backed toward the door.

"I'll let you get some sleep."

"That's what the rest of the guys are doing."

I let myself out and checked the hallway again. Then I opened the door to the stairwell and stepped inside. Narrow staircases zigzagged in a box pattern from the lobby to the roof. The metal rails and banisters reminded me of the parkour course the stunt coordinator had set up on the lot, and I wondered how quickly someone with a bit of experience could climb from level to level.

After searching for alcoves and hiding places, I didn't find anything that would work well enough to avoid detection if Scar or a member of his team was on the hunt.

Still, I checked every floor below Dinah's. At least it was a little easier going down the stairs rather than up. Briefly, I exited on Clay's floor. A sticky cam or surveillance device might have indicated how the stalker knew when Dinah was leaving the party and that she would be alone, but I didn't find anything.

The stairwell ran all the way to the parking garage beneath the hotel. With the support pillars and larger vehicles, a person probably could dodge the cameras and gain access, but that was iffy. They'd need to be quick and extremely careful. Still, it was the only explanation I had, unless Dinah was lying. I spoke briefly to the parking attendants, but no one saw anything. I hit another dead end.

When I completed my walkthrough, I knocked on a few doors. It was early, but most people were up. Lying, I said I was with the hotel and investigating complaints about a woman being loud last night. No one remembered hearing Dinah scream, and since these were the people who took the stairs last night, I asked if they remembered seeing anyone lurking in the stairwell. As predicted, they hadn't.

As I made my way to the lobby, I wondered how anyone would know Dinah wouldn't ask for an escort upstairs. Granted, I remembered her reluctance to take the elevator when she visited Cross's office, so I considered that might be commonplace for the actress and something anyone who was paying attention would pick up on. But Scar followed her around like a puppy, except when she was filming. No one should have assumed he wouldn't make the journey with her from Clay's room back to her own, unless her stalker found a way to maintain eyes on Dinah's security team. By the time I left the hotel, I was even less certain the incident actually occurred.

My next stop was the club. It was just before noon when I arrived. The place was locked up tight. I banged a few times against the door, but no one answered. Unwilling to give up that easily, I called Cross. Normally, this would be a job for one of the assistants, but he gave me strict instructions to call him. So I did.

Within fifteen minutes, a car drove into the alleyway. A

man stepped out. He wore leather pants and a linen shirt unbuttoned halfway down his chest. He had a goatee and sunglasses. The only thing missing was a gold chain around his neck.

"You Alex?" he asked.

"Yep."

"Lucien called. He said you wanted to look around." He unlocked the side door and held it for me. "Do you want the security footage from the door?"

"Please."

He flipped on the lights. "You want a drink?"

"It's a little early."

"Never too early." He went into the back while I surveyed the place. It was large. It could have been a high-end private club in Vegas with the velvet and suede couches, the gleaming hardwood tables, and the crystal chandeliers. The bottles behind the bar were three and four figures each. No wonder Clay chose this place to party.

"Any problems last night?" I asked when he returned with a thumb drive.

"Nope."

"No one tried to sneak inside?"

He laughed. "Not exactly. They waited the polite six feet from the door. My bouncers made sure of it."

"Drugs?"

He smiled. "Are you a cop?"

"I thought Lucien called."

He held the grin. "Right. Well, either way, I plead the fifth."

"No overdoses? No one passing out drunk? No brawls? No one getting too handsy?"

"It's a club, darling, but no one had that much fun last night. For actors, they were tame. I've seen what real actors can do to a place. Shit, I figured Lance Smoke would have turned this into a sex club, but things were calm." He sounded disappointed. "I will tell you the women in here were top rate. The men too." He looked me up and down. "You should have joined them."

"Maybe next time." I took the drive from his hand. "Did you hear any complaints?"

"Not a one."

"Thanks for your time." I looked around the room again. "Do you mind if I use your bathroom before I leave."

He pointed to a narrow hallway. "Help yourself."

I went inside, and after a quick check for illegal surveillance equipment, I searched the place. I didn't know what I hoped to find. Honestly, I was grasping at straws, desperately trying to determine if an incident even occurred. Answers weren't inside the club's bathroom, just some discarded condom wrappers, an empty glass vial with cocaine residue, and some blood red matte lipstick. For shits and giggled, I placed the items in a plastic baggie and stepped out of the bathroom. The owner was sipping rye. He toasted in my direction, and I nodded and left. Next stop, Cross Security.

"You have interesting friends," I said when Lucien's assistant led me into his office. My boss looked up, and I held out the baggie. "I didn't find much but thought we might want to run these for prints, just in case."

He looked at the items. "Where did you find these?"

"Inside the ladies room at the club."

"Any particular reason you think this is useful?"

"Not really."

His eyebrows raised in question, but he decided it was best not to inquire further. "What about the hotel?"

I shook my head and walked across the room to the large windows. Cross had a nice view. "None of it makes much sense. The hotel allowed me to review the relevant camera footage, but no one exited the stairwell around the time of the alleged incident. According to Scaratilli and his team, they investigated but didn't see anyone. I even asked a few guests if they heard or saw anything, but they didn't."

"You think it's bullshit."

"The dummy with the knife through its heart didn't look like bullshit," I turned away from the window, "but I think Dinah's story about footsteps might be bullshit. She was drunk, probably high, and undoubtedly tired. Her imagination could have run away with her."

"But you believe there's still a threat."

"Scar thinks so."

Cross pushed away from his desk. "He could be playing us too."

I'd only encountered Mr. Scaratilli three times, but he wouldn't ask for help if he didn't need it. He took himself and his job too seriously. He took Dinah's safety seriously. "What do we know about him, aside from your alpha male profile?"

"Parker, I prefer if you speak your mind. I don't have time to figure out what you're fishing for."

"Dinah said he's been with her since her early days modeling, but when he came here, he only referred to her as Miss Allen."

"Professional courtesy."

"That's what I thought, but when I spoke to him this morning outside Dinah's trailer, he called her Dinah. Twice."

Cross let out a disgusted growl. "Quick, call the etiquette police."

"That's not what I'm saying."

"I know what you're saying. He takes his job personally. I've done some digging. Scaratilli has a propensity for violence. Over the years, there have been a few police reports, but when the time came, charges weren't filed. The victims recanted their statements."

"Someone got paid off."

Cross pointed a finger at me. "That's what I like to see from my investigators," he said sarcastically, and I glared at him. "Her chief of security is protective, but there's no way of knowing if the situation warranted the aggressiveness of his actions."

"What about his private life?"

"He isn't married. From what I gather, his dating life is bleak. He lives and breathes Dinah Allen, just like the rest of her team. He's dedicated to the job, and she's the job. Make of that what you will."

"You have no fucking idea what to make of him either."

He snorted, coughing to hide his laugh. "None." Moving the stack of files to the coffee table, Cross dropped into one of the leather chairs.

"Can you ask Lancaster to find out where Lance Smoke

went last night after the club and what time he went back to the hotel?"

Cross didn't bother to glance in my direction. "You think someone worth eight figures, who is bankrolling the movie, and can have just about anyone he wants is stalking his costar? Do you realize how insane that sounds?"

"He wants her back, at least as far as the public is aware. It stands to reason if this movie is a success, he'll make far more as a producer than an actor, and a relationship might be the ticket to that type of success and a guarantee this one-shot deal turns into the next blockbuster franchise. If she's scared of the bogeyman, she might just latch onto him to feel safe."

"I'll have Lancaster do his best, but pitting ourselves against Smoke is asking for trouble. Broadway Films hired us, but if Lance wants us gone, they'll defer to him in the end. I don't want to be blackballed from the entertainment industry on nothing but some conjecture and a hunch. Is that clear?"

"Yes."

Cross put down the folder he was reading and reached for another one. "While you were on your little field trip," he said in a demeaning tone, "I finished going through Dinah's phone records." He removed several pages and held them out to me. "The techs are running the unfamiliar numbers and building profiles. Mr. Scaratilli's list proved to be a bust. For someone to get on the set, get inside Dinah's trailer, and possibly get to her inside the hotel, he must be close. I'd guess it's someone she confides in and speaks to regularly. He either belongs in her life, or it's someone whom she trusts enough to share personal details."

"Like her bodyguards?"

Cross turned. "Ooh, wouldn't that be interesting?" He took a moment to assess me. "Is that where you were going with your questions about Scaratilli?"

"He is responsible for her well-being, which one might confuse with love, which could then be confused with obsession."

"Then, by all means, dig deeper. In the meantime, take a

look at these." I took the pages, unsure what Cross wanted me to do with them. "Do you recognize any of those numbers?" he asked.

I scrolled quickly through the sheets. Why would I recognize any of the numbers from her call log? Stopping, I felt the pit in my stomach grow exponentially. Cross knew the number. Hell, he knew both of the numbers, and he knew I did too. When I lifted my gaze from the page, his eyes found mine.

"I'll take care of it," I said.

"I thought you might say that." He went back to what he was doing, and I headed for the door.

Halfway there, I stopped and turned on my heel. "Do you have copies of her text messages?"

"She wouldn't grant us access, claiming that would violate her privacy. I can get around it if necessary but thought it prudent to start with these first. Is that going to be a problem?"

"Not for me."

"Good. Let me know what you find."

SEVENTEEN

I knocked on the door and waited. The doorman told me he was here. Actually, the concierge at the front desk told me he was here when I phoned, but the doorman verified it when I asked two minutes ago. The fight was stupid. Whatever this was about was Martin's business, except somehow Cross had me sticking my nose into it. I was so screwed and not in the fun way.

Martin opened the door. "Did you forget your keys?" he asked, the accusation apparent in the hurt look in his eyes.

"I left them on the counter," I said, hoping to avoid further explanation. It wasn't a lie. I wouldn't lie to him. Not again. I just wasn't sure why he might be lying to me. "I'm sorry about the other morning."

"This isn't on you, Alex." He ran a hand through his hair. "I'm just glad you came home. When I saw your keys, I thought you were done. We were done."

"You want me gone, all you have to do is say it, and I'll go. But I'm not walking. Not again. Not from you. No matter what."

He smiled and brushed his thumb against my cheek. "Good."

I returned his smile and reached for his hand, brushing

my lips against his fingers before letting go. "However, it's nice to hear, for once, I'm not responsible for our fight."

"That wasn't a fight. We are far better at fighting."

Before the night was through, it would probably be a knockdown, drag-out brawl. He stepped closer, kissed me properly, and went into the kitchenette where dinner from two nights ago was finally being cooked. Too bad I didn't have an appetite. He filled two glasses with wine, pushed one across the counter toward me, and took a sip from his.

We remained in silence, which was rather uncommon, and I studied him. His posture, his movements, everything. He turned around and asked a question about salad. I asked about his day and let my brain analyze and interpret as he spoke. After two minutes, he stopped speaking and crossed his arms over his chest.

"Don't do that," he warned. "I'm not some perp locked in an interrogation room." He blew out a breath. "You know I hate it when you do that. Whatever it is, just ask." He worked his jaw, as if waiting to be tortured.

Steeling myself for the worst, I said, "Why have you been calling Dinah Allen?"

His green irises flashed disbelief, betrayal, and anger. "You pulled my phone records?"

"No."

"Then how the hell do you know I've been speaking to Dinah?" His eyes went to the folders I brought home. "God, Alex, did you get copies of my text messages and hack my voicemail too?"

"I didn't pull your records. I pulled hers. Or rather Cross did. And just so you know, I have never once looked into you. Even when I worked for you, Mark did the dirty work, not me, because I didn't want to know the things you didn't want me to." Even if, at this moment, I was reconsidering that stance based on his reaction.

"Jesus." He rubbed a hand down his face. "How in god's name did Cross get access to her phone records? She's a fucking movie star."

"She gave them to us." I stared at him. "This morning, Dinah Allen hired me."

He pressed his palms into his eyes. "You're joking."

I hated being behind on things. I waited for an elaboration, but Martin practically shut down. He went silent, his gaze shifting every few seconds from the files across the room to the food he was preparing, and not once did he look at me. "Why is your private number listed a dozen times in the last week alone? And the Martin Technologies number is listed another four on top of that. Martin, what is going on?"

He stopped what he was doing and gripped the edge of the counter. "I can't tell you."

"You better fucking tell me. If you don't tell me, Cross will have you investigated next."

"Why? What's going on?"

Deciding that asking questions wasn't getting me anywhere, I answered his. "Dinah's being stalked. We aren't sure how serious it is. One of the threats seemed blatantly obvious, but the more we dig, the murkier everything becomes." I eyed him. "Are you stalking her?"

He laughed, as if that was the most ridiculous notion in the world. Granted, he could get a little obsessed, but that involved projects and work, not people. My eyes narrowed, and I tried to figure out if there was any possible overlap between Dinah and his work. Could his top-secret project be related to her?

"Are you serious?" he finally asked.

"Sixteen calls and I don't even know how many text messages. Let me share with you a basic rule of thumb. You call once, it's normal. Twice, you're concerned. Three times, you're obsessed. Why don't you tell me what sixteen means?"

"It wasn't in one day. That was over the course of the week. Check the call duration. It was phone tag." He searched my face for some sign that I believed he wasn't stalking the movie star. "Tell me you don't think I'm responsible."

"Honestly, if you were, I'd cover it up and do everything I could to protect you, but I believe you. I know you wouldn't hurt her or anyone else unless provoked." My thoughts materialized into a pattern that didn't make a lot of sense. "She made you sign an NDA. God, she hands those things out like candy on Halloween."

He blinked, the surprise hidden, but I knew his tells. Depending on the terms, he might not be able to confirm. What the hell did he get involved in this time?

"It's me, Martin. I'm not going to say anything."

"I know, but your boss wants answers. Ask me something I can answer."

He always took his business agreements seriously. This time, a bit too seriously, but his response was enough of a confirmation. If I went about this the right way, I could get answers without him breaching their agreement. I just wasn't sure if I'd be able to maneuver around this minefield without getting in trouble or accidentally throwing Martin under the bus in the process.

"How do you know her?" I asked.

He put the bowls on the counter, drained his glass, and refilled it. "When she was in college, she interned for my mom. The fashion design school Dinah attended had some sort of program. We worked together. We were friends."

"With benefits?"

He cocked his head to the side and took another sip. Well, that answered one question. "It was a lifetime ago."

My fears from a few nights ago resurfaced. "Is there anyone on this planet you haven't slept with?"

"A couple of people here and there." He gave me a cocky smile. "Until you swooped in and stole my heart. Now I can't imagine being with anyone except you for the rest of my life."

I swallowed. Too much. Way too much. And it was damn distracting, which had probably been his goal — scare me into silence. But it wouldn't work. "Have you been in touch this entire time?"

"God, no. It's probably been fifteen or sixteen years since we last spoke." The notion irritated him. He nodded at the paperwork. "You can see when we got back in touch. Prior to that first phone call, we hadn't spoken since she left for Europe."

"Are you sleeping with her?"

He put the glass down, all of his energy focused on me. "Alex, come on. You know me better than that. You are the love of my life. I wouldn't do that to you." This time, the words weren't said to intimidate me. He meant every single one. "What's wrong? Are we okay?"

"Cross will want to know. This way, I can say I asked."

He reached across and squeezed my hand. "Talk to me."

"The perfume, the makeup on your sleeve and collar, the way you came home the other night," I let out a shaky exhale, "it was uncharacteristic. Something happened. I know it did, and while I know you aren't a cheater, I'm not wired to just turn a blind eye. What if I'm wrong to put so much faith in you? What if I'm just being naïve and stupid?"

"You aren't." He reached across and caressed my cheek. "It's my fault. You notice everything. You deserve answers, and I," he looked like he was fighting with himself, "am not in a position to tell you what you need to hear." He dropped his hand and let out a resounding sigh. "Maybe we should go back to therapy."

"Why? Are you going to be able to talk about it then?"

"No." He sounded defeated.

I snorted, finding this oddly amusing. "You really want to punish me just because I asked a question for my boss?" I teased, hoping to ignore the bomb we were skirting around.

"Lucien knows everything there is to know about everybody. He must know we're together. Does he get some kind of perverse pleasure in screwing with us? Is this payback because I didn't sign with his company years ago?"

"I'm not sure he knows. We were always careful."

"But we own property together. This apartment. There's a paper trail now. We have a paper trail," he declared proudly, as if it were a grand feat, and given what we'd been through, it kind of was. No wonder fate sent Dinah Allen into our path like a cyclone.

"The paperwork was probably filed around the same time Cross hired me. If he looked then, he might have missed it." I gave his hand a squeeze. "You're trying to change the subject. I believe you've been faithful, but what's the deal with you and Dinah?"

"You have really pretty eyes."

"Martin."

"And a gorgeous smile. And the way you move," he smiled devilishly, "just thinking about it makes me hard."

I jerked my hand out of his grip and glared at him. "Be serious."

"Oh, I am."

"Enough. We're talking about Dinah." I narrowed my eyes. "Is she the reason you came home ready to play the other night?"

His green eyes bore into mine as he tried to figure out what I actually knew and what I was guessing. "I wasn't lying when I said I'd been thinking about you the entire day. Even when I was in her company, my mind was focused on coming home to you. That's why I wanted to play. It had nothing to do with her. Being in close proximity to her does nothing for me."

"It did once."

Realizing being cute wasn't going to get me to change the subject, he let out an unhappy groan and went back to cooking. Now that he was annoyed, he was ready to play with fire. "It was more than once."

"See, now we're getting somewhere," I said sarcastically.

"In my defense, that was before you. Actually, even if I knew you then, it would have been illegal for us to be together because you would have been underage. That's how long ago this was."

"Can we stop talking about you and Dinah?"

"Sure, sweetheart, we can drop the subject." He turned off the oven and took out our food, using a wooden spatula to divide it up onto two plates. He put one in front of me. "How was your day?"

"It was fine until I came home and murdered my boyfriend."

"I'm sorry to hear that. Anyone new and exciting lined up to take his place? Maybe one of Hollywood's hottest hunks?" He took a seat next to me, scooting closer until our thighs touched.

"They are a bunch of douchebags," I glanced at him from the corner of my eye, "kind of like my dead ex. Maybe I will give one of them a call."

He held up his hands before putting a napkin on his lap. "You're right. I don't like this game either."

"You started it." I took a bite and washed it down with some wine. "Is there anything you can tell me that might help identify her stalker?"

"It isn't me." He chewed thoughtfully for a moment. "I don't see how anyone could get to her. She's surrounded by her team at all times."

Unless it's one of them, I thought.

We ate the rest of our meal in silence. When Martin finished, he turned to face me. "Why did she hire you? The last I heard you were working on a movie, presumably hers, but you said she hired you today. It's about the threat of a stalker, right?"

"Yes."

"But she has a security team. Why aren't they handling it?"

"You met them?"

He didn't give me a precise answer, but I knew it was yes. "They appear more than capable."

"They need help."

His eyes darkened, and he moved to clear away the dishes. "How exactly are you supposed to help? She better not expect you to bodyguard."

"No, only playboy millionaires hire me for that reason. I'm just supposed to identify the source of the threat."

He finished loading the dishwasher and turned back to me. "Well, you can mark my name off your list of potential hostiles."

"You were never on my list. I just wondered if she mentioned anything to you."

He didn't speak. It was hard for him to offer helpful advice when he wasn't even supposed to confirm or deny his interactions with the starlet. Finally, he said, "She mentioned an ex who was getting a bit aggressive."

"Lance?" I asked, and Martin nodded. "He's at the top of my list, but he stands to lose a lot more than he can gain by going all *Fatal Attraction*."

"Is that the one with the bunny?"

I snorted. "How the hell did you ever date an actress?"

"For the record, I didn't. She was a student. Someone my mom liked. Someone mom thought was talented and could go places, but those places were behind the scenes, not up and down the catwalk. Guess Dinah surprised us all."

"Do you know any of her designer friends? She mentioned someone from her past she recently reconnected with." My eyes narrowed. "I'm hoping it isn't you."

He winced, as if he were in pain. "Please, Alex, don't ask me these things and don't ask why."

"Okay, I won't." But I couldn't help but think he was one of the only people on this planet who could give me answers, and her attorneys silenced him.

EIGHTEEN

"Find out anything interesting concerning Mr. Martin's connection to Miss Allen?" Lucien asked once the conference room cleared out.

"He's not stalking her."

Cross gave me a look. "He visited the set the night the flowers were sent to her trailer. She also took him on a tour, showed him wardrobe and the hair and makeup trailer. It stands to reason he possessed the knowledge necessary." Cross's tone remained neutral, and I wondered what his game was. "Remind me, didn't he hire you to clear his name from a possible murder charge when a model was killed on his yacht?"

"He was innocent." I fought to keep my voice just as flat.

Cross scoffed. "Of course, he was."

"Martin wasn't responsible then, and he isn't responsible now."

"How can you be certain?"

"He has an airtight alibi for the night the dummy was planted on set."

"Very well."

"Anything ever surface with the items I recovered from the club's bathroom?"

"Fingerprints on the condom wrapper matches Lance Smoke. He was with someone in that stall, but there's no way of knowing who. We didn't pull any usable prints off the cocaine vial or the lipstick." He thought for a moment. "Was that Dinah's shade?"

"I've only seen her wear glossy. That was matte. But it's possible. I didn't see her that night." I stood, moving to the door. Dinah expected me at her hotel in less than an hour. She had the day off from shooting and didn't plan to go to set. I couldn't help but think the reason she wanted me there so early was to wheedle more information out of me concerning her role and my perspective on being an FBI agent, rather than identifying her stalker. I stopped in the doorway. "Are we certain this isn't an elaborate hoax?"

"No." Cross looked at me. "Lancaster asked Mr. Smoke about the club. Apparently, Smoke left with two extras, went barhopping, and didn't make it back to his hotel that night."

"He's Lance Smoke. He can make his own truth. Don't you think his money and stardom might be enough to convince hotel security to alter the footage or lose the recording if he was waiting for Dinah?"

"That is not beyond the realm of possibility. However, we have nothing solid pointing to it, and when it comes to these heavy-hitters, we shouldn't speculate. It's bad for business."

"The point of being a private investigator is determining things without the red-tape and required amount of evidence," I argued.

"Perhaps that's true in some instances but not this one." He gave me a warning look. "Under no uncertain terms are you to confront any of the actors or film crew. Is that understood, Miss Parker?"

"Yes, sir." I was annoyed. That was a pretty common side effect of my interactions with Lucien. And now we were back to addressing one another formally. It was his way of not so subtly reminding me who was in charge. I didn't like it, but that was nothing new. I didn't like the command structure in general.

*   *   *

When I arrived at the hotel, I parked my car and took the stairs. Looking up from the bottom, I couldn't help but think this would make an excellent parkour course, and my thoughts went to the stuntmen and Kurt Wen. The stunt coordinator had been one of the last people to leave set that night. He could have left the dummy on the soundstage. No one would have given much thought to him wandering into any of the trailers. He was supposed to be there, and he'd been in the industry long enough to be considered a fixture.

Making a mental note to check into him, I trudged up the first set of stairs, hoping brilliance would strike. On the next platform, I hoisted myself over the railing, lowered down, and swung my legs forward before letting go. I wasn't high enough to risk serious injury, unless I landed wrong and broke my neck, but I didn't consider that before I dropped. I landed in a crouch on the ground.

For someone trained, it would be possible to disappear quickly, but no matter how swiftly someone moved from Dinah's floor back to ground level, it wouldn't be fast enough to disappear. Stepping out into the lobby or any of the other hallways would have been instantly caught on camera.

As I went up the stairs, I wondered if it was possible her stalker had gone up instead of down. Still, it would have led to the same dilemmas and issues, unless there was someplace above to hide. Before I could explore further, my phone rang. I looked down at the blocked number and hit answer.

"Hello?" I asked.

"Alex?"

"Yes." I recognized Dinah's voice but didn't feel like boosting her ego by acknowledging it. "Who is this?"

"Dinah Allen," she replied haughtily. "Where are you?"

I exited onto her floor and smiled at Ty who was positioned just outside her suite. "At the end of your hallway."

"Well, don't just stand there. Come inside." She

disconnected, and I wondered if she would appear in the doorway. Instead, the door opened a moment later, and Elodie stepped out, spoke to Ty, pointed at me, and crooked her finger in my direction. "Is she here yet?" Dinah's voice traveled through the open door.

"Yes," Elodie said, ushering me inside.

"It's about damn time," Dinah said. She shooed Elodie away with a wave of her hand, and the assistant gave me a look as if to say, *it's your turn*, and walked out the door. "You're late."

I checked my watch. "Four minutes."

"Like I said, late."

I crossed my arms over my chest and stared her down. Until this moment, she might have acted a bit spoiled but not like a diva. This was new, and I didn't care for it. Is this what signing on the dotted line meant? Was this the type of shit Elodie, Cherise, and Scar put up with on a regular basis? "Is something wrong?" I hissed out.

"Shit," she smoothed her hair with her hand, "I'm sorry. My life is out of control. I need you to do something to fix it. Tell me you've found something. Lucien's been poking around in my affairs, insisting it will lead to something, but I'm not comfortable with the scrutiny. I hired you to figure this out. Not him."

"It's his firm," I said, "and he's under contract with Broadway Films. He won't tolerate threats being made to anyone on set."

She took a seat at the dining room table. She gestured at the chair across from her. "Please," she waited for me to sit, "I'd like a progress report."

"Currently, we're working under the assumption whoever is terrorizing you is someone you know. It's the only thing that makes any sense. Your security team is topnotch, so it's unlikely some random crazy managed to get onto the lot multiple times and access you at the hotel."

"Isn't that what stalkers do? Find out everything they can and follow people?"

"Yes," I admitted, "but protocols were in place to prevent unauthorized access. Whoever gained access to your trailer went through the front gate. It might have been a guest. We aren't saying it's someone on staff or a costar, but we are confident it's someone with whom you're close."

"But it could be a member of the cast or crew or someone one of us invited to set." She thought for a moment. "What do you know?"

"As usual, not much. Based on the posing of the dummy and the note left with the flowers, I believe there is a sexual component involved. That's common in stalking cases."

"That's why you wanted to know about my partners and exes."

I pulled out the copy of her phone records and placed them on the table. A few of the numbers were highlighted. Pushing them across the table, I waited for her to pick them up. "Tell me about those individuals."

"What about the rest?"

"We've already ruled them out."

"How?" She seemed genuinely curious. "I want to know how the process works, remember?"

I explained how we checked their alibis and Cross determined their locations, ruling out those too far away or otherwise occupied. Her finger stopped briefly on Martin's number. I bit the inside of my cheek, resisting the urge to ask about him. I could, but no good would come of it.

While she spoke about her hairstylist, accountant, and personal trainer, I made several notes. "Did any of them ever exhibit an unhealthy fascination with you?"

"Two of them are gay, and the other might as well be a monk. He's only interested in my investments, not in me."

"You're sure?"

"Absolutely."

"Okay." That brought us back to my previous list with a few addendums. "Tell me about Scar."

She leaned back and studied me through her lashes. "Why?"

"He's chief of security. He protects you. Have the two of you ever had any issues?"

"No."

"This is just a job? A paycheck? Nothing more?" She didn't speak, so I pushed on. "If it's just a job, is it possible he might be willing to look the other way if someone else were to pay him more?"

Her response was quick and vehement. "No. Scar is loyal. We've been together for years. We're friends."

"You ever kiss?"

"Excuse me?"

I shrugged. "A big, strong man like that whose mission in life is to protect you, that's hot. That's the stuff of romance novels."

She was good. I almost missed the dart of her eyes and the secret smile that tugged at the corners of her mouth before she regained her composure. She was an actress. She knew how to keep her cool. I wondered if she could beat a polygraph or if the calm was only on the outside. "Definitely not. That would be unprofessional."

"You can't lie to a federal agent, former or otherwise."

She opened her mouth to protest, but my eyes held a challenge and she gave in. "It's only happened a few times. It doesn't mean anything."

"Does he know that?" I asked, even though I felt certain she thought it meant something.

"Scar's the one who insisted it was nothing." She looked away. "Sometimes, I get the impression he just humors me." She turned back. "What do you think?" As if remembering the reason for the conversation, she added, "He is not stalking me. It isn't even possible. He couldn't be in two places at once."

"The stairs," I said, recalling the details. "You're positive the way it happened?"

"Yes. This psycho creep came from below. I screamed, and Scar opened the door from above. The man behind me vanished. Scar came down the steps and took me to my room."

"When did he check the stairwell?"

"The security team did the sweep after I was locked in my room. My safety is their first priority. Catching the guy is second. That's protocol."

Someone could have hidden somewhere below and went higher after Scar and Dinah left the stairwell. I bit my thumbnail, a bad habit I picked up from Mark Jablonsky. "Did Scar do the check, or did he stay with you?"

"I'm not sure. I went into the bedroom to change, and when I came out, Scar was waiting. He had questions. Then he went to speak to hotel security, and someone else took over. I can't be sure if he remained in my room the entire time, but like I said, he couldn't be in two places at once. Honestly, Alex, Scar wouldn't hurt me. If he wanted to, he could just come in my room whenever he felt like it. He has a key."

I knew those things but figured he might be smart enough to blame it on someone else. He was in the protection business and worked security in Hollywood. He knew how to fix problems or make them disappear. He would know better than to get himself jammed up, especially if he was the assailant. He'd done it before with the assault charges that magically vanished.

"All right, let's get back to basics. Who knew you were at the party?" I'd already run through the list she made and the timeline. Frankly, I didn't think anyone could be ruled out.

"Everyone on set. Clay invited *everyone*." She looked at me as if I should be offended that commoners were allowed to rub elbows with the A-listers.

We spoke in depth about the party, the security, the club, and the transportation back to the hotel. At no time were outsiders able to gain access. Even if someone followed the party back to the hotel, the security on each floor was tight. The hotel was doing its best to keep the movie stars segregated to their own floors and sections. By the time the conversation was over, I knew this wasn't some random whack job. If Dinah Allen was being stalked, it was being done by someone working on the movie or working for her.

"If news of your stalker were to become public, what would that do to the film?"

She chuckled. "It'd probably guarantee an even bigger buzz. The press tour would focus a lot on that. It would hit more outlets because it's a crime drama where one of the actors was the victim of a crime. It might become actual news. Social media would be alight. They might even ask us to do some PSAs about asking for help or warning signs to watch for."

I leaned back. "Then why do you want to keep this a secret?"

"I don't want to be known for this. I don't want to be a joke on the late night talk shows. I don't want any publicity or accolades to come from something sick and twisted. Whatever I get, I want to earn."

"Is that why you're obsessed with handing out NDAs like lollipops at the bank?"

"That's part of it."

"And the other part?" I pried.

"It's because the last time this happened, we went through a lot of work to have the police reports buried. I didn't want it to come out, especially when it looked like a hairbrained scheme my manager devised."

"Was it?" I knew what everyone's stance on the matter was. I just didn't know what Dinah thought. Scar said she probably believed whatever her people told her.

She twirled her hair absently. "The police said there was no threat. Scar conducted a threat assessment and found nothing solid, but I swear to you, someone was inside my house." She looked away and swallowed. "I know I sound crazy. Nothing was on my security system, but I think whoever came inside erased it or bypassed it." She looked up at me. "Do you think the same person is stalking me now?"

"Stalkers normally don't escalate and back off only to escalate again. That being said, anything is possible."

She studied me. "You think I made it up before. That's how it would have played out in front of the press, but I know someone was there."

"Were you dating Lance at the time?"

"Yes." She thought for a moment. "Do you think it's him?"

"I think he has producer credits and wants to do everything in his power to make this movie a huge success. But I'm unclear of his intentions toward you."

"That would make two of us."

NINETEEN

After lunch, Dinah had a massage scheduled. As soon as the masseuse arrived, I returned to the stairwell. The hotel had more floors than I cared to count. It was probably a good thing I was used to running the stairs in my apartment building. Whoever was after Dinah wouldn't have had much time to escape to an upper level. Scaratilli and his security team weren't away from the stairwell more than a couple of minutes.

However, at the top, the stairwell let out onto the roof. I opened the door and looked around. There wasn't much to see. I found a coffee can filled with sand and cigarette butts and used it to prop the door open. I wasn't positive if it locked from the outside, but I didn't want to find out. From the looks of the place, I suspected some of the hotel staff took their breaks up here. A few discarded bottles and snack wrappers littered the ground.

I moved to the edge of the roof and looked down, reminding myself just how much I hated heights. Stepping away from the ledge, I assessed the area. In this part of the city, the buildings were wedged tightly together. The building to the east was only five or six feet away. An easy enough leap, if someone were so inclined. At the moment, I wasn't in the mood to jump from building to building in a single bound, but perhaps this was how the alleged stalker managed to vanish into thin air.

After a quick check for surveillance equipment which proved pointless, I went back inside. Kurt Wen was staying in the hotel. Even though he wasn't the talent, he was revered enough to have scored one of the nicer suites, but unlike Dinah, he was working today. He or one of his stuntmen could have vaulted up and down those stairs like nothing, and none of them would have given a second thought to jumping to the neighboring roof. Hell, the course they created was much trickier than the setup inside the hotel.

"What do we know about Kurt Wen?" I asked when Cross answered the phone. "He's the stunt coordinator."

"I know who he is. He's considered one of the best in the business. He's at the higher end of the pay scale for his particular job title, but he has a lot of debt. I believe the term degenerate gambler was used."

"By whom?"

"His second and fourth ex-wives. Is there a reason for your question?"

"The hotel stairs lead to the roof. Based on the stunts he devises, he or one of his guys could have used the roof access to disappear."

"What about the average human?"

"I'm not sure. Someone in decent shape with some training probably could pull it off, but I can't be certain."

"I'll see if I can pin down minutes and seconds based on the hotel's security system. That's assuming they will cooperate, which is unclear. I'll call you back."

"Hey, Dinah," I said when I returned to her room, "who's doing their own stunts on the film?"

"We all want to do as much as we can," she said, her face surrounded by the cushioned pillow while the masseuse worked on her shoulders. "Why do you ask?"

"Curiosity."

She pulled the sheet tightly around her before sitting up. "Bullshit." She smiled, proud of her own deductive reasoning skills.

"Bravo," I said, hoping to keep her distracted.

She took a bow and climbed off the table. "Thanks, Mindy." She watched me for a moment. "It looks like you might benefit from a back rub. My treat."

"No, thanks."

Dinah gave me a final uncertain look before dismissing the masseuse, who folded up the table and carried it out the door. Ty held the door while she exited, tossing a smile in my direction before securing it.

Dinah went into the bedroom to dress, calling out, "Why the sudden interest in stunts?"

"I may have missed my calling in life."

"Puh-lease. You were meant to be an investigator. That's the only consistent thing you've said about your personality and this job since the day we met."

I didn't think that was accurate, but I let it slide. "Someone might have been able to vault over the railings and basically drop level by level very quickly. It's the only conceivable way they could have escaped Scar's notice. Afterward, they probably raced up to the roof and vaulted across to another building."

"You do believe me." She sounded triumphant. "That does narrow things, doesn't it?"

"It might."

"Lance and Clay trained on that course. The stunt guys have been all over it, and I don't know how many extras and assistants tested it out during breaks. Apparently, they think the set is a jungle gym. Neil bitched everyone out about it yesterday. If the studio knew, they'd shit a brick. Insurance does not cover things like that. Fortunately, no one got hurt."

"I do recall Kurt suggesting I take the course for a spin."

She appeared in the doorway. "He's the one behind the crazy antics. Could that be because he's covering his tracks?"

"It's possible."

Now that Dinah had a rubdown, she actually seemed more interested in devising her own theories than hearing mine. I suspected she wanted to solve this on her own or with my guidance in order to feel like she could competently portray an investigator. It was stupid but a little endearing.

She opened a bottle of sparkling water and took a sip. "Doesn't this mean my phone logs are irrelevant? You know it's someone who's trained to do jumps and stuff."

"Not necessarily."

She put a hand on her hip. "Isn't that how this works? You collect clues and narrow down suspects. Why would this be any different?" She reached for her notepad and pen.

"You don't have to be a stuntman to race up the steps or climb down the railings."

"But you said they must have vaulted to the next building."

"What about Scar? Don't you think a formidable man like him would be capable of pulling off the exact same thing?"

"But we ruled Scar out," she protested.

"I know. He's just an example."

She dropped into a chair, looking utterly disgusted. "Anyone who's fit and obsessed with me could do this. We haven't made any progress. How do you ever make any progress?"

"It's a pain in the ass, isn't it?"

She glared at me. "I expect results in a timely fashion. Cross Security is supposed to have some of the best investigators around. At the moment, I'm not impressed."

Scary words, I thought sardonically. Frankly, I wasn't impressed with the supermodel actress who slept with my beloved. My expression hardened, and she switched tactics.

"In the meantime, I still need to prepare for my role."

"You've already shot several scenes. I'm sure you're doing a bang-up job."

"Why didn't you want a massage?"

"What?" Now she was jumping around like a professional acrobat.

She raised one eyebrow in a perfect arch. "Answer the question."

"Nice." I approved of her interrogation technique. "It's nothing personal. I just don't let strangers touch me."

"Because of your scars?"

"Partly."

Feeling brazen on account of my compliment, she jerked her chin up. "Show me one of them."

I took a seat across from her and held out my wrists. "See these," I pointed to the faint pink bands, "these are the result of being bound."

"Like handcuffed?"

"Like tied up."

She grinned. "Kinky."

My tone went cold and hard. "No. Tied up and tortured."

She sat back and swallowed, uncomfortable with how dark the conversation became, which was why I said it. I didn't care to talk about the investigation. I just didn't want to talk about me. "When did it happen?"

"A couple of years ago, and a few weeks ago."

"You're kidding me?"

"Wish I was."

She thought for a moment. "You weren't an FBI agent a few weeks ago."

"I was not."

"Holy hell."

"Cross hires topnotch investigators, and investigating is dangerous, particularly when you are on to something. This isn't a joke. Your stalker means business. You need to realize it. Your team knows to be vigilant, and Cross Security is taking every precaution. This isn't a movie. It's real life."

"I get it." She sounded solemn. "I will be more careful, and I'll try to answer your questions without protest or as much protest."

"Thank you."

"Maybe you could try to do the same. We're in this together, Alex."

Even though I didn't want to admit it, she was right. How the hell did I end up working for one of Martin's early conquests? I forced myself not to cringe. It was hard to look at her and not think about them. Sure, I briefly worked for his ex-fiancée, but I'd been in such desperate need of a distraction at the time that it barely registered. This was different.

"Do you want to see what a gunshot looks like?" I asked. She nodded, and I turned around and raised my shirt.

She blew out a breath. "Wow. Are all those scars from bullets?"

"No."

"Why the hell are you still doing this damn job?"

"I was just thinking the same thing." I lowered my shirt and turned around.

She frowned, biting her lip while she tried to figure something out. "You're crazy."

I pinched my thumb and pointer finger together. "Little bit."

"No. A lot. If I'd been through any of that," she waved her hand at my body, "I would turn my entire house into a panic room and never leave. It's no wonder you quit the FBI. I would have run away and found some deep, dark hole to hide in, but you're still doing the same job. That's insane."

"It is." I wondered if that might be her stalker's motivation for terrorizing her. If he put her through the wringer, she'd drop out of the film and maybe disappear from the limelight altogether. That possibility greatly broadened our suspect pool.

She flopped back in the chair as if she just finished running a marathon. "That's what I've been missing all along. My character, her motivation, her backstory, I totally get it now. Tragedy strikes, and she goes off the deep end with an obsessed need for justice."

"Hey, now," I held up my palms, "I never went off the deep end, and I don't have an obsessed need for justice. This is the job. Hell, look at police officers or firefighters worth their salt, and you'll see they're doing the same thing. They face danger or the potential for danger every shift, but they go to work the next day as if nothing happened."

"Maybe," she didn't look convinced, "it's about putting others' well-being above your own. I can see that, but I'm not wrong either. And it's my character. I can play her however I want."

"So you don't need me anymore?"

"Not for the attitude or backstory." She gestured at the memoir and her notepad. "But for the rest. This is only the beginning." Getting up, she went to the hotel phone and picked it up. "This calls for a celebration, and I'm starving." She lifted the handset to her ear and ordered a snack for herself and her security team; then she turned to me. "You weren't here for lunch. You have to eat. What do you want?"

"California Cobb salad, no bacon," I said.

As she was relaying my order, the window in her bedroom shattered. Immediately, I dove for cover, pulling her down with me. My gun was in my purse, which wasn't ideal. I grabbed my bag off the chair, pulled my gun, and made sure she was okay before moving into a crouch.

Security burst through the door. Ty followed closely behind Scar. "Dinah?" Scar asked.

"She's okay," I said.

Scar used hand gestures rather than verbal instructions. I wasn't sure why. Did he really believe a tango was inside the room? Ty diverted to Dinah, shielding her as he led her into the hallway and to another location. Gripping my gun, I moved toward the bedroom. Scar kept to the walls, moving faster in order to enter the room ahead of me.

He aimed, sweeping from left to right. No one was inside, just the shattered glass. I kept low, figuring it might have been taken out by a sniper. Windows in high-rises didn't just shatter. Hell, they rarely even opened.

"There." Scaratilli fired before I had time to voice a protest, and the remote-controlled drone fizzled and popped, pausing momentarily in mid-air before plummeting.

I leaned out the window, careful of the glass, and watched it career to the ground, praying no one was below. Getting hit with anything from this height would result in serious injury. Before I could berate him, Scaratilli left the room.

TWENTY

In the hallway, Scar barked orders to his team as he beelined for the stairwell. The heavy door slammed behind him, and I pressed the button for the elevator. While I waited for the doors to open, I checked on Dinah. Then I stepped inside the car and rode down to the lobby. Unsure if I beat Scaratilli down the steps, I went out the door and jogged to the spot where the drone had crashed to the ground.

Several bystanders crowded around, and I dismissed them with a quick wave. The paparazzi remained close. Pulling out my phone, I snapped a few quick photos of the group and called Cross. We needed containment.

Whoever launched this thing at Dinah's window had to be close. I looked at the mangled metal and plastic. One of the legs was covered in black duct tape. I didn't have gloves, so I didn't touch it. A few minutes later, Scar jogged to my location.

"Did you find the drone operator?" I asked.

He shook his head and crouched down. "I'm guessing one of the paps launched this skyward in the hopes of scoring some video footage or photos."

"Maybe." I grabbed his hand before he could touch it. "Don't contaminate our only lead."

He snarled and rocked back on his heels. "We don't need the publicity." Several of the onlookers had their cell phones pointed in our direction, and the paparazzi were snapping shots like there was no tomorrow.

"Fine." I looked around. The drone was large and bulky. "Take off your jacket, toss it over this thing, and let's move it inside." I would have suggested he try not to damage it, but he shot the damn thing out of the air. It was too late for that.

He did as I said and carried it back inside. A member of his team was already speaking to hotel security. Scar promised he'd be back in a moment to discuss matters. We waited for the elevator, rode up to Dinah's floor, and went into the adjacent suite.

Ty knelt at Dinah's feet, asking her questions. Scar put the drone on top of the table and shook out his jacket. His eyes found Dinah's, and I watched the unspoken exchange. She gave him a tight smile and a small nod, and he disappeared out the door. I studied the drone, hoping to determine if it was still broadcasting.

Ty climbed to his feet and stood beside me. "The lights aren't on. I don't see any indication any part of it is operational." He nudged me. "How could this toy break a window?"

I pointed to the taped area. "I can't be positive, but that looks like the tip of an emergency hammer." He reached for it, and I batted his arm away. "Don't touch." I was starting to feel like a museum curator dealing with kindergarteners.

He withdrew his hand. "It looks spring-loaded."

"Probably. I doubt this flying contraption could be launched at the window with enough force on its own to cause the glass to shatter." A thought crossed my mind. "I need the key to Dinah's suite." He handed it to me. "Wait here."

I went back inside. The phone was off the hook, and I replaced it before moving into the bedroom. Tiny glass pieces littered the carpet. No sharp shards. The few pieces that remained around the frame practically crumbled under my gaze. Tempered glass. The window had probably been marked by one of those dark stickers in the top corner. The drone operator had been staking out Dinah's window for a while, saw the telltale fire safety designation, and got creative.

When I returned to the security suite, Dinah was in front of the drone. Her hand shook slightly as she pointed at it. "What would be the point of breaking the window?"

"To scare you or deliver some kind of message."

She looked at it. "I don't see anything."

"You might have if Scar didn't shoot it out of the sky," I muttered.

"He was just doing his job," she insisted.

"It was a threat. He addressed it," Ty added.

"Yeah." I narrowed my eyes and fought the overwhelming urge to cover the entire thing in tinfoil. The first thing I needed to determine was the range on this thing.

Dinah paced the room. "Ty, will you check to see what the hotel is going to do about this?" He gave me an uncertain look. "We'll be fine. Alex won't let anything happen to me."

"Yes, ma'am." He wrote his number on the hotel stationery and handed it to me. "In case anything else goes wrong."

"Thanks."

She waited for the door to close before speaking. "You dove on top of me."

"Sorry. Reflex."

"Not many people would do something like that."

"Your security team would."

"Regardless, thank you."

"No need." I took a seat on the couch. Cross or someone from the office would be here momentarily. After back-up arrived, we'd have a better chance of canvassing the area. Someone must have seen something. With all those cameras outside, one of them must have caught something useful. "You didn't happen to notice this thing hovering outside your window when you got dressed."

"Do you think one of the paps was looking for a money shot?"

"Could be."

"But you doubt it."

I shrugged.

"I think my stalker found a new way to keep tabs on me," she declared. "Do you think he meant to break the window?"

"We'll know more once this thing is dismantled. My people are prepared to deal with this, but I'm not sure Scar wants to turn it over. It's up to you."

"I've seen your labs. You are in a much better position than we are. My security detail won't be a problem." She looked around the room before letting her gaze settle on me. "Not to sound dramatic, but now what do I do? I can't stay here. At the very least, I can't stay in my room. And quite frankly, I don't think I want to be in this hotel."

"Doesn't your security team have contingencies in place?"

"You're looking at it. They move me to a secure location, and we shelter in place until the threat is identified and removed."

It sounded like someone read the Secret Service handbook. It was a sound plan, if one didn't consider how freaked out and agitated Dinah was. She hadn't stopped fidgeting.

"You dove on top of me," she said.

"Yes, we established this. I'm sorry if I wrinkled your blouse." I didn't know why she felt the need to repeat it.

She ignored my glibness. "Why?"

"Again with the questions? Didn't you already determine I'm a lunatic? It's probably part of my crazy personality. Some people find it endearing."

"If you knew it was a harmless drone," she gestured at the machine which looked rather sinister with its gleaming black metal legs, broken and askew, "you wouldn't have forced me into cover. The only time Scar ever did that was when he thought there was an active shooter." The color drained from her face. "You thought someone shot out my window."

"It crossed my mind, but you shouldn't worry. You're safe." I said it to keep her calm, but I didn't believe it. From the look on her face, she didn't either.

Thankfully, I was saved by Scaratilli and Cross storming

into the room like two paratroopers on a black ops mission. Cross glanced in my direction, gave Dinah a brief apology, assured her Cross Security was on top of it, and surveyed the broken drone. He pulled a RF reader from his inner jacket pocket and scanned the device to make sure it wasn't emitting a signal. The thing was dead as a doornail.

"Nice shooting," he said sarcastically to Scar. "My techs will take it from here." Cross pulled me into the hallway and nodded at the two techs. "It's on the table, gentlemen." They entered, and while Dinah's security team was occupied, he asked, "What the hell happened?"

I gave him a rundown. "Once we know the distance for the remote control, we'll need access to security footage. With any luck, the drone operator was caught on camera, and if not, a dozen paparazzi are outside filming everything. One of them must have seen something."

"Go talk to them. They've been on Dinah's tail since her arrival. They've been outside the set, outside the hotel, and outside the club. It's possible one of them knows who is stalking her. Get everyone's name." Cross reached into his pocket and pulled out a money clip. Peeling off two dozen hundred dollar bills, he handed me the cash. "Try to buy their memory cards. They take photos to get paid. It shouldn't matter who pays for them."

"They stand to make a lot more by selling to the tabloids and internet sites."

"Then promise them more where this came from. You know how to be persuasive, and you know what to do if that fails. Now get to it."

I went downstairs, surprised to find hotel security had taken the liberty of placing the paparazzi inside one of the conference rooms. I couldn't be certain they corralled all of them, but Scar must have overseen it. He wouldn't let anyone slip away.

"Gentlemen," I said, entering the room, "how are you doing today? Did any of you get my good side?"

A couple of them chuckled. They were used to being hassled and harassed. "Do you have a bad side?" one of them asked.

"I do," I smirked, "and you don't want to get on it."

"Ooh, snap," another one retorted.

"Who are you?" another asked.

"I'm someone who might just make those hours you spent standing outside this hotel worth it. First, let's get the introductions out of the way, and we'll take it from there." I pointed to the one at the end of the table. "You first, sir."

By the end, Cross was $2400 in the hole and I was in possession of half a dozen memory cards. No one saw the drone operator. They didn't notice the device until it came crashing down. Based on the camera gear slung around their necks and thrown over their shoulders, none of them was in possession of a telephoto lens. Their focus had been the front door, not the windows of the suite. It was also reasonable to assume they didn't know if any of the actors were at the hotel. This group must have just stayed behind in the hopes of getting lucky.

"What about Reaper?" the one known as Pat asked. "He's always been a bit crazy. I bet he has a drone."

"Reaper? Is that his real name?" I asked.

"No. It's," Pat's brows scrunched, "fuck, what is his name?" Pat turned to the rest of the group, hoping someone could help him out.

"Isn't it Chaz something?" another replied.

Pat shrugged. "Sorry, lady."

"When's the last time any of you saw Reaper?" I asked.

The group exchanged glances. "Um, I guess it was outside the club two nights ago. We got a tip everyone was going out to party, and twenty or twenty-five of us showed up, hoping to catch a glimpse. Reaper was one of the first ones there, but he left early. It was weird. It's like he couldn't wait to take some pictures, but he didn't stick around long enough to get anything good."

"Okay, thanks for your time and the memory cards. If anyone remembers anything, please leave a message with the hotel, and we will get in touch. Like I said, any information will be handsomely rewarded."

"Exclusive photos?" one of them asked.

I smiled. "I promise it will be worth your while."

As they walked out, I made a mental note about each of

them. Since I entered the room, I'd scribbled down their descriptions, their names, and their alleged whereabouts at the time of Dinah's previous threats. They all seemed outgoing and personable, which I imagined was a necessity in their line of work. They did this long enough to know how to get in and out of places without being seen or stopped. I greased their palms, but that didn't mean they didn't do plenty of greasing themselves. I couldn't trust a word any of them said.

Cross waited in the lobby, watching the group file out. He appeared to be a businessman playing with his phone, but he was taking photos of each of them in the event they lied about who they were or where they were. I collected business cards, but those were easy to fake. As the last of them staggered out under the watchful eye of hotel security, I made my way to Lucien.

"Here." I held out the memory cards, each in a separate envelope with the photographer's name. "No one said they caught anything of value, but we can't be too careful."

Cross took the envelopes and flipped through the names. "I'll have these analyzed. The techs moved the drone back to the office. They've dealt with that particular model. It has a range of a hundred meters. HD video capabilities. It broadcasts the feed directly to the controller, but the techs are hoping something might be saved on the internal drive."

"So this wasn't an attempt to video Dinah naked?" I asked.

"I'm not sure. We'll know more once they get it opened up, but if that was the point, the operator wouldn't have broken the window."

"Unless it was causing a glare." A hundred meters was in the ballpark of three hundred feet. Dinah's room was on the fifteenth floor; that was at least half the distance. Damn, this might be the first time I ever used trigonometry in real life to determine the angle and distance. My brain was already drawing triangles from her window outward when another thought invaded my mind. "He could be in a nearby building or on a roof, even this roof."

"I'm aware." Cross looked outside and then back at the

elevator. "Dinah's being moved to a different floor."

"Good idea."

"However, she has another thought in mind." From his tone, I knew I wouldn't like it, but he didn't give me a chance to protest. Instead, he took my elbow and steered me to the stairs. "While I'm here, we should make the most of it. According to the hotel footage, it took two minutes and fourteen seconds for Dinah's security team to return to the stairwell after Scar evacuated Dinah to her room. Let's see how much time it takes to get to the roof." He glanced at me. "I'll race you to the top."

We made repeated attempts, or at least I did. Cross was far too fond of maintaining an accurate time count and had zero desire to get sweat stains on his shirt, so he left me to run the stairs alone. At a full-out run, we reasoned it was possible someone could make it from the twelfth floor to the roof in the time allotted. He had to be in great shape or utilizing some kind of wicked vaulting technique. That would help narrow our suspect list; unfortunately, it didn't rule out many of our known potentials.

TWENTY-ONE

"Anything?" Dinah asked.

Resisting the urge to look up from my desk, I said, "Not since you asked five minutes ago."

"It's been more than five minutes."

I massaged the bridge of my nose. This was pointless. Dinah insisted on coming back to the office with me, saying it would be safer and less conspicuous than if she stayed in the hotel. Scaratilli agreed after being assured Cross would exercise the utmost care with the movie star's safety, and since yours truly was stupid enough to dive on top of her when the glass shattered, she decided I would make an excellent temporary bodyguard.

"Alex," she whined, and I dragged my focus away from the computer screen and watched her flop lazily on the shorter end of my l-shaped sofa, "talk me through it. What do you think?"

That I should have tossed her out the window after the drone. "Whoever launched the drone knew which suite was yours and was paying enough attention to know the window was made of tempered glass in the event it needed to be broken in an emergency."

I closed the search box I'd been using to research the

paparazzi. They each had an assortment of charges, including trespassing and assault. Several had a handful of restraining orders and violations to said orders. While they might have technically been stalkers, I didn't think any of them actually posed a physical threat to Dinah. They didn't look like they could barrel up the hotel stairs fast enough. I'd done a search for Reaper, but with nothing to go on, I abandoned it. Cross was making some calls to see if he could track down the man, and I was happy to let him handle it.

"But what are *you* thinking?" she asked.

Rocking back in my chair, I propped my feet up on an opened drawer. "I want to know how the drone operator came to know these things. The hotel swears no one ever gave out your room assignment. Your security team is questioning the bellhops and maids to make sure no one talked, so unless one of them gave you up to an obsessed paparazzo with a drone, I think this is a waste of time."

"It's someone from the film. If I'm correct in believing whoever's stalking me is the same person who broke into my house in L.A., then it isn't some local with a camera."

From the conviction in her voice, she had a theory. "Who is it? Who would do this to you?"

"The only person I know who is obsessed enough to do something crazy is Lance, but he's filming."

"Could he have hired someone? Maybe sent his assistant?"

"Possibly." She reached for her phone. "Let me find out what he's been up to all day."

While she was distracted, I pulled out a pad of paper and went back to my theories. If this was an elaborate hoax, Dinah, Scar, and the rest of her staff were involved. That would explain everything, including the reason Scar shot down the drone. One of the security guards could have been remotely controlling it from the adjacent suite, and I would never know. It could also explain how they knew about the window and even made certain Dinah was given a room they could break into from the outside. But as I watched her nervously pace and speak animatedly, it became clear she wasn't involved, or she was the world's best actress. And I'd seen enough clips from her indie debut to know that wasn't the case.

I closed my eyes and tried to silence the voices in my head. What was my gut telling me? I took a deep breath. Dinah was convinced someone was out to get her, and it was the same person who terrorized her in Los Angeles.

She hung up the phone. "Turns out Lance wasn't feeling it today and changed the order in which the scenes are being shot. He spent most of the afternoon in his trailer."

"That would be easy enough to verify." I hit the speaker button and phoned the security team at the front gate, asking for the visitor log. Within moments, I had my answer. "Turns out Lance went on a little field trip from one to three."

"It could have been him," she said, a mix of triumph and confusion in her voice. "But why?"

"Okay, let's not jump to conclusions." Now I felt like I was channeling Lucien. "Something's been bothering me since this started. When you received the flowers, you seemed angry and annoyed. You didn't seem frightened."

"I'm just tired of this bullshit. I'm tired of being objectified and bullied. That was the second flower delivery I received. They both had similar notes attached with no way of discerning where they came from or how they got there. It was more frustrating than scary. They were flowers, not bombs."

"A bomb could have just as easily been left."

She swallowed, the thought never occurred until I voiced it. "I didn't think of that. I don't think in those channels. Who the hell thinks like that," she scowled, "besides you?" Before I could defend myself, she was up and moving around my office like a toddler on a sugar high. "I'm not going back to that hotel, and until we identify the actual culprit with a hundred percent certainty, I refuse to go back to Scar and the boys. You seem to think it could be Scar, so we need to make sure it isn't."

"Dinah, it's not Scar."

She put up a hand to silence me. "No. He didn't listen in Los Angeles. He treated me like I was crazy, and I'm not crazy. This is serious. Someone wants to knife me or enjoys knifing my likeness. Now windows are being broken. What if the drone had a gun attached instead of a little hammer?"

"Gun drones are mostly in movies."

"But they do exist." She was on a tear, so I let her go. She was spinning and would tire out eventually. "Even now, I don't believe Scar would risk jeopardizing me, but maybe he believes what they told him. And if he's not helping, then he's hurting."

"What are you going to do? You can't exactly find that deep, dark hole and hide away. You're in the middle of shooting a movie."

"True, but when I'm not on set, I can go off the grid." Her eyes brightened. "I'll just find someplace to stay that no one would ever suspect, and I'll make sure the paps and the rest of the cast and crew think I'm still in my room."

"Where will you go?" I asked.

She looked expectantly at me, but I kept my mouth shut. Cross mentioned she thought I should be her babysitter until we had a solid lead. That wasn't something I wanted to do. I'd promised Martin I wasn't hired to be her bodyguard; I wouldn't let Lucien or Dinah make a liar out of me.

"I know plenty of people here. Hell, I used to live here. Someone will put me up for a few nights." She bit her lip and thought. Then she went to her phone and scrolled through her list of contacts. "It should be someone you've already ruled out." She came closer and scanned the papers on my desk. "Where's my phone log? The ones you didn't highlight are clear, right?"

I had no idea who she planned to call, but it better not be Martin. Over my dead body would I allow her to stay at his place. That wasn't happening. I set my jaw. "You can't be positive whoever you contact won't leak your presence."

She thought for a moment and smiled. "Yes, I can. In fact, I know just the guy."

The NDA. Shit. "No. You can't." I relented, cursing my paranoia. She probably knew plenty of guys, and I was just being irrational. "I know a place where no one would ever think to look. It doesn't have room service or housekeeping, and there might be mold on the stairs. But no one's died there recently."

"You're stashing me in the ghetto?"

I laughed. "It depends on what Cross thinks. He's in charge."

*   *   *

Letting Dinah stay at my apartment was never something I planned. If jealousy hadn't reared its ugly head and I hadn't panicked at the prospect that she might ask Martin for a place to hide out, I never would have come up with such a ridiculous idea or given in to her ridiculous idea. Hopefully, she'd hate it and go running back to the hotel. The problem being she was more afraid of her stalker and not knowing who he was than a possible rat or cockroach sighting, even though my apartment didn't have rats or cockroaches. But somehow, she'd gotten the idea in her head, and I didn't bother to correct her.

She looked around the room while I locked the door. "Is this one of Cross Security's safe houses?" She went to the fire escape and looked out. "A sixth floor walk-up doesn't seem particularly secure to me."

Ignoring her, I went into my bedroom to make sure nothing private was out in the open. Unlike most normal human beings, I kept my living space devoid of sentimental things. No matter how hard she looked, she wasn't going to stumble across any framed family photos or pictures of Martin. I kept those things at our apartment since he was the far more civilized and human one in the relationship and enjoyed seeing proof that there was an us.

I stuffed some clean laundry into my drawers, changed the sheets on my bed, and replaced the pillows with the crappy spares I kept in the closet, deciding I'd be damned if she had a good night's sleep on my pillow. Then I went into the bathroom. Dinah didn't pack when she left the hotel. She actually didn't think this through. She just wanted to be away from the danger. I could relate to that kind of thinking, but unlike me and most federal agents, she didn't have a go-bag packed and waiting.

"Here," I opened the drawer and pulled out a stash of

hotel-provided toiletries from a few of my rendezvous with Martin and put them on the counter, "in case you need a toothbrush or something."

She entered the bathroom and looked at the items. Since Martin always picked ritzy places, the toiletries were rather nice, which was why I had nicked them. "I'm just now beginning to realize I didn't plan this out very well."

"It's not too late. I'll give you a ride back. Your security team is on alert. They have a new room waiting."

"Maybe tomorrow. For now, I'd just like to wind down. Is that okay?"

"Sure." I went into my room and came back with an oversized t-shirt, yoga pants, and pajama shorts. "I'm not sure about size. They should fit, but the pants might be more like capris so you might want to go with the shorts."

"I'm sure they're fine. I just want to take a bath and decompress. My energy fields are out of whack, probably from the shooting and the stress."

Energy fields. I resisted the urge to mock. "I'll order dinner. Low-carb, gluten-free. Any other restrictions?"

She shook her head. We'd already discussed our meal options on the way back to my place. She wanted sashimi. She'd circled the items she wanted on a takeout menu she found in my glove box.

I closed the bathroom door behind me and went into the kitchen. Picking up the phone, I called in our order, opened the fridge, and stared at the emptiness. My cupboards were just as bare. I had a water pitcher and some salad dressing. It would suffice. She was an actress. They weren't supposed to eat, so she shouldn't complain.

I put my pillows on one end of the couch, kicked off my shoes, and put my gun on the end table. It's only for the night, I said to myself. Her phone rang, and I turned toward the sound. It was in my bedroom. I debated checking to see who was calling, but before I could grab it, the delivery guy knocked on my door.

After paying him and taking the bags inside, I put the fish in the fridge and pulled out some plates and flatware. I didn't want Dinah to think I was a barbarian. The phone rang again, and this time, I went to see who it was.

According to the display, it was Scaratilli. However, the device was fingerprint encrypted. I went back to the living room and flipped on the TV. Lance was supposed to be giving one of the programs a set exclusive, but I couldn't find it. Perhaps it wasn't scheduled to air yet, or he rescheduled.

The hairdryer turned on, and I raised the volume a little and put on the local news. None of the stories were about the hotel, the drone, or the movie being shot. Granted, movies were filmed here all the time, so it wasn't newsworthy. But with the way things were going, I couldn't rule out the possibility someone might leak something to the press.

Dinah emerged twenty minutes later. She looked completely different. Her hair was stick straight. Her face was devoid of makeup. Her lips were pale and unimpressive without the bright red lipstick I'd grown accustomed to seeing, and she was dressed in my lounge clothes.

"Did I hear the phone?" she asked.

"It rang a couple of times. I'm guessing Scar is checking up on you."

It occurred to me someone with Scar's abilities could ping her phone and determine her location, but we ruled Scar out as a threat. And Cross said Dinah's security team was clean. Belatedly, I wondered if her stalker had her number or the foresight to trace her phone.

She called him back, promising she was safe and wasn't going anywhere and would see him first thing in the morning at the lot. After she hung up, she took a seat at my dining room table, and I took the food from the fridge and placed it in front of her. She opened the container, expertly maneuvering it out of the plastic and onto the plate. She daintily placed a napkin, even though it was paper, on her lap and reached for a set of chopsticks.

"This is your place, isn't it?"

"What gave it away?" I asked.

She tugged on the front of the t-shirt. "The clothing." She looked around again. "It's cozy." She ate a few bites and put the chopsticks down. "How did you know I'd end up here?"

"I didn't."

"Right, so I'm supposed to believe you just happened to clear out your knickknacks and photos on the same day I end up in desperate need of someplace to hide out."

"This is it." I looked around. "I'm a minimalist."

Deciding this might be another key to understanding the psyche of a federal agent, she dug deeper. "Do your former colleagues at the Bureau live in a similar fashion? Is it a security thing? Or maybe protocol?"

"Despite the regulation attire and hideous shoes, we aren't a cult. We each have our own lives and live them as we see fit. No two people fit into the same mold."

"May I ask why you live like a nomad?"

I told her about long-term assignments and undercover work. I told her about unplanned trips and the need to be ready at a moment's notice, and I mentioned it wasn't a bad idea to have a go-bag. She agreed.

Afterward, the conversation turned back to the hotel and her stalker, but it was basically just rehashing everything we'd already gone over. After another look out the fire escape and a glance at my front door to make sure it was locked, she went to bed.

I tidied up and went to work behind the computer. I had no choice but to believe the things she said. Whoever stalked her in Los Angeles must be the same person who followed her here. I needed official police reports, news and tabloid stories, and accounts from her people. Luckily, the time difference was on my side.

TWENTY-TWO

My phone rang for the sixth time in the last thirty minutes, and I glanced at the display before hitting answer. "Dammit." I cringed, realizing my mistake a little too late.

"Are you okay? Where are you?" Martin asked. His voice came out rushed and clipped, which meant he was worried I was lying in some ditch, bleeding out.

"I'm okay. Something came up at work."

He let out an involuntary breath. "No problem. When do you think you'll get home?"

"Maybe tomorrow."

"Alex," the worry was replaced with annoyance, "I thought we were past this. Honestly, you have no reason to be mad."

"I'm not." I got up from behind my desk and peered into the hallway that led to my bedroom. The door was closed, and I figured Dinah must be asleep since she was expected on set in a few hours. "I'm babysitting. Right now, your other girlfriend is in my bed."

"I thought you said you weren't doing that."

"Things change. It was beyond my control. It's just one night. Think of it this way, it's my turn to see how much fun she can be."

"Normally, I'd say I have no desire to share you, but if this is something you need to do so we'll be even, I guess I can accept it. Though, I wouldn't mind watching," he teased.

"Is that really what you want to say to me?"

"No. Why is she there? Is everything okay?"

"It's fine. We're having a sleepover, so we can stay up late and talk about boys. Apparently, you used to be a terrible lay. I really should thank her for teaching you a few things."

"You're joking."

"You better hope so."

"Sweetheart, I'm sorry. Look, if you want me to answer your questions, fuck it, I'll do it."

"No. I don't need to jeopardize whatever it is you're doing. I just hate this. I hate it when we can't talk to each other."

"Me too." Silence filled the space between us. "Is she okay?"

"Yes. Unfortunately, I'm filling in for her security team until they get their shit together." Martin knew being a bodyguard was the last thing I wanted to do, so he didn't waste his breath asking any more questions. My phone beeped, telling me I had an incoming call. "I have to go. The sooner I figure out what's what, the sooner she'll go back to her hotel and I can come back to you."

"Be careful. I love you."

"I know."

The incoming call was from the lead detective on Dinah's stalking case. He gave me the official story, which was the same thing I'd already heard several times. However, he remembered the scene in vivid detail. It wasn't his first stalking case. He'd worked several, usually in instances of minor local celebrities, but this was different. And he wanted to do it right.

No one suspicious ever appeared on the security feed. The few packages and other deliveries that came to Dinah's estate were left at the front gate where a guard was stationed. The perimeter was under surveillance, and there were no obvious signs of a break-in. None of the windows were broken. The alarm wasn't triggered, but the house didn't look right. The inside was off. The detective remembered seeing indentions in the carpet from where furniture had recently been moved.

"The weirdest thing was this flower vase. It was right in the middle of the table, but there was a smaller centerpiece shoved off to the side. It didn't make any sense, and the flowers were fucking hideous. They were these half-dead, dark purple things that stunk to high heaven. I don't know what kind of flower they were, but no one in their right mind would put those in their kitchen."

I thought back to the flowers that had been delivered. They'd been dark in color too, but I was never close enough to smell them. A thought nagged at the back of my mind, but I couldn't figure out exactly what it was.

"Allen said there was a note." He opened and closed a squeaky drawer, the squeal practically making me deaf. "Whoever wrote it fancies himself a poet."

"What did it say?" I asked.

"*You're mine. I'm yours. What we share is beyond love.* That's it. Nothing particularly threatening, but I don't think this guy needs to write for a greeting card company either."

"Ever come up with any suspects?"

He chuckled. "You realize this was solved. It was a publicity stunt. Her agent and manager concocted it."

"Before they came forward, did you have any leads?"

"It read like an inside job. I assumed the stalker was someone she knew and trusted like a friend, boyfriend, girlfriend, or someone who works for her. Whoever it was knew how to get inside and how to dodge the security system."

"Like her manager and agent?"

"Yep." I could hear him smile. "Case closed."

"Do you think they disabled her security system?"

"I wouldn't doubt it, but I can't be certain. You could call them and ask."

"Did you check alibis?"

"Why would I?"

Forcing myself not to say something snarky, I

considered my next words carefully. "You said something seemed off. Maybe you started checking before the truth came out."

"Nah. We didn't know exactly when the alleged break-in occurred. Nothing was on the security system. Miss Allen had been away. The flowers could have been left at any point. It's hard to say. They were dying, but they were ugly to begin with. That might just be the way they always looked."

"Thanks."

"Yeah." He waited a beat. "Someone already asked about this. Am I going to get jammed up over something here?"

"Nope. Just performing my due diligence." The way he should have.

"Sure, sure." The detective disconnected, and I pushed away from the computer.

Dinah was right. Whoever was stalking her in Los Angeles was here, and this time, they weren't stopping at flowers.

Sinking into the pillows, I grabbed the throw off the back of the couch and curled into a ball. Flowers, the prop dummy, the man in the stairwell, and now the drone through the window. It was escalation. The stalker was getting closer to his target. I sent a text to Cross with my expert opinion; Dinah's stalker was real. Why would her staff take the hit and cover it up? That didn't make any sense.

I closed my eyes and hoped to get a couple hours of sleep, but I twisted and turned, trying to come up with a reason for the deception and some idea of who could be stalking Dinah. According to the detective, it was someone close to her. I whole-heartedly agreed.

That left her costars, the crew, and the dozens of people she employed. Those were the only people who had access to her trailer and her hotel room. A chilling realization coursed through my bones. If Lance was responsible, would it even be addressed? Throwing off the blankets, I went back to my computer and searched for his contact information.

It only took a few minutes to discover Lance was represented by the same agency as Dinah. I reached for the phone and left a lengthy voicemail for Cross. There was no way he missed this. Was my boss going along with some Hollywood conspiracy for a few bucks and to keep his reputation intact? I didn't know Lucien well enough to be certain how he operated, but my friends in the police department warned me about him. And Mark Jablonsky had done the same. Maybe they were right. Good thing I didn't give a rat's ass about appearances or the company line. I just wanted the truth.

The overhead light flipped on, and I jumped, automatically reaching for my nine millimeter. Dinah was ghost white. The phone was pressed to her ear, and she was trembling.

"Please," she begged.

I didn't know if she was speaking to me or the caller, but I eased the phone from her hand and hit the speaker button. A modulated robotic voice asked, "Why did you run away, Dinah dear? It isn't safe to wander around. Something terrible could happen."

I snatched my phone and texted Cross with a 911. It was the only way I could guarantee he would respond. *Trace the incoming call to Dinah's phone. It's the stalker.*

Keep him on the line, Cross sent back.

"Dinah, where did you go?" the voice asked again. She shivered, and I led her to the couch and wrapped her in the blanket. "Answer me."

"Sorry, Dinah can't come to the phone right now," I replied, "but I'd be happy to take a message." I met Dinah's eyes and put a finger to my lips.

"Ah, I see Dinah has a new bodyguard."

"Who said I was a bodyguard?"

The caller laughed. The robotic interpretation came out more like a coughing bark. "You can't hide forever. People like you can't disappear into obscurity. You won't leave the limelight."

"Once again, Dinah's not here," I repeated. "Is that the message you want relayed? Who should I say called? If you'd like a call back, I'll need your number."

"Don't play games," the robot said. The monotone voice dampened the threat. I checked my phone, waiting for verification from Cross. "I know she's there. Give her the phone."

"Do you love her?" I asked.

"Of course. I take care of her and protect her, but I can't do that when she runs and hides. Why didn't she tell me where she was going? Why would she go with you? You're a stranger."

"Did you send the flowers?" I asked. The voice hesitated, and I worried the caller might be getting wise to the delay tactics. "It was thoughtful. However, I don't understand knifing a dummy dressed to look like Dinah. That was a little crazy, don't you think?"

"That was a warning. People who take pleasure from the flesh will hurt her in the end." The call ended, and I double-checked the display before handing the device back to its owner.

"Jesus," Dinah whispered. She was shaking like a leaf.

"Any idea who that might have been?" I visually checked the two deadbolts and security bar. No one was getting inside my apartment.

She shook her head and swallowed.

My phone buzzed with an incoming text, and I picked it up. *The call originated from the hotel. No way to determine what room.*

"Dammit," I swore.

Dinah's eyes shot up. "What is it?"

"Your stalker is a fan of horror films of the '90s," I said.

"What does that mean?"

"Nothing you need to worry about." I went into the kitchen and poured some water into a pot to heat. Martin always tried to calm me down with tea, so perhaps it would work for Dinah. I found a dusty box of chamomile in the cabinet and pulled it out. "Has the caller made contact before?"

"No." She looked at the phone as if it betrayed her, which, in a way, it had. "I need to call Scar."

I couldn't stop her. I wasn't even sure it would be wise to encourage her to keep her security chief in the dark. She hit the speed dial and waited. And waited. Eventually, it went to voicemail, and her voice shook as she left a message for him to call her back immediately. She put the phone down and turned to face me.

"He didn't answer," she said. "That's never happened before. Never."

An uneasy feeling wormed its way through my body, and I grabbed a second mug from the cabinet and put a teabag in each of them. I poured water into the mugs and brought them to the coffee table. "Here."

"Thanks." She dipped the bag up and down. "How do you think that thing got my number?" Her gaze flicked to her phone.

"While you were sleeping, I did some investigating. The responding officer to your home invasion believed whoever gained access was someone close to you, like a friend or someone who works for you. The stalker had to know about your security system and how to circumvent it. He probably has your number."

"No one broke in, remember?" she said bitterly. "That's what everyone told me."

"Yeah, but you don't believe that. And neither do I." I watched her take a sip of the tea. "Why did your management team decide to take the blame?"

"I don't know. My publicist said it would be bad. Dealing with the PR would be a nightmare, and I didn't want to be known for that. I didn't want to be labeled a victim or the girl who cried wolf, or worse yet, some prima donna who freaks for no reason."

"I mean no disrespect, but you need a reality check. This is serious."

"I know," she snapped.

"Is it possible your management team had someone else's best interests in mind? I did some digging, and Lance is represented by the same agency."

"So are a lot of celebrities. What's your point? We were together when the break-in occurred. We just came back from Maui when I found the flowers in my house. It couldn't have been him."

"Are you absolutely sure?"

"I'm not sure of anything right now." Dinah's phone rang, and she reached for it. The display read *Scar* which she flashed in my direction before hitting answer. "Did you get my message?" He said something, and her eyebrows furrowed. "Hold on. When did that happen?" The shaking intensified, and she whispered, "Talk to Alex," and thrust the phone at me.

"Parker," Scar sounded perturbed, "I just got a call. Untraceable number. Modulated voice. The caller said if I didn't protect Dinah, something awful would happen."

"Anything specific?"

"No, but the caller meant business. I want Dinah back at the hotel."

I prepared for an argument. "That's a bad idea."

"Dinah's to be brought back to the hotel immediately." Scar said something to someone else that I didn't entirely catch. "Whoever this shithead is, he's going to make another move. I need to stop him."

Giving Dinah a reassuring look, I went into the bathroom and shut the door, turning on the shower to drown out my voice. "Listen to me. This asshole just called and freaked her the fuck out, but we ran a trace. The call originated from somewhere inside the hotel. Bringing her back there is the same as handing her over to him."

"Are you sure about that?"

"It was the hotel's main line. We're guessing the call was placed from within one of the rooms, but we can't rule anything out." I took a breath. "How much do you trust the men on your team?"

"How much do you trust the people you work with?" Scar retorted. He let out an exasperated snarl. "My mission is to keep Dinah safe. Under these circumstances, you'll need to take over until something more permanent can be arranged. Whatever you do, keep her away from here."

"Did you call the police?" I asked.

"That will be up to Miss Allen to decide," he replied.

"Well, that's what I would recommend, but I'll let you discuss it with your client." I returned to the living room and held out the phone.

While they spoke, I called Cross. Maybe he would be

able to talk some sense into these people who thought they were too famous for the likes of local law enforcement. I didn't know who this asshole stalker was. All I knew was he was inside the hotel and knew enough about Dinah's safety protocols to call Scar. It was a power play designed to force her security chief to demand her return. When that failed, the stalker would try something else, and the only other place Dinah was guaranteed to be was on set.

TWENTY-THREE

"You should reconsider," I said for what felt like the millionth time. "The phone call was a threat. It put you in direct contact with whoever is terrorizing you. We should assume matters will continue to escalate."

Scaratilli and Dinah exchanged glances. Based on her body language, Dinah was on the fence, but Scar wasn't convinced. It might have been a point of pride, or he'd been in the business long enough to know police involvement would turn the entire matter into a circus.

"They don't need the police," Cross retorted. "That's why they hired us." He offered our clients a sheepish smile. "Please excuse, Miss Parker. She's new and has yet to fully grasp the services Cross Security provides. It's from her conditioning as an FBI agent."

Dinah met my eyes. I could read the apology on her face, but she agreed with Cross. "That is why I signed with your company, despite already having a private security detail."

"My team will maintain a constant presence until you have identified and removed the threat. Should another attempt be made, we will notify you immediately." Scar opened the door to the conference room and waited for

Dinah to exit. Ty Johnson was just outside the room, and another one of the guards was waiting near the elevator at reception. "Keep me looped in," Scar insisted.

Cross nodded, and we remained silent until Dinah and Scar were halfway down the hall. Cross dropped into a chair and rubbed his eyes. It wasn't even five a.m. Dinah hadn't slept after the phone call, and since she had an early call time, we decided to meet before she went to the lot at a safe location – the Cross Security offices.

"All right, here's what we're going to do," Cross said, fighting back a yawn. "I have teams inside the hotel. We will figure out where the call originated, even if we have to bang down every damn door. I don't care if the other security teams don't like it or think we're violating their clients' privacy. They can get over it."

"Great." I wasn't sure how he was going to make those things happen, but it would be unwise to question him.

He looked up, as if realizing he wasn't just verbalizing his strategy for his own benefit. "You spoke to the stalker. We need a workable profile. Get on that."

"What are we doing about Dinah?" I asked.

"Her security team is taking point. I have a secondary unit shadowing them, and several additional units providing around-the-clock protection at the lot. Even if one of her associates is responsible, we're keeping a careful watch. No one will be able to get to her. We're doing checks at the gate. No weapons will get on set."

"What about the ones that are already there?"

"The guns are props, so are the knives."

"Not the ones at craft services."

He practically rolled his eyes. "I'll ask them to switch to plastic. Anything else?"

I didn't like it, but Lucien knew the security business inside and out. And Scaratilli was no slouch. They would keep the actress safe. I just had to figure out who wanted to cause her harm.

"Do you think one of the medics upstairs could hook me up to a caffeine drip?" I asked.

Cross chuckled and rose from the chair. "Get to work, Alex. No one should be here for another hour or two. The breakroom is yours."

Returning to my office, I set to work creating a profile. Cross and I had already created a preliminary profile the night we found the dummy posed on the soundstage, but after speaking to the stalker on the phone, I had a few additional details to add. Over the course of an hour, I came up with what I imagined to be a workable lead.

Based on the phone call, the stalker believed he loved Dinah. He was clearly jealous of her sexual partners. However, that confused matters. Was he a jealous former flame or someone she rejected? Either option fit, but since we were unaware of Lance Smoke or Neil Larson receiving any threats, I was baffled. The stalker insisted he wanted to protect Dinah or save her from these men and these bad decisions. He didn't want her to be used, or so he had communicated through his note and phone call. Why didn't he do something to the men who hurt her and used her? Why target Dinah?

He's probably a weakling, I figured. If he were physically strong or formidable, he would strike out against them. He would want to be her protector. Her hero. But he didn't do that. Instead, he was attempting to fancy himself more of a lover than a fighter by delivering flowers and warning her away from these powerful men. It's the type of thing a good friend would do.

"Shit." I wasn't sure that theory fit. Whoever was after Dinah had vaulted up the staircase and disappeared onto the roof, assuming that's what happened. He had to be in some sort of shape. Maybe I made a mistake, unless Lance or Neil was responsible. The star needed the director just as much as the director needed his star. Due to the nature of their working relationship, neither could target the other. They would only be able to focus their efforts on Dinah.

The only other alternative was the stalker's access was limited to Dinah, not the cast or crew. At least not to the same extent. That would indicate it was someone Dinah employed or one of the men she was speaking to outside of the film.

"Anything?" Cross barged into my office and took a seat,

checking the time.

"This is bullshit. I've just gone in a complete circle. We still don't know enough. We don't have any idea who's stalking her or what his endgame is."

"Did you manage to rule anyone out? You had a list of several possibilities from set."

"Lance has made several attempts to win Dinah back. Even though he has his own stardom and the most to lose, he makes the most sense. Neil Larson could just as easily be responsible, and since he couldn't act against Lance on Dinah's behalf, he'd be stuck threatening her to stay away from Lance and maybe even the production."

"The director is the reason Dinah was granted a ride-along. He wouldn't appease her if he wanted her to abandon the movie, and he wouldn't have paired her up with an investigator if he was going to terrorize her. That doesn't fit." Cross leaned over and scratched his name off my list. "Logically, it just doesn't."

"This isn't logical."

"It doesn't matter. It isn't him. It doesn't feel right, and if you think about it for a few minutes, I'm sure you'll agree."

"You're right." I looked down at the names. "If it was the stunt coordinator, he could probably kneecap Lance and make it look like an accident. If he was stalking Dinah, he would make it known and take credit for his chivalrous tactics to protect her. Kurt talks a lot. He wouldn't be able to keep his mouth shut." I scratched off his name.

Cross smiled. "See, that's progress."

I frowned at the paper. "Not really. We already decided it wasn't Scar, so the only name left on the list is Lance Smoke."

"Unless it's someone we have yet to consider. In theory, it could be anyone on set. Maybe even someone behind the scenes. Most stalkers are nameless, faceless nobodies who blend into the background and are never seen or noticed. That's why they do what they do and how they manage to get away with it. You need to broaden your scope."

I gave him a look. "You don't think it's Lance?"

"It's possible. But we need to be certain, and the only

way is to rule out everyone else."

"Easier said than done," I mumbled.

He ignored me and pushed a thumb drive closer. "Here's what my search for Reaper has unearthed. You can get started on that while I lead the morning meeting. It might be time I bring in a few more investigators to assist."

"You think?"

He glared and went to the door. "I will speak to you when I am finished."

Great, now I was in trouble. Me and my big mouth. Shaking it off, I plugged the drive into my computer and waited. In moments, Reaper's entire life filled my screen. His name was Chaz Relper. His parents actually named him Chaz. It wasn't short for Charles, and an easy misspelling is probably what led to his nickname. Based on his arrest record, he had been in and out of the criminal justice system. As a kid, he'd done some petty things. By the time he hit twenty-five, Chaz had been charged with extortion, B&E, trespassing, vandalism, public nuisance, harassment, lewd behavior, and public urination.

Besides his criminal record, Relper's or Reaper's credit card statements, phone records, and family connections were included. Access to most of these things was difficult or illegal to obtain, but Lucien didn't follow the rules. I was convinced there was a line, but I had a feeling my boss wouldn't agree. Instead of allowing the moral and ethical quandaries to be debated in my brain, I parsed through the details for relevant facts.

By the end, I knew Reaper had recently purchased a drone. In addition, he had several recent transactions at a local hardware store, but I had no way of determining exactly what he bought. I wrote down the VIN and license plate of his vehicle, along with his home address and phone number. I didn't want to call and risk tipping him off. Instead, I thought I'd pay him a visit.

When Cross returned to my office, I was in the middle of shrugging into my shoulder holster. He didn't seem surprised I was on my way out. He also seemed to have mellowed since our previous conversation or simply forgot he intended to chew me out.

"Where are you going?" he asked.

"To see if I can pin down Reaper."

"His phone's been turned off for the last three days. I tried to track it, but it was impossible."

"I'll let you know what I find."

"Excellent." Cross stepped back into the hallway, and by the time I picked up my keys, he was gone. At least I finally had some autonomy.

When I arrived at the apartment, I knew why my boss had made such a hasty retreat. The drive to Chaz Relper's apartment took far longer than it should on account of morning traffic. His place really was in what Dinah would call the ghetto. It was a sketchy neighborhood. Several homeless people were asleep on the sidewalks and in the alleys. I dropped a few dollars into someone's coffee can on my way to the apartment building while I wondered if there were any spare blankets in the trunk.

The building was old. Several of the windows were broken, covered with cardboard and tape. The front door was hanging off one hinge, and I pushed inside, afraid of what I might see. Even at this early hour, I could hear people arguing, a baby screaming, and what sounded like three or four cats fighting or mating. With cats, sometimes it was hard to tell the difference.

I went up a few flights of stairs, stepping over some questionable patches that might have been old rust spots or recent bloodstains. When I reached Reaper's apartment, I pounded against the door. No one answered. I tried again. After glancing around, I saw a woman peeking out from behind her door.

"Excuse me," I said, and she slammed the door shut. "Ma'am," I knocked gently on her door, "I'm looking for Mr. Relper. Have you seen him?"

"Why do you want to know?" she asked, her voice barely more than a cackle. "You a bill collector?"

"No, ma'am. I'm a friend."

"That asshole doesn't have any friends," she said from behind the door.

"Everyone has friends," I said. "When's the last time you saw him?"

"He left four days ago, middle of the night. He hasn't been back since." She cracked the door open again and stared at me. She was a tiny woman with tightly curled gray hair. "Are you a cop?"

"No, ma'am." I offered a friendly smile.

She eyed me suspiciously. "You look like one of them. They were here earlier. You just missed them."

I raised an eyebrow. "The police?"

"Yep." She gave me a challenging look. "If Chaz is one of your friends, you might want to warn him that they're looking for him again."

"Thanks." Before I could even get the syllable out, she slammed the door in my face.

Taking a step back, I waited for her shadow to disappear from beneath the door before I returned to Reaper's apartment. Why were the police looking for him? They didn't know about the situation concerning Dinah Allen or the incident at the hotel. At least, that's what I had been told. However, I wasn't positive the hotel hadn't filed a report. After all, they sustained property damage. They might have been obligated to file a police report for insurance purposes.

Unsure why the police might want Reaper, I figured they'd be back eventually. If he was wanted for a crime, they'd return with a warrant and search his place. I needed to look around first. This way, they couldn't remove a potentially important piece of evidence before I had a chance to see it. For all I knew, he might have a shrine dedicated to Dinah Allen right inside.

Convincing myself this was necessary, I removed the lock picks from my purse and set to work. His lock, like the rest of the building, was in poor shape. The door opened without putting up much of a fight, and I slipped on some gloves and tied back my hair before stepping inside.

Small didn't even begin to describe it. The rear wall had a fridge, sink, and oven. The counter jutted out maybe two feet, and the front door scraped against it. A loveseat was against the very back wall with a TV tray in front of it. The bathroom was in the back, and a cot took up the rest of the living space. The counter, tray, and furniture were covered in camera equipment, and the closet was packed full of clothing, coats, a sweeper, and mop. The food in the fridge had gone bad, and I wondered if it was possible Reaper hadn't been home in more than four days.

I didn't find a drone or any photographs of Dinah Allen. All of the camera equipment was broken. Carefully, I checked each one for a memory stick. Most were empty, but I did find two and removed the cards. I went through the pockets of Reaper's clothes. He had a parking stub from the hotel garage dated five days ago, so he had been staking out the hotel and possibly Dinah Allen. Other than that, I didn't find anything of use. I didn't find the drone, Reaper's phone, or any indication that he might be able to identify the stalker.

Feeling defeated, I let myself out of the apartment. The parking stub meant he'd been home sometime in the last five days, so his neighbor's timeline appeared accurate. I just didn't know if lengthy absences were commonplace for him. The man lived in a sardine can. He probably only went home when it was absolutely necessary.

When I made it out of the building, I checked the nearby streets for his car, but I didn't find it. He wasn't home, and wherever he was, he probably had his car. A sick feeling washed over me. I wasn't sure why, but I was worried, even though I didn't spot any threats. No one was after me, but I couldn't help but think someone had come for Reaper. He really should have found a better nickname. The irony might just mean his death.

TWENTY-FOUR

I clicked through the photographs on the memory cards. The first card contained several images of the exterior of the studio. Reaper had obviously spent some time walking the entire length of the fence, taking shot after shot as he went. He even captured the small defect at the bottom of the fence. Several zoomed in shots of the trailers were taken, but from this angle, I couldn't tell one from the other. It was possible he'd pinpointed Dinah's trailer, but without anyone in the shot, I couldn't be certain. However, from these vantage points, even zoomed in, I was positive Reaper never made it onto the lot.

Moving on to the second memory card, I scanned through those photos. These were taken at the hotel. Several caught glimpses of the actors entering or exiting. The celebrities were always flanked by security and assistants with their heads ducked as they dove into their cars. Lance, Clay, Gemma, Dinah, and a dozen other lesser knowns were photographed. Based on clothing and the light patterns, the photos on this card had been taken over the course of several days.

I kept scrolling. Almost all of the shots were taken from nearly the same position, just to the left of the hotel doors.

I minimized the photo viewer and checked the file information to see when each photo was taken, but the camera Reaper used wasn't properly programmed. The date was listed at 1/1/00, and the time was 0:00:00. Neither detail was accurate or useful. Perhaps the techs could do something about it.

The memory card contained over five hundred photographs. Most were nothing more than blurry images. I clicked through even faster, wondering if the stalker might have been caught in one of these blurry shots. Cross and I had wondered the same thing about the memory cards we had purchased the day the drone went down, but those were a bust. I had a feeling this would be too. If these cards contained anything of value, Reaper wouldn't have left them with his broken camera equipment. His building wasn't exactly safe, so anything of value must be elsewhere, probably with him.

As I neared the last third of the photos, I stopped on an image. It was the exterior of Dinah's limousine. It was dark outside, either late at night or early in the morning. She was stepping out of the car, but someone remained in the back seat. Her security always exited first, so I knew it wasn't Scar or Ty. Zooming in, I stared at the pixelated image for a few moments. The only identifiable part of her companion was his right arm. I highlighted a section of his wrist and hit the enhance button.

The computer slowed considerably in protest, but eventually, it sharpened the area in question enough that I could make out the design of his cufflink. I knew those cufflinks. Hell, I bought those cufflinks. I clicked through the remaining photos, but Martin wasn't recognizable in any of them. For a moment, I thought about deleting that one photo, but I hesitated. No more secrets.

I fished out my phone and dialed Martin. It was around lunchtime, so there was a good chance he'd have time to chat. We only spoke a few minutes, just long enough for me to ask some questions about Dinah. He might have seen or heard something important, and even though he didn't want to discuss these matters, I convinced him otherwise.

We hung up fifteen minutes later. Apparently, he had

gone to set the same night the flowers were delivered. She had taken him on a tour. She never officially introduced him to anyone, and he didn't recall anybody paying them any particular attention. Afterward, they shared a ride to her hotel during which they discussed matters to which I was not privy. Scar and another man from her protection detail had been inside the limo with them.

Martin never went inside the hotel. He simply went from her car to his, having told his driver where to pick him up. She had given him a hug, supposedly resulting in the makeup transfer to his shirt. The paparazzi hadn't caught that on camera because it happened inside her limo, and he didn't get out of her car until it was parked in the hotel garage. When Dinah stepped out at the front door, the paparazzi swarmed her, as they usually did, and that was it. Martin was never spotted by the camera brigade.

I stared at the photo another moment. Cross's people would realize someone was in the car with Dinah, but they wouldn't be able to ID him from the photo. Deleting it would just draw more attention to it, which I wanted to avoid. Martin didn't seem worried about the photo. The only thing he was concerned about was what I was going to do with the information concerning his arrangement with Dinah. Nothing. It wasn't Cross's business, and it had no bearing on the investigation. It was irrelevant, just like these memory cards.

Deciding I wasn't ready to share them with my colleagues, I phoned the paparazzi I interviewed the previous day. No one had seen Reaper or had any idea where he'd be. He wasn't waiting outside the lot, and he wasn't at the hotel. The annoying buzzing nagged at the corners of my mind, and I went upstairs to update Cross on the situation.

"You have friends at the department," Cross said. "Find out why the cops are looking for him. Discreetly."

"I'll try."

"You are under contract. Nothing is to be divulged under any circumstances. Do I make myself clear? Should you encounter resistance, contact Mr. Almeada. I will notify the defense attorney that he should make himself available to you."

"Sure." I didn't know why Cross thought I needed to have the city's best defense attorney on speed dial, but from previous encounters, it was probably to scare the police into submission.

On my drive to the precinct, I picked up a tray of fancy coffees. Although bribing a police officer was illegal, I couldn't show up empty-handed. That wouldn't be particularly friendly, and I needed someone to be in a friendly mood in order to do me a favor.

I parked the company car in the rear lot where a fleet of police cruisers were waiting. Before going inside, I decided to make one final attempt to find Reaper on my own and dialed his phone number. The voicemail picked up automatically. Obviously, his phone remained off.

Exiting the car, I entertained the possibility Reaper could be Dinah's stalker, but he was a native. Based on his credit card records, he hadn't made any trips to California, and I was operating under the assumption whoever was after Dinah followed her across the country. Plus, he just didn't have the access.

"May I help you?" a rookie officer asked from behind the desk.

"I sure hope so." I hadn't considered exactly how I wanted to play this. "I'm here to see someone in major crimes."

"Do you know who specifically?"

I held back my chuckle. None of the boys upstairs would be pleased to see me, which is why I came bearing gifts. "One of the detectives. If you could just let them know Alex Parker is here with a coffee delivery, someone will buzz me up."

He gave me a funny look but didn't bother to protest. He picked up the phone and dialed the upstairs extension and repeated what I had just told him. If it hadn't been for a recent attack on the police department, I probably could have slipped upstairs without a problem, the way I always had. But things were different now. Hopefully, one day soon the city would be safe enough for the protocols to become laxer.

The rookie hung up the phone. "It'll be just a moment."

By the time he had gotten the words out, Detective Nick O'Connell appeared at my side. He didn't hesitate to select a vanilla latte from the tray. He sipped slowly, eyeing me over the lid, and led me to the stairs.

"Do I even want to know?" O'Connell asked, sounding tired and resigned.

"Can't I just stop by for a visit?" I jiggled the coffee carrier as we went up the steps. "I thought my friends could use a little pick-me-up."

"Uh-huh." He was far from convinced. We pushed through the double doors and made our way to his desk. His partner, Thompson, was stabbing away at his keyboard. "You sure you don't want me to write it up?" O'Connell asked him.

"I got it," Thompson growled. He never looked up from the screen. "What do you want now, Parker?"

"I brought coffee."

"We can get our own coffee," Thompson retorted, but he held out a hand while he continued to type with the other. I put a large coffee with cream and two sugars in his waiting palm. He took a sip, never acknowledging that I remembered his preference.

I glanced around the bullpen. "Is Heathcliff around?"

O'Connell leaned back in his chair and put his arms behind his head. "He just ran down to records. He'll be back in a few minutes." He cocked an intrigued eyebrow. "You planning on asking him for a favor instead?"

"Jealous?" I crossed to another desk and put a cappuccino next to Heathcliff's nearly empty mug.

"Call it hopeful," O'Connell said, but he knew I'd been doing my best to avoid Derek Heathcliff after our last two encounters had caused him a few personal and professional difficulties. "You still working for Cross?"

"Yep."

"Which is why you're here," Thompson muttered.

Nick gave me a look and jerked his chin at an empty chair. I pulled it up to his desk and took a seat. "Talk to me. How are things?"

"Couldn't be better. You can't tell anyone, but I'm consulting on a movie," I said.

"Have you met anyone famous?" Nick asked.

"I can't say. It's all very hush-hush."

He dropped his arms and reached for his latte. "I'll bet. Is Martin freaked out?"

"Why would he be?" I asked, wondering if O'Connell knew something I didn't.

Thompson coughed. "Hall pass."

I turned in my chair to look at him. "What?"

"Shut up," O'Connell said.

Thompson glanced up at his partner and then at me. "I'm sure they must have an understanding. Her boyfriend knows everyone who's anyone. His hall pass probably only involves foreign nationals who are denied access to this country."

"What are you talking about?" I asked again.

Thompson snickered, took another sip, and went back to typing, this time not nearly as angry as before. O'Connell sighed, hoping I'd just get to my point instead of wasting time trying to shoot the shit and pretend this was strictly a social call.

But I was stubborn and refused to give in, so Nick finally said, "A hall pass is a made up list of five celebrities you're allowed to mess around with if the opportunity presents itself."

"You and Jen each have a list?" I asked in disbelief.

"It's something we joke about, but I'm pretty sure if she got one of those pretty boy actors on her list naked in the hospital, she'd take advantage." He gave me a look. "It's just one of those stupid what ifs for fun. It doesn't mean anything for us normal folks. For those of us not involved with millionaires, the likelihood of running into one of the people on the list isn't even remotely possible, so it's something to tease and threaten."

My mind went to thoughts of Martin and Dinah, and I cringed. Nick quirked an eyebrow, but I shook away his question.

"Sure, loads of fun. Sounds like a blast," I said.

Nick took another swallow from his cup and stared at

me. "I need to get back to work, so would you mind telling me why you're really here?"

"The paparazzi have been out in force lately. They wait outside the studio and the hotels. They are a real pain in everyone's ass," I said.

"Yep." Nick continued to stare. "Are they causing problems? We might be able to force them to disperse."

"Actually, I was hoping to speak to one of them in particular. I dropped by to see him, but he wasn't home. His neighbor said the police came by to talk to him."

Nick put the cup down and clicked his mouse a few times until he was on a different screen. "What's his name?"

"Chaz Relper." I spelled it, and O'Connell scanned the details for a moment.

"Let's see," O'Connell's eyes narrowed slightly as he read, "a BOLO's been issued."

"Why?"

"Says here he's wanted for questioning. Apparently, he inflicted property damage, caused an accident, and fled the scene." He read a few more lines. "Officer Mitchell took statements and issued the BOLO. It's his case. You want to know anything more than that, you'll need to ask him."

"Where can I find Mitchell?"

"He's a beat cop," Thompson supplied before O'Connell could respond. "Dispatch should have a twenty."

O'Connell reached for a radio and pressed the button, asking for details. Once he had the information, he was patched through to Mitchell. "I got a lady here wants to buy you lunch. Just say when and where." The staticky response came back, and O'Connell scribbled it down on a sticky note and stuck it to my arm.

I looked down and read the note. "Now I have to buy this guy lunch?"

Nick shrugged. "You said this was a social visit. Go be social."

Thompson kept his eyes on his screen, but he smiled. "Too bad you didn't put Mitchell's name on your hall pass."

"Last time I bring you coffee," I snapped.

"One can only hope," Thompson replied.

O'Connell laughed. "If you want, I can radio back and tell him you're a badge bunny."

I glared at the two of them. "Thanks a lot, boys."

"Don't mention it," Nick insisted, "and next time, don't waste your breath saying this is a social call. We all know you're incapable of such things."

"I am not."

"Fine. Put your money where your mouth is. We're having poker night at my place next Saturday. You're invited, and feel free to bring Martin."

I took my note and headed for the door. "I'll let you know about poker. I'm surprised it's not just for the boys."

"Can't be," Nick retorted. "Jen will be there, and Thompson's dating a girl cop. We have to be inclusive."

"They aren't called girl cops, O'Connell. They're called cops," I said.

He grinned. "So I hear."

TWENTY-FIVE

"Why are you interested in Reaper?" Mitchell asked, the words barely recognizable as he chewed. He slurped his strawberry milkshake and eyed me. "You famous?" His brows scrunched, and he put the cup down, wiping his mouth on his sleeve. "You can't be. O'Connell doesn't know anyone like that."

Aside from introducing myself and paying for his meal, which consisted of two double cheeseburgers, a strawberry milkshake, a side of onion rings, and a cup of chili, the only words I'd uttered to Officer Mitchell were, "What can you tell me about Chaz 'Reaper' Relper." And since then he'd done nothing but talk and eat, mostly at the same time.

When I didn't answer, he looked at me expectantly and reached for an onion ring. "You sure you don't want something to eat?"

"No, I had a big breakfast."

"Suit yourself." He popped the onion ring into his mouth and shoveled a mouthful of chili in after it. "How do you know O'Connell?"

"You might call it a working relationship." Changing the subject now would be best. A career beat cop wouldn't bother giving a private investigator the time of day, even after she spent far too much on his artery-clogging euphoria. "Any leads on Reaper?"

"Not really. I dropped by his place several times this week while I've been out on patrol, but he's never there. We tried calling. No answer. We issued an alert on his car, but we haven't gotten any hits there either." He stopped eating and sat back. His eyes suddenly grew keen, and his body shifted. "How do you know Reaper?"

"I don't."

Mitchell exhaled. "I'm gonna need more than that. You are aware I'm under no obligation to discuss an ongoing case with any outsiders, and quite frankly, I don't know O'Connell well enough to owe him any favors. So what's the deal?"

"I'm in the private sector. He's a paparazzo with a drone. That poses problems for my client." It was vague. He might think I was an agent or manager, a private eye, or in the security biz. The fewer facts I divulged, the better. "O'Connell and the rest of major crimes will vouch for me. I'm not looking to get anyone jammed up. I just want to pin down Reaper's whereabouts."

"You and me both." He picked up the second burger and took a bite.

"Is it out of line to ask what he's accused of doing?"

Mitchell chuckled. "Sure, innocent until proven guilty and all that, but this asshole flies his drone right into this lady's windshield. Broke right through the glass, scared the living bejesus out of her. What the fucker didn't count on was the dashboard cam she had hooked up. She caught the whole thing on camera."

"And you identified Reaper from the footage?"

"Nah," he took another bite, swallowed, and picked at something caught between his teeth, "this putz stuck a label on the front of his drone. *If found, please return.* He put his name, home address, and phone number right on the thing."

"Do you have the drone in evidence?"

He shook his head. "Craziest thing. It breaks through her windshield. She slams on her brakes. Gets rear-ended. The drone is still in flight, busts out her rear window, and flies off. A couple of people who saw the accident caught its departure on their phones. Talk about crazy shit."

"Was anyone hurt?"

"The woman driving got cut up pretty bad when the drone busted through the glass, and the hit from behind was enough to push her into a parked car. It set off her airbags. She has a busted nose, and she's claiming whiplash." He rolled his eyes at that one. "She's out for blood. She wants this Reaper guy dead to rights. I'm thinking she's hoping the criminal charges stick to strengthen her civil claims." He took another bite. "It shouldn't be that big of a deal. This guy should have just come forward at the time. Now he's evading us, which pisses me off. I want to find him. If he doesn't show up soon, we'll probably step up the search and take a more active approach than just knocking every once in a while." He took another sip of his milkshake. "I got a call into the DA's office. We're thinking it might be important to search his place. If nothing else, we need to confiscate that drone before he does more damage. Just imagine if he'd flown that thing into one of the cars on the bridge or in a tunnel during rush-hour. It would take hours to get it sorted and cleared."

His radio squawked, and he turned it up and tilted his head to the side while he listened to the call. After grabbing another quick bite, he wiped his hands on a napkin, pushed the button, and responded that he was on his way.

"I gotta go." He looked at me again. "O'Connell got your info?"

"Yeah."

"If I need something from you, I'll be in touch."

He left in a hurry, and I stared at the few morsels left on his tray. His story didn't give me much to think about. I needed additional details, so I called O'Connell while I cleaned up Mitchell's mess. According to the police report, the accident happened a few blocks from the club the same night Clay booked it for his private party. Based on the 911 call, it happened just after one a.m. From what I recalled, things should have been underway, but it was still early enough in the evening that most of the cast hadn't gone back to the hotel yet.

Pondering if any of this information was relevant, I returned to the office. My first stop was the tech department. Without access to the actual dashboard camera footage, I couldn't say with absolute certainty this drone and Reaper's were the same, but they did find adhesive residue attached to the front from what might have been a label.

"It's a cheap model. No GPS. No way to determine coordinates or location. If it's the same drone the police are looking for, then I can see why the guy who owned it would put a label on it." Amir glanced at the machine. "We're going to dust the tape for prints. It'll be done in sections since we have to unravel it. We might even find some kind of trace or a hair."

"But no photos?"

"Just one. Someone removed the internal memory card. The only image we were able to pull was the last thing the drone captured before it seized." He tapped the spacebar on the closest computer and a fuzzy image popped up. "That blur is the bullet that killed it," Amir said gravely.

"Let me know when you finish the autopsy," I said, finding his sentiment comical.

He snickered. "Will do."

After updating Cross on the situation, I returned to my office and went back to the stalker's profile. I read through my possible suspects, but since everything was speculation, it was hard to make much progress. The actual facts I possessed were few and far between. Maybe Dinah Allen was being stalked by an apparition. At this point, that made just as much sense as anything else.

Reaching for the phone, I dialed Pat the paparazzo. He remembered Reaper leaving the club early that night. Reaper had been there when the celebrities arrived and took several shots as they entered, but he didn't hang around to wait for them to leave.

"I thought he had a hot tip on something else," Pat said.

"Have you seen him since?"

"No."

"Do you remember an accident that night?"

"Can't say that I do." He waited a beat. "Was one of the actors involved in something?"

"Not that I know of."

He didn't believe me. "You said if I cooperated, you'd make it up to me. Why do you care so much what's going on with Reaper? Is he getting sued again?"

Without answering his question, I said, "Do you think the drone that crashed outside the hotel was his?"

"I didn't see him that day, and I don't think he'd just leave a piece of hardware like that on the street. He'd go back and get it."

After thanking him for his time, I hung up and paced my office. When brilliance failed to strike, I grabbed my things and drove back to the club. Reaper had been here. It was the last place anyone remembered seeing him. Maybe I'd find some hint as to where he'd gone.

On the way, I wondered if flying the drone into that woman's windshield had been a test run to see if the safety hammer attachment would break the glass. Perhaps Reaper planned on breaching the club and getting some shots of the party inside. None of his competition would have gotten those snapshots, and based on the items I found in the bathroom, it might have been worth the risk.

He flew the drone away from the scene of the accident, so he must have been close, just not close enough for the freaked out woman or the other driver to have noticed him. I parked in the alley beside the club and looked around. The place was closed. From the outside, it didn't look like much, but I did see a few small windows rather high up. They weren't broken, but if they weren't made of tempered glass, the drone wouldn't have been powerful enough to break the window.

I checked the rest of the alleyway where Scar had waited for Dinah, but I didn't find anything of interest. The front of the club was more exotic than the side of the building with blacked out doors covered in bars. The sign was flashy, and at night, it lit up in bright blues and neon purples. During the day, the nearby shops and buildings did a decent business, so if something obvious was out in the open, it would have been noticed and picked up.

I moved outward from the club, circling and expanding a block at a time. This would have been easier if Officer Mitchell had given me a location for the accident, but he didn't. Based on his age and demeanor, I'd guess he'd already put in his twenty. He was seasoned and not about to share intel with some woman he didn't know, so I was lucky to have gotten as much out of him as I did.

When I failed to determine the location of the accident, I headed back to the club. Since I knew the distance for the remote-controlled drone, I could estimate how far away Reaper must have been. Even though Pat and the others saw him leave, they weren't paying enough attention to their surroundings to be considered reliable. Reaper could have been sitting inside his car, flying his drone, and they wouldn't have noticed. At night, it'd be almost impossible to see the contraption flying through the sky.

I checked the nearby streets for his car. That was another dead end. I checked down a few of the nearby alleyways, but since garbage pick-up hadn't happened in a few days, no one was illegally parked near the overflowing dumpsters. I needed a better strategy.

What if this was just a wild goose chase? We weren't even certain if the drone Scar shot down outside Dinah's window belonged to Chaz Relper. And since Reaper was MIA, we couldn't exactly ask him about it. The fact that he vanished didn't sit well with me. His place didn't appear tossed, but there wasn't anything to toss. Everything of value was out in the open, but the memory cards were missing from his equipment.

Unsure what to do and tired of running in circles, I returned to the office. From what I recalled, Reaper didn't have much in the way of family or friends. Would anyone notice if he disappeared? Was this behavior common for him? I phoned the local hospitals to see if he'd been admitted. The hospitals didn't have any record of him, and I was running out of ideas. Perhaps I should see if anyone filed a missing persons, but I nixed that idea. If Reaper caused the accident, it might explain why he went into hiding, but something told me he wasn't hiding.

My desk phone buzzed, and I picked it up. "Mr. Cross

would like to see you," the assistant said.

A feeling of dread took hold. "What happened?" I asked.

"He's waiting for you upstairs."

"I'm on my way."

His assistant was on the phone but held up a finger, indicating I should wait. I crossed my arms over my chest and resisted the urge to tap my foot impatiently.

"I'll let him know." The assistant hung up the phone and pressed the intercom button. "Lucien, the details on the phone call will be forwarded to your e-mail momentarily, and Miss Parker is here."

"Send her in," came Cross's disembodied voice.

The assistant looked up. "You heard the man."

I opened the door and stepped inside, pulling it closed behind me. "You summoned."

"Have a seat."

That was never good, but I did as I was told. Lucien clicked his mouse a few times and glared at the computer screen. "Last night's call came from a courtesy phone in the hotel gym. It's a twenty-four hour gym. The keycard used to gain access was Dinah Allen's room key."

"That's not possible. Dinah was with me."

Cross gave me an incredulous look. "Obviously, her stalker gained access to her belongings. I've contacted Mr. Scaratilli. We need to determine how this happened."

"What about security footage?"

Cross hit a button, projecting his screen onto the large monitor against the wall. A slight figure dressed in baggy sweats and a hoodie entered the gym. The hood remained up, concealing his face. He never looked at the cameras. He went to the phone, attached something to the handset, and dialed a lengthy number. "We're assuming that's a voice modulator."

"Good guess," I replied giving him the same look he gave me.

"Still, it's a start."

After the call concluded, the unsub went into the attached locker room. No cameras were inside for obvious reasons. However, he never came out. Based on what I knew of the hotel, the locker room also led to the showers which had another exit to the outdoor pool.

"We need to know who went out through the pool," I said.

"Cameras were misaligned. Whoever did this planned it out carefully."

"Dammit," I hissed, staring at the frozen image on Cross's screen. "Who the hell is this guy?"

TWENTY-SIX

My phone rang, and I blindly hit answer while my eyes remained glued to the camera footage from the hotel. For the life of me, I couldn't figure out who was beneath the hoodie. The person wasn't built like a refrigerator, so that definitely ruled out Scar and the rest of Dinah's security team, who all resembled football players. The baggy sweats concealed everything about his build. The guy could have lean, sinewy muscles like Lance and Clay, or he could be soft with a tiny potbelly, like the director. Cross had the techs working on precise details, but we put the person in the hoodie in the ballpark of 5'9". Lance was roughly three inches taller, but I didn't think it was enough to completely rule him out.

"Hello?" I asked while I pulled up the profile on Reaper. According to his license, he was 5'9" and weighed 155 pounds, which fit perfectly with the image but not my theory. Most of the men in Dinah's life had the wrong physique, except for Bernardo Nykle, the designer. He was a slight man, but he didn't have access to the set, and according to Cross, Nykle was in Europe when the prop dummy had been left. Something was wrong, either with the footage or the profile. Whoever this guy was, he had used Dinah's room key to access the gym. Scar had sent over a list of people who had come and gone, but no one stuck out.

"I'd like an order of General Tso's chicken, fried rice, not steamed, beef and broccoli with a side order of spring rolls, extra duck sauce, and an order of moo goo gai pan and won ton soup, extra dumplings."

Confused, I wondered why Det. O'Connell was calling me with his takeout order. "Did you dial the wrong number, Nick?"

"No, but since you're on your way to the precinct, I thought you wouldn't mind picking up dinner." Someone said something in the background. "Oh, and a platter of spare ribs. They're supposed to be an appetizer, but if you ask for a platter, not the pu pu platter, but just a platter, they make it into a meal. You are going to Dynasty House on Seventh, right?"

I blinked a few times. "Don't they deliver?"

"Yes, but it's always cold by the time it gets here."

"I'll fetch your dinner on one condition."

"What's that?" Nick asked.

"Tell me why I should schlep all the way back to the precinct."

"We found Chaz Relper."

"Good answer."

O'Connell was waiting on the stairs when I arrived. He took the bags and poked his head into one of them. "You didn't get anything for yourself?" he asked as he led the way upstairs. I shook my head, and he eyed me with that all-knowing detective look of his. "Martin's ruined you." At his desk, he divvied up the orders and rummaged through his drawer for some plastic silverware.

"Not to be a pain, but can't that wait?" I asked.

"Relper's not going anywhere, and I don't want this to get cold. That's why I asked you to deliver it, remember?" He went into the breakroom to get a paper plate, and I trailed behind him.

"Do you want to tell me what's really going on?" I asked.

He glanced out the door into the bullpen. "After your luncheon with Officer Mitchell, he decided to do a bit more investigating. He got the watch commander to sign off, and he took a squad of newbies to the scene of the accident to perform a canvass. They found Reaper behind a dumpster."

"Hiding?" I asked, even though I knew it was a stupid thing to say.

"Homicide took over. Mitchell's pissed. He wasted days trying to find this guy, and as soon as he did, someone else swoops in to work the case. He isn't too happy about it, so he blabbed about you to the detective who caught the case. Apparently, you would have been Mitchell's prime suspect."

"Where is he now?"

"Mitchell? He's out on patrol, looking for Relper's vehicle." O'Connell looked guilty. "Homicide wants to talk to you. They were prepared to barge into your office and ask questions, but I volunteered to save them a trip and the wrath of Lucien Cross."

I glared daggers. "Wasn't that nice of you?"

"Look, Parker, it's nothing personal. You and I are good. We always will be. But you work for Cross, and that causes the department problems. Cross doesn't share intel. He doesn't play ball. He sends us the clowns in Tom Ford who tell us to back off or risk seven figure lawsuits. A man is dead, and we don't have time for this shit."

"We really don't." My thoughts went to the phone call last night. "Do we know the cause or TOD?" A part of me almost hoped Reaper had been the stalker and Scar eliminated him. At least that would mean Dinah was safe, even if she was employing a killer.

"ME has him on the table now. We'll know more once they finish processing the evidence and get him opened up. Preliminary reports suggest blunt force trauma." O'Connell brushed past me and back to his desk. "Jacobs," he called to the detective who just came up the steps, "take Parker to see our friends in homicide."

Jacobs offered a tight smile. We'd worked together a couple of times. The last time was during my final case at the OIO. We were comfortable enough with one another that he didn't feel the need to chitchat. He led me through the doors to homicide and straight to an office in the far corner of the bullpen. After a quick introduction, he excused himself and went back to work.

It took less than two minutes to reach an impasse. I wasn't willing or able to divulge the precise reason why I wanted to find Relper, and unlike my friends in major crimes, the homicide detective wasn't nearly as lenient. His opinion of me was already jaded by whatever unkind remarks Mitchell had made, and to think, I bought that prick lunch and watched him gobble it down.

"Let's try this another way. What do you know about Chaz Relper?" the homicide detective asked.

"His friends call him Reaper. Now that just seems like it's in poor taste." I tapped my fingers impatiently on my thighs. "He's a paparazzo. He owns a drone. Did you happen to find it?"

The detective's stare grew even harder. "No."

"What about his camera equipment? It's my understanding he wouldn't go anywhere without it."

"How well did you know Mr. Relper?"

"I didn't."

"But you expect me to believe it's just a coincidence you asked about him the same day we found him dead?"

"No. My asking is what caused Officer Mitchell to double-down on his search. You probably wouldn't have found Reaper if it wasn't for me." I narrowed my eyes. "Where exactly did you find him?"

He leaned back in the chair and steepled his fingers while he scrutinized me. "Why are you sniffing around?"

"I might have heard rumors he was wanted for questioning."

The homicide detective didn't say anything, but his attention went to the screen in front of him. For a moment, he did nothing but watch. Then he hit pause. "You went to a club in the middle of the afternoon. Any particular reason why? Did someone tell you to go there?"

I blew out a breath. "This conversation isn't helping either of us. By now, you've had time to run my background. You know who I am and what I do. If I had anything solid on who killed Reaper, I'd tell you. Until ten minutes ago, I didn't know he was dead. We both know he had enemies. Powerful people don't like their dirty laundry sold to trashy websites, and in his line of work, competition is cutthroat. Unless you tell me more, all I can do is speculate at this point. Maybe it was a mugging gone wrong. I don't know," I assessed him carefully, "and I don't think you do either."

"What kind of powerful people?"

"Take your pick. It could be the royal family for all I know."

"Are you hoping to spend a night in a cell?"

"You can't charge me with anything because I haven't done anything."

"I could probably book you for obstruction."

"And I could call Mr. Almeada and have him assist me in answering your questions, but neither of us wants that." Name dropping was normally Martin's schtick, but Cross slipped an ace up my sleeve, so I might as well use it. "This doesn't need to be unpleasant. What I can tell you is I'm consulting on a stalking case. I don't know who the stalker is. For all I know, it might be our buddy Chaz, or Chaz might have taken a few snapshots the stalker didn't appreciate. It's hard to say for certain."

"Who's being stalked?"

"That's privileged."

"Has your client filed a report?"

"Not locally."

"Nothing indicates Relper's left the city in the last year and a half, so if I'm reading this situation correctly, the stalker you're chasing might have just crossed the line to murder. You need to give me everything you have."

"I can't. I'm sorry." I stood. "Listen, I understand you have rules and regs to follow. And I can't offer much in terms of sharing or a quid pro quo, but once we ID the stalker, I will turn that information over to you."

"Even if the stalker isn't the killer?"

"It's not my job to find a killer, Detective. My job is to identify a stalker. If that person is one and the same, then so be it. It's your job to figure it out and prove it. Not mine."

He climbed to his feet and stuck his hand out. "Thanks for coming down, Miss Parker. You can see yourself out."

I shook his hand and placed a copy of my business card on his desk. I wasn't sure what to make of this.

TWENTY-SEVEN

Several hours later, I received an e-mail from an address I didn't recognize. It contained copies of the police and coroner's reports. Reaper's cause of death was widespread blunt force trauma. Based on the contusions and bruise patterns, he'd been hit by an SUV. The ME estimated it happened roughly thirty-six hours ago. A broken camera was found underneath the dumpster, but according to the evidence report, it didn't contain a memory card.

The paparazzo must have caught the stalker on film and died because of it. For a moment, I tried to imagine what Reaper could have seen that would have provoked someone to kill him. Reaper must have been out flying his drone the night Clay hosted the party at the club. The stalker must have been there. He probably stole the memory card and drone.

I scanned through the rest of the inventory. Reaper's wallet and credit cards were still in his pocket. He didn't have any cash, but I had a feeling the paparazzo already spent it or used it as a bribe. The police never found his cell phone, but since Reaper had professional-grade equipment for capturing the money shots, I doubted there would be anything useful on his phone anyway. His car was still missing. Strangely enough, the cops didn't find any keys with the body, not even his apartment keys. In some ways, the murder did look like a mugging gone wrong, but why leave the wallet and credit cards?

As I made my way to Lucien's office, I thought about the things that were taken. Dinah's stalker got sloppy and got caught near the club, so he killed the paparazzo who could have identified him in order to protect his identity. That made everything more dangerous. I swallowed, fearing what the stalker would do next. The call last night was ballsy. If the police were closing in, the stalker would have to act soon or risk permanently losing access to Dinah.

After I updated Cross on the situation, my boss picked up the phone and asked for an update on the progress made identifying the caller from last night. We knew the call came from the courtesy phone in the gym, and the exterior cameras didn't catch a glimpse of the stalker leaving.

"I'm working on an alternative solution," Cross said. "Maybe one of the paparazzi noticed something. I've offered a reward to the first one who turns over valuable information."

"Any takers?"

"Not yet."

"Do you think Dinah's security team might know more than they're letting on?"

"I'm not sure. Scaratilli might be keeping key facts to himself in order to address the issue on his own. He knows everyone who had access to Dinah's room and her room key, and he has yet to provide any valuable leads."

"How do you think he would address the issue?"

Lucien stared me right in the eye. "Are you afraid our investigation might lead to murder?"

"It already has."

"You know what I mean." I didn't answer, and his wary gaze lingered a moment longer. Finally, he said, "After Dinah is finished filming for the day, I will be meeting with her and her team to address her security concerns. She can't remain at your apartment indefinitely."

"I agree."

"The best way to get rid of your unwanted houseguest is to figure out who's obsessed with her."

*   *   *

"I've arranged new lodgings for Miss Allen," Scar said. The four of us were in Cross's office. "We checked in under a new alias. The credit card on file is my personal card. Nothing will trace back to Miss Allen or the studio. I booked an entire block of rooms. We have the floor to ourselves. I even checked the windows in the suite. It's safe."

Dinah sighed dramatically and focused on me. "Did you discover anything new since this morning?"

"A few things," I said, hoping Cross would intervene.

"Out with it," Dinah insisted.

"We believe your stalker was present at the club the night you were chased up the steps. We're getting closer," Cross said.

Scar narrowed his eyes. "Was he inside the club?"

"That is yet to be determined," Cross said.

"But he was there," Scar retorted. "He followed us back to the hotel and waited for an opportunity to get Dinah alone. Fucking A." She shivered, and he put his hand on her forearm. "I'm sorry. I shouldn't have left you unprotected."

"It's not your fault. I insisted. I was in one of my moods." She grasped his hand. "You know better than to argue when I'm like that." Taking a deep breath, she remembered where she was and abruptly stiffened. She removed her hand from atop his and straightened her blouse. He retracted his hand immediately and circled the room, placing some distance between them. That made their exchange even more obvious. "What do you think he wants, Lucien? Do you think he's dangerous? Last night, he threatened me, threatened the people close to me."

"I won't let anything happen to you," Scar interjected.

Cross did his best to be diplomatic. "We should assume he's dangerous. He's spiraling. His actions are becoming erratic, desperate. It's best that you stay with Scar. With any luck, we'll identify the stalker before he locates you a second time."

"He won't," Scar insisted.

"No," I interjected, "he will, but we'll make it as difficult as possible. Don't go directly from the studio to your hotel. Don't tell anyone on the set where you're staying."

"I can't do that," Dinah said.

Scar looked at me. "We'll be selective."

Cross licked his lips. "We know whoever's responsible had access to Dinah's hotel room. Allowing the same people access to her new location is asking for trouble."

"I'm aware," Scar replied.

Cross had dealt with these situations often enough that he knew better than to waste his breath. His clients would do whatever they pleased. "We'll find this asshole, Miss Allen. You have my word."

"Thank you, Lucien." She offered him a smile. "I'd like Alex to accompany me to the hotel and check for any possible security issues." She already sensed Scar's protest and quickly added, "It wouldn't hurt to have a second set of eyes review the measures in place."

"Of course," Cross said. "Whatever you need. I'd be happy to send one of my security teams to assist your detail."

"That won't be necessary," Scar said, and Dinah agreed. "We should get going."

I trailed after Dinah and Scar as we exited Cross's office, picking up Ty on the way to the elevator. In the garage, a third member of her security detail joined us. Unlike our previous encounters, Dinah's limo was parked beneath the building to avoid unnecessary attention. Scar's eyes scanned the area, but aside from a few business types who worked in the building, no one lingered.

Scar held the rear door open, and Dinah slipped inside. After the door was closed, he told Ty to make sure to stay close and keep an eye out for follow vehicles. "Are you riding with us?" Scar asked.

"I'll take my car, not the company car. We don't need to draw any unnecessary attention. I'll follow a few car lengths back and make sure no one's nearby." I already knew the destination. "I might need someone to meet me in the hotel elevator so I can gain access to your floor. I assume you chose an executive suite that requires keycard access."

"You assumed correctly. Not even authorized personnel will be able to get to Dinah without my say so." He gave me a look, glad that Dinah couldn't hear our exchange. "No disrespect, but I have this under control."

"I'm sure you do."

He climbed into the front of the limo beside Dennis, the driver. Ty shot me a friendly smile and hurried off to the dark SUV waiting for him. Perhaps if they didn't want to draw unnecessary attention, they shouldn't parade around town in a limousine. A town car would be much more subdued, but Scar had it under control. What the hell did I know?

No one followed the limo or the SUV. Honestly, I didn't think that was the stalker's style. Still, the twitchy feeling lingered in the back of my mind. The stalker was at the club. The stalker killed Reaper a block from the club, probably stole the man's drone, his car, and his house keys. After dialing O'Connell, I put it on speaker and tucked the phone in my cup holder.

"Is anyone sitting on Chaz Relper's place?" I asked.

"Parker, he's dead. That was the entire reason I had you come down here. Did you forget?"

"Answer the damn question."

"No. Homicide sent a team to check the place out. Not much there, except a giant mess."

"Did anyone talk to the little old lady who lives next door?"

"Why do I get the feeling you know more than you do?"

"Regardless, I don't know enough, but the killer took Reaper's keys and could have gotten his address off his license. I bet he stopped by to make sure he'd never been caught before and maybe to grab some things while he was there." I nearly told Nick the killer would have wanted photos of Dinah, but I remembered the contract and shut up.

"Nice theory. I'll run it by homicide. Any chance you

noticed some surveillance cameras around Relper's apartment building that might make this easier?"

"They don't exist."

The limo and SUV pulled into the hotel parking lot. Dinah's driver ignored the valet stand and entered the garage. A few spaces were reserved near the elevator so Dinah could go from the car to her floor without any chance encounters. The SUV parked behind it, and I checked my mirrors again to make sure we were alone. Unlike the others, I stopped at the valet stand and put the car in park.

"I have to jump off here. Homicide didn't seem fond of the idea of exchanging favors, so the way I see it, you owe me for dinner. Let me know what they find." I disconnected just as he began to voice a protest.

"Ma'am," the valet said as I handed him my keys, "are you checking in? Do you have any bags?"

"Just visiting." I buttoned my jacket to make sure my shoulder holster remained concealed and entered the lobby.

I'd been here before when I was evaluating security at a conference and again as a guest when Martin and I were trying to figure things out. From what I recalled, the room service prices were steep and the bed was squishy. Hopefully, Dinah wouldn't have the same complaints.

Casually, I circled through the lobby. The front desk was busy, but the staff was attentive. I continued past the decorative fountain and indoor garden display and made my way to the bar. It was like most upscale hotel bars, full of expensive furniture, top-shelf liquor, and businessmen. The group near the back I pegged as lawyers, sitting in leather club chairs and drinking. The rowdier group with the roaming eyes near the picturesque view were either stock traders or investment bankers. I wasn't positive since they tended to attract the same personality types. Several women were seated together at the high-tops, drinking martinis. They wore expensive clothing, but everything about them was understated. They didn't want to stick out or draw extra attention to themselves. Probably corporate bigwigs. The few possible working girls seated at the bar were high-end escorts. They knew how to keep secrets and keep off the hotel's radar, or I was jaded and they were lawyers or doctors just out for a night of fun. In a place like this, it was hard to tell the difference.

No one stuck out. No one sat alone in the corner drinking or watching people. If Dinah's stalker knew about her relocation, he wasn't staked out in the bar. I circled around and went out the way I came in. Luckily, it had been crowded enough that no one questioned me or tried to buy me a drink. After that, I double-checked all the side doors and entrances. Every one of them required a keycard for entry, and each had a security camera posted above. Based on my quick check, everything looked good.

When I felt as confident as possible, I checked the stairs. No one was hiding out. In fact, no one was in the stairwell. I ducked back into the lobby and pressed the button for the elevator. When it opened, I punched in the floor several below Dinah's, exited, checked the stairs again, and went up to her level. Even the stairwell door to the executive floor required keycard access. You could leave without a keycard, but you couldn't enter.

For all intents and purposes, no one should be able to get to Dinah Allen without the hotel's permission or hers. The problem was I didn't necessarily trust Dinah's judgment, and I wasn't sure how trustworthy the hotel employees were. Maybe the night manager had a sick kid with lots of medical bills piling up. Or maybe the housekeeper wanted to remodel her bathroom and needed some extra cash. There were always weaknesses and loopholes, and I was certain if the stalker located Dinah again, he'd figure out a way to get to her, even if it meant rappelling down from the roof.

Fishing out my phone, I dialed Scar. "I checked out the place. It looks good. I'm three floors below you, outside the elevator. Mind letting me join you so I can finish my evaluation?"

"Ty's on his way." Scar clicked off.

Four minutes later, the elevator arrived. Two people got off, offering apologetic smiles as they brushed past me. The car was empty, so I continued to linger while I waited. They went down the hall to their room, pulling their rolling luggage behind them. The elevator returned a minute later, and Ty was inside.

"Get lost?" he teased.

"I wish." When we were alone, I asked if he noticed anything strange. He said no, but I knew he wouldn't say otherwise. Still, I had to try. "Who knows where Dinah is right now?" I asked.

"The security team and your people." He shrugged. "I'm not sure about anyone else."

"What about Dinah's manager and agent and masseuse?"

He fought to stifle his chuckle. "Honestly, I have no idea. You'll have to ask her. Miss Allen has a habit of doing things without informing us. If she told someone about her relocation, she might have neglected to mention it."

That was the last thing I wanted to hear. "Great."

"Don't worry so much. It's nothing we can't handle." His confident assurance was the kind of attitude I had when I was his age. It was blissful ignorance. If shit happened, he'd feel like a dumbass for ever being so naïve and stupid. Truthfully, I hoped he'd never have that kind of epiphany.

"Dinah," I could hear Scar's growl before we even made it inside her suite, "we discussed this. That compromises everything. We should relocate again."

Ty slid the keycard into the slot and pushed the door open. Dinah and Scar both turned at the sound. Scar's hand lingered just above his weapon, but he didn't draw. Dinah let out a sigh of relief and beelined for me.

"Alex, tell him he's being unreasonable."

"What happened?" I asked.

She rolled her eyes and waved her hand in the air like he was the most infuriating man on the planet. "I have matters to which I must attend. I've been in talks for the past week on a lucrative venture, but Scar thinks it's a mistake."

"She just told someone where she's staying," Scar snapped. "The only way this hotel is secure is if no outsider knows about it. Didn't you listen to a word we said in Cross's office?"

She didn't even look at him. "It's fine. Really." She implored me to take her side, but she saw the expression on my face. "No, really, it is. I only gave out the information to one other person, and you vetted him."

"Who?"

"James Martin."

TWENTY-EIGHT

I was hallucinating. There was no other explanation for the name that just passed through her lips. I was mental. A nutcase. I should probably have the men with the white coats and butterfly nets come and take me away.

"Why?" I asked.

She shook away the question and made her way through the suite. The drapes were drawn, and Scar made it abundantly clear that wasn't to change. Due to the drone attack, Dinah readily agreed and dropped onto the couch and glanced back at Ty who was standing uncertainly in front of the closed door awaiting Scar's orders to evacuate the suite and move to a tertiary location.

"Ty, sweetie, would you mind pouring a whiskey sour?"

Scar gave a barely perceptible nod to Ty before grabbing my elbow and dragging me out the door. "Is it true?"

"Is what true?" I asked bewildered, my heart racing for some inexplicable reason.

"That you vetted this Martin guy? Does he pose a danger? Is he going to broadcast this meeting of theirs to the world?"

"He isn't a danger, but this is a bad idea. You have to talk her out of it."

Scar snorted. "Less than twenty-four hours ago, some shithead calls and threatens her. She should have gotten on a plane first thing this morning and went home. Instead, she told her agent about it when she arrived on set. By lunch, Cherise had put the perfect spin on the situation in order to get Dinah to go along with this hairbrained idea."

"What idea?" Scar's tone and derisiveness filled me with dread.

"Cherise decided Dinah would be an excellent role model for women reclaiming their power. I heard her discussing book options and interviews to schedule after the press junket for the film runs its course."

"Wait a minute. Dinah told me she didn't want to be the victim."

"The wind's changed. By the time her current project wraps, goes through post, and the press tour finishes, we're talking at least a year from now. This hiccup won't even be a blip on the film's radar. It will be a story in and of itself, and Dinah will be able to control the narrative. Plus, it'll give her time to write a book on these experiences and use the movie as a springboard to greenlight future projects."

I felt woozy. "You should know," my mouth went dry, and I swallowed, "one of the paparazzi was found dead outside the club. He's been there for days. I bet Dinah's stalker did him in."

He stared at me, not finding this detail at all surprising. "I know."

"How?" Reaper was killed by an SUV, like the one Scar's security team drove.

His brow furrowed in confusion. "Cross told me." His gaze went to the suite door. "Miss Allen doesn't know, and I don't want to worry her."

"Maybe she should know. Then she would take more precautions."

"She's doing her best. It's my job to worry about security issues. I told her I'd find a way to keep her safe, and I will. I just don't want potential threats traipsing onto this floor and into her suite. I'll ask you one more time, does James Martin pose a threat?"

"No." Obviously, naïveté was running rampant through

the security team. "But who knows about the next person Dinah invites over. You better show me what measures you have in place, and we'll take it from there. It looks like, from here on out, we're in this together."

He pressed the button on his earpiece and requested someone else guard the outer door to Dinah's suite. As soon as a second guard was on duty, Scar took me on a tour of the floor, showing me what he had set up. One of the other suites connected to Dinah's, which would allow for an easier escape and two-way access should a breach occur. The other suite on the floor was full of surveillance equipment. They stuck pinhole cameras on the stairs, near the elevator, and throughout the hallway. No one would get to Dinah without security noticing.

"I spoke to the hotel. Maid service has been suspended. They will be given the all-clear only after Dinah has left the building, and we will sweep for bugs after the maid finishes. Room service orders will be called in from a room I reserved on the floor below, and one of the members of my team will bring them up after the bellhop leaves. No hotel employee has access to Miss Allen."

"Show me the room you have downstairs," I insisted.

We went down a floor. It was just a regular room with two double beds. Nothing special about it. A few duffel bags were tossed in the corner, and I gave him an odd look.

"The team will be using this to sleep. We will be six on and two off until the stalker is identified. We're rotating shifts on a six hour basis."

"What about Dinah's people?" I asked. "Who knows she's here?"

"Cherise knows, and so does her assistant. Elodie has to bring the sides and scripts over at the end of the night, so Dinah can prepare for the next day. But Elodie is legally bound to keep those facts to herself." Scar didn't sound pleased. "I tried to convince Dinah otherwise, but she wouldn't know how to navigate the set or be prepared for the day without Elodie. It was a necessity."

"She's the client. She gets what she wants."

He scoffed, muttering under his breath, "More like what her manager wants."

With little else to do, I returned to Dinah's suite. The newest guard, who I didn't recognize, opened the door without a word, and Scar and I went inside. Dinah was sipping her cocktail and absently flipping through the channels. She looked up when we entered, and for a moment, I saw the fear. If I told her it wasn't safe, she'd most likely pack up and follow me home again.

"What's the verdict?" she asked, the mask slipping into place.

"Alex didn't find any issues," Scar said. He looked at her for a moment, acknowledging the tension between them. "I suppose your impromptu meeting will be acceptable, but he'll need to be searched before he's permitted to enter. And I want to remain present while he's here."

"Fine." Dinah stared at him, and Scar practically bowed and went out the door, leaving me in the lion's den. "I know what you're going to say. To be honest, I'm not sure how I went from utterly freaked out and ready to call it quits to this." She yawned and finished her drink. "I'm worn out. Maybe I'm just too tired to care."

"That happens," I said, perching on the chair across from her. "What happened on set today?"

"Nothing. We shot a few scenes. Neil didn't like the way Kurt's choreography looked on yesterday's dailies, so most of today was reshoots. Since it was a showdown between Clay and Lance, I spent most of my time in the trailer. My personal trainer came, and we did an hour of yoga. I thought I could use the time to re-center myself."

"Did anyone mention anything about last night's call?"

"No one knows, and whoever does is too smart or scared to confront me in person. I just don't understand. Last night, this whack job threatened me, and today, it's like nothing happened. If you hadn't been around to hear the phone call, I might have thought I dreamt the entire thing. It doesn't make sense. Is this how stalkers normally behave?"

"I don't know. This isn't my area of expertise. Generally speaking, stalkers want to isolate the object of their fixation. It's about control and domination."

"But the notes and the call don't make the stalker sound

strong. They make him sound weak and desperate," Dinah said, "like he's obsessed with getting close to me." The light bulb went on, and her mouth formed an oh. "The call made me come here. Could that be part of his plan?"

It was something I hadn't considered. The point of the call was to get Dinah to tell him where she was, and when she didn't, he called her security detail in the hopes of convincing Scar to force Dinah back to the hotel. I had my own ah-ha moment. "I need to make a few calls."

"You're on to something."

"I don't know yet."

"Well, when you do know, I want to hear how I helped you crack this case wide open." She blinked. "That is what you'd say, right?"

"Yes."

She looked proud of herself. "Cool."

Taking my phone, I ducked into one of the other rooms and called the office. Whoever the stalker was, he knew enough to contact Scar. The number of people who had access to her security chief's phone number and Dinah's room key couldn't be that extensive.

I requested someone get started on analyzing Scar's phone records. I should have realized it sooner. Dinah's stalker called the security chief after calling her which meant the stalker had to be in a position to know key details about Dinah's routine. Hell, he might have even known about the quasi-relationship between Scar and Dinah. It could make Scar a target, albeit an unlikely one.

It took nearly an hour to get the details sorted. The entire thing would have been easier if I was in the office doing it myself, but instead, I was babysitting again. Just to be thorough, Cross was going to obtain phone records for every member of Dinah's security team. There was the possibility the stalker had called before without the voice modulator and under the guise of whatever his normal role in Dinah's life was. The one thing I was certain of by the time I hung up was Dinah's stalker was regularly present. He knew her routine. He knew the people in her life, and he knew precisely what strings to pull.

"Hey, Dinah," I said, opening the bedroom door and

stepping back into the main room, "I'm going to need a list of everyone you encountered today. Actually, you should do that for the entire week."

"You can start with him," Dinah said, smiling. My attention went to Martin who was seated in the chair I had vacated. "This is James Martin."

"Alex?" he asked, clearly surprised to see me in Dinah's suite.

"You two know each other?" she asked.

"We're acquainted," I supplied before Martin opened his mouth.

Martin gave me a funny look. "You could say that."

"How?" Dinah asked.

"Actually, I wanted to talk to you about that," Martin began, but I gave him a sharp look.

"He hired me as a security consultant," I said, communicating with my eyes that he need not elaborate further.

"Oh." Dinah sounded disappointed. Then she said, "*Oh,*" like that tidbit was the missing piece of some puzzle. She turned to him and gripped his forearm excitedly. "You must have stories."

"No, he doesn't," I supplied.

Martin grinned like the cat that swallowed the canary, his eyes never leaving mine. "I'd love to stay and regale you with tales of Alex's heroics and wicked deductive skills, but I actually have several overseas calls to make. I'll have the contract drafted tomorrow and messengered over in the afternoon. Is that acceptable."

"Of course, it is, Jamie," she replied.

The nickname made me bristle, and I turned around and pretended to take great interest in reading the instructions for the in-room coffeemaker. The only other person who I'd ever heard call him Jamie was his ex-fiancée.

"I am truly sorry. I wish I had known sooner or realized what was happening. I would have done something to stop it, but it all happened so fast. She really was the best. It would have been her year. I'm glad you reached out when you did. Christian was planning to auction it off as his own," Dinah said sadly.

"I know." A dark cloud came over Martin, and he stood. His eyes fell, and he shoved his hands into his pockets. I saw the heartbreak and failure in the way his face contorted, and I could hear it in the way his voice dropped "That was nearly fifteen years ago, and it's taken me this long to track it down. If it wasn't for you," his eyebrow twitched, and the joint in his jaw jumped, "it might have been another fifteen years." He looked up, hiding the anger that burned in his green eyes like the showman he was. "It really was lovely to see you again, Dinah. I appreciate all you've done. This means the world to me." He gave her a polite kiss on the cheek.

"I hate that you have to run off. Promise we'll get together again for an entirely social engagement before I leave town. Shooting wraps at the end of the month. We'll have plenty to celebrate by then."

"Sure." He winked at her and strode to the door, moving close enough that his fingers brushed against mine. "I'll see you later, Alex." My eyes searched his for a moment, silently asking if he was okay. He nodded and ducked out of the room.

I went back to the coffeemaker, and Dinah let out a knowing hum behind me. "What was that about?" I asked, turning to see her sprawled out on the couch, her manicured nails tapping a rhythm on the backrest. "Business or pleasure?"

She let out a soft laugh. "For now, business."

Deciding to play with fire, I dug a little deeper. "Is he the guy you were texting the other night? The one that made you smile?"

"That depends."

"On what?" I asked.

Before she could answer, an alarm blared and a white flashing light filled the room. "What the hell is that?"

"The fire alarm," I replied.

This was precisely why I should keep my mouth shut; my question set off the damn alarm. I didn't smell smoke, but I didn't believe this was a coincidence. My mind raced through the possibilities. Dinah's stalker didn't like her interactions with men, and Martin was one hundred percent male. Shit. Was the stalker escalating again?

"Shouldn't we evacuate?" Dinah asked.

Scar swallowed. "There isn't any smoke. The sprinklers haven't turned on. I think someone pulled the alarm intentionally. We should assess the situation before we take action." He pressed the button on his radio and sent two members of his team to investigate.

"I'll go check it out," I declared, running for the door.

"Phone us when you know something," he called after me.

Like Scar, I had a feeling this was another elaborate attempt by the stalker to lure Dinah out into the open, but my priority wasn't on saving the client. It was on saving the man I loved.

TWENTY-NINE

Martin left two minutes ago. He couldn't have gotten far, but he wasn't waiting in the hallway for the elevator. Dammit, the car must have already been stopped on this level from when he arrived. I raced down the stairs, which were quickly filling with people evacuating the building per the broadcasting instructions. I did my best to go around them, but I gave up and burst through the door on one of the floors below. A group waited for the elevator to return, and when it did, I climbed into the packed car and rode to the lobby. This was taking too long. Impatiently, I dialed Martin's number, but he didn't answer. Service was spotty inside the metal box. I needed a better carrier.

What if the psycho was outside with a gun trained on Martin? The stalker made it clear he didn't like the men in Dinah's life. That probably meant all the men. They were his competition.

The doors opened, and I pushed my way through the crowd and out the door. Most of the guests were being herded to safety across the street. Jogging past the hotel staff who tried to corral me away from the building, I darted to the side, hitting speed dial as I ran. Pick up, pick up, the words looped through my mind.

"Sweetheart," Martin said, and I sighed in relief, "what's going on?"

"Where are you?"

"Outside. The alarm went off when I was in the elevator. The staff forced me outside. Is everything okay?"

"Get to your car. I'll meet you."

Martin's town car had bullet-resistant glass, and with any luck, his bodyguard would be waiting inside with his driver. Like they said, there was safety in numbers.

Spotting the town car, I sprinted to it and climbed inside. Without a word, I put my arms around Martin and kissed him. "Listen, I don't have much time." My eyes went to the exterior security cameras. Cross would inevitably watch the footage. And being in Martin's car would be next to impossible to explain, but at the moment, I didn't care. "Dinah's stalker killed someone a few days ago. We just found out about it. Last night, he called and threatened her." My gaze briefly drifted to the evacuating hotel. "I can't believe this is a coincidence. I want you to stay at our place. I want Bruiser with you at all times. Stay away from the windows and keep the drapes drawn. This guy's crazy. I don't know what he'll do. I don't know what you and Dinah are involved in, but you need to stay away from her until this thing is settled."

"Is she okay?"

"I'll keep her safe."

"That's not what I meant."

"It's okay," I insisted. "I just need you out of here and away from this. Whatever business you have, do it through an intermediary."

He shook off my instructions, as he so often did. "What about you? I don't want you running into a burning building or going toe to toe with a psychopath."

"For once, being a woman has its perks. I'm not a threat. He won't target me."

"How can you be sure?"

"I just am." I opened the car door. "I have to go. Get the hell out of here and stay safe. I'll get home as soon as I can, but it might be an all-nighter. Don't worry about me, just watch your back." I leaned toward the front seat and gave

Marcal, his driver, instructions on how to navigate around the mess.

I closed the car door and headed back into the thick of things. Halfway to the front door, I turned and watched the town car disappear from sight. After I was positive Martin wasn't being followed, I forced my way back inside the lobby, despite the protests and pushy hotel staff.

The hotel manager was at the front desk on the phone. I went up to her. "I work private security for one of your guests. What's going on?"

She looked exasperated. For a moment, I thought she was going to have me removed, but at this point, she had so much to deal with that I was the least of her problems. "Someone was smoking in the restrooms. It started a trash can fire which set off the smoke detector. One of the staff put it out with an extinguisher, but it's protocol to evacuate the entire building until the fire department gives the all-clear."

"I'm going to need copies of your security footage."

"Are you insane?" she asked. "Who the hell do you think you are?"

"I appreciate your position, but in a few minutes, a guy that does a mean impression of a refrigerator is going to come down here and ask the same thing. I'm not sure what kind of mojo he's going to work, but you might agree to his demands. If not, my boss will be down here, and quite frankly, he's just a pain in everyone's ass."

"First off, don't try to intimidate me. And second, you need to wait outside with everyone else until the fire department says it's safe to come back inside." She signaled to hotel security who hovered around me. The guard knew better than to touch me, but he herded me toward the exit.

Giving up, I went out the front door. The first call I made was to Scar. After alerting him to the situation and the likelihood the fire department or hotel staff might try to force them to evacuate, I hung up and dialed Lucien. He would get access to the footage one way or another.

In the meantime, I had a job to do. Dinah's stalker was here. He had to be. I just wasn't sure if he was hiding somewhere inside the hotel or if he was out here with the crowd. I sent a quick text to Scar since I couldn't exactly do a sweep of the hotel floor by floor to see if the stalker was inside. His team was already on it. The bastard probably hoped to corner Dinah in the chaos, if his plan wasn't to knife Martin in the back. If Scar's team was half as good as they claimed, they might be able to sniff him out. If he wasn't inside, that meant he was out here. Waiting. If he was here, I'd find him.

Skirting the edge of the crowd, I scanned for familiar faces. The hotel guests were clustered into small groups, talking amongst themselves. A few were angry. Most were nervous or scared. The bar-goers had dispersed once the hotel evacuated. The group of women headed down the street toward another watering hole, and I looked around but didn't see any of the lawyers or investment bankers in the throng, not that I suspected any of them.

Movement at the periphery caught my eye, and I saw a dark shadow disappear around the corner. Dashing down the street, I turned and saw a figure in a dark hoodie walking along the sidewalk. It was hard to tell from the back, but the build was a close approximation to the person who placed the call the previous night.

"Excuse me," I yelled, hoping to catch up to him. "Sir, wait."

At the sound of my voice, the figure broke into a run. The man ran into a public parking garage, and I pursued him. Chasing suspects into parking garages always resulted in injury, usually mine. I slowed my pace and reached for my weapon.

He clicked the remote on his keys, and headlights flashed on a green SUV. He jumped behind the wheel and gunned it. The tires squealed as he shifted into drive from reverse. He drove right at me. I dove out of the way, rolling and coming up in a crouch with my gun raised. I didn't fire. Instead, I tried to read the license plate before the SUV vanished into traffic. I only got a partial plate, but it would have to be enough.

On the trek back to the hotel, I called O'Connell. "Tell Mr. Homicide Detective I have a lead on Relper's killer.

Some bastard just tried to mow me down with his SUV." I gave him the plate number, a description of the vehicle, and what little I could discern about the driver.

"I'll pass this along and get it to dispatch. We'll pick up his trail," O'Connell promised. "Thanks."

"Remember this the next time I ask for a favor."

After checking the garage for any clues as to who this guy was or how long he might have been waiting, I headed back to the hotel. A fire truck was parked at the main entrance. The lights were on, but the siren was off. The guests were still waiting across the street for the go-ahead to return inside.

The announcement came over the PA system that it was safe to enter. The hotel was comping the guests a free breakfast for the inconvenience. I hung back and called Scar to tell him to expect incoming. I wasn't sure exactly how they managed to remain inside, but it might have involved a bribe or hiding in the room.

After the last of the guests went through the front door, I made my way into the lobby. I wasn't surprised to spot Scar at the front desk. Ty was with him, and they were speaking to the manager.

Scar noticed me and excused himself. He asked for a detailed account of what I knew. I had a feeling it would be another long night and told him about the man who escaped in the SUV.

After listening to my description of the man and the vehicle, Scar scratched his cheek. "That sounds like Dinah's stalker. How did he find her so quickly? I've taken every precaution." Leading the way upstairs, Scar showed me into the security suite. He had photographs of everyone working on the film. "You saw him. You have to identify him."

It was pointless to protest, so I flipped through the photos, stopping on an image of Lance's assistant. "He was built like this guy, but I didn't get a good look at his face, just that he had dark hair."

Dinah opened the adjoining door. She put her hands on her hips and remained in the doorway. "Well, now what do we do? I don't see how changing hotels again is a great plan, and even when I stayed with Alex, he still found a way to harass me. I want this stopped."

"We're working on it, Miss Allen," Scar replied. "He didn't breach this level, and he didn't catch a glimpse of you during the evacuation. I think it's best if you remain here."

"What do you think, Alex?" Dinah asked.

"It's up to you ma'am." It wasn't what she wanted to hear, but I didn't have a solution.

"You don't think James Martin is behind this, do you?" she asked. It was the first thing Scar had asked me.

"No, I don't, but you need to realize whoever you invite into your life could be targeted."

"What about Elodie? She's on her way with tomorrow's sides. Should I call her off? I need her. I can't do this without her."

"We'll ensure Miss Smith's safety," Scar promised. "We'll let you know when she arrives."

Dinah went back into her suite and closed the door. Scar and I continued to work through leads and theories, but he didn't know anything more than Cross Security. When Elodie arrived, Ty met her in the lobby and brought her to the security suite.

"Miss Smith," I said, gesturing to the chair, "we haven't gotten a chance to speak. I was hoping to ask you a few questions. You are aware of Dinah's situation."

Scar had separated the photos to include only individuals who fit the profile and description of the caller and the man I saw earlier this evening. "Have you seen any of these men paying particular attention to Dinah? Do you know if any of them had access to her hotel suite?"

Slowly, she flipped through the photos. Her face flushed, and she looked up with fear in her eyes. "Is this my fault?"

"Why?" Scar asked. "What did you do?" His voice was harsh, and she cringed and cowered. I gave him a sharp look and took a seat next to her.

"It's okay. You're not in any trouble. Just tell us what you know." I looked at the photo. It was of Jett Trevino, Lance's assistant.

"I let him into Dinah's suite a few days ago. He's Lance's PA. We hang out sometimes. All of us do. Other PAs get it, but regular people just don't. Our jobs are crazy. It's hard to make friends or have a life outside of work." She looked sheepish. "Not to say that I don't love my job because I do. I really do. It's just lonely sometimes."

"Does Jett own a dark jacket and jeans?" Scar asked.

"With a hood," I added.

She shrugged. "I don't know. I guess. He had on one of those waterproof slickers earlier today. They have hoods, right?"

I hadn't considered him in the list of potential stalkers, but that's because I'd never seen him interact with Dinah. "Do you know how long he's worked for Lance?"

"A couple of years. He went to college to be a director. He took all these film classes and was working on some indie projects in the hopes of getting noticed, but he never had any luck. He knew some people who got him hired on as a production assistant on one of Lance's other films. Lance liked him enough to hire him on as his personal assistant. He uses Jett on all of his movies."

"You seem to know a lot about him."

"And Carrie, Johnny, Vince, Louisa, and Bonnie," she said. "Like I said, we all hang out after work."

"Have any of the other stars been targeted?" I asked.

She thought for a moment. "As far as I know, it's just Dinah. No one's said anything."

"Have you said anything to them?" Scar asked.

She blushed and looked away. "You don't think Jett or one of the others is involved, do you? They would never do anything like that. We each have skin in the game. We wouldn't jeopardize our future careers over something stupid." She gasped. "Is Dinah going to fire me? Jett wasn't in her room that long. He was with me when I dropped off some things for Dinah. We weren't even there two minutes. I know he's had to sign NDAs for Lance too, so I didn't think it'd be a problem. Shit. Don't tell her what I did. I'm not sure how those things even work, and I can't afford to lose this job or get sued. I'm just biding my time and making contacts while I work on my screenplay."

"No one's getting fired," Scar said, "but I need to know if you've told anyone where Dinah is staying."

Elodie blinked a few times, shaking her head. Even though she denied it, I had a feeling she probably shared that information with her fellow PAs, believing it was no big deal. It was a very big deal, particularly if one of them was the stalker.

THIRTY

Until today, we never had enough information. Now, it seemed like we had too much. Not that such a thing was possible, but it would take a lot of time to sort through. My neck hurt from the crooked way I had my head propped in my hand as I read through phone records, police reports, and suspect profiles. Amir pulled some prints off the tape on the drone which matched Chaz Relper. At least we knew for certain we had the right drone; too bad it didn't lead us anywhere.

It appeared Jett Trevino had, on one prior occasion, placed a call to Mario Scaratilli. That call happened during Dinah and Lance's trip to Maui. Based on Trevino's credit card information, he remained behind in Los Angeles. Perhaps he had taken a liking to his boss's girlfriend. That liking turned into obsession, breaking and entering, and stalking, with a side of homicide.

According to the DOT, Trevino was five foot eight, a hundred and fifty-five pounds, and drove a white pick-up truck. However, upon arrival here, he rented a blue SUV. I thought the SUV that nearly drove over me was green, but with nothing but streetlights to provide illumination, I could have gotten it wrong. Or it might have been teal. For some reason, the rental agency refused to give me the plate number, so I was stuck waiting for the cops to find the car and driver. If they didn't find him tonight, I'd check the parked cars at the studio in the morning.

Jett could have started the fire, freaked when he spotted me, and took off. Since Lance wasn't staying at this new hotel, Jett had no excuse to be there. He was spotted, so he had to flee. Apparently, that was the stalker's M.O. Starting the fire was daring. I just wondered about the timing. My initial gut reaction, which might have been an overreaction, was the stalker saw Martin, recognized him from his previous meeting with Dinah, freaked out, and set the fire to get Martin away from her. I just didn't know what he planned to do afterward. Kill Martin? Lure Dinah out and abduct her? Kill them both? I didn't know the answer to that, but I was great at jumping to worst case scenarios.

"It'll be another few hours before my guy can get the hotel footage. I spoke to the manager, but she doesn't want to cooperate," Cross said as he entered my office. "We should have considered the assistants and set helpers sooner. It's always the ones we don't notice. Tomorrow, while they're filming, we'll search the entire lot, but the studio's adamant about its privacy. I don't want to piss them off, so we're going to do it quietly." He dropped into one of my chairs. "Dammit, why didn't we consider Jett sooner? He fits the profile."

"We ran backgrounds on Dinah's team, but the men came up clean. We never thought to look into Lance's guys because it never made sense they'd have the type of access needed to know these things about Dinah or get her keycard."

"Yeah, but Lance does. And the assistants have access to everything Lance does." Cross flipped through some of the paperwork. "I feel good about this one." He pointed to a photo of Jett. "Have you noticed him around?"

"Just on set with Lance."

"I sent his photo to the club owner. Jett was partying with the rest of them. That places him in the area around the time Reaper was killed. After he tied up that loose end, he could have gone back to the hotel and waited for Dinah. Since Lance was club-hopping, he wouldn't have had any idea what his assistant was up to."

"We know how he might have been able to get a hold of Dinah's keycard in order to get into the hotel gym. But why wouldn't he have just used his own or Lance's?"

"He's smarter than that." Cross thought for a moment. "You called the police. They have cause to bring him in for questioning after he nearly ran you over. Once that happens, we'll convince them to look a little deeper, and then we'll be certain."

"Sounds easy enough." I narrowed my eyes. "I thought you didn't believe in working with the police."

"They have their talents. I have mine. Overlap is not something I enjoy, which is why I never take murder cases. Unfortunately, the stalking issue was unforeseeable. Had I known, I might not have signed the contract with Broadway Films, but I did. And here we are. I'm just glad you're here to liaise between the police department and my firm."

"I should get a raise."

"Or maybe I should fire you, seeing as how I never had these problems before you started working here."

I quirked an eyebrow. "Go ahead."

We stared at each other in a game of chicken, but I wasn't backing down. Plus, I was seventy-five percent sure Cross was joking. Eventually, he blinked. "You should call it a night. We'll have a lot more data to sift through in the morning. I told Renner to tail Lance Smoke until he gets eyes on Jett Trevino. Right now, we don't know where they are, but Smoke's appearance always causes a buzz. We'll track him and find Trevino. If Jett makes another attempt, at least we'll know about it before it happens. Get some sleep. You look like shit."

At least Cross had a plan. It was more than what I could say for myself. I grabbed a few files off my desk and made my way home. The one thing I had that Cross didn't was access to a possible witness.

When I opened the door to the apartment, I heard a gun being cocked. "Exciting night?" I asked.

Bruiser put the safety back on and returned the gun to its holster. "Only for the last two seconds."

I smiled and put the files on the kitchen counter. "That's sweet of you to say." I looked around but didn't spot Martin. "Where is he?"

"In the bedroom, on the phone. From what I gather, it's not going well."

"What's going on?"

"I don't know, and it's not my business."

"I ought to make that my motto." I checked the locks, poked my head behind the curtain, and stared into the dark night. When I failed to spot a drone or sniper, I slid out from behind the curtain. "Were you with him when he met with Dinah Allen?"

"Both times I waited in the car."

I grabbed the files off the counter and sat down next to him. "Would you mind looking through some photographs to see if you remember spotting any of these people? It's strictly off the record. I know you were probably told not to mention anything about the visits and I've been told not to discuss these matters with anyone, but you and I can't follow those instructions and do our job."

"Our job?" he asked. "You mean protecting Mr. Martin?"

"Shh." My gaze bounced around, but the door to the bedroom remained closed. "Our mission is top-secret, Mr. Jones. He must never find out."

Bruiser laughed. "How very cloak and dagger of you. And here I thought you forgot my name." He flipped through the photographs of what I had deemed to be our suspect list. "Isn't he a famous action star?"

"Uh-huh."

"Well, I didn't see him." He flipped through the photos of the director, stunt coordinator, and the DOT photos I pulled of Dinah's team. "I saw these guys." He pointed to photos of Scar and one of the other guards. He flipped through a few more images, slowing on the one of Jett. "Maybe him, but I'm not sure."

"Tonight?" I asked.

"No. I didn't see anyone tonight. That was from last time."

"What was the game plan tonight?"

"Martin got dropped off at the front entrance, and Marcal and I circled the block a few times while we waited for him to finish. I didn't see anyone." An angry growl came from behind the bedroom door. "Does this have anything to do with whatever's going on in there?" Bruiser asked.

"I have no idea." I closed the folder. "I probably should find out. You can call it a night, but I'd appreciate it if you were waiting in the lobby for him in the morning. If you happen to spot anyone suspicious, let me know."

"Good night, Parker."

I locked the door behind him. Then I knocked on the bedroom door before opening it. Martin was pacing back and forth in front of the bed. One hand was rubbing the back of his neck while the other held the phone to his ear. He barely glanced in my direction.

"I don't care about the ramifications. It doesn't matter." Whoever he was speaking to was arguing and interrupting. "Don't get started on that bullshit. It was her intellectual property. It should have never been sold." He dropped the hand from the back of his neck and rubbed his eyes. "I understand that. I don't know what I'm planning to do with it. I just want it back. I want the rights." Another annoying interruption caused Martin's fist to clench, and I wasn't positive he wouldn't put a hole through the wall. "No, I don't want to sue. In that industry, it's next to impossible to win those types of cases. You're my fucking lawyer. You should know that." He let out an exasperated huff. "If I were concerned about sound investments, I would be talking to my accountant instead."

"I can go," I whispered, pointing at the door.

Martin shook his head. "Listen. No, you listen." He walked out of the room, realizing we were alone so he had the rest of the apartment in which to pace and argue.

So much for asking him about Jett Trevino and Dinah Allen. I listened to the sound of his angry, annoyed voice, but the words didn't quite carry. It was clear he didn't want me to hear what he was discussing. I remembered the look on his face right before he left Dinah's suite. I didn't know what they were talking about or what this was about, but it was clearly a bone of contention for Martin.

Reluctantly, I ducked into the bathroom to shower and get ready for bed. Maybe he'd be off the phone and in a better mood by the time I came out. After drying my hair, I came out of the bathroom in a pair of pajama shorts and a slouchy tank top. At least I didn't hear any arguing.

I found Martin leaning over his laptop. He had a glass of scotch next to him and the bottle beside it. It was one of those nights.

"Are you okay?" I asked.

He glanced up. "Huh? Oh, yeah. Fine." Before I could say anything else, the phone rang, and he grabbed it. "Is it done?" he snapped.

We needed to talk about his business with Dinah and if he'd seen Jett or anyone else, but now wasn't the time. I went to the kitchen and plucked the notepad off the fridge. Leaving him a note, I separated the photos from my files and took the rest of the paperwork and placed it in a box and tucked it into the bottom of the linen closet. I just needed him to identify the men he'd seen around Dinah.

I gave him a concerned look which he didn't notice on account of his furious mouse clicking. "I'm going to bed," I said. "I left something for you on the counter, if you get a chance later."

After he acknowledged he heard what I said, I left the room. It was obvious he didn't want the company or an audience. Truthfully, he probably didn't even want to be here, but he was here for me. The least I could do was give him space. I had never been very good at figuring out what was wrong, particularly when it came to him, or how to fix it. But right now, I wanted nothing more than to fix whatever was going on. He was angry, and for no reason I could understand. In Dinah's hotel room, I'd seen it flash over him. The hate. The contempt. I had no idea what she had been talking about or why it triggered that response, but it had only gotten worse in the last few hours.

Closing my eyes, I listened to the slam of drawers and his deep voice berating and arguing with whoever was on the other end of the line. The only thing I could do was get this stalker situation with Dinah wrapped up in the hopes that it would somehow make his arrangement with Dinah easier. My last thought before drifting off was that he shouldn't have an arrangement with Dinah, but I had no right to dictate terms on things I didn't understand.

The vibration of my phone woke me, and I squinted at the time. It was 2:30. Renner had located Lance and Jett. The star and his lackey were at one of the premiere nightclubs. From the photo he texted, Lance's leftovers would be easy pickings for Jett, so why the infatuation with Dinah? It was pointless to try to get into the mind of a psychopath.

I put my phone down and looked at the spot next to me. Martin never came to bed. After listening for the sound of his voice, I decided to see if he was still here. At this point, I wouldn't put it past him to sneak out in the middle of the night again.

With the exception of the table lamp, the lights were off. He was seated sideways on the couch with my files strewn in front of him. The closet door was open, and I couldn't help but feel his actions were a total invasion of my trust and privacy. He'd made a sizable dent in the bottle of scotch, but he didn't appear inebriated. His green eyes looked sharp as he sorted through the paperwork. His anger and irritation had been replaced by a quiet brooding.

"What the hell are you doing?" I asked, realizing he was searching for something.

"Didn't you pull Dinah's phone records?"

"Yes."

"Where are they? What did you do with them?" It sounded like an accusation.

I wasn't used to that tone. "Why?"

His eyes found mine. "I need to see something."

"They're at the office."

"Oh." He examined each piece of paper before placing it back in the folder, as if I might be lying. "Could you get them?"

"Now?"

"No, tomorrow. Bring them home with you, okay?"

An uneasy feeling settled in the pit of my stomach. In all the time I'd known Martin, I had never been suspicious of him. But something was going on, and I wasn't sure how much longer I could ignore it. He said it was business. That he couldn't talk about it. But he was snooping through my files in the middle of the night. That wasn't normal.

"Why do you want to see them?" When he didn't answer immediately, I nudged him. "Hey, talk to me."

"I'm looking for a number. It's not a big deal."

"It sure as hell seems like one." I crossed the room and picked up the stack of glossy photographs. "Did you look through these yet?"

"Yep." He put my files back in the box and crossed to the kitchenette. "This stack I've met. These I haven't."

One of the piles contained all the men on Dinah's security team, her personal trainer, stylist, Kurt, Neil, Lance, and Jett. I snorted. Martin had gone to the lot. Of course, he saw them.

"Did you see any of them earlier tonight?"

He glanced up at me. "You know who I saw. That guy Scar, Ty, and that other one." He pointed at a third member of the detail. "You were there."

"But not this guy?" I held up the photograph of Jett.

"No." He wrapped his arms around my waist, oblivious to the fact I was miffed about his snooping. "What happened tonight at the hotel? You told me someone was killed and the killer is stalking Dinah. Why would you think he'd target me?"

"You've been hanging around Dinah a lot."

"I've met with her twice. Briefly. It doesn't make sense I'd be a target. Are you positive you're not in any danger?"

"No more than usual. Honestly, you're scaring me, James. You have to tell me what is going on."

The use of his first name hit my point home. He scooted closer, and I turned to face him. He was practically trembling, and I put a hand against his chest, feeling his heart racing beneath my palm. I didn't know what was going on, but for the briefest moment, I was terrified of what he was going to say.

He must have seen the fear in my eyes because his thumb stroked over my cheek, and he offered a calming smile. "This has nothing to do with you or your case. It has everything to do with Dinah and our shared history."

"Why did seeing her today upset you?"

"Seeing Dinah didn't upset me. The situation did."

"Me being there?"

"No, sweetheart. I wanted to tell her precisely who you are to me and get her damn stipulations removed, but you didn't want me to say anything. Maybe if we tell her, she won't care if you know what's going on, and then I can tell you everything and clean up the mess I've made."

"It's not a good idea to broadcast our relationship, particularly under these circumstances." We were getting sidetracked from the issue. "So what set you off? Should I be worried that you ordered a hit on whoever you were talking to on the phone?"

"Damn, now you know why I was looking for a phone number," he teased, continuing to skirt around the issue, but I didn't give up that easily. "It's complicated. She has contacts, connections, that I require."

Even though I didn't understand the intricacies, I already figured that's why he wanted access to her phone records. Before I could ask for an elaboration, my phone rang. "Now what?" I grabbed it off the counter, expecting a call from Renner. Instead, it was the precinct. Officers brought in the driver of the green SUV. They picked him up on his way home from work, and he had a very different version of events. The arresting officer wanted me to come down for questioning. Didn't anyone sleep anymore? "I have to go."

"Is everything okay?"

"Sure."

He released me. "I'm going to get some sleep. I'll see you later. Don't forget the phone records."

THIRTY-ONE

The man who I spotted outside the hotel, who I chased into the parking garage, and who almost ran me over with his SUV, was not Jett Trevino. In fact, he had no ties or connections to Broadway Films or Dinah Allen. He wasn't involved. He hadn't even been at the hotel when the fire alarm went off. He was just some guy who went to grab a quick bite.

According to what he told the officer, he was at one of the nearby restaurants where his roommate was a cook. He ate in the kitchen with the staff, several of whom had already verified his alibi. On his way back to his car, he realized someone was following him. He claimed to have felt threatened. I'm not sure the officer believed it, but the guy said he thought I was a mugger or carjacker. So he ran to his car and drove away. He would have called the police, but he was on his way to work and didn't have time.

His SUV was indeed green, not blue. He was just a local who worked at a bar across town. He'd been slinging beers during Dinah's club foray, and he'd been at work at the time the stalker made the threatening phone call. Since he couldn't be across town at a bar and inside the hotel gym at the same time, I knew he wasn't our guy.

When the police first brought him in, he wanted to press charges against me, but the officer talked him out of it. If he pressed charges, I would press charges, and it would all come out in the wash. Instead, we called it a draw. I promised to stay away from him and not sneak up on people, and he promised not to run over the next person he thought was trying to jack his SUV.

By the time the situation was sorted, it was nearly five a.m. Bennett Renner remained on Jett's tail. As of his latest social media update, Lance, Jett, and several women were cruising around town in the back of the limo. They even stopped to take some creepy selfies at a cemetery. Hollywood really was full of weirdos. From a few of the other posted photos, it appeared Lance didn't have a destination in mind, and I wasn't positive I wanted to know what he and his entourage were doing in the chauffeured car. On the plus side, they were far away from Dinah.

Once I was free to go, I let myself into my office and looked around. Dinah's call logs were in my drawer. Martin had no right to ask me to do this. It was a breach of professional ethics, even if I wasn't entirely sure private eyes had any ethical guidelines. But I did. Why couldn't he just ask her for the number?

I skimmed through the list again. Every other call was to or from Elodie. The next most frequent number was her agent, followed closely by her manager. Martin was the fourth most frequent caller, at least over the course of the last two and a half weeks. I went down the list, but no one stuck out. Jett never phoned, but a few calls came from Lance. I needed to get to the lot and check out the SUVs. Whoever killed Reaper had to be a member of the production team, and everything pointed to Jett. We just had to prove it.

It was early, but a few of the grips and stagehands were already hard at work, readying the backlot. Since Cross Security was in charge, the guards on duty allowed me access to anything and everything. Broadway Films was a different story. They didn't want anyone poking around, particularly since it might jeopardize their film or an actor's credibility, but as far as I was concerned, murder trumped everything else. If we didn't stop Dinah's stalker soon, the death toll would rise. It was just a matter of time.

I surveyed the rows of vehicles. A third of the lot was already filled, and since Jett was riding around town with Lance, there was a decent chance his rental might still be here. I grabbed the flashlight out of my trunk, made sure I had an extra magazine in my jacket pocket, and began at one end of the lot. As I walked up and down, checking for damage, more people arrived.

Hitting the radio, I requested to be informed when Lance and his entourage showed up. The last thing we needed to do was spook the stalker. On a set like this, he might feel the need to act, and someone could get hurt. I finished examining the final row of vehicles, finding no signs of recent accidents. I thoroughly checked the two blue SUVs, but I didn't know if either belonged to Jett. Another thought shot through my brain; what if he wasn't our guy?

Jett Trevino had no criminal history. No one ever filed any official complaints against him. For all intents and purposes, he was clean. His student loans were in the hundreds of thousands, and he put up with a lot of shit from Lance and the studio for the opportunity to be here. If he was willing to deal with that on a daily basis, why risk it all over a twisted obsession? Jett had the access, the opportunity, and fit the physical description, but something didn't fit. Maybe I was wrong. Obsession was an overpowering force that could make a man do anything.

After requesting someone keep an eye on the incoming cars for any signs of front-end damage, I set off for the trailers. It was time someone did some digging. The trailers were considered private property, and Cross Security had been forbidden from entering or searching them. It was one of the first things Lucien had wanted to do after the Dinah dummy was planted, but the studio said no. Their legal team had been up in arms, particularly when they feared the actors' individual representatives would sue the studio. Cross might have wanted to look around, but he deferred to the studio's wishes on the matter, believing it was more important to keep the client happy. I had no such qualms, but it would still be best not to get caught. Lance Smoke was vindictive enough to press charges and have me arrested for B&E, and given who he was, even my friends in the department wouldn't be able to sweep it under the rug.

Glancing around, I waited for one of Gemma's assistants to finish prepping her trailer and head for the soundstage before I approached Lance's trailer. Slipping my lock picks out of my back pocket, I set to work. A few seconds later, I pushed the door open, knocking as I entered.

"Hello?" I called out. No one answered, so I closed the door behind me.

I didn't flip on the lights for fear it might attract attention, so I used my flashlight to look around. The fridge was filled with expensive, imported water. Lance had a video game system and large-screen TV with a fancy massage chair in the main room. In the corner was a weight bench and assorted free weights. He also had a punching bag and jump rope. The bedroom had enough lube and condoms to make me think he was personally responsible for soaring stock prices.

"Eww, gross." I slammed a drawer shut when I found a large collection of women's underwear. Maybe Lance had a fetish or liked to cross-dress, but more than likely, those were trophies from his conquests. I cringed and checked the closet and the tiny desk.

I found a phone number and several receipts for flower deliveries. I wrote down the number and the order details and snuck out of the trailer. I closed the door behind me and went down the three steps. I was halfway to Dinah's trailer when the front gate alerted me to Lance's arrival. Not a moment too soon, I thought.

I continued to Dinah's trailer and let myself inside using my lock picks. The overwhelming scent of flowery perfume filled my nostrils, and I practically gagged. I knew that smell. Martin said it was Samantha's perfume, but that was a lie. Hitting the light switch, I took a step back at the sight in front of me. The entire trailer was filled with flowers. Purplish, nearly black, roses that stunk to high heaven.

Who the hell did this? Carefully, I took another step

back. I had inadvertently stumbled into what might be a crime scene. I had to make sure not to contaminate the evidence. I went outside, scanning the doorframe and the exterior of the trailer for signs of who might have been here. The pavement and metal steps didn't allow for shoe impressions, and no footprints were visible. The door didn't appear to be tampered with. I had just picked the lock, and even that was undetectable.

I wore my hair in a braid, but I tucked it into the back of my jacket anyway. Then I donned a pair of gloves, wishing I had a breathing apparatus before venturing back into the trailer. Roses were among the most fragrant flowers. Aside from allergies, the smell occasionally made me nauseous. It was probably a psychosomatic response, a residual effect from one too many funerals.

After taking a deep breath, I cautiously entered the trailer. The flowers were in vases. There had to be over a hundred in the tiny trailer, making the air practically unbreathable. I scanned the various vases for an attached card but didn't see one. My head pounded, and the room started to spin. My stomach churned, but I pushed forward. I stumbled into the bedroom, finding even more flowers. A quick glance into the bathroom assured me the trailer was empty. Whoever did this was gone.

When could this have even happened? I exited the trailer. My eyes felt puffy and had started to water. It wasn't even six a.m., but it was going to be a bitch of a day. I hit the radio, relaying what I'd found. Then I dialed Lucien and left an update on his voicemail. I closed the door to the trailer and headed for the front gate. I made it to the dumpster before I heaved, hoping we wouldn't need to search it later for evidence.

"Alex?" a concerned voice asked. "Hangover?" A hand held out a tissue, and I took it and wiped my mouth.

When I pulled my head out of the dumpster, I looked up at Elodie. "Not quite. Have you been inside Dinah's trailer today?"

"I was going to head that way after I got everything together. I just have to stop in at the writers' room to make sure they didn't change anything since last night, and then

I was going to stop at crafty and have them get to work on her breakfast." She quirked an eyebrow. "Is something wrong?"

"Just stay away from the trailer."

Elodie put her hands on her hips and stared down at me. "You can't tell me that. I work for Dinah. I have responsibilities, duties, that I can't neglect."

"I know." I sighed. "Dinah received another flower delivery. Security is on its way to investigate. Until then, no one goes in or out."

"More flowers?"

"Yeah."

"Shit." She sniffed in my direction, probably catching a whiff. "How many more flowers?"

"A lot. You can probably smell them on me." I couldn't smell anything but those terrible things. Most women liked the smell of flowers. Early in our relationship, Martin would regularly send bouquets. I always kept them segregated in the corner. Eventually, he realized I hated them and stopped sending them, replacing his gifts with silk flowers, if the occasion required flowers, or wine and other treats. "Excuse me." I stepped past her and went to speak to the two members of the Cross Security team who were making their way through the parked trailers.

"Parker," one of them said, glancing at the trailer, "when did this happen?"

"You tell me. You were keeping watch. Do we have surveillance footage?"

"I already have people working on it," he said while the other security guard went to the trailer and checked for signs of a break-in. "Did you go inside?"

I told him what I saw. "Have you contacted Dinah Allen's security chief?"

"He's been notified. We're to seal off the area until he and Cross have a chance to confer."

I turned around to make sure Elodie wasn't planning on rushing the trailer, but she had wandered off in the direction of the soundstage. "Dinah's assistant was adamant about having everything ready for Dinah's arrival, but I told her the trailer was off limits. However, I wouldn't put it past her to try to clear the place out. Make sure she stays away."

"Dinah's assistant? Tall, black hair in a pixie cut?"

"That's her," I said.

"She just came through security, not even five minutes ago. She's a sweet kid. Brings us snacks from craft services whenever she has to run errands. I'm sure she won't cause problems."

I gave him a skeptical look. Maybe I was just in a bitchy mood. "Here's the thing," I narrowed my eyes, my thoughts racing, "there are over a hundred flowers inside the trailer. It would have taken time to get them inside. Someone had to carry them in. With the way the trailers are situated, a car or delivery van couldn't pull up to the door. It could get close but not close enough. Only golf carts are small enough to zip between the trailers. You had to have seen something."

The guard exhaled. "Do you see that?" he pointed to the backlot. "Workers have been here all night moving those sets around. They couldn't get the pieces in through the front because it was too narrow, so they had to open up the side gate where the fence slides. Our view's been obstructed most of the night."

"Son of a bitch." Anyone could have bypassed the gate. I wondered if his head was next on Cross's chopping block. "I need a list of everyone who left set and returned during Dinah's absence, and I need it now." With any luck, the stalker might have gone out the front even if he snuck in through the side.

We jogged back to the front gate. By the time Cross and Scar arrived, I had several leads. The flowers in the trailer were Black Bacarra roses. Only a handful of local florists had that variety available, one of which was the florist Lance had used for his orders. They told me they had received several orders in the last day for that particular flower, but not in the quantities needed. After a few more calls, I realized several shops had filled orders for dozens of the roses. The flowers had been paid cash on delivery. The store owners offered to put me in touch with their delivery drivers as soon as they showed up to work. That was a start. Once we had a description of the buyer, we'd know exactly who was behind this. In the meantime, the shop owners gave me the delivery address. Every shop had sent the bouquets to the cemetery, which didn't exactly arouse suspicion, but didn't anyone have any sense of etiquette? Weren't black flowers and death a little too on the nose?

Shaking it off, I finished checking the list of people who'd left after Dinah or returned sometime during the course of the night or early this morning. Lance left set after Dinah but just returned. Jett, on the other hand, had come and gone several times before finally hooking up with Lance at the club. He could have brought the flowers in bouquet by bouquet. Maybe that's why they stopped at the cemetery.

THIRTY-TWO

"Stick with Dinah for a bit," Cross insisted. "Let's see if we can make this bastard nervous. Once they start filming, I'll have Lancaster keep on him. I'll make a few calls and have someone get you a keycard to Jett's hotel room. I want you to head over there and look around. Don't get caught."

"No problem." Okay, it might have been a problem, but that wasn't an option.

"After that, meet with the delivery drivers face to face. I'll head to the cemetery and see what I can find. Let me know the moment you find something."

"Copy that."

Cross glanced at Scar. "I can spare a few guys."

"We have it covered."

"Okay. You should be aware, when we identify this psycho, I'm turning him over to the police. They're already investigating a homicide. Stalking is a step down, but they'll be pleased to have a suspect." Cross focused on me. "If they call you with an update, I want to know about it," he narrowed his eyes, "but don't run your mouth to them until I say so. Is that clear?"

"Crystal." I didn't like being treated like a toddler, but Cross always liked to micromanage and make his commands known. There was no second-guessing with my boss when it came to six-figure contracts. I focused on Scar. "Where's Dinah now?"

"I left her in the makeup trailer with Ty and Raoul. She's protected."

"A little extra firepower can't hurt."

Cross nodded, and I headed across the lot. After acknowledging her security detail, I entered the trailer. The smell of hair products was a welcome relief to the floral hell from earlier. I watched as the makeup artist applied a set of fake lashes that looked real even at this distance. Someone else was working on Dinah's hair, trimming the split ends and making sure her highlights hadn't grown out.

Folding my arms over my chest, I felt the bunch of my jacket at my back, and I put my hands on my hips instead. Normally, I kept my gun in a shoulder holster at my side, but I tucked it at the small of my back so it wouldn't be as noticeable. I'd been granted access to carry on set, but I didn't want anyone to know it, particularly since I had no idea what Dinah's stalker would do next.

Elodie dashed into the trailer and handed Dinah the script and took a seat in the chair beside her. The two spoke at length about the shooting schedule. Dinah told her what she wanted to eat for lunch and when she planned to take her breaks. After making a few notes, Elodie settled farther into the chair and the two ran lines until Gemma entered.

"Are you ready for me?" Gemma asked.

Elodie politely apologized and surrendered the chair. "Miss Parker," Elodie edged into the back corner of the trailer, hoping to be unobtrusive, "Mr. Scaratilli wanted me to tell you Dinah's trailer has been cleared. He'd like a word before you leave for the day."

"Thanks."

She gave me a final glance in case I had any requests. The radio on her hip hissed, and she pushed the button and spoke to another PA as she pulled the door closed behind her. As far as I could tell, flowers or not, it was just another day on set.

For the next twenty minutes, a stylist covered Dinah's

head in assorted rollers. It looked painful and antiquated, but it didn't phase Dinah in the least. After she exchanged a few words with Gemma, she closed her eyes and fell asleep while the experts transformed her into an on-screen beauty.

The trailer door banged open, and Dinah jumped, scaring the hairstylist. My eyes zeroed in on Jett, Lance, and some girl who hung off the celebrity's arm as if she'd been surgically attached. Lance wore dark sunglasses and smelled of spirits. From the way he and the woman stumbled inside, I wasn't sure either of them was sober.

Lance flopped into the empty seat on the other side of Dinah, and I took a protective step closer. The girl on his arm knelt on the ground beside him, never letting go of him. I took another step closer, my eyes on Jett who had been rapidly clicking buttons on his phone ever since they entered. He looked nervous, and I wondered if he knew we were on to him.

"Mr. Smoke," I said, my tone hard as nails, "did you have a busy night?"

The girl giggled. She was wispy and blonde with bubblegum pink lips. From the way she acted, I suspected her bra size far outmatched her IQ. "Busy," she stage-whispered, bursting into a fit of giggles.

He slid his sunglasses down his nose and looked at me. "Feeling left out?" he asked. "Ol' Dinah here just isn't as much fun, is she? What were you ladies up to last night? Let me guess, you were running around playing cops and robbers." His gaze flicked to Dinah. "I missed you last night."

The blonde tugged impatiently on his arm, growing bored now that his attention was elsewhere. He snapped his fingers at Jett. Jett tucked his phone away and helped the blonde to her feet, dragging her out of the trailer. Now I was the only person who no longer belonged. Unfortunately, I couldn't run out after Jett without causing a scene.

"Where were you?" Lance asked Dinah. "I didn't see you at the hotel."

"Did you even go back to the hotel?" I asked, even

though his gaze remained fixed on Dinah who was, by all accounts, ignoring him.

Since she wasn't speaking to him, he realized he'd have to talk to me instead. "I popped in for a moment before partying 'til dawn. I picked up Candi at one of the clubs, and we drove around." He leaned over the arm of the chair, clearly speaking to Dinah. "You should have been there. You would have loved it."

Her fingers gripped the arms of her chair. "No, Lance. Seeing you screw around is not something I love."

"I'm not the only one who screws around, dear."

"Did you have any alone time?" I asked. "Or was Jett with you all night?"

Lance looked at me, as if he'd forgotten I was in the room. "Why is that any of your business?" His eyes narrowed further. "What exactly are you implying?"

"Nothing. I was just wondering how you could film all day, spend the entire night out, and come back and film. Don't you need to sleep?"

He shot me a charming, practiced smile that probably had his female fandom dropping their panties. "Are you impressed by my stamina?"

"Absolutely," I replied, "so I take it you didn't need Jett to fill in for you. Is he just your lapdog you drag around for fun?"

He glared. "He works for me, just like you work for Dinah. He handles my business, so I have time for a life. I don't care what he does as long as he does his job." He glanced at Dinah. "Why is she talking to me? They have their place." My place? I resisted the urge to tell him exactly what I thought of that, but his attention was solely on Dinah. He leaned closer to her. "You promised to stop by so we could talk. When is that going to happen?"

"Don't you dare speak to my people like that," she growled. "You want to abuse someone, go beat up on poor Jett. That boy is a saint or a masochist for putting up with the likes of your shit."

"Sorry," he muttered.

She glared at him with the ferociousness of a mama bear. "I'll consider having a conversation with you whenever you decide to stop whoring around and getting drunk off your ass."

Gemma coughed. "You know, I can go."

"No," Dinah replied, "it's fine." The hairstylist removed the final roller, and Dinah turned in her chair, tucking one foot beneath her as she faced him. "Tell me the truth. Did you look for me at all yesterday?"

"I said I did."

"Why, Lance? Were you looking to hit this?" Dinah rolled her eyes, and her voice grew quiet. "What happened to us? I thought we had something real."

"This is the real me." He shook his head, trying to clear away the buzz. "We need to get back together. I need you. The film needs us. But you won't talk to me. You have to talk to me. We need to get on the same page."

"What about Candi?" Dinah asked.

"Shit, Dinah, she's nobody." He reached for her hand, but she pulled away. "You're somebody."

"Is that what you told the interviewer?"

"No, I rescheduled the set tour. I said we were behind on shooting. I can't give the interview until you and your team get on board. I spoke to Cherise. She was all for it. Why the hell aren't you signing off on this? Haven't you spoken to her?"

Dinah turned in her seat, studying her reflection in the mirror. "We'll talk," she finally said. "Maybe around lunchtime, unless you're too busy."

"I'll be there, and I expect to see you. If not, I'll send Jett to get you. I'd prefer if we did this in private." He narrowed his eyes at me, but I could read the words on his face. *Stay the hell out of my business.*

I smiled back at him, hoping he could read my expression just as easily. The one thing that didn't sit right was his threat about Jett. Honestly, if the assistant was happy being Lance's puppet, he might be acting on Lance's behalf. The threats, the flowers, the stalking could all be on Lance's order. I needed to get answers, and I needed them fast. There wasn't a chance in hell Dinah was walking into Lance's lair without protection, and I wasn't talking about a rubber.

THIRTY-THREE

Stepping out of the elevator, I looked both ways and headed for Jett's room. Cross had given me his room key, and I didn't ask how he'd gotten it, probably the same way he'd gotten copies of the surveillance footage. I slid the card into the slot and waited for the light to turn green. Then I turned the handle and pushed my way inside.

This was a single room with a double bed. I closed the door and flipped the lock. That would buy me some time in case Jett or housekeeping came knocking. The first thing I did was photograph the entire room. After I tossed the place, I wanted to make sure I was able to put everything back where I found it. Then I started my search.

The nightstand drawer contained an assortment of pill bottles and supplements. Allergy medicine, sleeping pills, anti-depressants, a plethora of herbal remedies, and tons of energy shots. With this mix, Jett must feel like a yo-yo. I noted the name of the prescribing physician and closed the drawer.

Beneath the mattress, I found a dime bag of coke and several rolled joints. In the dresser was an entire drawer of magazines. Each one featured Lance or Dinah. Among the collection were several dated tabloids featuring news of the sex tape and the scandal involving the A-list couple. And here I thought most people hid their dirty magazines under the mattress.

I located Jett's planner and flipped through the pages. He had a list of important numbers, and I photographed the page. Scar's number was handwritten, along with numbers for Dinah's manager, agent, and assistant. I skimmed through the rest of the planner. It was written in some type of shorthand I didn't understand. It was initials and symbols with times written beside them. If Jett was dumb enough to write anything damning in his calendar, we would find it. It would just take some time to decipher. I'd let the techs at Cross Security handle that. Replacing the planner where I found it, I finished searching the drawers but didn't find anything else.

I went into the bathroom and looked around. It was a typical hotel bathroom. Jett had his personal care products on the vanity. I checked beneath the sink, in the shower, behind the toilet, and even in the toilet tank but didn't find anything. He just looked like some guy who had settled in for an extended stay. I was just about to leave the bathroom when I noticed the robe hanging on the back of the door. I checked the pockets but didn't find anything. Instead, I noticed something taped to the door behind it. I moved the white terrycloth out of the way and stared at a poster of Dinah from her modeling days in nothing but a bikini bottom, stiletto heels, and strategically holding a small designer handbag against her chest. Obviously, I knew what Jett liked to think about in the shower.

It wasn't exactly a smoking gun, but it did register on the skeevy scale. I clicked a quick photo of the poster and replaced the robe on the hook. Before I left, I checked the closet. Jett had most of his clothes hanging up, and I went through the pockets, finding a bracelet for admittance to one of the clubs, several receipts for fast food and liquor, and a copy of his rental car agreement. Jackpot.

Pocketing the sheet of paper, I gave the room a final glance to make sure it didn't appear disturbed. Then I headed for the garage. Since I failed to locate Jett's vehicle at the studio, there was a good chance he might have left it at the hotel. I just needed to find it.

The garage was nearly full. A few parking attendants were near the exit, taking a break. They paid me no heed, but they might not have been aware of my presence. I scanned the rows of cars, looking for a rental with front-end damage. I had the make, model, color, and license plate number. It shouldn't be that hard to find. What I found instead was Chaz Relper's car wedged into a corner spot at the far end.

Did Reaper leave his car here? Or did the killer park it here to avoid detection? Frankly, how it came to be in this parking garage was unimportant. Glancing around, I tugged on the door handle, but it was locked. I tried the other three doors, just in case, but they didn't budge. After carefully considering my options, I went back to my car and opened the trunk. Returning with a slimjim, I slipped the thin metal between the window and waterproof sealant. After some maneuvering, the lock popped. I opened the driver's side door and crouched down to examine the interior.

I had no doubts the vehicle contained evidence. I avoided touching the steering wheel, gearshift, and adjustment knobs. If the killer drove the car here, he might have left a print or hair. It would just be a pain in the ass to find. The car was a mess. It was in worse shape than Reaper's apartment. The paparazzo must have eaten his fair share of meals in the car and never cleaned up after himself.

I dug through the piles of crap, finding a random sock, a half-filled bottle of what looked like pale apple juice, and an instruction manual for the drone. Slipping around to the other side of the car, I searched underneath the seats, finding a lens cap, some empty plastic memory card holders, a detachable camera flash, and lots of loose change. No cameras. No memory cards. No sign of the stalker.

Flipping down the visors, I found the vehicle registration, insurance information, and some parking stubs. Deciding those might be useful, I wrote down the timestamp and locations. Then I opened the glove box.

Inside, I found a pair of fingerless gloves, regular winter gloves, earmuffs, and registration for a gun and a carry permit. The only thing I didn't find was the gun. Since it wasn't found with the body, I had to assume the stalker took it. Whoever had it out for Dinah was armed and clearly deranged.

I put everything back where I found it, locked the doors, and called a tip into the police. When I finished my search of the garage, failing to locate Jett Trevino's rental, I pondered my next move. Jett's SUV wasn't here, and it wasn't at the studio. Where the hell did he leave his car?

While I waited, I phoned several body shops in the area. A lot of SUVs had recently been brought in for repair, but none of them were rentals. The police would have checked this avenue, but they probably gave up the search as soon as they found the owner of the green SUV. Like Cross always said, we were on our own. I placed a call to the office, hoping someone could find out if the rental had an anti-theft system or GPS. If it did, we could track it. Finally, the cops arrived which was my cue to leave.

When I stopped at the first of the flower shops, I took a moment to slip into a light vest. Cross outfitted his personnel with whatever equipment he thought we'd need, and while I would have preferred something more tactical, this was better than nothing. I put it on beneath my shirt, checked my appearance in the side mirror, and went to speak to the delivery driver and the shop owner.

By my fifth stop, I expected to hear the same story again. The flowers were delivered to the mausoleum at the cemetery. A woman from the funeral home paid in cash. From the description, the woman in question was tall and thin with long blonde hair. One of the guys had seen her business card on the table. Gwendolyn Moore. I relayed that information to Lucien, who was currently at the cemetery, speaking to the caretaker. He would check into Mrs. Moore. Her name had never surfaced during the course of my investigation, so I wasn't sure how she fit into any of this. Perhaps the stalker happened across a funeral and decided to steal the flowers. It made about as much sense as anything else.

I stepped into the last flower shop, the one that linked back to the orders Lance Smoke had placed, prepared to hear another rendition of what I'd already been told, but I was wrong.

"Black Bacarra roses," the owner said, "we sell a few every once in a while. They make elegant accents to mixed bouquets, but it's rare to get an order for just those, unless it's a wedding. It's weird. I've had several orders in the last week and a half." She clicked through her order log. "They were all internet orders." She laughed at the name. "The most recent was made by Lance Smoke." She snorted. "I had no idea a celebrity was interested in my flower shop." She rolled her eyes. "Probably someone wanted to keep his identity secret."

"Where were the deliveries sent?" I asked.

"A hotel. Um," she tapped the down arrow, "a design firm, and two office buildings. The four of them went out first thing this morning."

"How were these orders paid for?"

"Credit card." She scanned the details. "Would you believe the credit card matches the name on the order form?"

"Can I get the card number for verification?"

She hesitated, and I offered my brightest, most helpful smile. I had already seen the receipts from Lance's trailer. Obviously, he must have ordered flowers. It couldn't be a coincidence.

"I don't see what harm it would do." She flipped the screen around so I could see the authorization codes and numbers.

The last four digits on her screen matched the last four digits on the receipts. It was Lance's card. Although, that didn't necessarily mean Lance placed the orders. It was possible Jett had access. "I need to know exactly when and where the orders were sent. Is there any mention to whom the flowers were intended?"

She was getting a bit squirrely at the prospect that I was asking for a celebrity's private information. "I really can't say, but you should speak to the driver."

"Thanks for your help."

She went to assist a group of women, who were picking out flowers for a wedding, and I dropped a fifty in the gratuity jar and went to speak to the delivery guy she pointed out when I arrived. He was at the back of the shop, loading the refrigerated van with outgoing orders. He didn't stop working even as I asked where he'd been this morning, but he seemed perfectly capable of multitasking.

"The black roses went to four different locations." He loaded a large vase with daisies and sunflowers into the back. "The addresses are programmed into the GPS. You know how to work one of those?"

"Yes."

He jerked his head toward the front of the van. "Go check it out. I got to get this done. These have to get to the hospital by noon, and I'm already running behind."

"Sure, no problem." Except after checking the GPS, I realized we had a very big problem.

A dozen Bacarra roses was delivered to Lance's hotel. Another batch was sent to a fashion designer uptown. A bouquet was sent to the Cross Security offices, and the last was delivered to the Martin Technologies building. Shit. How did he discover her connection to Martin or the designer with whom I assumed she was flirting?

The first thing I did was call my office and ask about the flowers. They were at reception. They hadn't been addressed to anyone in particular, just Cross Security. After giving strict instructions to have someone from the lab analyze the card and the flowers, even though I doubted they'd find anything damning on them, I disconnected and called Scar.

"Someone using Lance's credit card sent flowers to Dinah's old hotel. I don't know if they've been delivered, but you should have someone check."

I could practically hear him growl. "Is Lance Smoke responsible? She's supposed to meet him for lunch later. I'm not leaving her alone with him. What are you people doing about this?"

"We're working on it. Just keep a close eye on Lance and his assistant. Don't leave Dinah alone with them, and you should know, there's a decent chance the stalker might be armed."

Scar cursed and hung up.

When I dialed Lucien, he didn't answer. He was working on leads and might have been in the middle of something. I hung up and sent a text letting him know we had a problem. After that, I dialed Martin. When he didn't answer, I called the main line and spoke to the security executive, Jeffrey Myers. The flowers were delivered sans card, but they were addressed to Martin. They didn't set off the metal detectors, and since Martin was running from meeting to meeting, as was his norm, the flowers remained at the security desk.

"Keep them there. Someone from Cross Security or the police department will drop by to pick them up. Just know they are meant as a warning or a threat, and you need to be extra watchful of any unauthorized persons entering the building. I'm going to send you a few photos. If you recognize any of these people, do not let them near Martin. Is that understood?"

"Yes, Miss Parker," Jeffrey said. "What should I tell Mr. Martin about the situation?"

I knew Martin and how he reacted to threats or potential threats. It would be pointless to say anything without hard proof. "That's your call," I said, knowing Jeffrey's helpfulness in the past had nearly cost him his job. "Just keep him safe."

"Yes, ma'am."

We hung up, and I considered my next move. Following up with the fashion designer probably wouldn't lead to anything useful, but I felt the man should probably be aware he might be in danger. However, the biggest known threat was to Dinah, and right now, I had proof Lance Smoke's credit card was used to purchase the bouquets. That was definitely enough to warrant a conversation, so I whipped the car around and raced back to the studio. Based on this morning's conversation, Lance wanted to talk to Dinah in private, and if he was behind the stalking, that would be the perfect time to make a move.

THIRTY-FOUR

I paced nervously along the side of the building. They were shooting on the backlot. Scar and his team waited on the sidelines, watching everything. My eyes scanned the area for Jett, but I didn't see him. Most of the PAs lingered nearby in case they were needed. So where was Lance's assistant? Lancaster was supposed to be shadowing him, but Jett had given him the slip.

Ducking onto the main soundstage, I looked around. Several of the writers and camera crew were talking. I heard snippets of their conversation. Apparently, they would be shooting on location later in the day and for the rest of the week. Some things couldn't be recreated in a studio. Maybe that's why the stalker was desperate to act. He felt his window of opportunity slipping away. Although, they still had weeks of shooting ahead after this. He must be freaking out because we were closing in.

On my way to the trailers, my phone rang. It was Cross. "Alex, I sent a security team to Christian Nykle's fashion studio and another team to Martin Technologies. Scaratilli says he has Dinah's security handled, but I told our guys to be vigilant. You're certain Lance Smoke's credit card paid for the bouquets?"

"I found receipts in his trailer this morning, and the florist verified it. What did you find at the cemetery? What about Moore? How does she fit into this?"

"The flowers were delivered to the cemetery two days ago per the instructions of a ninety-three year old horticulturist who died of natural causes. She had made her wishes known about the floral arrangements years ago. She's entombed in the mausoleum and wanted the entire place brimming with dark purple flowers. The caretaker knew her personally and knew of her intentions. They made sure to abide by her wishes. Moore coordinated everything from the mortuary. I've already run backgrounds on the dead lady and Moore, but neither has ties to anyone involved with Broadway Films or Dinah Allen. It appears to be a coincidence."

"Those don't exist," I muttered.

Cross grunted, seemingly losing his train of thought.

"Are the flowers still at the cemetery?" I asked.

"No." He sounded distracted and unfocused which was unusual for him. "The caretaker was surprised to find the entire mausoleum emptied out when he checked this morning. He called the police, but they have yet to show. It wasn't exactly a grave robbery, so they aren't too concerned. I watched the security footage. A dark-colored SUV came through the front gate just after eleven last night and left around midnight. I couldn't make out a plate, but it's our best bet. Did you locate Trevino's vehicle yet?"

"No. The techs are hoping to crack into the anti-theft system to get a location, but I haven't heard anything." A thought crossed my mind. "How did the stalker know about the flowers? Do you think he murdered the woman?"

"She was ninety-three. It appears to be natural causes, but I'll check. My guess is the stalker must have phoned several flower shops and found the roses sold out. He probably inquired why. It's speculation but entirely possible." A disturbing, shrill noise sounded in the background. "I have to go. We'll meet up at the lot. Make sure Dinah remains safe. I trust you can handle that."

I continued on the path to the trailers. This would be a lot easier if I could just get Lance into a room and question him about his recent credit card activity and who had access to his accounts, but since that wasn't going to happen, I had no choice but to track down Trevino and force him to spill his guts.

No one was near the trailers. I knocked on Lance's but didn't get an answer. It was too risky to break-in again when the lot was bustling, so I detoured to Dinah's trailer, hoping to make sure it remained safe. Someone from her security team remained outside. The door to the trailer was wide open, as were the windows. He offered a nod, and I returned the gesture.

I turned to leave, but a thought that had been nagging at me for quite some time surfaced. "Hey," I turned around, "any idea why those roses might be significant?"

He thought for a moment. "I'm not sure. Have you asked Miss Allen?"

"Not yet." I'd failed to ask a lot of people a lot of important questions lately. "Have you seen Lance Smoke or Jett Trevino?"

"Sorry, ma'am. No one's been by the trailer since filming began."

Unsure where to go from here, I circled the perimeter. It took almost an hour, but I didn't spot Jett or his SUV. Cross had yet to arrive, so I found a quiet spot near the side of the main building and pulled out my phone and tried Martin again.

"I was just about to call you back," he said. "Would you like to explain why your office sent a security team to my building?"

"Are they still there?"

"I had security escort them off the property, but I was told we gave them a parting gift."

"Have you spoken to Jeffrey?"

"Yes."

"I didn't send the security team," I began, fearing he would think I was overstepping without consulting him. "Cross did. We believe the flowers are a threat from Dinah's stalker. You weren't the only one targeted."

"Who else got roses?"

I exhaled. "Christian Nykle."

"He's in the city?" Martin seemed far too excited by that prospect.

"As far as I know. Cross should be at his shop now." Martin's question brought to mind several other questions. "What do you know about Nykle? Is he dangerous? Could he be involved in this?"

Martin snorted. "Doubtful. He lives in Milan but has boutiques in several of the world's so-called fashion conscious cities. He's the one who originally put Dinah in front of a camera."

"That doesn't mean he might not have a grudge. He could be a jilted lover or jealous of her rising stardom."

"I'm the reason she's back in contact with Christian," Martin hissed. "You can check, but I doubt she had any interaction with him prior to a couple of weeks ago. Honestly, if he's also on the stalker's radar, then it's someone who knows about our dealings."

"What dealings?"

He hesitated. "She's brokering a sale between the two of us."

"Any significance to the flowers?" I asked, blinking as I processed through what this meant. "Black Bacarra roses. They're more of a dark purple, actually."

I heard faint clicking. "Let me see. I'm sure I ran across something about roses."

I waited patiently, listening to the click of his typing. "Whose number did you want off her phone records? Was it Nykle's?"

"She said he was in the city, but nothing indicated that. My sources said he was still in Milan. I don't know when he arrived, but it was kept quiet, not that I blame him. He wouldn't have wanted the news of what he has to get out. It could ruin him."

"What are you talking about?"

"Nothing. It won't help you identify the stalker."

"It might," I insisted.

"Sweetheart, we really don't have time to get into this right now."

I wasn't used to Martin playing these games. "You're the Great Oz, and even you didn't know Nykle was in town or how to get in touch with him. You've been actively searching and had no idea he was here, so how did the stalker stumble upon that intel?" I didn't need Martin to answer that question; I knew the answer. Dinah was compromised. Her phone could have been hacked or cloned. It would explain everything. "I have to talk to her chief of security. You find something on those roses or you suddenly realize we're on the same side and you'd like to come clean, you know how to reach me."

"Alexis, I promise I'm not withholding anything relevant. I wouldn't do that to you."

"Just do me a favor and stay away from Dinah until this thing is wrapped up. You can't deny you're a target."

"Y'know, he could have seen me at the hotel last night. You seemed certain he was there. That could be why I received the flowers. Are you sure Christian didn't show up after I left?" Martin asked.

"I'm not certain of anything right now, not even you." I clicked off, regretting the words as soon as they left my mouth.

I was tired of this. All of this. This wasn't how I conducted an investigation or myself. I didn't wait around for other people to tell me what to do or provide solutions to my problems. Working for Cross had confused issues and me. The damn, domineering prick had me twisted around, convinced I'd be fired or sued if I stepped out of line, even though he'd promised me autonomy.

Dialing the precinct, I waited for O'Connell to answer. "I screwed up," I said.

"What else is new?"

"Shut it, Nick. I called in a tip about Chaz Relper's car. By now, I'm sure it's been searched and impounded. Has any progress been made on that or the body?"

"Not that I know of, but you're calling the wrong division."

"I'm calling my friend." I took a breath. "I need help finding a car. It's possible the driver may be responsible for Relper's murder. I don't know. But I can't find the SUV, and at the moment, I can't find its driver either."

"Do you have a plate or VIN?"

"Both." I dug the rental agreement out of my pocket and read off the numbers. "As soon as you locate it or Jett Trevino, let me know. Trevino should be at the studio, but I haven't seen him since this morning."

"Any reason to think he might be in trouble or considered dangerous?" O'Connell asked.

"Relper's gun wasn't in his car or at his place. I'm guessing whoever killed him took it."

O'Connell whistled. "We'll consider Trevino armed. We'll issue a BOLO, and I'll toss this information over to homicide. Someone will call you if they find something, but Parker, you better do the same. If you find Trevino and he's safe and sound and not involved, let us know, so we can call off the hounds."

"Thanks, Nick."

After hanging up the phone, I checked the time. Lucien should have been back by now. The film crew was set to break for lunch in forty-five minutes, and I hoped for a solution before that happened. If not, I'd accompany Dinah to Lance's trailer and conduct my own interrogation. Dinah would be over the moon, and Lance, well, he'd probably have me forcibly removed. It was a good thing I worked for the same company as the security guards.

Wondering if Jett might have been making a snack run for Lance, who seemed to have very specific dietary needs, I wandered over to craft services. They were busy getting everything ready for the impending rush, and I stayed out of their way, watching as they worked.

Elodie ran up to me and lifted her radio, pressing a key. "I found her."

"What's up?" I asked, fearing her answer.

She shook her head and led me away from craft services, afraid one of the workers might overhear. "Scar said he thought he saw someone heading into props with more of those flowers, but he doesn't have the manpower to spare and thought you would want to investigate."

"Tell him I'm on my way." I thought for a moment. "Have you seen Jett?"

She bit her lip, her brow furrowing. "Lance sent him to get a different FBI badge. He was convinced the one he had yesterday was different from the one today." Her face grew ashen. "He sent him to props. I'll go with you."

"No. Hang back here. I'll check it out."

THIRTY-FIVE

The props department wasn't in a trailer. It was actually in building C, which contained a smaller soundstage and a few larger rooms. The set for Lance's character's apartment was here, along with the set for the FBI field office. I pushed the door open and carefully stepped inside. Unlike building A, which housed the main soundstage, craft services, several offices, and was bustling with people, building C was empty. My footsteps practically echoed in the cavernous expanse.

I looked around, failing to spot any signs of life, human or floral. Props was tucked in the far corner, and I checked the few openings and rooms as I searched for signs of Jett. If he came to get a different badge for Lance, he might have already left, or he was planting more flowers to make another macabre threat for Dinah. I wasn't positive what was going on, but the vacant building was eerie. It felt like I was walking into a trap.

My phone rang, and I jumped. Grabbing the device, I silenced it and glanced nervously around. No one lurked in the shadows, and I waited a moment, listening for sounds of footsteps. Once I was convinced I was alone, I answered. It was Amir.

"We analyzed the bouquet. Black Bacarra roses. No card. No note. Only one set of prints on the vase, and those belong to Becky in reception. She said the delivery guy was wearing gardening gloves."

"What about the bouquets sent to Nykle and Martin?"

"Nothing but roses. A dozen each. No card. No indication of the sender."

I blew out a breath. "The florist said the orders were placed using Lance Smoke's credit card, but without an obvious threat, I don't know if that matters. It might be circumstantial."

"I'll see what I can do," Amir said.

Thinking about the other loose ends and hoping to find something to connect the flower deliveries, I asked, "How's the hotel footage coming along from last night? Did Christian Nykle drop by Dinah's hotel?"

"I'm not sure. I've been focused on figuring out who started the fire."

"Way to bury the lead. Do we have an ID yet?"

"Negative. All we know is the fire started in the public restrooms just outside the lounge. The ladies room to be precise."

"Huh." Several thoughts went through my mind, but before I could voice my theory, a rustling sound came from the back of the room. "I'll call you back."

Pushing open the door to the props department, I glanced around at the cluttered, yet organized shelves. "Hello?" I called. "Anyone here?"

My hand rested on the butt of my gun, but I didn't remove it from beneath my jacket. I'd encountered the prop master briefly on another occasion and didn't want to give the man a heart attack. I turned the corner and found a large bouquet of black roses.

"Son of a bitch." Warily, I moved closer. These had a card:

I'm sorry. Love, Lance

Unlike the other flowers Dinah received, the note was handwritten in a flowing script. It'd be easy enough to match it to a handwriting sample, but I doubted the A-lister would deny they were from him since he went to the trouble to sign the card. This bouquet was different from the rest. The vase was blown, red glass in the shape of a heart, and small white tulips and pale violets accented the arrangement.

"What the hell are you doing?" Jett asked, startling me from behind.

I spun, my gun at the ready. "Drop it."

He cocked an annoyed eyebrow and gave my gun a look of utter amusement. "You first." He spun the handgun on his finger, and I saw the orange strip. It was one of the studio's facsimiles. "Does Dinah want to practice her shooting again?" he quipped, pushing past me as he searched one of the plastic tubs on the second shelf. "She's such a perfectionist." He let out an annoyed exhale, muttering to himself.

"Did you have anything to do with the flowers?"

"You weren't supposed to see those." He dug out a badge and a few other items and put them into the box he was carrying. "Those are none of your business."

I moved around the shelf, positioning myself between Jett and the door. He wasn't going anywhere until I got some answers. "Did you put the flowers in Dinah's trailer this morning?"

"What are you talking about? I picked up Lance's delivery and brought it here." He pointed at the vase. "Does this look like Dinah's trailer to you? Don't you dare tell her about them."

"Fine, you want to play that game, I'll bite. Why don't you tell me where the hell you parked your SUV?"

He hefted the box and stared at me. "Get out of my way. I have to get these back to set. They're in the middle of filming."

"Answer my question."

"I don't know." He tried to shove me with the box, but I pushed back, sending him into the stack of shelves. "You'll pay for that. Lance will have you banned."

"And you'll be arrested. I'm pretty sure in this scenario I win."

"Arrested for what?" He appeared genuinely confused. "What did he do now?"

"He?"

Jett dropped the box at his feet and rubbed a hand over his forehead. "He took my SUV four days ago when we were leaving the club. He didn't want to go back to the hotel, and he didn't want the paparazzi to follow him. I took his limo, and he took the truck. I haven't seen it since. He said he forgot where he left it. What happened?"

"Lance didn't go back to the hotel that night?"

Jett shrugged. "I don't think so. I waited in his room, but he never showed. He called me at five a.m. to pick him up from a diner near the wharf." He reached into his pocket, and I aimed at him. He looked up, still unaware my gun was real. "Seriously? Isn't that federal agent routine getting old?" He pulled out his phone. "Just tell me what the damage is so I can get someone to clean it up. We have people who handle these situations." He hit a few keys on his phone and stared at me expectantly.

"A professional fixer," I surmised, tucking the gun back into my holster. He wasn't armed, and I was confident I could take him without resorting to shooting him.

"It's part of the business."

"Is stalking part of the business?"

"Lance isn't being stalked."

"No kidding. Dinah is."

Jett chuckled. "Oh, that?"

For a moment, I was convinced I was trapped in the *Twilight Zone*. "Why are you targeting Dinah?" He looked at the door, itching to escape. "I'll let you go just as soon as you clear this matter up."

"That was a stunt to gain publicity and keep Dinah on the front of the magazines. As long as she stays in the limelight, anything she and Lance touch is gold."

"Why the flowers?"

"They're from Lance, as an apology. He figures he needs to woo her in order to get her to agree to go public with their relationship. She keeps bucking him when he explains it rationally, so we thought turning up the charm might work."

"And you think a hundred roses isn't overkill? Were you planning to suffocate her?"

"What hundred roses? There's a dozen and some tulips and violets. That's it."

"Not those flowers. The ones in her trailer." I was losing my patience.

Jett glared at me. "I don't know what you're talking about. I need to get back. Lance is waiting."

"You're not going anywhere." The hairs at the back of my neck prickled, and I glanced around, feeling as if someone was watching me. "I saw the poster, Jett. I know you've been inside her room. Are you jealous of your boss, or are you acting on his behalf?"

Jett reddened. "What?" He blinked rapidly as a sheen of sweat developed on his upper lip. He'd been caught, and he knew it.

"Tell me what happened after Dinah left Clay's party."

"How the hell would I know?"

"You chased her up the stairs, didn't you? And you called her in the middle of the night."

"You're insane," Jett squawked, his voice cracking on an unmanly octave.

Footsteps sounded behind me, and I turned to see Lance storming toward us. Jett took that moment to scurry past, but the star didn't turn or break stride. He waved away Jett's muttered excuses and continued on his intended path. I attempted to pursue Jett who was now sprinting for the exit, but Lance blocked my path and grabbed my arm. He shoved me back into the prop room and slammed the door.

Despite Cross's warning not to confront Lance with the allegations, I had no choice. I didn't get anything out of Jett. Either Lance was responsible, or he was employing a psychopath. Either way, I thought he ought to listen to what I had to say.

"I warned you to stay away from filming," he snarled. "What are you doing holding up production? I should have you removed." He looked down at the gun at my side. "You aren't authorized to be armed on set. That's a direct violation. I'll have your job."

"I'm doing my job. I was hired to protect Dinah."

He moved deeper into the room, checking to make sure

his flowers were still tucked safely away. "You need to stay away from Dinah. I know what's best for her. You're confusing her."

"You sent the flowers."

"That isn't a crime."

"Threatening phone calls in the middle of the night are."

He narrowed his eyes. "I never threatened her. Sure, I might have called to hook up, but who hasn't done that?"

"Killing a man is a crime."

"What the fuck have you been smoking?" he asked. "That's a movie, honey. Not real life."

"So you didn't hit someone with your SUV?"

His Adam's apple bobbed, and he glanced away. "What are you talking about?"

That sounded like a confession to me. "After you left the club, you hit someone. Jett already said you took his SUV. The police found a body. Does that ring any bells?"

"Shit." He blew out a breath. "You can't be serious. I didn't do that." But something in his eyes told me he wasn't sure.

"Then Jett did."

"No." He swallowed. "That's not possible."

"Too high to remember? You were doing blow with whoever you took into the bathroom. Maybe I should ask her what happened that night."

He licked his bottom lip. "I'm not saying a word to you. Stay the hell away from me and my assistant. You're just some crazy bitch who misses the glory days of being an actual cop."

"Fine, let's talk about the prop dummy that was dressed like Dinah and stabbed through the heart. That's a threat, Mr. Smoke. Any idea who might have done it?"

"Someone did that?" he sounded dumbfounded. "No wonder Di's been so out of it lately."

"You took credit for the flowers, but you deny that?" Even as I made these accusations, they felt wrong. Lance didn't go back to the hotel after the club, so he couldn't have chased Dinah up the stairs. Jett was there, but he seemed to be unaware of a lot of things. Or he was great at playing dumb.

"Flowers are romantic. They are an *I'm sorry*, not an *I'm going to stab you, eeek, eeek, eeek.*" Lance made a stabbing gesture and mimicked the sound from *Psycho*. "Do I look crazy to you?"

My phone buzzed in my pocket, and I reached for it, keeping one eye on Lance. It was the police. They found Jett's SUV abandoned near the water. The front fender was badly dented and showed signs of blood and hair. Forensics was analyzing it now.

"Have you checked for prints?" I asked.

"It's been dusted. We've found several sets. They're being run through IAFIS now. I'm guessing you sent us to look for this car in connection with our DB."

"Yeah." I stared at Lance, who was fidgeting uncomfortably.

"Thanks." The homicide detective reconsidered hanging up. "Our lab experts were able to recover a single image from the internal memory of the camera found beneath the dumpster. It's pretty blurry and pixelated from the recovery, but I'll text it to you. Maybe you can make heads or tails out of it."

"Sure." I tucked the phone back in my pocket. "Are you sure you don't want to tell me what's going on? The cops found the SUV."

Lance squeezed his eyes closed. "I'm not speaking to you. If they have questions, they can talk to my attorney. We're done. And so are you." He pushed his way out of the room.

"We're not through."

"Yes, we are."

He detoured to the stage, and I followed after him, unwilling to let him out of my sight until this matter was resolved. I already lost Jett. I wouldn't lose my other potential suspect. Grabbing my phone, I called security and told them to detain Jett. Lance crouched down in the middle of his character's living room and reached for something on the floor. From this angle, I couldn't see what was on the ground in front of him, but I heard the sudden staticky buzz and saw Lance drop.

I took a step closer, seeing the live wire spark and jump

momentarily before the circuit breaker overloaded and the lights around the set went dead. I dialed 911. While I relayed pertinent facts, I knelt next to Lance and felt for a pulse. Shit. I put my phone on the ground, listening to the operator as I began chest compressions. After what felt like an eternity, he gasped, and I let out the breath I'd been holding.

"He's back. Get that ambulance here ASAP." I hit the disconnect and dialed the security station. The studio had medics on standby who'd be able to help a lot faster than emergency services. "Lie still. You're okay. Help's on the way."

He didn't say a word. He just winced and closed his eyes. I noticed the flashing image on my phone's screen. It was from the homicide detective. It was a blur of pale skin and dark hair. Basically, a photographic Picasso of a person's likeness which was entirely indecipherable unless you knew who you were looking for. In that instant, I knew who was stalking Dinah Allen, and it wasn't Jett or Lance.

THIRTY-SIX

"Is he dead?" Elodie asked from somewhere in the dark.

"Lance, don't speak and don't move," I whispered. "Help is on the way."

"Alex, is he dead?" she repeated more forcefully.

"Where are you?" I called, removing my gun and chambering a round. With my other hand, I grabbed my phone and flipped the flashlight on. It didn't do much to illuminate the dark, expansive studio, but it might be enough to lure Dinah's stalker out into the open. "It's safe. You can come out."

"He was ruining her life," Elodie said, and I moved laterally around the stage in the direction of her voice.

"He can't hurt her now," I said. Elodie didn't speak, but I heard shuffling near the back corner. "You only wanted to protect her. She'll be grateful."

"You're hurting her too."

"Me?" That was a surprise.

She let out a derisive snort. "I saw you last night with him. In his car. You're conspiring against Dinah."

Martin. Of course, she'd seen us. She was in the lobby. She set the fire. It had been her the entire time, but we overlooked it because Dinah said he chased her. Elodie used Dinah's key to get into the gym and make the call, and she had access to Dinah's trailer and the set. She must have found a way to sneak in and out without us noticing, or she enlisted the help of her clueless friends. She used Jett to point us in the wrong direction. Her friendship with Jett must have been how she got access to Lance's credit cards.

"No, I'm not."

"You're a liar," she screamed from behind me.

I spun, but it was already too late. She barreled into me with a heavy metal object, and I heard and felt the ka-thump followed by jolting pain. Ka-thump. Ka-thump. Batting the nail gun away from my chest with my elbow and forearm, I aimed and fired at her, but she skittered away into the dark.

I dropped to my knees. I couldn't breathe. The flashlight was inches away, but I didn't dare make a move for it for fear that it would give away my location. I swallowed, looking down at the three nails sticking straight out of my chest. I tugged on the top of my vest and looked down. They didn't penetrate.

My eyes searched the pitch black while I struggled to get my lungs to fill. After several wheezing gasps, I climbed to my feet. Scooping the flashlight off the ground, I held the light beneath my gun as I swept the area. Lance remained in the middle of the set. I wasn't sure if he was still conscious or even alive. His heart might have stopped again.

Spotting a few drops of blood, I cautiously moved in the direction Elodie must have gone. "Elodie," I called. She was wounded. Maybe I could convince her to give up.

Something clanged inside the prop room, and I edged to the doorway. With all the shelves and clutter, it would be nearly impossible to spot her, but I wasn't going to give her the opportunity to sneak up on me again. I killed the light and slid along the wall, moving silently toward the sound. She was looking for something, probably Reaper's gun.

"She wants to be just like you, Alex. She listens to what you say. You told her the person who sent the flowers is evil. You told her the diorama was a threat. You poisoned her against me."

"You dressed a prop up in Dinah's likeness and stabbed it. It looked like a threat."

"It was a warning," Elodie insisted. "She spreads her legs and lets these...these men," she said it as if they were disgusting vermin, "do whatever they want. They take advantage. They use her. First for modeling. Now for acting and gaining publicity. The new one just wanted her to make a deal, but you wanted him for yourself." She laughed. "Maybe I should thank you for that. At least he didn't spend the night like the others."

"Why did you send flowers?"

"It's their funeral. It's only appropriate."

The sound of my voice tipped her off to my location, and she fired in my direction.

"Where'd you get the gun?" I asked, hoping the muzzle flare I'd seen was just a prop.

"I had to take it from that disgusting snoop. The one who takes the pictures. God," she sounded exasperated, "they post such filth for the world to see. These paparazzi sickos think it's great to show Dinah being preyed upon by Lance in the most depraved of ways."

I crouched down and hit the flashlight on my phone, sliding it across the room. She fired again at the moving light, and I rounded the corner, returning fire where I'd seen the muzzle flash. She let out a surprised shriek.

"I don't want to hurt you, Elodie, but I will if I have to. It doesn't have to go like this. You were protecting Dinah. Anyone can see that. We'll get this sorted out, but first, I need you to drop the gun."

"Don't worry, Alex. I have everything under control. The perfect cover story." She bumped into one of the shelves, and I followed the movement, finally able to decipher her from the shadows. I stepped backward, making myself less visible as I focused on her position. "You thought Jett was stalking Dinah, but you were wrong. It was Lance. The two of you had words, and somehow, you ended up killing each other."

"Except he was electrocuted. That's a pathetic storyline for someone who's supposedly writing a screenplay."

"Stop it," she screamed. "You don't know anything."

"What about Dinah?"

"Dinah's confused. He confused her. The men confuse her."

"Elodie, put the gun down," I tried again. "No one else needs to get hurt. You need to walk out of here, so you can tell Dinah how these men have hurt her. She needs to hear it from you." Negotiation wasn't my forte, but I didn't want to shoot her. She was sick. She needed help.

"You lie."

The lights suddenly came on, and I was no longer concealed by the dark. I aimed, my hand steady, even as hers shook. "Put it down. Don't make me put you down."

"I don't have a choice. Bye, Alex."

I knew my mistake in an instant. I waited too long, trying to talk her out of it. It didn't work, and I dove to the side. A force pulled me backward, but I managed to keep my feet beneath me and returned fire.

She crashed backward into the shelves and fired wildly. She shot through the crate I was using for cover as she went down, and I moved toward her. My body felt sluggish and unresponsive, but I kicked the gun out of her hand and knelt to check her pulse.

It was rapid and thready. Her eyes fluttered, and she made a gurgling sound. One of my bullets had gone into the lower part of her neck. A wave of dizziness crashed over me, and I fell back onto my butt. The jarring nature of my stumble sent a sharp pain into my chest, and I looked down at the wet, red stain on my shirt. Dammit.

I made a few futile attempts to suck air into my lungs. Finally able to catch my breath, I pressed my hand against my side and kept an eye on Elodie. She wasn't dead yet. She was barely breathing and still bleeding. She wouldn't last long.

Voices were in the main room, and I realized the medics who came to help Lance must have turned on the overhead lights. Twisting, I put a hand underneath me, and I tried to push myself off the floor. "Careful, there's a live wire on the stage."

"Parker," Cross hurried to me, "shit. Don't move."

"Funny, I told Lance the same thing."

"Where are we on that wire, guys?" Cross yelled to them, realizing the danger had yet to be removed. Someone shot him a thumbs up, and he turned his attention to me. Cross lowered me onto my back, and I winced. He tore open my shirt, relieved to find the vest underneath. "The nails didn't penetrate." He turned and barked orders to the security team who had guns trained on Elodie while a second team of medics raced into the building.

I lifted my head and looked down, seeing blood. "You can't say the same about the bullet."

"You took one to the side." He put a hand beneath my hip and lifted. "A through and through. Small caliber. It's just a flesh wound. No big deal. You'll be fine."

I shuddered. "Lance?"

"They just put him on a backboard. He'll be taken to the hospital. The police have been notified. They should be here momentarily, so I'd like to know what the hell is going on." He looked at Elodie who was unconscious. Her gun was across the room, halfway beneath one of the shelves. She no longer posed a danger.

"Elodie confessed to killing Reaper. She stabbed the dummy through the heart. She set the fire in the hotel. I still don't understand the fucking flowers or who Lance ran over with Jett's SUV." I tried to sit up, but Cross put a hand on my shoulder, which was the equivalent of sending a white hot poker through my chest. "Asshole move," I mumbled.

"Sorry." He removed his hand. "Stay put until someone checks you out."

"You mean getting shot might be a big deal?"

He cleared his throat. "The flowers?" he asked impatiently.

"I don't know. Lance paid for them. There's a bouquet over there," I pointed to the back of the room, "but I don't think he had anything to do with the dozens in Dinah's trailer or the ones sent to Martin, Nykle, or our office. That was Elodie, but I don't know why. You'll have to ask her." More EMTs came into the room, and I watched as they prepped her and slid a backboard beneath her. "Is she going to make it?"

"Her chances are pretty slim," the medic said.

One of the radios chirped, and Cross turned it up. "The police are here."

"Good," one of the EMTs said, "we'll need them to accompany us since she's the shooter." They glanced at me, as if making sure the right person was going into custody.

"I'll let them know you're coming out," Cross said, relaying a message into the radio to his guards who must have been with the cops.

They lifted Elodie off the floor and left the room. I made another attempt to sit up, managing to make it before Cross could interfere.

"I need to talk to the police," I said.

"Mr. Almeada is on his way. I don't want you answering any questions without him present. There's a good chance Elodie Smith won't survive. I don't want you getting charged with homicide for a good shoot."

"Not a problem." I held out my arm, hoping he'd help me up, which he did.

"My medical team is on the way. You really should sit down, Alex."

"I'll just walk it off. It's no big deal."

THIRTY-SEVEN

I stepped into the lobby of our apartment building, cursing my own idiocy. The police had arrived at the same time as Cross's mobile medical unit. I spent the entire afternoon in the back of the van, getting x-rayed and stitched up while answering a million questions.

The police were building a case against Elodie. The photo was proof she killed Reaper, but they also found her prints inside his stolen car and on his gun, the same gun she used to shoot me. I didn't understand Lance's role in any of this, and Mr. Almeada made certain I didn't offer any speculation to the police. The homicide detective took pity on me, probably on account of the surgeon suturing my side, and lobbed softball questions for most of the interview. The officer in charge of securing the scene took my weapon into custody.

When I was finished getting stitched up, an officer gave me a ride home. I offered a few off the record tips as to what might be going on, but the only thing I was certain about was Elodie had been stalking her boss. Several officers were already at the hospital following up with Lance Smoke. Production at the studio was halted until further notice. The authorities would get this sorted, and I should take the next few days to recover.

However, now that I was home, reality set in. My car, my keys, my wallet, and my phone remained at the studio. I offered a tired smile to the concierge. "Do me a favor," I said, "call Mr. Martin's office and let him know he should come home."

"Yes, Miss Parker." He reached for the phone, cocking his head to the side. "Anything else I can get you?"

"No."

Despite my insistence, he signaled to the doorman, who called for the elevator and pressed the button for my floor. I rode to the proper level and stumbled out. I'd been holding my jacket strategically against my side in order to hide the bloodstains. The bullet hadn't done much damage. It had gone in a few inches above my hip bone and exited cleanly, but I had dribbled blood down the leg of my jeans and over the front and back of my shirt. It looked much worse than the wound itself. Or maybe I just thought that because I was zonked on painkillers.

I tried turning the knob to our front door, but it was locked. It was a good thing we took our home security seriously. I slid to the floor and draped my jacket over me, wondering if Martin was mad. Honestly, I wasn't even sure how I felt.

I dozed on and off. When the elevator dinged, I held my breath, hoping it wasn't one of our neighbors. Martin stepped out, and I smiled. His brow scrunched in confusion. "Are you okay?"

"I left my keys and phone at work," I said.

"And you forgot how to pick a lock?" he teased.

"I forgot my picks at work too."

"The building manager would have let you in." He unlocked the door and knelt next to me, not believing that was the entire story.

"I didn't think about it." I sighed. "I'm sorry about earlier. I shouldn't have said those things to you. I didn't mean it."

He brushed my hair from my face. "You have no reason to apologize." I moved my jacket, and he saw the remnants of my showdown with Elodie. "Alex?"

"I'm okay. It's no big deal."

"It looks like a big deal."

I chuckled. "Yeah, I said the same thing to Cross." I looped my arms around Martin's neck, and he slowly stood, hauling me to my feet. "You'll be pleased to hear Dinah's fine."

"Good, but I'm more concerned about you."

"Eh, the actual wound is less than an inch, but it bled like a son of a bitch." I let go of him and went into the apartment. "Crap. You wanted that phone number."

"Alex," he watched me carefully, "that isn't important."

"It was last night." Shaking my head, I took a breath and felt the bruise. This wasn't worth fighting about. "Thanks for letting me in. You can get back to whatever you were doing."

"The hell with that."

"No." I stared into those fiery green irises. "We aren't doing this. I'm okay, and whatever your priorities are, this doesn't change them. It shouldn't. You've put me through hell this week, so you damn well better see it through. Or all of this agony and doubt has been pointless, and I'll be fucking pissed." He didn't speak, which was new for him. "I'm going to get washed up. I'll see you later. Bring dinner home."

I went into the bathroom, closed the door, and flipped the lock. I heard him linger just outside. After a few minutes, the shadow disappeared from beneath the door, and I knew he was gone. For a moment, I wish he stayed.

My thoughts were jumbled. I wasn't thinking straight. My mind would clear as soon as the painkillers wore off. I finished cleaning up, grabbed a glass of water, and went into the bedroom. Turning on the television, I flipped on the local news. The main story involved the incident at the studio, but Broadway Films and Cross's public relations team had done a great job concealing the truth. All that was known at the moment was an accident occurred on set and Lance Smoke was recovering from electrical shock. There was no mention of a stalker or a shooting, and I wondered when or if that information would leak.

Turning off the TV, I closed my eyes and drifted off to

sleep. An hour later, I heard the front door. "Are you back?" I called.

"Yes." Martin came into the bedroom. "It's taken care of."

"What is?"

"Everything." He offered a wry smile. "I'm going to tell you everything. I'm tired of keeping secrets. To be honest, I don't give two shits about Dinah's NDA or its stipulations. I realized that I cared way too much about the end result. Frankly, I don't even know if it was worth it. God," he sighed, "I feel like I'm losing it." He sat on the edge of the bed. "I can't lose you over this, Alexis. And I can see it happening. I see the pattern, this cursed, fucked up pattern, and it doesn't make sense. None of it does. None of it ever did. I didn't get it then. And now," he let out an ironic laugh, "history is repeating itself, and I don't know what I'm supposed to do about it. It's so stupid. The whole thing is really stupid."

I sat up, tucking my left leg in and scooting closer. I pressed my lips against his shoulder before resting my forehead in the exact same spot. "I'm here. I'm not going away this time."

He put his arm around me, rubbing my back gently. "It bothers me the label my mother worked so hard to create is gone. It's like it never existed." He swallowed. "Like she never existed." He dropped his hand from my back and rubbed his eyes. I hated seeing him tormented. Any discussion concerning his mom always tormented him, but this wasn't just grief and sadness. This was contempt and loathing. His face contorted, but he fought to calm his emotions. "I've spent years trying to track down my mother's work, her drawings, notebooks, samples. Most of it was scrapped. Dinah has contacts. She heard what happened and where it ended up and how to get into contact with the right people."

"Christian Nykle?"

He bit his lip and nodded. "My lawyer thinks I'm insane. Verification is nearly impossible, and it's been so long. Fifteen fucking years. Everything is worthless, except to collectors. But I just couldn't let it go. And Dinah's thrown a gag order over the entire thing. Even the little tidbits I've told you are enough to nullify our agreement. If I lose my chance to get back the ashes of my mom's company, I don't know what that will do to me. But the terms are straining everything else in my life. I've barely been able to focus on Martin Tech, and you have questions. Serious, life and death questions. You and I," he swallowed, "we've been through so much. My mom's label was the utter destruction of two relationships. It will kill me if it's the destruction of ours too. Tell me what to do, Alex. I'll do whatever you want."

"You don't have to say anything. We have an agreement on the past, remember?"

"I want to tell you." He shifted to face me, pulling his left leg up on the bed. He held out his arms. "Come here first." I crawled into his arms, and he squeezed me, breathing in the scent of my hair. A tremor cut through him. "I love you. I'm sorry for being such a dick."

"Then don't squeeze me so hard."

"Shit." He let go. "Lie down. Get comfortable." His eyes darted around the room. "Are you hungry? We can eat first." He stood suddenly and took a few steps to the door. "We should eat first." He lingered in the doorway. "Do you want to eat here or in the kitchen? You never told me exactly what happened today."

I grinned. There was the slightly manic, overprotective man I loved. "We'll eat in the kitchen." I pulled myself off the bed. "I'll tell you mine, and if you want, later you can tell me yours."

"Deal."

I finished my story, focusing more on the sautéed vegetables on my plate than making eye contact while discussing the firefight with Elodie. "I can't believe I missed it. It was so obvious. The figure in the video footage was her height and thin. I know Elodie ran the free run course, and her prints were the only other set on the first flower delivery. She had access to the trailer. She knew about Dinah's wardrobe and makeup." A jumble of inconsistencies ran through my mind.

"You're a sexist," Martin teased. "Why did you assume it

was a man?"

"Dinah said *he* chased her up the steps, and the romantic connotations to the card had us convinced it was a dude."

"People can love whoever they want," Martin said. "But over eighty percent of violent crimes are committed by men. Most of the time, that isn't a bad assumption."

"Except in this case." The gnawing continued to drive me a little crazy.

As usual, he read my expression easily. "What is it?"

"Lance practically confessed to running someone over, and Jett, his assistant, didn't seem at all surprised by that prospect. Plus, Lance's credit card paid for the flowers that were sent to your office, Nykle's, my office, and the batch he saved for Dinah. He even wrote out the card."

"You think they were working together?"

"Unlikely. Elodie hated Lance. She wanted Dinah away from him and anyone else who wanted to use her or hurt her." I stabbed at a mushroom. "I'm missing something," I deflated against the chair, feeling achy now that the meds were wearing off, "but I'm not going to figure it out tonight."

Martin was clearing the table when the intercom buzzed. Placing the plates on the counter, he went over and pushed the button. A messenger had couriered over a package that required a signature. Martin gave the okay to send him up and waited in the doorway. A large, thin, rectangular crate remained wedged in the open doorway while Martin signed the clipboard and tipped the messenger.

"What is it?" I asked as he slid the crate inside and latched the door.

He didn't answer me. He found a claw hammer we had for hanging pictures and pried open the crate. Reaching inside, he lifted up a leather portfolio case, aged and worn. The thing was three feet by two feet. He brushed off the coffee table with his arm and put the portfolio case down. As the seconds ticked by, he just stared at it. Slowly, he eased onto the edge of the sofa and undid the clasps. His fingers traced the indentions, and he glanced up at me.

"It's my mom's. This made her so happy, even though the label barely got off the ground before she took ill. I went to work for her then, wanting to make sure she got to see her dream realized."

"You were a good son."

"After she passed, my dad sold it off. It was the first thing he did. It's like he couldn't stand having any remnants of her around. He got rid of her designs, her studio, everything. He just threw it all away. Six months later, the people who bought the label and her existing line ran it into the ground. Years of hard work destroyed in a matter of weeks."

"Martin." I crossed to him and sat beside him on the couch, snaking my hand around his forearm. I could practically feel the blood racing through his veins. "I'm so sorry."

"Dad didn't even care it was destroyed." He pulled his arm free and opened the case. Dozens of sketches filled the interior. Some were nothing more than pencil marks on yellowing paper, and others were in full color. They were amazing. He smiled bittersweetly. "He used the money from the sale to expand his own business. To take care of his interests. The only thing he focused on was his work, and the rest of us, we could just go to hell. It wasn't always like that, but that's how it was at the end."

"Are these her drawings?"

He hadn't taken his eyes off of them as he slowly flipped the pages. He took in a ragged breath. "The first thing I did when I took control of his company was dismantle it. Then I built mine out of the rubble. I just wish I had done something before it was too late. Had I realized what he was going to do to my mom's designs, I would have filed for an injunction or fought for control. It just happened so fast. The only thing I was able to do was treat his business the same way he treated hers."

"Martin," I tried again, but he was lost in his memories, "you were just a kid. You didn't know what you know now."

"I was twenty-two years old, Alex. I should have known something." He scowled. "At the time, Dinah warned me there were whispers someone wanted to buy the label, but I dismissed it. I should have listened. When she told me that, she was on her way to Europe. I figured it was just gossip, and then we lost touch. My time and attention were spent on school and mom and eventually Francesca. Shit happened. More shit happened, and my life went to hell. By the time I got my bearings, everything had been resold. I couldn't track it or find it. I figured it ended up trashed or in someone's private collection, but I always had people keeping their ears to the ground for it. When Dinah hit it big, news of her humble beginnings surfaced, and details started to emerge."

"This is why you've been keeping secrets." I watched him fondle the edges of the paper. "Why did Dinah feel the need for secrecy?"

"It's complicated, but suffice it to say, Dinah influenced a lot of Christian Nykle's early designs based on some of the work she'd done with my mom. Nykle's fame came from my mother's work. His reputation would be destroyed if this came out. The NDA was to protect them both."

"Your lawyer wants you to sue."

"The law doesn't recognize fashion as a valid form of art, which makes establishing intellectual property rights difficult. It's why knockoffs can get away with only making minor changes. I don't blame Christian or Dinah. I just wanted to have something of my mom's." He tore his eyes away and looked at me. "But never at the cost of jeopardizing your safety or our relationship. These sketches are cursed. They showed my father's true colors and tainted my view of the man I had always thought of as my hero. And the way you've been looking at me this week, I hate to think what kind of irreparable harm I've done. Maybe it wasn't worth it."

I kissed him. "It's over now, Captain Ahab. You finally got your white whale. We'll be okay. Give it a day or two for the sting to wear off." I got up from the couch. "I'll let you have some time alone, but just for my own sake, do you still need that phone number?"

"No. The deal's done. The matter is never to be discussed, but I wanted you to know the truth. I should have told you the first time you asked. I was just scared it would come out, and I would lose this again."

"That's why we're working on rebuilding trust, right?"

THIRTY-EIGHT

"What are you doing here?" Cross asked.

"Working," I retorted. "We're still missing something."

His annoyed eye roll was practically audible. "What's the problem now?"

Your attitude, I almost said. I sifted through the reports. Lance was expected to make a full recovery. Production was halted, except for a few film crews shooting B-roll of several city locations. Elodie was in the ICU. Her condition remained touch and go, and Mr. Almeada was fielding questions from the police and doing his best to shield me from visiting the inside of an interrogation room. I should have been happy to let it go, but I wasn't.

"Lance practically confessed to vehicular homicide. Who's the victim?"

Cross laughed. "The blood and hair on the front of Mr. Trevino's SUV were canine."

"He hit a dog?"

"It appears so."

"Then why did he freak out over the possibility he mowed down Chaz Relper?"

"If you recall, Mr. Smoke has been known to drive while under the influence. That vial you found in the bathroom had trace amounts of his saliva. He was probably high when he took the car, hit something, freaked, and abandoned the SUV. He probably convinced himself it was a bad trip or a dream, but that resolve was shaky."

"Okay," I said, even though I felt as though Cross was seeing the world through rose-tinted goggles. "So why the flowers?"

"Actually, the printed receipts you found and Smoke's credit card were covered in Elodie's fingerprints. Jett admitted to letting her hang out with him in the trailer when they were hiding from their respective celebutantes. She might have swiped the card, made the purchases, planted the evidence against Lance, and replaced the card. According to Jett, Lance had one apology bouquet sent to the hotel but changed his mind and had it brought to set. Jett mentioned it to Elodie who probably decided it would be easy to use Lance as a scapegoat."

"Sure, that wraps up nice and neat."

Cross cocked an eyebrow. "You don't believe me?"

"Your job is to protect Broadway Films. Lance is a considerable asset."

"I don't protect murderers or stalkers," his stern conviction was enough to convince me, "and I don't cover up violent crimes." He blew out a measured breath. "We should have realized Elodie was responsible sooner, but Scaratilli insisted Dinah's team was clean. She had no prior record. No history of violence or instability. And she could have struck out at Dinah at any point but never did."

"She freaked when Dinah switched hotels and didn't tell her."

Cross agreed that's why she made the desperate call in the middle of the night and probably why she set the fire when she realized she couldn't get to Dinah without the security team being present. "The police searched Elodie's hotel room. They found a voice modulator and the memory cards from Chaz Relper's drone and camera. He had caught her bringing the first flower delivery to Dinah's hotel, and he caught her looking none too happy with Dinah inside the club. I believe the police called it murderous rage."

"No wonder she killed him. He saw her for who she

really was. Do we know what set her off?"

"The weekend of the break-in at Dinah's house, Elodie's sister died, but because of Dinah's sex scandal, Elodie wasn't at the hospital or the service."

"She stayed at work to take care of Dinah." I thought back to what I knew. "The roses must have been significant. That's the first time Dinah received them."

"Actually, the police and I did some digging. Elodie's credit card activity showed a purchase of red roses and a get well balloon for her sister. She bought them three days before Dinah returned from Maui. By then, the sex tape hit the internet, and it was all hands on deck. Her sister died from unforeseen complications, and the flowers did too. So she left them at Dinah's house. The black, dying roses became significant in her mind, but since she can't exactly buy dying flowers, she found a replacement."

"Damn, we missed a lot."

He studied me for a long moment. "I'll leave you to conduct your own investigations in the future. Perhaps this was a case of too many cooks in the kitchen. But you figured it out in the nick of time."

"The police did."

He picked up his phone and scrolled through the photos, stopping on the image I forwarded to him that the police had sent to me. "I know what Elodie looks like. So do the men in our tech department. And this image is entirely indecipherable. You saw what you already knew."

He held out the photo, and I stared at the white and black blur drizzled in a swirl of neon from the club's sign. It looked nothing like the photo I saw inside the prop room. Confused, I reached for my own phone and looked at the same image.

"The police based everything I said and Elodie's guilt on this. If it's meaningless, why would they do that?"

"Because it wasn't meaningless to you." He smiled. "Good job, Alex."

*   *   *

Four days later, production resumed. The actual events

that transpired remained a secret, but news of Elodie's condition had spread. Hospital security and the police were working overtime to keep the paparazzi away. Her condition had improved to the point that she was no longer in intensive care, but she had yet to wake up. If she did, she'd find herself under arrest.

Dinah felt slightly responsible for Elodie's mental break, and in the event she survived and wasn't imprisoned, Dinah would see to it that her assistant received the psychiatric help she needed. It was a kind and forgiving gesture, but the cynical part of me wondered how much optics played a part in that decision.

Speaking of optics, I tugged on the hem of my dress, cringing when my bandage got stuck to the fabric and pulled at my stitches. "I'm not going."

Martin came into the room and gave me a look. "I thought Cross specifically asked you to."

"I don't care." I pulled the zipper down and carefully stepped out of my dress. "I haven't been wearing crop tops all week because I was hoping to revive fashion from the early nineties."

"I thought it was your way of teasing me with flashes of excess skin." He moved to the closet and slowly flipped through the hangers.

"Explain to me again why you were invited."

"Dinah asked me to go, and after she went through the trouble of brokering the deal for my mom's sketches, I can't say no." He held out a blue dress with cutouts. "Try this. It shouldn't pull at your bandage or stitches."

"But everyone's going to see the bandage."

"So?"

Grumbling, I put on the dress, holding my hair up, so he could zipper it. "I'm leaving as soon as possible. I don't even know why they are throwing a party after what happened."

"For the press," Martin said, clearly knowing a lot more about this situation than I did. "She and Lance are going public on their relationship. The party is supposed to be a celebration of his recovery and continuing production, but really, it's so the media will get wind of their union. It's to shift focus from the hospitalized assistant and the electrocuted leading man."

"Damn, I miss a lot when I avoid the office." The day after the shooting, Cross barred me from the office for the following seventy-two hours. He had called late last night to tell me Dinah expected me at this party, and he said we'd both be there.

Martin straightened his tie and tugged on his cuffs to make sure his jacket sleeves fell perfectly. "Are you ready to go?"

"I guess."

Arriving at the hotel, I stayed in the car while Martin stepped out. Even though we rode together, I didn't want anyone to see us show up together. Martin wasn't concerned, but this was work. I wanted to maintain some distance.

Marcal circled around a couple of times before dropping me off. I stepped out and entered the lobby. The celebration was being held in Lance's penthouse suite. He had the entire upper floor at his disposal, along with a rooftop pool and bar. The hotel provided catering, and I walked in to find Cross in a corner speaking to Scar. Martin was in the center of the room speaking to Dinah, Lance, and a group of film executives.

"I'm here," I said, nodding at Scar.

Cross shook hands with Scar and led me outside to the bar. "Relax, Alex. This isn't an assignment. This is a party. Dinah requested your presence."

"Actually," Lance came up behind us, wearing an untucked white shirt, opened at the throat, "I wanted to thank you." He held out his hand, waiting for me to give him mine. When I did, someone took a photo. He looked back at the photographer who was consulting the view screen. He nodded, and Lance thanked him. "Positive publicity, in case details emerge." He glanced at Cross. "Don't worry. We're not planning on using those unless necessary."

"Noted," Cross said.

Lance narrowed his eyes at me, and I realized the thanks was faked. "Enjoy the party." Without another word, he wandered off, plastering another phony smile on his face as he schmoozed with some entertainment reporters.

I felt Martin's eyes on me. He was inside the suite, looking polite but bored. Dinah had left him with a couple of models or movie extras. Cross gestured to the bartender and ordered a drink.

"Alex," Dinah bounded over and hugged me, "it's so good to see you." Her gaze shifted around. "Thank you." She looked at the white gauze against the backdrop of my blue dress. "You look stunning." She lowered her voice and slipped onto the stool. "Is that where you were shot?"

"Yep."

Cross took his drink and stepped away, making sure no reporters were close enough to overhear our conversation.

"I'm so sorry this happened. I really do appreciate everything you've done. No one could have seen this coming, but Lucien told me what you did, how you must have figured it out without even realizing it. That's crazy, but I absolutely love it. I've talked the writers into putting something like that into the script. It'll be great."

"Glad I could help."

She didn't mention Elodie's name, and neither did I. Someone called to her, and she looked up. "Just one second." She lowered her voice again. "Lance and I called this party so we can do an interview. It'll be good for the movie and good for me. It will keep the truth from coming out. It's so twisted. I feel responsible. Maybe once I have time to process, I'll come forward and work on the narrative."

"You mean the book deal?" I inquired, feeling jaded and annoyed.

"Maybe."

Lance called to her this time, and she hopped off the stool. "I don't expect you to come by set after what happened, but let's get together before I go back to California. I'd like to properly thank you."

"That isn't necessary."

She gave me a look. "Yes, it is. I'll be in touch." She fluffed her hair and put on that sexy, shy smile of hers and headed for Lance, looping her arm around his waist while a photographer took some photos before they started talking to the interviewer.

I watched the two of them talk while guests mingled about. I spotted Clay and Gemma working another section of the crowd, but my eyes kept drifting back to Martin who was in full business networking mode. He knew how to work parties like this.

Cross retook his seat beside me. He scooted closer and boxed me in. "What are you doing?" I asked, swiveling to face him.

"Testing a theory."

"Does it involve getting slapped for invading my personal space?"

He chuckled. "James Martin's here."

"I noticed."

"He and Dinah are old friends. I did my research. They knew each other before either of them was anybody. His mom gave Dinah her start."

"Is that why you assigned me to be Dinah's technical consultant?" I asked.

Cross didn't answer my question. Instead, he looked down and brushed a finger against my bandage. "If you'd like, I'll schedule an appointment for you with my tattoo artist. She does wonders covering scars and injuries with elaborate inkwork."

"Is that the reason for the tattoo on your back?"

"Tales for another time." He grinned. "Looks like my theory is about to be proven correct."

"You still haven't told me what it is."

Cross had a sly grin. "James is surrounded by attractive women, models and actresses, stuff of men's fantasies, but he hasn't been able to take his eyes off you. He's been clocking your movements since the moment you stepped through the door."

"It's pretty easy when I haven't moved from the bar. He probably just wants a drink, and I happen to be in the way."

"We're about to find out," Cross whispered. Martin came up on my other side, asking the bartender for a scotch. "Make that two," Cross said.

Martin turned. "Lucien. Alex. I didn't expect to see you here. How are you both?"

I hid my smile, turning away from Cross. Martin might not care if the world knew of our relationship, but he still did a good job of covering it up.

"We were just discussing Alex's recent injury." Cross took a sip of scotch. Martin asked what happened, and Cross gave a vague explanation. "I hate that my people are often in danger. Alex could have been killed."

"I thought it was no big deal," I muttered, wondering what Cross was doing.

"What are you doing to protect her? Them?" Martin asked, correcting himself.

"Actually, that's what I wanted to talk to you about." Cross climbed off his stool. "I heard you were doing some R&D with biotextiles. The research shows a lot of promise in strength and ballistic protection. I was hoping we could discuss some things." He led Martin to an empty area near the end of the pool, and I blew out a breath. Everything Lucien Cross did, including hiring me, had something to do with Martin. I just wasn't entirely sure why.

Twenty minutes later, I ducked out of the party, wishing Scar a good night. I sent a text to Cross, telling him I was leaving, went downstairs, and took a cab home. An hour later, Martin joined me.

"What did Lucien want?"

"Honestly, I think he wants us to go into the fashion business together."

"What?"

Martin snorted. "He was hoping my research could be used to mass produce bulletproof attire using biotextiles. The problem, which I tried to explain to him, is it isn't possible to harvest the amount of materials needed for an endeavor like that. Needless to say, I had to agree to put a meeting on the books for next month just so I could duck out of there." He began taking off his suit. "That asshole made me miss my favorite part."

"What's that?"

"Peeling your dress off." He grinned licentiously and

crawled up the bed and kissed me. "How are you feeling?"

"Good, hoping you'll get me to great."

"I'll get you to fantastic." He kissed me again. "I love you." He pulled my ponytail free and studied my face. "What's wrong? You look like you want to say something."

"It can wait."

"We've been doing enough of that lately."

"Okay, but I warned you." I swallowed, hoping it wouldn't ruin the mood. "Given what I now know about your parents' relationship, why on earth would you ever want to get married?"

"They weren't always like that. And I'm not my father. I know whenever we're ready, it won't be anything like that. You're my everything. Not Martin Tech or Cross's silkworm vests or whatever the future might bring."

"Unless we're cursed."

He continued working on getting us both naked. "I'll consult a gypsy in the morning, just to be on the safe side."

DON'T MISS THE NEXT INSTALLMENT IN
THE ALEXIS PARKER SERIES.

SIGN-UP TO BE NOTIFIED OF THE LATEST
RELEASE.

http://www.alexisparkerseries.com/newsletter

ABOUT THE AUTHOR

G.K. Parks is the author of the Alexis Parker series. The first novel, *Likely Suspects,* tells the story of Alexis' first foray into the private sector.

G.K. Parks received a Bachelor of Arts in Political Science and History. After spending some time in law school, G.K. changed paths and earned a Master of Arts in Criminology/Criminal Justice. Now all that education is being put to use creating a fictional world based upon years of study and research.

You can find additional information on G.K. Parks and the Alexis Parker series by visiting our website at
www.alexisparkerseries.com

Made in United States
North Haven, CT
29 April 2023

36031946R00186